Massive Impact

Sam Strait

DISCLAIMER:

This is a work of fiction. Any resemblance to actual persons or events is purely coincidental. Sam Strait is the pen name of the author.

Table of Contents

PROLOGUE

My name is Sam Strait. I am a personal injury lawyer in Seattle. My story begins in April 2007, when I was twenty-nine. I had only two years' experience in personal injury after three years as a King County prosecutor.

Rodney Mammon hired me to be his only personal injury litigator four days before my story begins.

Rodney breezed into my office with a Traffic Collision Report and tossed it on my desk with a flourish. "Bro, this client's husband got killed riding with some stoner going 90 in a 30 who spun out and hit a tree. Torso got squished like an egg in a vise. Hubby was a crab fisherman pulling down 150K in great health in his early forties, so primo damages. Wife is already signed up, and the probate is pending with Bonus Malone. You know Bonus, right?"

My blood pressure went to 1000/800. I was excited and scared and excited. "I know Bonus. Bald, moon-faced, always upbeat. Great probate lawyer. Trustworthy, too."

"Bingo." Rodney flipped through some notes, his blond gel-stiffened porcupine hair bristling. His suit today? Pale silver sharkskin with lavender tie and pocket square. Rodney liked tailoring. "Widow's name is Saralee Nillsson. Realtor The perpetrator's name is Byron Cleverly.

Dude. You can't make this shit up." He flipped through the notes. "I hired the Delta Force of collision reconstructionists, guy named Don Meissner. He picks you up downstairs in ten minutes to visit the crash site." He pointed finger-pistols at me. "Go get 'em, tiger."

I went to the men's room and splashed cold water on my face, and straightened my blue paisley tie. At work, I always wore the same thing—gray suit, white shirt, blue paisley tie. With tie clip.

Ten minutes later, Don Meissner picked me up in his white Yukon Denali. I was still excited and scared and excited. I couldn't wait to visit THE SCENE.

In personal injury law, the scene is where your client got hurt. But THE SCENE is where your client got killed.

Don looked over at me and smoothed down his white walrus mustache.

"Why do you drive a Yukon Denali?" I asked.

He winked. "Because mass wins." The Yukon smelled like spearmint and fresh rubber. Don was about fifty-five, burly and genial, short silver hair with a big bald spot. He wore khaki cargo pants and, a green fleece pullover, and a fisherman's vest with many mysterious pockets. He looked like he'd been around the block a few times.

I hadn't been around this particular block at all.

Don handed me his curriculum vitae to read as he drove us to Kent. He had been a collision reconstructionist for the National Transportation Safety Board, reconstructing the worst crashes in the US to establish what caused them. He would get the total station data from the police to establish where the vehicles collided and where the vehicles (or pieces of them) wound up afterward. Then, he'd load the data into a computer using PC Crash or another program and reconstruct what vectors and forces caused the vehicles to go from the impact point to the resting point. Then he'd conclude who had been going how fast, in what direction, and who was the "causing driver."

When Don was with the NTSB, he never rolled on something less than a quadruple fatality.

But after he went private, he could do this for any plaintiff's attorney. Rodney did only criminal defense—he only employed a personal injury lawyer for the extra money. Rodney defended DUIs and, vehicular homicide, and other car-related crimes. He knew he'd need a good reconstructionist to prove the defendant killed Mr. Nillsson.

The back of Don's Yukon was filled with aluminum cases for cameras, camcorder, laptops, and laser sights. Don Meissner was loaded for bear.

At THE SCENE, Don parked about a hundred yards back on the narrow shoulder. The road was two lanes, narrow gravel shoulders, and a high crown. It climbed a steep hill into a thick maple forest. Two squirrels watched us, twitching their tails, and overhead a crow commented. Something cynical, no doubt.

Don squinted at me. "I hear this one's your first?"

"My first fatality. Yup. Kinda scared over here."

He clapped me on the back. "You'll never forget your first fatality. Just like your first girl. C'mon. First thing I do is walk the scene in the direction the defendant was going to see what the defendant saw."

We started strolling up the hill.

Don paged through the Traffic Collision Report. "Witnesses say the defendant was doing about ninety when he lost control," Don said. "This steep hill is where the local idiot high school kids try to get airborne."

"But the defendant was forty-five," I said.

"Yup," he said. "The defendant was taking his buddy, the crab fisherman, out for a spin in his new Mazda roadster. A spin is what he got, all right. He wanted to show how well the Mazda could jump. Defendant crested the hill going ninety, touched down, and immediately swerved to avoid a woman running on the right shoulder with her golden retriever. She saw the whole thing."

The sky was clearing, showing wisps of royal blue behind sweeping white clouds. The maples around us were budding. The crow commented again. A few Steller's jays called as the sun came out. The trees seemed to be breathing. I thought, *So it begins.*

As we walked uphill toward THE SCENE, a sudden wind ran through the maple trees overhead. It sounded to me as if they were whispering, "Useless, useless."

The light got brighter. Every variation of green shimmered up ahead.

I wondered whether I was good enough to handle this. I'd done criminal jury trials and smaller personal injury trials. But this was playing at the big table—the private room in the back of the casino where there was no betting limit, and the gamblers were cold-blooded indeed.

We reached the crest of the hill. The light brightened again. "Note the orange spray-paint marks on the pavement," Don said. "They start where the rubber marks show him beginning to skid left, then right, as he overcorrected."

I nodded. It seemed that the temperature dropped about forty degrees. It wasn't a cold day under the rustling maples. But I shivered. The light at THE SCENE turned brilliant.

"So he swerves left to avoid the pedestrian and the canine," Don said, walking me through the marks. "Then he attempts to swerve right to stay on the road. But he turns the wheel too suddenly, and he spins."

Don tapped an orange mark on the pavement on the left side of the road with the toe of his boot. "He leaves the roadway surface here. Probably still doing seventy, maybe more." I looked at the skid marks zooming off the precipice.

Don looked down the steep slope covered with saplings and bushes into a deep ravine. "You can see the swath after that."

I looked down, three hundred feet down a near-vertical slope. The torn bushes and saplings showed pale brown wood and the silvered undersides of leaves. The twelve-foot-wide swath went all the way down, three hundred feet down, to the bottom. Where a huge Madrona tree had a bite taken out of it. A bite big enough to be made by a great white shark. The Madrona tree still bled.

"Note the debris field," Don said, pointing.

The Madrona tree was the center of a debris field—dozens of fragments—plastic, metal, and glass. The debris field exploded out a hundred feet in every direction like an asterisk. An asterisk of silver glitter. The wreck had been winched up the slope four days before. But the fragments centered on the Madrona tree told the story.

"We'll view the wreck later at the State Patrol impound lot," Don said. "You can expect copious amounts of blood."

"I can handle that," I said. "I did hostile boardings in the Coast Guard in the Gulf of Mexico. Drug interdictions and human trafficking. I've seen blood."

"How many hostile boardings?"

I shrugged. "I did some, but my buddies did more."

Don clapped me on the back, a paternal gesture. "Attaboy. Keep it modest. Keep your shit tight."

Because I'd been orphaned at seven, paternal gestures like this always bucked me up.

I knew the epilogue. The crab fisherman had been "emergently transported by Medic One" to the local junior high school soccer field, where an Airlift Northwest helicopter had flown him to Harborview Medical Center. They'd slaved over him for two hours in a crash suite but couldn't save him.

The Autopsy Report was pending. But the trauma surgeon told the victim's wife he'd had eight broken ribs, all on the right side, which punctured his lung and lacerated his liver. He also had multiple avulsed fractures in the extremities and a severe traumatic brain injury.

Again, it sounded like the maples were whispering, "Useless, useless."

But a surge of exultation swept through me. I hadn't done a fatality before. But I was stoked. I was going to win this thing. The defendant was the useless one, not me.

In five minutes, I'd gone from scared to excited. I wanted to do everything at once—get the Harborview records and the Autopsy Report, get the tax returns, and get an economist working on the victim's lost income. If there were four of me they would have all been busy.

Don pointed at the debris field. "You see how the fragments flew a hundred feet?"

I nodded.

"This was a massive impact."

CHAPTER ONE—HELP FROM THE GHOST

The next two days after I visited THE SCENE with Don Meissner, I ran around like a manic squirrel gathering evidence and planning. I read the motions chapter of my auto accident deskbook and listed motions to file. One motion in particular fascinated me and I downloaded the forms. I got the supplements to the Traffic Collision Report with the witness statements. I got the press accounts online. I ran the defendant through my favorite stealthy database and pulled his criminal history, assets, and aliases. He had two prior DUI convictions and several arrests (but no convictions) for felony drug possession. He owned a house with a lot of undeveloped land right on the edge of the suburbs. The database showed no aliases. But I knew all this wasn't definitive.

For the definitive read on this guy, I'd have to see The Ghost.

Once I had rounded up the initial evidence, I scheduled a visit with Duvonda Marshall to bring her coffee and get some advice.

I need to explain about Duvonda. She was my mentor and best friend. She was a fierce Black plaintiffs' lawyer who looked a lot like Tina Turner. She dressed to the nines in splendid skirted suits and usually a leopard-print or tiger-print silk top. She'd been a King County prosecutor for six years longer than me. Then, she became a plaintiffs' attorney, running her own practice five years ago. She gave me sage advice, called me "son," and wiggled her toes when she was delighted. I called her Auntie Duvonda.

I loved legal research and writing, so sometimes I'd write a brief for her. I also sometimes came up with ingenious or nutty ideas about strategy. But she had taught me most of what I knew about personal injury. She gave me far more than I gave her. I dreamed of working for her, or maybe with her, someday. I dreamed of getting away from Rodney Mammon and his Greek chorus of polished criminal defense attorneys, even though I'd only just started with Rodney. I once told Duvonda she was my "spirit animal," and she ruffled my '50s-style black buzz cut and said, "Aw shucks."

She had told me her favorite joke: "So a horse walks into a bar, and the bartender says, why the long face?"

We first met at a Trial Lawyers Association convention. Duvonda had recommended that I take the job with Rodney Mammon but warned me, "That man is a snake. Cancel that—I've met snakes with more heart. Work there, learn stuff, but don't trust him."

So I took my treasure trove of stuff up to Marshall & Associates, Duvonda's office in One Union Square near Mammon & Associates in downtown Seattle. As I walked into One Union Square, I noticed there was a guy (I suppose) in a pink gorilla suit playing drums in the plaza. A bunch of well-dressed fans kept cheering and putting money in the derby hat he had in front of the drum set.

Why a derby? It's what the well-dressed pink gorilla was wearing this season, I guessed.

Since tech companies had flooded into Seattle, and homeless junkies followed right behind, the weirdness quotient had gone up.

Duvonda didn't have any associates currently, just a couple of paralegals and a semi-employee, semi-boyfriend who was a private investigator. His name was Silent Mike. He'd done SWAT with Seattle Police before burning out and going private. I'd learned to use Silent

Mike for difficult process service because he could get at people that nobody else could get at. He always did service on video using a button cam. He was a master of disguise. I'd known him to dress as a security guard, a Rastafarian, a doctor, a Hare Krishna, and what have you. Many process servers make one feeble attempt and try to upsell you into paying for expensive alternative techniques. They screw up very often. Silent Mike cost more upfront but he never messed up and never gave up. I hadn't had him fail to find somebody yet. Rumor had it he still had contacts in law enforcement.

I sat down with Duvonda and handed over her triple mocha with extra whipped cream. This week, her nails were leopard pattern. She leaned back in her fawn-colored side chair across from me, took off her calfskin pumps, and put her stocking feet up on the coffee table. She took a deep swig, leaned back in her chair, and squinted at me. "So what's the situation, son?"

"My client was riding with a buddy in the buddy's Mazda roadster. The buddy got it up to ninety in a thirty-miles-per-hour zone, trying to get it airborne on a hilly two-lane road down in Kent. He got it airborne, all right. As he landed, he swerved to avoid a woman running on the shoulder with her dog and spun out down a slope and sideways into a Madrona tree about three feet in diameter. It hit on the passenger side. My client got airlifted to Harborview, but he died on the table."

She took another sip. "Hell," she said. "Widow or kids?"

"Widow, no kids. She's a realtor. Great with people, you know, realtors. The victim was a crab fisherman pulling around two hundred grand a season in the Bering Sea. Big lost income."

She nodded. "So what can Auntie Duvonda do for you, son?"

I said, "So here's the deal. Defendant's been charged with vehicular homicide. He's out on bail. He's being represented by Aloysius Miller."

Duvonda winced. "That one. Let me tell you, Sam. When I was prosecuting, we used to say in Felony Trial Teams that Rodney Mammon was the second biggest scumbag in the defense bar. The second most likely to buy off witnesses, hide evidence, phony up alibis. Guess who was the first?"

"Aloysius Miller. Just my luck."

"Yes, he's the worst. But here's the nice thing about Aloysius Miller. He's conceited and greedy. Make that two nice things. Wears excellent suits, always flipping his blond forelock, always has a studio tan and whitened teeth. Funny thing about Aloysius—you give him one solid kick in the balls, and it confuses him. At least for a little. Can't say that about your boss, Rodney Mammon. That boy can take a punch and not even blink."

"So why is this good news about Aloysius Miller?"

"This early in the case, the defendant's insurer has appointed an adjuster, but if you haven't served the defendant yet, there's no defense counsel. So you have to be ready to blitz with everything right at the beginning before there is an insurance defense lawyer. Serve the defendant with the Summons and Complaint and also with Interrogatories and Requests for Production of Documents and Requests for Admission of Facts. Then the day after you serve the defendant, serve everything on Aloysius Miller, his current criminal defense counsel. Include an innocent cover letter stating that you consider him civil defense counsel until and unless somebody else appears. Aloysius thinks he knows everything. His firm does a little bit of personal injury and a little insurance defense. But when it comes to the Civil Rules, Aloysius Miller doesn't know shit from Shinola."

I nodded. "Okay. But because the defendant's facing criminal charges, I can't take his deposition or, make him answer interrogatories, or produce documents, or provide any discovery. He can't be forced to incriminate himself by providing any evidence under the Civil Rules."

She winked at me. "He can't be forced to provide discovery. But you can ask for it. Worst thing they can do is say no and file a Motion for Protective Order. You think not having leverage to force discovery is a bad thing. But if you look at it sideways, it can be twisted into a good thing." There was a strained silence. This was why Duvonda was a good mentor. She wanted to guide me to figuring it out, not spoon-feed me the answer.

My mind raced. Would he blunder and just answer the discovery requests? Would he waive his Fifth Amendment right against self-incrimination? I doubted the defendant would do that with a criminal defense lawyer on board. I shrugged. "Call me dense, but I can't see how."

She leaned over and slapped my knee. Then she told me how.

"That is frigging awesome!" I said, gathering up my stuff.

When I came out into the plaza, the pink gorilla had gone. But reclining in the plaza lay a white homeless guy with dirty skin blond dreadlocks, growling, "Cash for chemo" on an Army blanket. For some reason, he was wearing a fleece jumpsuit. He looked and smelled like a heroin addict. The Big Gulp cup in front of him was almost full. Some beggars in Seattle made forty bucks an hour in a good spot. What did they spend it on? They already had free food, free shelter (which they usually refused because it required sobriety), free healthcare, yadda yadda yadda. So, what did they need cash for? Cigarettes, alcohol, and street drugs. The cash mostly went for that stuff. I'd learned that from prosecuting.

Seattle had attracted thousands of homeless addicts lured by free stuff and lax drug enforcement, the way feeding pigeons in the park attracts more pigeons.

Next, I had to see The Ghost.

***

And now I need to explain The Ghost.

I'm all thumbs when seeking romance. I'm sincere and monogamous and clumsy as Hell. My twin sister Catherine had gone straight into a therapist career for reasons which will become obvious. She said I was a clumsy lover because of our orphanhood and rotten upbringing in foster care. (Therapists, right? They often drag stuff back to childhood.)

I'd somehow landed exactly one great relationship. My law school girlfriend Suzanne. When dating after Suzanne, I'd ask myself, "Is she a Suzanne?" Suzanne the sly and shy. Black curly locks, deep brown eyes, hooked Roman nose, Jewish and Reform. We'd studied together, and I'd fallen in love the only way I could—with her personality. She'd been in the same year at University of Washington Law School. We'd been inseparable, but she'd confessed she was going straight home to New Jersey after graduation. I had confessed I wouldn't ever in this life live in New Jersey. So, it had an expiration date, which welded us together.

Face it, Suzanne was clinically shy. For some reason, she couldn't talk freely with anybody, but she could talk freely with me. I met her at a grad school dance when she asked me to dance. We talked all night and wound up kissing a lot until we were both covered with the invisible pink snow of affection. We both loved Hemingway. She would end our conversations by saying, "That's it, finito." We traded volumes of *Bad Hemingway* and quoted from them. Suzanne was the one if such a thing existed. I was hopeful now there was more than one for me.

When we graduated, she moved straight back to New Jersey, no hesitation. Only kid, total star and her dad was leaving her mom for a twenty-eight-year-old cupcake. When I kissed her goodbye at the airport, I said, "I'll always love you."

She had said, "Me too, but we need a clean break." Tears flowed down her cheeks. "Best to rip off the Band-Aid, Sam."

It hadn't felt like ripping off a Band-Aid. It had felt like somebody ripped off my arm and slapped me with the wet end.

I didn't even try to date for years. Suzanne got married, started having kids, built a promising career in pharmaceutical patent law. She moved on.

Now we're coming to The Ghost.

I went on some online dates. Blech. Not quite as bad as a root canal without anesthesia. If I liked a woman, she wouldn't want a second date because I was "too needy." If I didn't, she thought I was Mr. Wonderful. I wasn't good at pretending to not particularly like a woman that I particularly liked.

As you'll see, I could play it cool only when I'm doing legal work. The rest of the time, I'm obvious. When I got excited or mad, the scar where a drug smuggler had shot off my right earlobe glowed red. Not subtle.

In one online date, I'd met somebody worthwhile. Shocking. I met her at a dimly-lit artsy espresso place in Magnolia out by Elliott Bay at about eight on a rainy night. (In Seattle, there are lots of those.)

Hmm. Slender, pale, fine blonde flyaway hair, ironic smile, hazel eyes. She wore a vintage blue evening gown and a fake fur jacket. She took a sip of her latte and studied me. "So what's your lifestyle?"

I shrugged. "I work a lot, and I hope to find a woman to spend quality time with. I'm pretty much romantic and monogamous. When I get excited, the scar on my right ear, where I lost my earlobe, turns dark pink. Obvious, right?"

She chuckled. The Ghost was going to do a lot of chuckling with me. "No, I meant your sexual lifestyle."

I shrugged again. "I'm a one-woman man. I like to express myself passionately. But I'm rather conventional. Someday, I'd like to get married and have kids."

The Ghost leaned forward. Small and velvety breasts. Mole on the left breast. The room grew hotter. "Let's start with something simple. Have you ever tried poly?"

I'd read the local alternative magazine. I knew some of the terms; they just didn't apply to me. "I'm not polyamorous. If I'm with a woman, I don't want either of us having sex with somebody else."

She twirled a lock of her blonde hair around her finger. I liked that her nails were cut short and not polished. "Not a deal breaker. What's your stance on DP?"

I smiled and shook my head. "I'd have to know what that is, I guess."

She looked straight at me. This was an audition, all right. "DP. Double penetration of a woman."

"You mean two guys? With the woman? At the same time?"

"No, silly," she said, slapping my hand. "One man. He goes into her vagina or her anus. And a toy of some kind goes into the other hole at the same time. Vibrators optional." Sly smile. Audition.

Now I was blushing. "I haven't tried anything like that." I tried to recover. "So, are you polyamorous?"

She leaned back, again covering the velvety breasts. "Now and then. I was with my ex. He liked me to play with his friends while he watched. He was a cuckold boy. But that's been over for a couple of years. I'm pretty…versatile."

"Okay," I said. Not a Suzanne. Whole different animal. "So, what kind of relationship are you looking for? To put it your way, what is your lifestyle?"

She nodded. This was the ground she wanted to cover. "I'm an S&M D/s switch, occasionally poly and bi, who wants to play inside the relationship with strict agreements and safe words. The only thing off limits is caca and blood sport."

I gaped at her. She laughed. I'd read enough of the alternative magazine to know she liked sadism and masochism, dominance and submission, and just about anything except playing with feces and blood.

I had liked her eerie intensity.

I grabbed for a conversational lifeline. "Do you like to play Scrabble?"

She burst out laughing.

It turned out she did like to play Scrabble. I'd been playing Scrabble with her weekly ever since. She beat me more than I beat her. And after we'd been Scrabble friends for several months, I asked her what she did for a living.

That's when I learned what made her The Ghost.

The Ghost had a great backstory. She'd been the only child of an exceptionally domineering divorced mother, an electronics engineer who kept a log—an actual log—of every single thing The Ghost did as a child. The Ghost grew up abnormally self-conscious.

This explained her lifestyle. She was attempting to obliterate self-consciousness with extreme sexual experiences.

The Ghost got hired by Tacoma Police. While in the Patrol Division but off-duty, she had to fight back in a bank robbery and ended up fatally shooting both robbers. More on that later. Then she developed multiple sclerosis and, took a disability retirement, and became a private investigator specializing in web research.

The Ghost treasured her privacy. And taking sex off the table with me actually made us better friends.

The Ghost wasn't showing significant signs of MS yet. But I knew the prognosis. Occasionally, she tripped or stumbled. She was very careful of where she put her feet. Her hands and the rest of her body weren't affected yet.

When she was diagnosed, she used her online skills and found out every possible treatment for MS. She got the best. This reignited her love of online research. She started her own private investigator agency. Limited to investigating rotten people for plaintiffs' attorneys and the "kink community." She found the defendants' aliases, their criminal history, their spare passports. Often even their overseas bank accounts. She augmented the online work with a little of what she called "pretext calls" and "social engineering"—contacting people with cover stories, lies really, to coax out more information.

She got some of her information from "playmates," who I never asked about and didn't want to know. Some of them were apparently very well connected. In Seattle, a lot of rich and powerful people "played" in the "kink community."

The Ghost could find unfindable things and unfindable people. The only problem was finding some legal way to explain what she'd found so I could use it in court. But The Ghost helped with that too, sometimes even posting the stuff she found in obscure places online so I could claim it was "on the web." She called it "acceptable cover."

The Ghost only took on a project when she thought the target was a "total waste of oxygen." That was her term. If the target should not be using up oxygen, she was in. She cost a lot and she was worth it.

I'd hired her three times before. I always paid her out of my own pocket. I didn't want clients or, coworkers, or bosses knowing about The Ghost. I kept The Ghost in my back pocket.

You know that thing called "Googling yourself"? I've done that. But I never asked The Ghost to look into my own past. I didn't want her to feel sorry for me. Because of orphanhood and abusive foster care and whatnot.

I hated to be pitied, and I never pitied myself.

Self-pity is poison. There's a Sam Strait generalization for you.

I didn't want The Ghost to know everything about me. Funny, right? She was the one who was into kink, but I was the one who was ashamed. The Ghost was totally comfortable with her identity and her life. I was the one who was not.

We became close. I confided in her about loneliness and work because she was loyal and secretive. We branched out from Scrabble. We met for coffee. We went to movies. I'd go for walks with her, so long as the footing was easy. Her MS was starting to make her stumble at times. We sardonically made each other our emergency contacts for healthcare stuff, and we went out on Valentine's Day if she didn't have a kink date. It went without saying that I seldom had a date.

I once told her, "If the MS really goes to hell, I will be there for you."

She had covered my hand with hers. "I know," she said.

I will not name The Ghost in this book. She wanted to be a ghost for her own reasons.

So, the night after I saw Duvonda, I went to see The Ghost. She lived in a nondescript condo in Magnolia, out by the north end of the harbor. It was cold and foggy. A couple of ships' horns sounded out beyond the grain elevator. The air smelled of salt water, and out in Elliott Bay, bells rang on buoys. A homeless white guy in an Arctic parka stood on the corner near her house singing "A Pretty Girl Is Like A Melody" in strong baritone. Somewhere out there, seals barked.

When The Ghost let me in, she was drinking Earl Gray tea.

"Want some?" she asked. She always sounded like a viola.

"Sure," I said.

She closed the living room closet door. "I'm not letting you see the Toy Closet because that's just paraphernalia for my paraphilias."

"Nice phrase," I said. "Euphonious."

The Ghost called her living room The Playroom, where all the action happened. Her bedroom was just for sleeping. The living room closet was the Toy Closet, presumably stocked with lingerie and handcuffs and vibrators and dildoes (and things I've never heard of). She liked teasing me by leaving the Toy Closet door open just a little. It was part of our whimsical dance.

I smelled sandalwood incense and noted that Sade's "Smooth Operator" was playing on her Kenwood stereo in the teak entertainment center. She'd cleared the white leather couch and white leather armchair of clutter and had vacuumed the bearskin rug. Seriously—a real bearskin rug. She'd also had *The Garden of Earthly Delights* print reframed in muted gold. The sideboard showed Grey Goose vodka and Jack Daniel's whiskey.

I put my preliminary investigation stuff on the kitchen table. She brought the tea and started looking through what I had. "Nice TCR," she said. "But this other stuff is, well, it's jejune. Somewhat pedestrian."

"Scrabble player," I jibed.

I had put Post-Its on the printouts from my database search showing the defendant's criminal history and his property. I would have to sell her the idea that this guy was a waste of oxygen.

"So what makes this guy a waste of oxygen?" She arched her eyebrows at me.

"You see in the TCR where he was going ninety in a thirty when he got airborne on a hill, swerved to avoid a runner with her dog, and spun out into a tree? Well, his passenger died. His friend. And now Aloysius Miller is going to argue that the dead guy was driving, and the defendant was really in the passenger seat. The old DUI 'I wasn't driving' defense."

The Ghost rolled her eyes. If intoxicated drivers couldn't dispute intoxication, they disputed driving. It was customary. Rodney Mammon and, Aloysius Miller, and all the criminal defense attorneys argued that. I'd prosecuted lots of "phantom driver" cases.

I plunged ahead. "The Mazda was a convertible, and the top was down. They were both thrown. Aloysius thinks he can make this 'I wasn't driving' defense fly, oddly enough, because the crash made both of them literally fly."

She smiled at me. "Aloysius Miller, huh? Now that guy is a real waste of oxygen." I stared at her, hoping against hope she'd take it on. Not to be tiresome, but this was my first fatality, and I wanted to crush this.

Showing my usual craftiness, I said, "This is my first fatality, so I want to crush this."

She sighed. "Oh, Sam. You're such a Boy Scout." She liked that I was idealistic about my work. I called it my mission. She teased me about it, but that was also part of our whimsical dance. When I saw her, she always found a chance to call me Vanilla Boy or maybe Boy Scout. "Okay, I'm sold," she said, again sounding like a viola. "This guy is a waste of oxygen. I will run it for you and tell you what I found in one to two days."

We hugged. We always hugged, saying goodbye. I kissed her forehead. I always did that, too.

For some reason, The Ghost and I were two of a kind.

***

I gave The Ghost two days to work. In the meantime, I got the widow Saralee Nillsson into the office. She wore a black skirted suit. Her face was stamped with sorrow, her honey-blonde hair lank, her baby-blue eyes rimmed in red. She had an upturned Scandinavian nose laugh lines on her face. She looked like a burned-out house that had been a pretty happy house until somebody threw a Molotov cocktail in.

I'd done some death notifications in the Coast Guard because of boat sinkings and, worse, boat piracy by drug smugglers. My skipper had told me: "These people will have a thousand gallons of sorrow injected into them under pressure by this news. The best thing you can do? Just listen to them. For hours if need be. Listen, and they can offload some of this cargo onto you. After that, they might be able to stand up and continue life."

What a skipper. So when I sat down with Saralee Nillsson, I said, "You can start anywhere. Take all the time you need." She squinted at me, wondering if I was trying to fake her out. I let the silence thicken. Silence is like nature…it abhors a vacuum.

I got her settled in the conference room and shut up, and she plunged in. "I gave him that nickname, Buzz," Saralee murmured. "He didn't like his legal name, which was Sigurd. I met him the summer we were nineteen, at a cheesy video game arcade at Ocean Shores down at the coast. I challenged him to a game of Frogger, and I won. Then he took me to a shooting arcade, and won a stuffed animal for me. It was a bumblebee with cartoony eyes. That's when I named him Buzz. That was our first night together. He loved all the kid stuff—mini golf, go-karts, pinball, Halloween. So why the hell wouldn't he have kids? We got married a year later, and he got onto a crab boat because he knew a guy. Not this idiot driver who killed him, Byron Cleverly—Byron's dad. Crab fishing in the Bering Sea is crazy dangerous. Those guys have a much higher death rate than cops. But he loved the risk, the big money, the brotherhood. I got my real estate license to stay busy until we had kids. Yeah, right."

I gave her a box of tissues. I let the silence thicken so she could keep filling it up.

"When Buzz died, we were on our second separation. The first came after he got a vasectomy and didn't tell me; he just got drunk one night and told me I could go off the pill. I asked why, and it came out. He got a vasectomy and didn't tell me. I poured him another drink to soften him up and said what about sperm donors? Then he said he didn't want kids because he would fuck them up the way his family fucked him up. I moved out for two weeks, but I came back because, you know, he was the irresistible Buzz. The guy had charm. He made me feel like the best woman ever."

Now I needed a tissue. I kept silent.

"I thought I could circle back to the kids issue. Then I started hearing from the other Boat Wives, that's what we called ourselves, that he was doing coke and hookers up there. But most of the Boat Guys were doing coke and hookers up there. It's crazy dangerous. They make serious money. Some of the Boat Wives said they made the Boat Guys use condoms, and I thought, what for? He's got a vasectomy!"

More tissues. I still kept silent.

"The last separation came a year ago when he brought home a nifty case of gonorrhea and didn't tell me, and sure enough, I got it. You know how humiliating it is to go to your doctor and tell her yes, I'm square married lady, but now I have gonorrhea, and it feels like peeing broken glass, and I need a prescription? I filled it, and at the pharmacy, the pharmacist explained in a loud voice that I had to take the entire prescription even if it felt like my gonorrhea symptoms were gone and everybody in that long line was looking at me, and I slunk out of there half dead from humiliation, and I changed pharmacies, but it burned, not just when I had to go pee, but my face was burning too because Buzz had humiliated me. So I moved out for two months. Never filed for divorce. I told Buzz it was condoms for everything from now on. He apologized and gave me the big grin, and we went out for steaks and good wine. But I held the line on the condoms. I just wanted Buzz. I wanted kids with Buzz. If maybe I could talk him around. We had time. Until he rode with Byron Cleverly, and now we don't have time.

More tissues. I kept silent.

"We died that day. Now, there's just me. My minister says I need to forgive Cleverly. He says it'll burn inside if I don't forgive him. I said I'll forgive Cleverly when I get photographic proof that he is roasting in Hell, and the Devil gave him a seat right next to the furnace. Does that make me a bad Christian? Am I a bad person?" She pinned me with her eyes.

I blew my nose and wiped my eyes. "I don't think you're a bad person. Because you didn't do anything wrong."

"I know, right? But I'm wondering if I'm a bad Christian because I haven't forgiven Cleverly. I changed pharmacies, so maybe I need to change churches too, but they were my companions when Buzz was up in the Bering Sea, and maybe the boat would sink because they often sink, and I really needed my church friends in case Buzz drowned. But maybe I shouldn't forgive Cleverly until he's actually gone to prison and the lawsuit you're filing is done. Maybe he needs to do penance. Then maybe I can forgive him and be a good Christian again."

I nodded. "You should do whatever reduces your misery. I'm miserable just hearing your story. You're a victim of a terrible crime.

Vehicular homicide? It's still homicide. It's a type of murder. I just want to get you something for your misery. Has your doctor thought about giving you a trial of Xanax for a while, just to take the edge off?"

She glared at me. "She offered Xanax. I'm not going to take anything. This damn thing happened because of drugs. I'm going to the gym every day and pounding myself. I'm talking to my sister. She never liked Buzz because she said he was an addict, and she's in recovery. So, no medication. But what can I do other than what I'm doing now?"

I know squat about therapy. But I had one possible idea. "Have you ever heard about MADD? Mothers Against Drunk Driving? They have free victim support groups. It might help if you met with other people who've been down this road."

She wiped her eyes. "I used to do Al-Anon when Buzz was drinking a lot, which was every time he came back from the Bering Sea. I can try that." She stopped. "What else should I tell you?"

"I want you to say anything that is on your mind. I'm your attorney. So, anything you say is confidential. Just like your doctor or your minister. So you can say anything. Not just now. All through the case. Here's my cell phone number." I wrote it on my card and gave it to her. I'd never given a client my cell phone number before. But I'd never had a widow on my caseload before, either. Desperate times call for desperate measures.

She sighed, shivered, and put it in her pocket. Then she sat up straight, now less wounded. "So how does this lawsuit work?"

I said, "I'll sue him and see if I pry out some evidence before the judge shuts me down. When a defendant is facing criminal charges, he doesn't have to provide a deposition or any evidence in a civil case until the criminal charges are resolved because he doesn't have to incriminate himself."

The widow brushed back her carefully frosted hair and straightened the seams of her trim black suit. Already, I was getting the feeling she'd been too good for her late husband. He was a crab fisherman who did drugs and blew money on hookers up in Alaska. She was a realtor who just wanted a secure income and a couple of kids. But they hadn't had kids. She was perceptive, foxy, and smart. I wondered what had brought them together.

She murmured, "So what recourse do we have if this driver spends or hides all his money?"

I patted her hand. "That's the trick, isn't it? I have a plan. I'm going to fake him out, so he shows his cards and then I'll try to seize his money and his assets. I'll file a Motion for Prejudgment Writ of Attachment." I sketched an outline.

She regarded me. I could tell her late husband had had lots of brilliant ideas that hadn't worked out. "How can you even find his stuff?" she wondered.

"I know an investigator who is so good she scares me," I said. "She's a friend. I've used her three times before, and she's found stuff that seems impossible to find. I'd sure hate to have her on the other side." I remembered where I was and lowered my voice because Rodney Mammon's lobby outside was usually full of criminals. "Fortunately, she doesn't work for criminals or people who defend criminals. Sorry, I can't identify her, but those are the ground rules. I pay her out of my pocket, so she doesn't cost you or the firm anything."

"And how do you know you can fake him out?" she concluded.

I shrugged. "I'm not certain. But I'll take the shot. I've done some reading up on this. Also, I have a mentor, a woman who is one of the best personal injury lawyers in the country. Not Washington State. The country. We worked out a plan. No promises, but it's the best chance."

"So, the personal injury lawyer you're talking about? That's not Rodney Mammon?"

I laughed. "Hell no. Rodney and the other lawyers here do strictly criminal defense. Rodney doesn't even want to look over my shoulder.

He just wants the nice green money. But this kind of case is what I was born for."

She stood. "In a big real estate deal, I know there has to be one person I can trust. Or else it will all fall apart. This case is my sorrow. But it's also a big deal." She snapped shut the brass locks on her briefcase. "I've decided I'm going to trust you. It sounds like you have two smart women who are experts, and they trust you, so I will, too."

I walked her to the door. Rodney was leaning against the new receptionist's desk, and murmuring, with his gel-stiffened blond porcupine hair, his tailored dove-gray suit, his capped teeth shining. The new receptionist? A blonde ex-stripper with large fake breasts displayed in a revealing maroon top. Rodney seemed to be loitering around her. I'd bet serious money he'd met her while defending her in a lap-dancing case. I'd bet non-serious money he was "boinking" her. His word, not mine.

Rodney held out his studio-tanned hand to the widow. "I'm Rodney," he droned. "I'm so very sorry for your loss." An amoeba would have known he was insincere. I had to bite my lip to keep from laughing.

"Thanks," she said, giving his hand one businesslike pump and letting it go. "I have a feeling I'm in good hands."

"You are," he said, glancing at me. "Sam Strait is one gnarly kick-ass litigator. I always turn to him when the chips are down in civil court." I'd been in his employment for about a week. Rodney turned back to the widow. "We're going to get a boatload of cash from that dude," he said. "And by the way, you look stunning in black."

He watched her as she left. Because he was checking out her ass.

I went back to my office to see if The Ghost had anything for me. Turned out she did.

I knew The Ghost's real name and address only because I was one of what she called her "real friends." Other than Duvonda, I suspected there weren't many. I didn't have her real cell number or email. She was extremely careful about how she used phones and the internet. She liked to say, "cell phones are radios." She never used public Wi-Fi and laughed at those who did. Given her expertise, it was understandable.

So when we needed to contact each other, we would log into a Gmail account she'd set up just for us two. Only we had the password. I would log in as VanillaBoy6969 and see if there were any draft emails. If there was one, it was from her. I would read it, delete it, and then write a draft for her to read as a response. That way, nothing between us ever went out over the Web. She liked calling me Vanilla Boy because kink people call non-kink people "vanilla."

There was a draft, all right. *Mama has supper ready. Come by at 7:30.* I deleted it and wrote my own draft. *I'm hungry. See you then.*

When The Ghost met me at her door, she winked. Tonight, she wore dark-gray velvet lounging pajamas with her blonde hair in a black velvet bow. I guessed she had playtime later that night. She smelled of White Shoulders, my favorite perfume. "Hello, Vanilla Boy. Turns out your defendant is a rather major waste of oxygen. I found lots. But some of it I can only show you, I can't let you take it with you. You'll see why."

We sat down at her kitchen table. Her tuxedo cat Guinevere looked up at me, blinking, and said a rusty "Meow."

"Meow yourself, sweetie," I said, scratching her on the nape of her neck as The Ghost laid out her documents.

The Ghost cherished showing off, and I cherished letting her do it. "Okay, first, let's get the ordinary stuff out of the way," she said. "Here's his property with the mortgage, promissory note, etcetera. There's a land use application pending. He's looking to subdivide his acreage into fifteen lots for building new houses." She pushed the documents across to me. "Here's his bank account at Chase. A hundred grand in checking, twenty grand in savings. Strange that there's so much in checking, but leave that aside. Now for the good stuff."

She pushed another sheaf of documents across the table and waited while I leafed through them. I whistled. She said, "I know, right? He has three actual Social Security numbers. The US government verifies that."

I didn't want to know how she knew this. "How did he get those?"

"Until about the mid-'80s, if you said you'd lost your Social Security card, the Social Security Administration would give you a new card with a brand-new number. Perfectly legal. So, if you got in deep doo-doo, you could just start using another Social Security number and be somewhat invisible. It's not perfect. The new numbers are issued under the same name. But it's good. The federal government and most big companies track everybody by Social Security number. Only if they get very curious about you do they go deeper."

"Okay, but no aliases."

"Nope. None that I can find. But here's the kicker." She pushed another sheaf of documents across the table.

I leafed through them. This was juicy. "A passport from Dominica? I thought that was that Spanish-speaking half of the island that also has Haiti. What's special about that?"

"You're thinking of the Dominican Republic. Dominica is a separate island in the Caribbean. They sell passports for twenty-five thousand, the cheapest legitimate passports in the world. A Maltese passport, the Cadillac of shady passports, costs ten times as much. And Dominica has no extradition treaty with the US. He got this fifteen years ago. He's been preparing an escape hole for a very long time." She handed over one final thing. "And he's got an account in Grand Cayman for $1,200,000. Maybe there are more I couldn't locate. I can let you have the passport and the Grand Cayman bank statement. I'll give you an explanation for how you found that stuff later."

Grand Cayman. A serious banking haven. They didn't report anything to the US government, and many of the world's smartest tax cheats and crooks stashed some money there.

I said, "But I thought our defendant was just a small-time dealer in coke and meth who sold our victim and his shipmates a little product when they were working twenty hours a day on the crab boats."

"Not small time. Mid time. He's probably working that angle on lots of fishing boats and fish processors, too. He's got to be in bed with people who are big-time. Maybe some of that money in the Caymans is theirs. Who knows? Now, here is the stuff I cannot let you have. I can only show it to you. This guy is somewhat dangerous, Sam."

The Ghost didn't go in for hyperbole. She pushed the final sheaf of documents over to me but kept a finger on it. I wasn't going to take this stuff. I was pretty sure I didn't want to.

It was a printout from the Drug Enforcement Administration entitled *Known Associates*. I scanned down through it. Yup. There were large cartel people listed. I recognized a couple of family names from way back when I was in the Coast Guard. I guessed he got his product wholesale from them. There was a lot of supporting documentation, too, including transcripts of several wiretaps.

Our defendant was in deep doo-doo. But if I screwed up, so was I. Cartel people didn't mind murdering anybody who interfered with their business. Sometimes, they took people apart with…home improvement tools.

"Motherfucker," I said as I slid those back to her.

"Can't prove that yet," she laughed, "but the night is young." She took my hand. "This stuff is spicy, Sam. You've done some good personal injury work, but you just joined the NFL. Can I ask what you're planning to use all this for?"

I gave her a brief summary of the plan I'd worked out. She clapped. "That's nice," she said. "Your idea?"

"Mostly mine," I said. "But as we just confirmed, just now, I think best when I've got a good woman as a sounding board."

She rose. We hugged, and the hug lingered. "We could have such fun if you weren't a Vanilla Boy," she said.

I nodded. "But I am. My childhood wasn't so great, just like yours. I'm not sure what romantic love is, apart from the thing with Suzanne. But that's what I want."

She walked me to the door. "I get it. You told me some of the story."

I hugged her again, and again, it lingered. What a complex creature The Ghost was! I couldn't imagine what it would be like to have a mother constantly surveilling, snooping, logging your every act.

My childhood had been quite the other thing.

"I'll let you know how it turns out," I said. "I'll take you for goat cheese tortellini and a rousing game of Scrabble." I kissed her forehead.

As I walked to my battered Subaru Outback, ships were hooting out in the dark harbor, and a fog was turning into rain. Again, the seals barked. The homeless baritone had disappeared.

First I was going to have a rousing game of something else.

CHAPTER TWO—AN IDEA SO CRAZY IT MIGHT EVEN WORK

The wrongful death case of *Saralee Nillsson, Personal Representative for the Estate of Sigurd Nillsson v. Byron Cleverly,* was going to require a lot of fancy dancing.

Usually, when a defendant kills a passenger while driving recklessly or under the influence, there's a standard sequence. You get the surviving spouse named as personal representative and get Letters Testamentary. Letters Testamentary authorize the personal representative to do business on behalf of the estate. We personal injury lawyers often call the Letters Testamentary the "hunting license." Then you round up the police report, photos of the scene and wreckage, the medical examiner's autopsy and supplemental report, and get an economist to estimate how much the deceased would have earned during his or her working life, reduced to present value.

When you have all this stuff, you write a detailed demand letter explaining the damages and asking for a huge amount. You enclose all the exhibits you gathered unless you expect sneakiness. In that case, you keep one or two good weapons in your back pocket. You send it to the defendant's car insurance company. Unless they have huge policy limits, if the fault is clear, they usually offer what they have and prove that's the limit. Then, you check to see if the defendant is rich and underinsured.

They usually are not. Rich people are usually smart enough to get enough insurance. Then, you go to the deceased's own car insurance, make an underinsured motorist claim, and "pop the limits" for both policies. If the defendant has major assets, you seek a personal contribution from the defendant's own assets.

That's the usual sequence.

But here's the catch—the personal injury attorney has to dig hard to verify that the defendant doesn't have big-time assets other than the car insurance. If the defendant is rich and underinsured, then you've got a war.

And if the defendant is charged with a crime, the defendant can't be forced to give any evidence to the plaintiff until the criminal prosecution is done.

Like a lot of things we humans do, it's a tug of war for money. Before the plaintiff gets to trial, the defendant can sell his house and assets and hide that money. Then his criminal defense attorney can charge crazy fees and pig out on the money. This often leaves the poor widow sitting there with nothing but the insurance policy limits, even if the defendant is loaded.

But sometimes, the plaintiff's attorney can do something fancy. That's what I worked out with Duvonda. Unless that BS "I wasn't driving" defense panned out—and eyewitnesses contradicted it—we could pop the limits. But I wanted to get Saralee Nillsson lots more. I thought Byron Cleverly should pay most of what he had.

So, I didn't send a demand letter. I just filed suit in King County Superior Court and sent Silent Mike, Duvonda's investigator and boyfriend, out to serve Cleverly. I wasn't serving just the Summons and Complaint, which is the usual tactic... I was serving Interrogatories and Requests for Production.

Interrogatories are written questions that the defendant has to answer under oath within thirty days (forty if they are served with the

Complaint). Requests for Production ask the defendant to produce the requested documents and state under oath that all requested documents have been provided, again within thirty days (forty if those were served with the Complaint).

And I also added a set of Requests for Admission. I love these things. They ask the defendant to admit that each statement in a Request for Admission is true within thirty days (again forty days if they are served with the Complaint). But if the defendant denies one, and their denial is proved to be a lie at trial, the defendant can be forced to pay attorneys' fees for time spent disproving the lie. Not every judge gives attorneys' fees for that. But it's a good lever because the risk is real.

So, I sent out the whole batch of stuff with Silent Mike out for service on Cleverly. I asked the defendant to admit he had been driving when the Mazda hit the tree. I asked him to admit he'd been driving over the speed limit when the Mazda left the road. Etcetera. Basically, I was serving notice that if he lied at all about the crash, I planned to request attorney fees on an hourly basis against him personally. My time was worth $300 an hour, and the hours would add up fast.

Silent Mike got Cleverly at dinner that night. (The best time to serve most defendants is at dinnertime.) The next day, my paralegal Nicky knocked on my door and laid a fax on my desk. Aloysius Miller was appearing for Cleverly as civil defense counsel for now. He was Cleverly's criminal defense lawyer, too. I wanted to rush everything and spook Miller before an insurance defense lawyer who knew the Civil Rules better got involved.

The next day I called Aloysius Miller and acted bashful. "So I'm wondering, Aloysius, what's your position on getting us the discovery responses on time?"

Aloysius sighed. "At the present juncture, I do not foresee any major difficulties. But Cleverly has been charged with felony vehicular homicide, so that may present difficulties," he said.

I quietly said, "Fair enough," and told him goodbye. I looked out the window. The trees in the plaza below showed new pale green leaves in the spring wind. The leaves looked like waving hands as they flickered. A flock of crows mobbed a hawk, driving the hawk away from the nest, I guessed.

The next day Nicky again knocked on my door and handed me another fax. Along with a messenger slip and a sheaf of documents. "Miller also e-served everything," she said. I checked my email. Sure enough. Faxed service wasn't even legal. I guessed he wanted to tell me in every possible way that he would stomp me.

I leafed through the pleadings—the defendant's Motion for Protective Order Staying All Discovery, Declaration of Aloysius Miller with Exhibits, and proposed order. I went right to the Declaration.

If Miller was going to goof up, it would be in the exhibits to the Declaration.

Hmm. Traffic Collision Report showing a pending criminal charge—to support the discovery stay—but it also stated the defendant had been driving. Tasty.

But he also attached the witness statements from the Traffic Collision Report. If a party omits part of a document, the opposing party can move to admit the rest into evidence. I'd expected him to play hide the ball. But he didn't.

The witness statements weren't so very great for the defendant.

Both statements said the dark-haired man was driving when the Mazda zoomed past them right before the crash. Cleverly's hair was dark. Nillsson's was bright red. They were in a Mazda roadster with the top down. Clear view. Solid evidence that Cleverly was actually driving. One witness was the female jogger he swerved to avoid. The other was an elderly guy checking his mailbox.

Why had Aloysius Miller included the whole Traffic Collision Report? He'd shown that the defendant was facing criminal charges and denied me the moral victory I would get from moving to admit the entire TCR into evidence. But it seemed to me he'd goofed. Maybe a paralegal wrote it. Maybe not. Trade secret—most criminal defense attorneys are not good legal writers. They stand up in court and argue. When it comes to pounding the keyboard, most of them aren't exactly Beethoven.

Nicky stood in the doorway, studying my face. "This is awesome," I said, for once sounding like Rodney.

"Why?" she asked, flexing her long piano-playing hands.

"Please sit," I said, and she did. Nicky had black curly hair, big brown eyes, and unplucked eyebrows. She was the only cerebral woman in the firm. The criminal defense lawyers were blond and shallow—both the women and the men. The criminal defense paralegals looked like they'd been taken from modeling school.

Nicky Schwartz was real. She stood out like a college professor at a sports bar on Wet T-Shirt Night. Suddenly, my throat was dry.

I took a big swig from the ever-present iced Americano. "I'm going to try something tricky called moving for a Prejudgment Writ of Attachment," I said. "I'm going to ask the court to seize all his assets—locking them up so they can't be sold or hidden—until the criminal and civil cases are both done. I can't do discovery while the criminal case is pending, because Cleverly has a Fifth Amendment right. Unless I can stampede him into waiving it."

"The right against self-incrimination?" Nicky said.

"Exactly. However, if I can show that the defendant is likely to be convicted because the evidence against him is solid, and there's some likelihood he might conceal his assets, then I can seize any of his assets that I can find and enumerate. If the judge grants the Writ, I just need to get a big bond to cover the value of the assets. In case of wrongful attachment. The defendant still owns everything. But he can't hide it or spend his money until the civil case is resolved."

"Is the writ hard to get?" she asked.

"Very. Usually, judges are reluctant to prevent somebody from using or selling their property unless they've been convicted of a crime or a judgment in a civil case is already entered against them. So, I have to show that he has the means to conceal assets and also that he's likely to get convicted. I tried once before, and I lost." I patted my briefcase. "But this time, I have something special."

"You mean the witness statements showing he was driving?"

"Bingo. That shows he's likely to get convicted. I'm also waiting for the police to run the tox screen so we can know if he had drugs in his system. Assuming they're willing to voluntarily give it to me. They might just be persuaded. If he was rolling dirty, then there are two ways to convict him—extreme disregard for human life and driving under the influence."

Nicky arched her eyebrows. "That sounds like half the people Rodney and the criminal defense people down the hall are representing," she said softly.

I took a deep breath. I was about to stick my neck out with her. I leaned in and lowered my voice. "Right. Our practice group, the Personal Injury Department, is really the Innocent Peoples' Department. The Criminal Defense Department down the hall is really the Guilty Peoples' Department."

Nicky laughed softly and looked over her shoulder with a naughty smile.

I said, "I prosecuted against Rodney a few times when I was a greenhorn up in juvie. He told me the only clients he ever worried about were the tiny percentage who were innocent."

Nicky leaned forward. "Did he really say that?"

"Yes. But I didn't believe him." I smiled at her. "The only clients he ever worries about are the ones that aren't paying."

She laughed, a cute yelp. "So what do you have showing Cleverly is likely to hide his assets or sell them?" she asked.

I slid several documents across my desk to her—copies of the three virgin Social Security cards and the passport from Dominica. I was keeping the bank account from Grand Cayman in my back pocket to use as the final bullet if I needed one. "Don't tell anybody here about this."

Her eyes went big. "Where did you get this stuff?"

I shrugged. "I have a very good investigator."

"Not ours," she said. Our firm had a private investigator on retainer who did the criminal defense stuff like finding and interviewing witnesses. He had worked for the public defender before he set up his own shop.

He wasn't bad when he was sober. Which was sometimes.

"Not ours. She is a friend of mine. She's done a couple of cases for me, and she's so good it's scary. And she's not cheap."

Nicky frowned. "Rodney doesn't like any vendor who's not cheap."

I nodded. "I'm paying her out of my own pocket. I want to win this."

Nicky said, "But you've told me you have a profit-sharing agreement with Rodney. Don't you know that all the criminal defense attorneys have that too? Don't you know he's never paid them a dime? Even Paddy, who's been here five years?"

I nodded again. "I've heard that. I know profit sharing may not come through for me. But here's the thing, Nicky. Have you met the widow?" She nodded. "I really want to win this for her. Her husband was violently killed. By a friend. She deserves this."

Nicky squinted at me. "I'm not sure you're going to fit in here," she said, "but I like it."

"Me too," I said. "I'm going to ask you to be a big help in the next few days."

"You mean writing pleadings? We did some of that in my paralegal course. I could do that."

I wagged my finger at her and winked. "Not yet. I write everything myself for now. No, I mean I'll need you to launch everything when I say, where I say. And proofread all my stuff before it goes out because you have a good eye. And I'll need you not to talk about any of this with the criminal defense people. I used to prosecute once upon a time. Criminal lawyers spend so much time in court and in the hallways waiting while the calendars grind on while the defendants take twenty minutes apiece to plead guilty. They gossip. Rodney and Aloysius are colleagues. Nothing we do or say will be secret from Aloysius Miller if it's ever disclosed to the criminal defense people. So I really need you to be super secret."

Nicky smiled. "I can be super secret," she said, holding up three fingers. "Girl Scouts' honor."

The defendant's Motion for Protective Order was granted without oral argument. Exactly what I expected. But my Motion for Prejudgment Writ of Attachment was specially set for oral argument.

All this happened so quickly that no insurance defense lawyer had appeared for Cleverly. Maybe Aloysius Miller persuaded the insurance company to hire him because he did do some insurance defense and some civil litigation. Maybe the insurance company just hadn't gotten the memo yet. That often happened. In some insurance companies, the left hand didn't know what the right hand was doing. It didn't necessarily care. "That's not my department," was the thinking. Bureaucracy, right?

So I was going nose to nose with Aloysius Miller. And my widow Saralee Nillsson was going to be sitting there beside me. I wanted the judge to see there was a human being involved here. Two, if you counted Byron Cleverly. But I didn't.

***

Cold rain and wind descended the day of the hearing. I met with Saralee and Nicky in the conference room and briefed them about what

I expected. Saralee was blonde, with a stylish short asymmetrical haircut sad gray eyes, wearing a black linen suit and pumps. She listened well. She was a realtor—able to get along with anybody, usually positive. But today, she was drenched in sorrow so potent I could smell it. Human beings exude pheromones that convey emotion. Those pheromones soak into everybody around them, straight from the nose into the limbic system, the emotional center of the brain.

I put a hand over hers when we were done talking. She scrutinized me, then nodded.

As I was loading the pleadings file and my tabbed exhibits into the litigation case, Rodney came in. "I thought I'd tag along and watch you kick some major ass, Sam," he said. Oh great.

I locked the litigation case, and we walked over to the King County Courthouse. My umbrella almost turned itself inside out in the wind. We were set before Judge Beth McCollum. I'd been in front of her several times as a prosecutor, and I was pleased she was the assigned judge. She'd been smart and witty every time I'd been in front of her. Better yet, I had only lost when I deserved to.

Aloysius and Cleverly were already there at the defense table, the one farthest from the empty jury box. Cleverly got up and limped around the table to pour himself some water. He was using a cane. Cleverly was a big, pudgy guy with lank black hair and, a gothic-script neck tattoo and gray circles under his eyes. He wore a jean jacket and cargo pants showing a wallet on a chain. To court.

It wasn't the worst defendant wardrobe I'd ever seen. Once, when cross-examining a juvenile defendant in criminal court, I'd asked him to tell the judge about the caption below the cartoon squirrel on his T-shirt. He had blushed and murmured, "It says *Rub My Nuts for Luck.*" Seriously, you can't make this stuff up.

On the front row bench, Saralee Nillsson sat quietly. We shook hands, and I swallowed hard.

Rodney opened his briefcase and took out a sheaf of papers with a pink Post-It on it labeled *SURPRISE* in big letters. I leaned over and whispered, "So what's the surprise?"

He held up the sheaf to me so the other side couldn't see it and flipped through the pages. They were blank. "Thought I'd fake them out," he murmured. Whatever. As long as he wasn't going to pull anything, that would ruin my argument. I hoped he wouldn't say anything at all, but he was the boss.

"All rise," said the bailiff, taking her seat. I jumped to my feet. "The Honorable Beth McCallum, presiding."

Judge McCallum swept onto the bench, put her long gray hair back in a scrunchie, and sat. "Be seated," she said, her gray eyes flashing. "We're here in the matter of *Estate of Nillsson versus Cleverly*. Plaintiff is moving for a Prejudgment Writ of Attachment. All parties identify themselves for the record."

I stood. "Sam Strait for Plaintiff, and I will be arguing for the Writ." I wanted to elbow Rodney out of the way. "I'm here with my fellow counsel, Rodney Mammon. Also present is Saralee Nillsson, the widow who is personal representative, and my paralegal Nicky Schwartz."

Aloysius stood and flipped his blond forelock. "Aloysius Miller present with Defendant Byron Cleverly. I apologize he cannot stand as he was seriously injured in the crash, which led to this case."

I'd just seen Cleverly stand. And walk.

Judge McCallum nodded to us and then focused on me. "Proceed."

"Your Honor, Plaintiff has met the test for this Prejudgment Writ of Attachment because she has shown that the defendant has a strong likelihood of being convicted of vehicular homicide and because he is likely to conceal or liquidate his assets given the multiple Social Security numbers he has and his passport from the Caribbean nation of Dominica, which does not have an extradition treaty with the United States."

Aloysius snorted.

"All right, Counselor," Judge McCallum said, glancing at him. "First let's explore the strong likelihood of conviction argument. Mr. Cleverly has been charged?"

"Yes, Your Honor. Exhibit Four to my declaration is the indictment for Mr. Cleverly."

She flipped through some pages and looked at me. "So regarding the strong likelihood of conviction, Mr. Strait. Along with your Declaration, you filed the Declaration of Aloysius Miller with exhibits in which he sought and obtained a protective order barring discovery until the criminal case is concluded." She frowned. "Isn't it somewhat unusual to use the defendant's own pleadings in one motion to seek relief against him in another?"

I nodded. "Yes, it is. I did that because Mr. Miller's exhibits, which he authenticates himself, inadvertently show that the defendant was driving when the crash happened. One statement is from a gentleman who was checking his mailbox one hundred yards before the crash scene. This crash involved a Mazda convertible, and the top was down. He saw a dark-haired man driving at about ninety miles per hour and a red-haired male in the passenger seat. Mr. Cleverly has dark hair. The photo of Mr. Nillsson, which is part of the funeral brochure, shows that Mr. Nillsson had red hair. There is no way Nillsson could stop the car, change seats, and then accelerate again to his excessive speed before reaching the point before he spun off the road and crashed."

Judge McCallum motioned with her hand. "And the other witness?"

"The other witness was the female jogger who was running with her dog when Mr. Cleverly crested the hill airborne, swerved to avoid her, and spun off the road and down the slope. She also confirmed that the dark-haired male was driving and the redheaded male was in the passenger seat. She saw the Mazda leave the road right before her eyes, only about forty feet away. This all shows likelihood of conviction."

She placed her hand on the exhibits and turned to Aloysius. "Counselor, what do you say about likelihood of conviction?"

Aloysius stood. This time, he didn't brush his forelock, which showed he was a little rattled. "Your Honor, the defendant is presumed innocent until convicted by a jury of his peers who need to find him guilty beyond a reasonable doubt. Also, the plaintiff should not try to use the defendant's own Declaration and exhibits against him. It's not only unconventional, it is unjust and outrageous."

Judge McCallum glanced at me. "How about that, Mr. Strait?"

I nodded. "Your Honor, there is a specific RCW that allows attorneys to make statements and offer evidence that their clients are bound by. Also, Mr. Miller offered the Declaration voluntarily, without any reservations, and it is a statement against interest under the Evidence Rules and therefore excluded from the hearsay rule. It is admissible evidence. It actually was admitted in considering the defendant's Motion for Protective Order. It shows that Mr. Cleverly has a strong likelihood of conviction. We don't need to show proof beyond a reasonable doubt because we're not trying to put him in jail. We're not even trying to obtain damages from him at this point. We just want to secure his assets so they won't be concealed before we can get to a judgment. The statute is expressly created for this purpose." Again, Aloysius snorted.

She nodded. "Okay, you've both given me something to think about. And next, I need to move on to the issue of Mr. Cleverly's likelihood of concealing his assets." She furrowed her brow and looked at me. I took a deep breath. Right here, I had to do some fancy dancing so I wouldn't have to reveal The Ghost.

Aloysius butted in: "Plaintiff has shown no dishonest conduct by Mr. Cleverly, and he has no evidence that Mr. Cleverly will conceal his assets. Mr. Cleverly proved he had strong ties to the community when he posted bail in the amount of half a million dollars. He has a house and property in Kent and is pursuing a very profitable subdivision of that property with a view toward selling lots for building houses. He has a stellar credit rating. I find it inexcusable that the plaintiff would accuse this injured man facing criminal charges with attempting to hide his assets when it hasn't been conclusively determined that he was even driving the car."

Judge McCallum held up a hand. "Enough, Mr. Miller. I was asking Mr. Strait for his position first. Please wait your turn."

I remembered a brilliant saying from law school—never interrupt your enemy when he is making a mistake.

I cleared my throat. "Your Honor, Mr. Cleverly has three separate Social Security numbers. That shows he has the capacity to conceal assets. There is no legitimate reason—not one—for him to have three different Social Security numbers. This is not innocent behavior. Regarding his passport from Dominica—when that is combined with the Social Security numbers, it shows Mr. Cleverly is very able to conceal his assets and to flee the jurisdiction of this court. He is facing a serious criminal charge, which could send him to prison. He has a passport to a country where he could flee and not be extradited."

Judge McCallum nodded. She leafed through my declaration, looking at the copies of the Social Security cards and the passport. I had her interested anyway. But my heart was in my throat. If somebody asked me how I got these documents, I had a flimsy cover story. But not a great answer.

I took a deep breath and looked over at Mr. Cleverly. Then I reached into my folder and took out the statement from his bank account in Grand Cayman.

I hadn't offered it into evidence. It wasn't before the court. That was deliberate because I wanted to hold it back in case I lost and had to move for reconsideration. Moreover, it might expose The Ghost. But I held it up and squinted at it so Cleverly could see the distinctive green palm tree logo on the statement.

Then I looked over at him. He'd turned pale. And I realized something. Aloysius didn't know about the bank account. Nobody knew except Cleverly, The Ghost, and me. It was a lever, and I just showed, silently, that I could press it if I needed to.

Then Cleverly turned even whiter, and I suddenly realized something else. This wasn't all his money. This was cartel money. Bad things happened to people who lost cartel money.

This was a better lever than I'd hoped for.

Judge McCallum asked, "So how did you get these documents, Mr. Strait?"

This was the fancy dancing part. "They are all public record," I said blandly. "It just took a little digging."

This was where I was taking a giant leap. The Social Security cards were government records. But they weren't public records. If either Aloysius or the judge called me on it, I was hosed.

I darted my eyes over at Aloysius, and he seemed distracted by Cleverly whispering in his ear. I looked back at the judge, and I caught a twinkle in her eye. Then she turned to Aloysius. "Counselor, what of it?"

Aloysius stood. He'd been distracted, and his opening had floated right past him. Under his studio tan, he was a little pink. "Your Honor, the plaintiff hasn't shown that Mr. Cleverly has done anything illegal or is contemplating breaking any law. Plaintiff hasn't shown it's illegal to have three Social Security numbers or a passport from Dominica. Plaintiff has not shown Mr. Cleverly is trying to conceal his property or has any plan to conceal his property. Holy smoke, his land is a major asset under development. You can't conceal that."

Judge McCallum nodded. "But you can encumber it. If Mr. Cleverly took out a mortgage on the property and concealed the funds, the money could just walk away, couldn't it?"

I remembered she'd done some securities litigation before she went on the bench. She took a big pay cut to become a judge. That meant she really liked the job. As they say, in Washington, DC, you either come here to be somebody or to do something. It looked like she wanted to do something.

Aloysius nodded. "But mortgages and deeds of trust are public records, too. There's no evidence before the court that Mr. Cleverly has taken out a mortgage or a deed of trust. There are no encumbrances before the court."

"Not yet," Rodney snorted.

Judge McCallum pointed at Rodney. "Mr. Mammon, you are not arguing this motion, are you?"

"No, Your Honor," Rodney said with elaborate humility.

"Then let Mr. Strait provide all remarks to the court for Plaintiff." She leafed through the papers again. "But Mr. Mammon makes a point here," she mused. "The purpose of a Prejudgment Writ of Attachment is to prevent property from floating away before a judgment is rendered. If it is granted, Plaintiff will need to post a bond for any damages resulting from attaching the property in the event she does not win her wrongful death case. If Plaintiff needed to show the property had already been concealed before getting the Writ, which is designed to prevent the concealment, that would be locking the barn door after the horse has escaped."

She looked around the room. "This is a sticky one. I am not going to rule today. I will take this under advisement, read the statute and some cases, and email you my order. If the Motion is denied, then it is denied with prejudice. I won't go through all this again. And if it is granted, I will only sign the Writ of Attachment after Plaintiff provides proof of a very sizeable bond as surety against wrongful attachment. The statute requires that, so the defendant isn't wrongfully deprived of use of his property without having a remedy."

She looked over our heads. "I will be in touch, folks. And now I have a routine calendar coming up after this. That is all."

I stood and turned around. Saralee Nillsson nodded to me.

While we'd been arguing, about a dozen lawyers had filed into the courtroom and taken seats in the back. I hadn't known they were there. This was good. In the prosecutor's office, they'd called it "having your blinders on." When you're in the zone, you get tunnel vision and that's when you perform the best.

I put my finger to my lips, and Nicky nodded. I didn't want us to talk until we were well away from the courthouse.

Rodney slapped me on the back. "I think Aloysius is shitting bricks," he murmured.

I nodded. But I didn't think Aloysius was shitting bricks. I thought he was playing for time while Mr. Cleverly put all his yummy money in Aloysius's trust account, where Aloysius could gobble it up defending the criminal case. I wasn't at all confident that we would win or that we would win soon enough.

Outside the courthouse, we ran the usual gauntlet of homeless drug addicts and floridly mentally ill people who clustered on the sidewalks there. To my right, three hollow-eyed junkies in track suits passed around a hand-rolled cigarette. Up ahead, on the street corner, an obese woman was singing the theme song from *Cabaret* while gesturing at the sky. She wore a threadbare and filthy T-shirt, her navel exposed. Under the dirt, it read *Take the Pepsi Challenge.*

Saralee walked closer to me on one side and Nicky on the other. The wind was roaring, but the rain had stopped. My blood was racing. Behind me, Rodney gave the junkies a dollar bill. Who knows? Maybe they were former or future customers of his. If they got promoted to dealing heroin or crack or meth and could pay the freight.

"So, how do you think it went?" Saralee asked me when we had crossed the street out of the weirdness zone around the courthouse.

I sighed. "I did my best. We have a good shot. But you never know until you know. We have a good judge and a good argument. But this is an extraordinary remedy, depriving somebody of use of property before he's been convicted or a judgment is entered. I lost the one other time I tried this. This time, our facts are better."

I looked at Saralee's shining eyes. "It made a difference that you were there. Looking at the widow in a wrongful death case gives us a lot of emotional pull. Judges deny that they are influenced by that. But they're humans. So they are influenced by that."

I rode the elevator up to Mammon & Associates. Rodney went sauntering back to the Guilty Peoples' Department but turned before he rounded the corner. He pointed at me. "I think you were a badass motherfucker today, Sam," he said.

"Thanks," I said. For once, I was glad that Rodney tended to overstate everything.

I walked Nicky back to her cubicle and pointed to her CD rack. "Nicky? Could you lend me a CD? Maybe a piano concerto? I need some classical music to help me decompress."

She handed me a disk. "Take two of these, and call me in the morning," she said with conviction.

This was the great thing about plaintiffs' personal injury cases. If you didn't deserve to win, you didn't sign the case, or you withdrew. Which meant you only went forward when you deserved to win.

CHAPTER THREE—LEARNING TO BOND

For three days, I waited for a ruling on needles and pins. I filled out the bond application. I submitted a check request to the firm bookkeeper so I'd have the premium fee if it was needed. Sometimes, I just stared out the window and watched the April leaves waving in the April wind.

I was meeting with Saralee Nillsson and explaining the next steps when Rodney came into my office. He sat on the corner of my desk, a little too close for my comfort, holding the check request. He always crowded people to make them uneasy. "This check is for five thousand bucks, hombre," he said.

"I know. I asked for it, so I'm ready to roll if we win the motion. It's the cost of the bond. It will secure attaching Cleverly's real estate and his bank accounts. We'll be locking up over two million dollars of assets to preserve them so we can get a judgment and levy on his assets. But if the Writ of Attachment is not wrongfully granted, we exonerate the bond and pay only twenty percent of the amount. So it sounds like a good deal."

He frowned. "Five thousand bucks? That's half of what I get for a DUI case. Seems pretty steep." He leaned in. I smelled his cologne—something sandalwood and musk. Saralee caught my eye and looked on, nervous.

I bit my tongue. I'd learned how to do that after getting reprimanded at my last firm. I didn't mention that Rodney spent almost three million dollars a year in advertising, and he handled hundreds of DUI cases per year. He got defendants to plead guilty in all but two percent of those DUI cases. His henchmen, like Paddy, tried the rest. They were misdemeanor trials which typically only took two days. Rodney had built a money-making machine. But he wasn't ready to spend even a little so he could be playing poker at the big table, where multimillion-dollar wrongful death cases were handled.

I was thinking about putting up the money myself. But there was no profit sharing in sight, despite our contract. Also I had paid The Ghost and Silent Mike from my own pocket, as I always do.

Saralee unzipped her purse, drawing Rodney's eye. "Sam, your contract says I am responsible for all of the client costs, right?" I nodded. "Then I'll pick up the cost. I'll be paying for it eventually, out of the settlement. I just need you to seize Cleverly's property. There's no need for your…boss…to get upset."

I showed her the bond application so she would make it out directly to the bonding company. I didn't want Rodney to get the money into his trust account and blow it on two more Pierre Cardin suits or whatever. "Problem solved," she said as she tore the check out of the book and handed it to me.

By now, Rodney had backed away and stood by the door. So long as he wasn't paying, he was satisfied. He left and closed the door without a sound. The guy could move silently.

I made a copy of the check and the bond form and put the check in my wallet. I handed her the copies. "I'll let you know when we hear about the motion," I said.

She shook my hand. Good handshake—firm, dry, one businesslike pump and done. She met my eye and nodded. She knew what I was up against, just as I knew what she was up against. A shared adversary unites people quicker than almost anything.

I walked her out through the lobby. Rodney leaned against the reception desk, murmuring to the receptionist/stripper. Again Rodney checked out Saralee's ass as she left. He fixed his flat blue eyes on me. "Let me know when the order comes in, hombre," he said. "This will be rad."

When he was gone, I refreshed my email. Oh God. There was an email from Judge McCallum.

I took a deep breath before I opened it.

I'd put Mr. Nillsson's photo up on the blank wall in my office. He stared back at me, redhead in sunglasses, wearing a baseball cap that read *Bite Me*, laughing on the sunny deck of a fishing boat at sea. He was the first specter in my office.

Then I opened the email and the PDF Order Granting Writ of Attachment. "Holy Moses!" I yelled.

Then I went to my window and posed like the guy in *The Karate Kid* when he finally learned Mr. Miyagi's best move. The Crane. I balanced on the ball of my left foot, extended my right leg with my toe pointed, stretched my arms out with cupped hands and splayed fingers.

Everybody needs a touchdown dance. The Crane was mine. Still is, in fact.

The door opened behind me. "Any word?" Nicky, of course.

I turned to look at her. Still did The Crane. "Motion granted," I said, still smiling.

She smiled and tucked her black hair behind her ears, cocking her head. Curious.

I explained The Crane. She nodded, indulging me. She sat down in my guest chair and threw a curveball at me. "So, what happened to your right ear?"

"It got shot off in a hostile boarding when I was in the Coast Guard. A drug interdiction."

"What happened to the guy who shot you?"

"Rusty Russ and Drunk Bob shot him many times, and he died. His shipmates surrendered. We found almost a ton of cocaine in the hold among a bunch of bananas. Lots of spiders in the hold, too. Spiders and bananas go together like peanut butter and jelly for some reason."

"Did it hurt?"

"It stung at the time. Like three or four bee stings. Not a big deal. But when I get mad or excited, the scar turns dark pink."

She tilted her head. "It's dark pink right now. I noticed it when you were doing The Crane."

I shrugged. "Not exactly subtle. But you knew that about me." I wanted to turn the subject back to her. "So, who's the guy in the picture in your cubicle? The handsome dude?"

She looked away. "That's just Fred."

"Boyfriend?"

"Supposed to be my boyfriend," she said. I noted her evasion. She was smoke-screening. No problem. I just wanted to get her off talking about my scar. Sometimes, I got self-conscious about it. Duvonda had told me my scar glowing dark pink was my "tell," like in poker. I knew that. But there wasn't a damn thing I could do about it.

Then I called the bonding company on speakerphone and got the okay to bring the application and the check over. And I printed out my Prejudgment Writ of Attachment, which listed the legal description of the Kent property and all the bank accounts we were seizing.

I was learning to bond.

***

I put the check and bond application in my briefcase and decided to walk over to the bonding company. Seattle has a phenomenon called "sunbreaks"—when the clouds finally break open for an hour or two. Everybody gets outside if they can to soak up some Vitamin D and maybe take the edge off seasonal affective disorder.

When I came out the front door into the plaza I noticed six Indian guys wearing serapes and fedoras with colorful hatbands playing wooden flutes in the sun. A Peruvian band. I loved those guys. Their leader stood in front, clapping in time, with a fedora on the pavement in front of him, filling up with cash. Sun-drenched the whole scene.

I stood in the sun. The Peruvian music swooped and swirled around the plaza, around a growing crowd of hipsters and business people. Every few seconds, somebody put more money in the fedora. I folded up a twenty, dropped it in the hat, and stepped back. I closed my eyes. The sun and Peruvian music soaked into me, dissolving the cortisol leaving nothing but peace. I was chronically undernourished with peace.

I opened my eyes again and stepped back next to a barista with a Boring Green Coffee apron. She smiled at me and crinkled her nose, her blonde braids dazzled with sunlight.

Then, a shadow fell over the fedora. A homeless guy with a shaved white head, long, tangled brown beard, cloudy blue eyes. He was compulsively chomping his jaws—probably because of antipsychotic medication. He wore nothing but a tan fleece blanket and hiking boots. He chomped and glared.

Then he knelt quickly, grabbed the fedora by the brim, and turned to run. The barista stuck out her foot, and he tripped and fell hard. He dropped the fedora, and the cash fell out. He staggered to his feet, glared at the barista, and bunched his fist.

I stepped in front of her. "I don't think so," I told him, bunching my own fists. I stomped once in his direction.

Then he fled, his fleece blanket flying out behind him like a non-superhero cape, revealing white boxer shorts with pink hearts on them. His hiking boots clomped down the sidewalk as he ran.

The barista and I knelt and put the cash back in the fedora. She placed it in front of the band leader. "*Muchos gracias*," he said, displaying a wide smile with several missing teeth. The barista walked back to me, and we exchanged fist-bumps.

I walked down the glittering glass canyon of Third Avenue, filled with sunlight and delight. Seattle. Just when you think you've seen it all? You realize you have not seen it all.

***

I got the bond and had the Writ issued. I went to the courthouse and got ten certified copies. Silent Mike started serving them on the banks so we could stop any withdrawals. I got the Writ recorded against Cleverly's property with a title company. Now I had this sucker wrapped up like a calf in a rodeo.

Aloysius Miller moved for reconsideration, of course. He was billing the insurance company by the hour, remember? They still hadn't replaced him as civil defense counsel.

In personal injury, there are two categories of defense attorneys. Most cases are handled by counsel employed directly by the insurance company. These people want to either win or settle with minimum wasted time because they aren't billing hourly. They are called In-House Counsel. They have no incentive to waste time because they aren't billing hourly.

Then there are hourly defense counsel, who have an incentive to file unnecessary motions, impose needless obstacles, and waste time with the court and the plaintiff's counsel. They run up big hourly bills, wasting the court's time and my time. I called them Outhouse Counsel. The term was spreading.

Aloysius Miller was Outhouse Counsel. Until the insurance company woke up and chose somebody who knew more about civil litigation, anyway. The Writ of Attachment might lead to him getting fired. In law, they call this "breaking opposing counsel's rice bowl." It means they can't get paid anymore. It's supposedly a bad thing. I loved doing that. It tended to hasten resolution.

Under the King County Local Rules, I didn't have to respond to his Motion for Reconsideration unless Judge McCallum asked me to. She wouldn't grant reconsideration without giving me a chance to respond.

She denied the Motion for Reconsideration without requesting a response from me. It was time to see if I could pop the insurance policy limits and intimidate Cleverly into paying a hefty sum from his own pocket to settle.

I leaped into high gear. I got the autopsy and medical examiner's report, including the photos of poor Mr. Nillsson lying on the stainless-steel autopsy table, eyes wide open. I got Don Meissner's crash reconstruction report. I'd need Don to nail the "I wasn't driving" defense down with a computerized collision simulation.

I asked Don: "Could you run an animation from the total station data for me? Actually, I need two animations. One which shows the movement of the two occupants if Cleverly was driving, and winding up where the medics found them. And the other one showing the motion of the occupants if, in fact, Nillsson had been driving and landing where the medics found them."

Don chuckled. It was a warm sound, like the feel of a sip of bourbon. "Can do," he said. "I'll get you a flash drive with the results. I was going to suggest you get both versions. I'm predicting the reconstruction with Cleverly as the passenger will defy the laws of physics. You'll enjoy this."

Four days later, Don came in and gave me the flash drive. "I want to watch you seeing this," he said. "Your first fatality? It's just like your first girl. You will not forget this. Cleverly is the red stick figure, and Nillsson is the blue stick figure."

I plugged in the flash drive and double-clicked on the reconstruction named *Cleverly driving*. Bang. The red stick figure named Cleverly driving the Mazda flies out of the driver's seat lands right on the star labeled *Medics Find Cleverly*. Straight line. Nillsson's blue stick figure slams into the tree on his right side, stops, and flops limp in the Mazda, right at the star marked *Medics Find Nillsson*.

Second version—*Nillsson Driving*. Nillsson's blue stick figure goes right through Cleverly's red stick figure, changes direction, and falls into the passenger seat. While Cleverly hops straight into the air, changes direction in midair going left, goes right through Nillsson, changes direction in midair again, and flies out of the car, landing next to the tree.

"Interesting, right?" Don was smiling and smoothing down his white walrus mustache.

I ran that one again. God damn. Impossible. I knew Rodney was going to tear into me when he saw Don's bill. I had to show him the reconstructions first. That might just shut him up.

Cleverly was driving.

I had a hunch my old coworkers at the King County Prosecutor's Office might like to see this. I made a few calls. Turned out they did want to see it. They got the Major Accident Investigation Team to run a simulation of their own for Cleverly's criminal trial. Same result. Identical. They shared it with me. Now, I had two magic bullets, not one.

Then, I got Mr. Nillsson's tax returns for the last few years and had an economist run a projection of lost earnings and accumulations over his expected life, reduced to present value. It was over a million dollars, even though the Nillssons were pretty big spenders.

I wrote a demand letter to Cleverly's insurance company explaining how Cleverly was unquestionably at fault and the massive damages suffered by the Nillssons. I sent it only to the insurance adjusters for

Mr. Cleverly's liability carrier and Mrs. Nillsson's underinsured motorist carrier. I was going to try to pop the limits and get Cleverly to put in a big personal contribution himself.

I did not send the collision reconstructions from Don Meissner and the MAIT team. I kept those in my back pocket. This kind of stuff is called "attorney work product" and is exempt from discovery. Also, Aloysius hadn't sent me any discovery requests. He was still maintaining that any discovery exchange between the parties was forbidden because Cleverly was facing criminal charges.

I didn't send the demand letter package to Aloysius. I wanted to sneak up on that bastard. Just sent it to the insurance adjusters.

After a few days, Aloysius called me, fuming. "How dare you contact my adjuster without going through me first," he said.

"The insurance company isn't a party to the lawsuit, counselor," I said. "I can contact them anytime I want. Even if it interferes with your attempt to bill the hell out of the insurance company. You have a pleasant day." I hung up on him. That felt pretty good.

I got limits offers from both insurance companies. This was called "popping the limits." But I wasn't going to take them without taking a big chunk out of Mr. Cleverly's personal assets as well. Cleverly didn't have enough insurance to pay for killing Mr. Nillsson. Not many people did. But Cleverly had major assets. The widow deserved the money more than Aloysius Miller did.

And that's when things got really interesting. I wondered if Cleverly would spend his money in Grand Cayman on Aloysius's criminal defense work. We'd seized his property in the US, but he still had that bulging piggy bank overseas. I wondered if he would draw on that and fight to the last bullet.

But I had a hunch that the Grand Cayman money wasn't Cleverly's alone. My long and sensitive nose smelled cartel money in that account. People who spent cartel money without permission tended to have… shortened life expectancies.

We couldn't accept the insurance money without signing a release excusing Mr. Cleverly from having to pay any of his own money. Saralee and I agreed there was no way we would do that. Cleverly had to ante up, or we would not settle.

Rodney was apoplectic. "Dude, you're totally screwing the pooch, big time," he yelled, pounding on my desk. He wanted to pop the limits and be done because that was low-hanging fruit. Rodney knew nothing about delaying gratification. But I didn't budge.

We were eyeball-to-eyeball with the bad guys.

But then they blinked. Aloysius apparently didn't get a new big retainer from Cleverly. In fact, Cleverly pled guilty to vehicular homicide in exchange for a mild reduction in sentence. He had turned out to be intoxicated—on meth and pot. He was sentenced to two years.

At the sentencing hearing, I sat next to Saralee, with Nicky on her other side. Saralee sat straight and kept her eyes forward, her jaw clenched. Stray tendrils of blonde hair escaped from her barrette. In her black suit and white blouse, she stared. I knew she would be okay until she had to speak or move.

Right before sentencing, Saralee got to give her victim impact statement. The part that still sticks with me was her telling about coming into the crash suite at Harborview just minutes after her husband died. "He had the most perfect feet," she said, wondering. "I just sat down by the foot of the bed and held his feet. They were still warm."

Then Cleverly was sentenced, and was taken into custody right away, right there. Apparently, Judge McCallum and the sentencing judge had discussed Mr. Cleverly's three Social Security numbers and his passport from Dominica. He wouldn't get a chance to run.

Cleverly looked at me just once, his hollow eyes with dark gray circles peering out under his lank black hair. He still had a limp and still used a cane. I wondered if maybe he did feel guilty about killing his friend.

After that, I worked out the settlement. The limits of the liability and underinsured motorist coverages together were four hundred grand. But with the Writ of Attachment on Cleverly's property, the subdivision could not go forward until it was resolved. No bank would lend money for the plat development on the land with the Writ hanging over it.

In the end I got another seven hundred thousand from Cleverly, some of it in cash, some secured by a Note and Deed of Trust on the property. The Note would continue to accrue interest until the property sold or a lender cashed us out.

Rodney got his standard fee of one-third. It was four times my annual salary.

The promised profit-sharing didn't show up. I was unsurprised. I'd just had an epic experience and gotten a million dollars' worth of education. I was happy. Also, I'd hooked up Saralee with a grief counselor, and she was going to do the DUI Victims' Panel with the court, where she and other victims got to talk to recently-convicted first-time drunk drivers to tell them how terrible the consequences of drunk driving could be. Sometimes, the DUI drivers were scared straight. It was the best prevention I knew of.

I took The Ghost out for goat cheese tortellini and a game of Scrabble in a local café. To be cliche, it was a dark and stormy night. She wore a red velvet smoking jacket, black slacks, and tortoiseshell glasses. She looked like a piece of German chocolate cake.

"So I have one unanswered question," I said.

The Ghost had just added BACK to my word TRACK and hit a triple word score. She smiled as she added up her points. "Do tell."

"Why didn't Cleverly take some money from his Grand Cayman account and pay Aloysius Miller to keep fighting to trial? Sure, the witnesses put him in the driver's seat right before the crash, and we had that great collision reconstruction. But why didn't Cleverly spend the Grand Cayman money and take the gamble?"

The Ghost took a big swig from her mocha. "My working theory is his suppliers, the fine gentlemen from the cartel, didn't want the prosecutors learning too much about him. They thought it was safer for him to plead out than to go to trial. Trial could expose the cartel members. I also have a hunch that some of that money in Grand Cayman came from his bosses, not from him."

I smiled. "I had the same hunch. I kinda sorta flashed the Grand Cayman bank statement at him during the Writ of Attachment hearing, and he turned white as a sheet of typing paper."

The Ghost patted my hand. "You bastard," she said with affection.

I nodded. I played ZERO and got a respectable score, but I wouldn't win this game. "So he took a dive because the suppliers wanted him to." I didn't use the word cartel. I didn't even want to think of the word cartel.

Those people cut people up with reciprocating saws while they were still alive.

I said, "Cleverly has such a nice job. He has more to fear from his business partners than from his fellow inmates in prison."

She nodded. "If you plead out and do your time, no problem. The cartel can shield you in prison. But if you don't obey the cartel, then nobody can shield you. Anywhere. Not even in prison. Especially not in prison."

I wondered if The Ghost was involved in "extreme play" with a DEA agent. I wondered how the hell she knew so much. But I didn't really want to know. If I didn't know, then I couldn't tell. And I would never want to tell on The Ghost.

CHAPTER FOUR—HORSING AROUND

I went to see my sister Catherine to debrief. She'd been my touchstone in childhood. I was happy about the Nillsson case, and I wanted to show off a little.

Catherine lived in Duvall, a town on the edge of farm country about ten miles east of Seattle, on ten acres. She counseled teens in a group practice in Bellevue, but when she thought a client needed to work with her horses, she brought them out to her place. I turned in by the sign that said, *Catherine Strait, M.A. Horsing Around LLC.*

She was out by the paddock, feeding something to her new horse, a retired racehorse named General's Daughter, who she called Jenny. I hadn't met Jenny before. Jenny had a glossy brown coat and a glossy black mane; Catherine loved grooming her horses. Because Jenny was a thoroughbred, she was extremely skittish. Catherine had been a horsewoman since forever, but I'd never been comfortable around horses. I was just too jittery. Horses get jittery around jittery people.

"So this is Jenny," Catherine said, pulling her hair back. Catherine's hair was the exact same color as mine—deep brown, almost black. But hers was shiny and shoulder-length and conditioned. Since the Coast Guard, I'd had a '50s-style buzz cut that I trimmed myself with electric clippers.

"Hello Jenny," I said to the big, velvety brown horse. Jenny raised her eyebrows at me and ambled away. "I've still got the old magic," I said sardonically.

"You'll get there," Catherine said. We sat down on a bench by the watering trough. "So tell me about the fatality."

I told her everything, except about The Ghost. Catherine was a great listener. She went totally still when she listened—she didn't blink, didn't fidget. Pretty much my opposite. She was a natural therapist. Her husband Jerry, a psychiatrist, said, "If all therapists were like Catherine, I wouldn't have to prescribe so many meds."

She looked down and nodded. "That's great. How is the widow doing?"

"All right. Except when I gave her the check, Rodney took her out for dinner after, and she got pretty drunk."

"Were you there?"

"Nope, she just told me afterward. She said she never really ties one on, but this time, she must have lost count, and she got plowed. But other than waking up with a bad hangover, she's really adjusting okay."

"And does she have a therapist?"

I smiled. "She does now. I got her hooked up with somebody on your list. It has to be horrible, losing somebody so quickly like that."

Catherine regarded me. "We should know."

That silence. Since we lost our parents when we were seven, we'd had this silence between us.

She squinted at me. "Your scar is bright red."

I protested, "That's because I'm happy. It gets red when I'm happy. Not just when I'm mad or upset."

Catherine put her hand on my knee and returned to an old subject. "I think you should talk to someone." She meant a therapist. Like some therapists, she thought everybody needed therapy.

"I do not think I need to talk to someone. I think my life's going great."

"I still think you might want to process what happened at the Malletts' Therapeutic Foster Home."

"Cat, we left that place in the dust a very long time ago. I'll never be helpless again. Now, I help the helpless people. Just like you."

"But I've done my work."

"Cat, not everybody needs therapy. Seriously. I don't need therapy. And I'm never going to talk to the Malletts' Therapeutic Foster Home with a stranger."

"A therapist isn't a stranger. Maybe you could process it with some help."

This was our same old argument. Most family members have one. "If it'll make you feel better, give me some names. If I decide to do therapy, I'll pick one."

"Coming right up." She reached into her fleece jacket and handed me a list. Of course, she had it handy. I stuffed it in my pocket. Truce. I never suggested she needed to sue somebody. So why did she suggest I needed to "talk to somebody"?

I looked across the paddock. Jenny stood a hundred feet away, still looking at me with mistrust. But I liked the good, honest smells—hay and horse manure and growing grass. I liked the swallows swooping low over the paddock, singing their microscopic songs. I liked the new leaves shivering on Redmond Ridge behind the paddock, showing the silver backs of their leaves, while a flock of crows flew north, calling raucous jokes at each other. I could forget that I needed to get outside. Often.

I cleared my throat and looked down. "So when I got home, the night after the Nillsson hearing, I was thinking about when we found out about Mom and Dad in the dining hall. I'm wondering if I remember it right." I felt shaky. I'd had a hunch for quite a while that I was doing personal injury because of the way my parents died.

She looked across the paddock, where Jenny was standing nonchalantly. The swallows kept singing.

Catherine said, "The camp director called us in. I thought I'd been busted sneaking out apples for the horses. You thought you'd been busted for writing graffiti with toothpaste on the inside of the cabin, even though everybody wrote toothpaste graffiti on the inside of the cabins. But when we saw there was a police officer with him, that seemed unlikely, even for stealing apples and toothpaste graffiti."

I nodded. Everything around us got dim and still.

"So the camp director says, kids, there's been an accident. And then the police officer said our parents had passed away due to a natural gas leak. He said they had gone to a better place. I didn't know what passed away meant. I didn't know what could be a better place. So I said, 'What, they're in Hawaii? And why didn't they take us?'"

Catherine laughed sadly. I did, too.

I took up the story. "And then the officer put us in his police car, and there were no door handles in the back. And he drove us to an IHOP and the social worker bought us pancakes for dinner. I always loved breakfast for dinner. Mom always hated it when Dad made us breakfast for dinner. He only did it when she was depressed and had been wearing pajamas for several days, but I loved it because he was stepping in. While we were eating, a frumpy social worker came and then she took us to the receiving home. And from there, it was off to the Malletts' Therapeutic Foster Home." It was a warm May afternoon, but I shivered. "So Cat? What were Mom and Dad really like? I worry that I can't remember them right."

Catherine pulled her hair out of the headband and let it hang on both sides of her face like a curtain. She did that when she wanted privacy—like blinders on a horse. "Well, Dad loved puns, and he loved putting together real estate deals. He wore Glen plaid suits. He smelled like Aqua Velva even though that was a totally obsolete cologne, even then." She smiled at the ground. "I ran into one of his old partners the other day. Ralph Combe? He told me that Dad was the dumbest smart man he ever met."

I frowned. "Why would he say that?"

Cat leaned forward more, her hair shielding her face. "He said Dad was smart because he could put together real estate deals that had ten different contingencies, and he did the Mensa puzzles for fun. He said he was dumb because he married Mom."

I knew where this was heading. I'd reached the same conclusion. Once, I was old enough to love truth even when truth hurt.

Just then, the street light in front of Catherine's house came on.

"Do you remember how Mom always told us to be home by the time the streetlights came on?" I asked. "But how could we know, before the streetlights came on when they were going to come on?"

Catherine was still hunched forward, her hair still curtaining her face. "She was always anxious. The whole thing was a setup."

I plowed on. "Once we came home after the streetlights came on, and Mom and Dad were both waiting, and Mom said, 'I was so worried about you! I thought you'd been run over and killed by a drunk driver!'"

Catherine leaned forward more. "That wasn't one time, Sam. That was about fifty times. Mom had anxiety attacks every day. Often more than one a day. Mom was like a smoke detector that goes off every time you steam broccoli. You can try to persuade the smoke detector that it's only steam, not smoke. But it's a failed mechanism. Failed mechanisms do not reason. They only react."

I started pushing my cuticles back. It was one of my nervous habits. "So what could have helped Mom? What could have made her stop freaking out?"

Catherine was pushing back her cuticles, too. We could prompt each other like that. Orphaned twins have a powerful hold on each other, especially when they don't get separated in foster care. "I talked that out with Jerry before we got married. I asked him what could have helped Mom. And I asked him how he could know that I wouldn't turn into Mom. You know what he said?"

"No, I didn't hear that story."

"He said that the only thing that could have helped Mom was medication. And he said that if I was going to turn into Mom, I already would have turned into Mom. I was twenty-five. Crippling anxiety is always present before the patient turns twenty-five."

I smiled sadly. "So that means you aren't going to turn into Mom."

She slapped me on the knee. "And you neither! Don't think I don't know that you worry about turning into Mom. I know."

I nodded. "But there's something I worry about more."

"Of course! Your biggest fear is that you'll marry a woman like Mom, and you'll wind up like Dad, always trying to soothe and placate somebody who can never be soothed and placated. Working extra hours just so you don't have to come home and be somebody's emotional outhouse."

I winced. "Emotional outhouse. That's harsh."

She slapped my knee again. "It's true. You know she was always demanding that Dad, and us, and everyone, make her feel safe. When she could never feel safe. She made everybody around her into failure because they couldn't somehow straighten out her fucked-up neurochemistry."

"And that's why we were always together outside."

"Exactly. But Dad couldn't stay outside with us, not long. He had to deal with her. That's why he was the dumbest smart man that his partner ever met. He married a broken smoke detector."

I shook myself and stood up. "I know better than to think this, most of the time. But I wish we could go back and have a good family. I wish Dad had somehow found some way to get Mom treated."

She stood, too. "You know self-pity is poison, don't you?" I knew. She'd taught me that way back when we were at the Malletts' Therapeutic Foster Home.

"Okay. So what are the two rules I tell my clients?" she asked, smiling at me.

"Rule One—you cannot ever change the past. Rule Two—you cannot ever control the actions of another person."

"Bingo. Let's go in. Jerry made dinner tonight. If you ever feel so inclined, call a therapist on that list."

Jerry was finishing up a stir-fry in the kitchen, the sleeves of his ever-present cardigan pushed up, his glasses steamed, his bald head shining. The kitchen smelled of peppers and, ginger, and soy. If I ever did jump the shark and need medication, I would see Jerry. He used only proven meds, and he loved to rant about new meds that were no better than the old meds yet had worse side effects.

Jerry looked up from the wok and gave me a brief hug.

"So what's the Poison of the Week?" I asked Jerry. I loved to get him going. He was pretty fierce about psychiatrists who hurt their clients with rotten meds.

"Zyprexa," he said. He picked up an issue of a psychiatry journal. "Atypical antipsychotic. No more effective than good old Haldol. Sometimes causes tardive dyskinesia, the compulsive movements of the jaw or face. Just like Haldol. But look at the additional side effects. Skyrocketing cholesterol and blood sugar. Not to mention gynecomastia."

"Not gynecomastia," I said, teasing. I had no frigging idea what that was.

He lowered his steamed glasses and looked over them at me with mock severity. "Gynecomastia is where male patients grow large and defined breasts. All this data came out years ago. But still some of my boneheaded colleagues prescribe Zyprexa. Imagine. You're hearing voices in your head. Your doc decides that good old Haldol will not do. So you get Zyprexa, and you need cholesterol drugs, you become diabetic, and you're suddenly a man with a big pair of boobs."

Catherine burst out laughing and threw her arms around him. I had a sliver of hope that I might someday have a happy marriage. That sliver was made of two things—my relationship with Suzanne, which had been over for six years, and watching Catherine and Jerry.

I drove home feeling like I'd had a vacation. Even if Jenny the horse shunned me, the way all horses shunned me. I was eager for the next set of intakes. And at least I didn't have gynecomastia.

CHAPTER FIVE—ANOTHER ARROW IN HER QUIVER

After my dinner with Catherine and Jerry, I had one of my periodic bursts of optimism about finding a good woman and settling down. The only lasting relationship I'd had was my three years with Suzanne in law school. I'd been alone for the six years since then. As I was driving my trusty battered Outback home from Duvall, I decided to check out TopFliteSingles.com.

But then I remembered my counselor's report when I'd been about twelve, living at the Malletts' foster home with Catherine. The Malletts told me and the social worker that I had to go to counseling for reasons I'll explain later, or they would require me to be placed somewhere else. They would keep Catherine. The threat of being separated from my twin sister was leverage enough, and I went dutifully. I would have stood on my head if they told me to.

Once, the counselor had gone to the washroom in the middle of a session, and I had sneaked over to his desk. My file was on it next to a bunch of cactus plants. Blue cardboard file with dogeared corners. It was open to his most recent progress report.

It had said, *Diagnosis: attachment disorder.* The narrative said *This patient is incapable of forming mutually beneficial bonds of love with any person other than his twin sister, owing either to the trauma of losing both of his parents when he was seven or a preexisting psychopathology. Prognosis is extremely guarded. Obsessive tendencies are marked. Fantasies of rescuing others from persecution are noteworthy. CONCLUSION: This patient is unlikely to ever form a dyadic bond leading to marriage.*

I had stared at the report, then heard the door close down the hall. I ran back to my seat and assumed a relaxed position. The counselor then once again started scraping away at whatever he thought was wrong with me.

I was in counseling because I'd done something right, not something wrong. I'll explain later. But those words had stuck to me. Attachment disorder.

Yes, I'd had the miracle of Suzanne. I sometimes wished I'd moved with her to New Jersey. I had even thought it was attachment disorder that made me decide not to move to New Jersey to stay in Seattle near Catherine instead.

So, I didn't consider myself a red-hot romantic prospect. I'd had some flings, sure. But nothing durable since Suzanne.

Nothing ventured, nothing gained. I set up a profile on TopFliteSingles.com and posted my best photo. I said I liked '80s music, spicy Thai food, road trips, and smart women. And then I dove into my matches.

I had dozens and dozens of matches, probably because I had a good education a good income, and I wasn't short. I'd recently read an amazing magazine story about dealbreakers for single women in the Seattle area. The number-one dealbreaker? Men who were shorter than them. The number-two dealbreaker? Men who were convicted felons. Convicted felons were more acceptable than short guys.

I was six feet tall—I wasn't short, even if I had a short circuit that made me *unlikely to form a dyadic bond leading to marriage.*

I looked at over a hundred profiles that night, looking for an apparently smart woman with brown eyes who apparently had a good career and something interesting to say. I found six. I emailed them all.

Based on prior experience, sending six emails would guarantee zero to one replies. I'd gone on some online dates before. The women who were worthwhile described getting hundreds and hundreds of emails. So I'd either have to e-bomb women indiscriminately or expect I would get very few replies. It was just the nature of the game.

And I got one. She had deep brown eyes, long brown hair, and a quirky smile. There was something piquant in her expression that reminded me of The Ghost. Remember, I'd met The Ghost through a personal ad, too. My match's name was Stella.

Stella suggested we meet at her favorite wine bar on Capitol Hill just east of downtown Seattle. I showed up early, wearing jeans and, a black mock turtleneck, and a blazer. The ambiance was dark—candlelit tables and cool jazz playing. I told myself not to be eager. I often ruined everything by being eager, or as the local hipsters called it, "thirsty." One of my failed personal ad dates once told me, letting me down gently, "Leave 'em wanting more."

Stella showed up on time. Unusual for a personal ad date. She looked just like her photo. Lush. She had big dark eyes, long, dark brown shining hair. She wore a low-cut maroon top showing splendid cleavage. Oh my. I stood as she came to the table.

"I'm Sam," I said.

"Stella." Her handshake was warm, filled with tingling.

The waiter asked me what Syrah I wanted. I said, "Just the house brand. Que Syrah Syrah." Stella laughed at that. We ordered Syrah and started chatting.

She made a few delicate probes into my career and seemed to like what she heard. I didn't ham it up. I'd found, to my regret, that when I described my idealism about work honestly, many women thought

I was a liar. Women dating online were universally skeptical. Then, I started asking a bit about her. Another failed date had told me, "Don't be interesting. Be interested." About that time, we were halfway through our glasses of Syrah.

Stella had a nice house in a good neighborhood, a Tudor. She'd never been married and had no kids. She didn't have any job she wanted to disclose. She had expensive tastes. Her favorite hobby was "nude archery."

About this time, my antennae went up. I had a hypothesis. I decided to check it out as artfully as I could.

"So, what sort of relationship are you looking for, Stella?"

She let the silence grow. She smelled like vanilla—the good vanilla that comes from vanilla beans. I was halfway fascinated and totally aroused. But I had to check out my hypothesis first.

Stella took a drink of the Syrah and licked her lips—sculpted dark pink lips. "I enjoy nonexclusive companionship with generous men," she said.

Hypothesis confirmed. She was a prostitute.

I wasn't mad. I just wasn't buying what she was selling. I'd actually been to see an escort just once, a year after Suzanne left. Afterward I felt almost ecstatic, like I'd robbed a bank and gotten away with it. But after a day, I felt morose for weeks. Did I really have to pay a woman to have sex with me? Wouldn't a worthwhile woman want to do it with me, even if she wasn't getting paid? So I decided not to do that again. It was like the one time I tried marijuana—immense rush, then a mournful backlash that lasted many times longer.

"Thanks for that, Stella," I said, "but I'm really looking for a woman to be exclusive with. I'm doing okay. But I'm not sure I could qualify as one of your generous men."

She nodded and winked at me. She passed me a business card with just her name, her email, and a, shall we say, very labial rose. "No harm done," she said. "Who knows? You might even reconsider."

I smiled at her. I really liked how artful and yet how direct she was. "I might even reconsider," I said. "You're as pretty as a hot fudge sundae."

She laughed, covering her mouth as I paid for the drinks. "Will you walk me to my car, monsieur?" she asked.

"Of course. This neighborhood isn't so great. I'd be delighted."

So we strolled back to her car, talking about music. She liked Billy Idol and the Talking Heads, and this delighted me. The moment of decision was past. Like almost every online date I'd ever had—and I'd had plenty—it was a mismatch. This time, a companionable one.

But she had one more arrow in her quiver. Pun intended.

She'd parked her car, a silver Mercedes, right next to the only Ferrari dealership in Washington State. When we got there, she turned and looked in the dealership window, admiring the shiny and sculpted cars. "They're really not that expensive," she murmured. "Not for a man of your means."

I bit my lower lip. "Charmed," I said as we shook hands. I waited until her Mercedes started and then walked back to my battered Subaru Outback. Still biting my lower lip.

When I got the key in the door, I couldn't hold back any longer. I doubled over laughing.

She was such a clever predator! Right up until the last minute, she was gauging my willingness to spend lavishly. I saw myself as the truly ridiculous figure I was, and it was hilarious.

The Ghost had once told me: "You're a heterosexual monogamous romantic man with a good job and a loyal heart who wants to get married and have children. In Seattle, you're a total freak."

I wiped the tears out of my eyes and drove home in my battered Subaru Outback to my anonymous condo near Northgate, which was crammed with '80s CDs and books and a whole lot of nothing else. I was a goddamned idealist with a diagnosed case of attachment disorder. I was *unlikely to ever form a dyadic bond leading to marriage.*

I was ready to sue the hell out of somebody again.

CHAPTER SIX—YOU NEVER KNOW WHAT'LL WALK IN THE DOOR

After I closed the Estate of Turner case, Rodney told Nicky to set up an Intake Clinic to feed more cases into the hopper.

Let me explain Rodney's system. He had a huge advertising budget, both for criminal defense and personal injury. He spent well north of two million per year on TV commercials, online ads, radio commercials, you name it. He had seven lawyers. So he had to make $300,000 per attorney just to pay the nut for the advertising—ignoring office rent, salaries, benefits, and his lavish profits. So he would walk through the office chanting, "Churn and burn." He lived for case turnover. He monitored us on the case management software for revenue produced year-to-date, caseload number, caseload aging, you name it. He liked to slice and dice the data. He called it "metrics." Totally rational. But because of the advertising budget, he lived on volume, not quality.

His criminal defense attorneys did mostly DUI defense, where he got paid $10,000 at the start, and almost everybody pled guilty. Two court appearances tops. Fewer than one percent went to trial, and DUI trials only lasted two days.

But with personal injury he went a different direction. Anything but a "Big Mama" case (or as I called it, a True Disaster), he sent to a high-volume, low-quality personal injury firm—a "settlement mill." He got a third of the fees—a third of a third of the recovery—for just doing an intake and signing the clients. This way, he kept overhead low—just salaries for Nicky and me—and got a steady stream of the cases referred out, plus the occasional juicy big fee from the True Disasters.

I'd been hired to do intakes and personally handle True Disasters only. That was the bait on the hook. I couldn't wait to jump on the True Disasters.

His model was a genuine cash cow. My predecessor had netted Rodney an average of seven hundred grand a year, even though he wasn't that motivated and spent much of his time on social media and watching porn on the web. I'd gotten Rodney half that much already, and I'd only been working for him about a week.

Rodney sure sold me when I interviewed with him. "Think of it, bro," he said, his eyes misting over. "Countless intakes per year. You pick the best cases and send out the rest to the settlement mills. You'll have a caseload of whopping catastrophes in no time." Rodney could read people.

For reasons I won't get into now, I'd wanted to help real victims and punish real victimizers ever since I'd been in foster care. That's why I'd aced the LSAT, why I'd gotten top grades at the University of Washington School of Law, why I'd passed the Bar Exam the first time. That was why I'd become a prosecutor. I'd been good at that, but I didn't get promoted because my boss called me a "true believer" right before he sent me to the Filing Unit, where dead-enders went to screen cases and file charges. People on the Filing Unit never went to court other than covering occasional arraignments, which a chimp could do. People got sent to the Filing Unit as the King County Prosecutor's Office's way of saying, "Start looking for another job."

After that, I'd gotten hired as a general-purpose litigator, a so-called "utility infielder," at a modest-sized general practice firm. I handled anything in litigation—real estate litigation, probate litigation, business litigation—anything except criminal defense and family law. My first firm called me the "knuckledragger" and the paralegals ridiculed me even though I brought in more fees than all but one partner. Profit sharing? Pathway to partnership? Not a chance. But I learned lots. I'd set my sights on moving to personal injury pretty quickly. I couldn't get stoked about somebody not making payments on a promissory note or failing to pay rent on their dental office. I needed True Disasters.

At the end of Rodney's interview, I wanted the job so badly I could taste it. He knew. I did insist on a written contract that paid me eighty grand a year and profit sharing. I wouldn't give up my old dismal job until I had ink on the contract. Rodney walked me up to the receptionist's desk and asked for my parking pass. "Can I validate you?" he asked.

"Yeah," I said. "Tell me I'm special."

He laughed a short crack and slapped me on the back. "Dude, that kicks ass." He wore a black suit that day and more sandalwood cologne than usual.

That joke probably got me the job. Rodney's motto was "hire fast and fire faster."

So, my first Intake Clinic. Nicky had lined up twelve cases at fifteen-minute intervals. I expected lots of ordinary cases, some genuine Barking Dogs (the cases that were so weak they were laughable), and if I was lucky, a True Disaster.

Since I'd been seven years old, I'd been on a first-name basis with disaster. I'd recognize it, all right.

Nicky lined them up and gave me a cup of coffee, her rose-scented hair brushing my shoulder. The first five were MIST cases. One notorious insurance company had coined the phrase, which meant Minimal Impact, Soft Tissue. Modest collisions with clear liability. The property damage to their cars had to be north of two thousand to be worthwhile. I'd learned at my previous job to ask, "Were you getting any treatment of any kind immediately before the collision?"

In Seattle, large numbers of people were getting what they called "maintenance chiropractic"—routine chiropractic adjustments that were necessary. According to the chiropractors. Anybody who was getting maintenance chiropractic when they were hit, I declined because they had a disqualifying preexisting condition. Unless they were really hurt in the crash and needed surgery. Nicky took down their names and addresses to send out decline letters the very next day, warning them of the statute of limitations and politely refusing the case.

I changed the decline letter—I made it very polite. If a potential client got turned down because they had a MIST case with maintenance chiropractic, they could come in with a real monster in a month or a year.

Nicky teed up the last two. The first was on the intake sheet as "gross fraud."

The potential client? A fiftyish obese woman with a permanent scowl. Middle school social studies teacher. She wore thick glasses and the air of resentment that spelled tenure plus middle school. She sat down with a heavy sigh and slid a single document across the table. "As I told your assistant, gross fraud," she growled.

I read the document. I bit my lower lip so I wouldn't burst out laughing.

It was a fake check that said in huge letters *YOU HAVE WON A MILLION DOLLARS*. Underneath that, in tiny type, it said, *If you have the winning numbers in our fabulous sweepstakes.*

"I opened this at lunch in the teacher's lounge, and I was utterly and totally ecstatic," she said in a monotone. "I thought all my problems were solved."

I nodded. She'd get her fifteen minutes. "Okay. But you did notice that statement underneath the big, bold type…"

"I can read," she said. "When I read that weaselly caveat underneath, I felt tragically and permanently forlorn." Again, with the monotone. Flat affect, as they say.

I nodded again. She had no case at all, but she had a pretty good vocabulary. "So you're alleging that the big, bold type was a misrepresentation, and you were harmed by a false sense of hope."

She leaned forward and patted the fake check. "Precisely. In a few minutes, my outlook on my entire life went from ecstasy to clinical depression."

I bit my lower lip again. Saralee Nillsson had sat in that same chair a few weeks ago and described the death of her husband. Rodney's incessant TV commercials brought in everything from pure gold to total shit.

'I'm afraid the damages in this case would not make it a profitable venture for us," I said, nodding at Nicky. Nicky took down her particulars for the decline letter.

The middle school teacher took back the fake check and put it into her large shoulder bag, which was, of course, decorated with tabby cat needlepoint. "That's what the last four lawyers said," she said, heaving her bulk to her feet. "Some people just don't recognize an opportunity."

When she closed the door to the conference room, I winked at Nicky, and she smiled. She'd been with Rodney for a year, and she had seen many barking dogs come in.

Nicky ducked out and came back with a couple—a bearded man in his forties and a gentle-faced Hispanic woman with a newborn baby in her arms. I looked at the intake sheet. Under *subject,* it read *possible medical malpractice.* Client name? Monica Fernandez.

Here's the deal about medical malpractice cases. A medical group called The Institute of Medicine recently published a study admitting that medical mistakes kill between one hundred thousand and two hundred thousand US citizens per year. The IOM Report was written by doctors. However, almost none of these mistakes resulted in damages being awarded to the patient. In Washington State, plaintiffs won only about ten percent of the cases that went to trial. Fewer than four percent of cases signed by an attorney went to trial. So, .4 percent of signed cases resulted in a positive verdict. A few settled, but most were dismissed when they turned as sour as two-week-old milk.

This is because of something called "defensive attribution." People think their doctors are smart, and they are. People think their doctors are well-meaning, and they are. People think their doctors are highly trained, and they are.

Defensive attribution is a strange phenomenon. When people are frightened by believing something, often they just simply refuse to believe it. They need to believe doctors don't screw up a lot because they depend on doctors. So they believe whatever makes them feel comfortable.

A very bright surgeon named Atul Gawande once wrote a book called *The Checklist Manifesto*. He made a convincing case that almost all medical mistakes occur because healthcare providers and organizations are disorganized. I'd read it and taken it to heart. We lawyers have to be organized too, or we will screw up a lot. I'd clinched my job at the King County Prosecutor's Office by telling the interview committee, "It's more important to be organized than to be smart."

So, I'd turned down almost every medical malpractice case I'd been offered because they were almost impossible to win. Along the way, the law firm would spend at least twenty grand on expert witnesses, sometimes ten times that much. But this couple deserved fifteen minutes of respectful listening, just like the disgruntled middle school teacher with a complaint about a small font.

"This is Monica Fernandez," the bearded man said. "I am Hector Fernandez. And this is our daughter Sylvia."

I got up, shook hands with them both, and looked down at Sylvia. She was adorable—a cloud of fine black hair, shining dark brown eyes, and a cherub's permanent smile.

Babies, right? All babies are cute, but this one was super cute. I smelled Hector's chewing tobacco, Monica's baby powder, and Nicky's rose shampoo.

I felt the temperature change. It got warm in the room. This is what happens when I'm getting the first whiff of a True Disaster.

"Monica is deaf," the man said. "She reads lips very well. I interpret for her because I can sign. Do you know sign language?"

I shook my head. "I'm sorry, I don't. Is it okay if we proceed with you interpreting?" I noted that both Monica and Hector had dark circles under their eyes.

Hector half-turned so Monica could see his hands. "Monica delivered by C-section at a small hospital down in the South Sound. Sisters of Mercy. You know it?"

I paused for him to sign. "Yes, I know it." My boss at my last firm had said, "I wouldn't send a dog I don't like to Sisters of Mercy."

Hector said, "A couple of days after she delivered, she started vomiting right after she ate something. I was working a lot at the time. I'm a welder in a shipyard. So our neighbor Helga had to take Monica to the ER at the hospital. Helga doesn't sign. The ER didn't have a sign interpreter, either. The law says they have to."

I let him sign all of this. Monica nodded energetically and put her hand on his wrist.

"So Monica took her notebook." He signed this, too. Monica reached into her purse and pulled out a black spiral-bound notebook. "She wrote notes to the people in the ER about what was going on with her. They wrote notes back because they didn't have a sign language person." He signed again. Monica patted the notebook.

"What does it say in the notebook?" I asked. Nicky was leaning forward.

"Monica went into the ER three times when she vomited after eating. Each time, Monica told them she had pain in her stomach, in her abdomen." He signed, and Monica pointed at her belly, again nodding.

"Go on," I said.

"Each time, they x-rayed her chest," he said. He signed again.

Monica reached into her bag and pulled out two bundles of documents fastened with binder clips. She slid them across the table to me.

I said, "Thank you," clearly so she could read my lips.

The first bundle was the chart from Sisters of Mercy. I flipped to the back, where the lab reports and radiology reports are. Sure enough. They had x-rayed her chest three times. They hadn't x-rayed her abdomen at all.

Idiots.

The second bundle was from Overlake Medical Center, a splendid hospital in Bellevue right near Microsoft. I flipped through until I found the Discharge Summary, which is the most cogent description of treatment.

Patient came in with emesis after ingesting solid food times two weeks after delivery by Caesarean section at another facility. Abdominal X-ray revealed incidental finding of retained surgical sponge in abdomen, wrapped around the small bowel. Patient's temperature was 103.5. Patient was taken to the operating room on an emergent basis without overnight fasting, and exploratory laparotomy was performed. The retained surgical sponge was discovered wrapped around the small bowel and appendix, and several feet of gangrenous small bowel and appendix were removed, the bowel being resected afterward. Pathology confirmed that the retained foreign body was, in fact, a surgical sponge.

Holy shit.

In medical malpractice law, the one kind of case defendants never want to fight is a "unintentional retained foreign body case." Surgeons hate to admit it, but thousands of times per year, they accidentally leave things inside patients—surgical sponges, needles, orthopedic screws, and sometimes even instruments like clamps and retractors.

The standard of care requires the operating room to have a nurse designated to count the "sponges and sharps"—the sponges and instruments—three times. First, before the initial incision is made. Second, when the surgery is done but before closing begins. And third, at the end of closing the final incision. The counts must match. If they don't, something got left behind, and the surgeon has to get an X-ray in the OR, then find and retrieve it before the patient leaves the operating room.

"I am going to bet next week's lunch money. I know what went wrong," I said. Hector signed it to Monica. She furrowed her brow. Sylvia shifted in her arms and gurgled.

I furiously leafed through the Sisters of Mercy chart. I found the Operative Report. Then, the Anesthesiology Record. It should come right after that…

Hell yes. They hadn't counted the sponges and sharps. In fact, they were missing the form for doing that.

Any hospital not operated by imbeciles has this form in every surgical chart.

This was the first surgical chart I'd ever seen that didn't have this form.

Not only didn't they do it. Probably, they NEVER did it.

My jaw dropped. Hector and Monica looked at each other. Nicky looked at them. Thick tension in the room.

"Okay, I think I've found a smoking gun," I said. "In every surgery, the circulating nurse is required to count the sponges and instruments on a form at three stages—before the first incision, again before closing the surgical incisions is begun, and finally after the last incision is closed. These counts all have to match to make sure the surgeon didn't leave anything inside the patient."

Hector signed everything to Monica, even though I was confident she had read my lips. Her brow furrowed again.

Hector leaned forward. "We knew they found a surgical sponge inside Monica at the Overlake place. So Sisters of Mercy didn't count the sponges and instruments on Monica's surgery?"

"That's right. And the form isn't even in the chart. Not a blank form. No form. I've never seen that before, and I've read plenty of surgical charts."

Hector signed. "So what does that mean?"

I leaned forward. "Sisters of Mercy committed medical malpractice and hurt Monica. It is possible they don't ever count the sponges and sharps. It is possible that Sisters of Mercy has screwed up like this before and is going to screw up like this again. I smell something interesting here."

Monica gasped and put her hand on Hector's arm. She signed to him a flurry.

Hector said, "Monica says, so this may even be a pattern?"

I nodded. "Yes, it might be. I want this case."

Hector signed, and Monica nodded. I respected how he deferred to her. It was ultimately her case, after all.

Just then, the door to the conference room opened, and Rodney came in. He was wearing a splendid sharkskin suit, a lemon yellow tie, and a strong whiff of sandalwood cologne. He sat down next to Monica and took her hand. "I'm deeply sorry for your trouble," he said, staring at her with his flat blue eyes in a strong display of totally bogus sincerity. He held that pose for a moment. The silence thickened as the rest of us thought, *What the hell?* Then he got up and left.

Hector and, Monica, and I looked at each other. "Who's that?" Hector asked and signed.

I rolled my eyes. "That's Rodney Mammon. He's the boss. But I do all the personal injury here. He just likes to say hello sometimes."

Hector leaned across the table and glanced at the door that Rodney had left through. He considered. "If we sign with you," he asked, "will we have to deal with that motherfucker?"

Nicky and I burst out laughing as Hector interpreted for Monica. She was laughing, too. I'd wondered if deaf people could laugh, and now I knew.

I wiped my eyes. "I promise you, my friends," I said calmly, "he only cares about money. I care about what happens to you. If you sign with me, you'll never see that motherfucker again."

Hector pulled the contract and authorization for records disclosure across the table. He and Monica read through it. "It says here forty percent of what we get is the fee," he said.

"That's the usual medical malpractice contingent fee," I said. "However, I think that's too high in this case." I looked at Nicky, who had her hand over her mouth. Nobody at Mammon and Associates had ever suggested a fee was too high before. "May I see that?" I asked, pointing at the contract.

Hector slid it over to me. I crossed out forty percent and, wrote *one-third*, and signed below the change. I then signed the contract. "I'll do it for a third," I said. "This case has very clear fault, unlike a lot of medical malpractice cases. The hospital will be humiliated when we sue them, unlike a lot of medical malpractice cases. You two are new parents, and you deserve a break. We'll still make plenty of money."

Hector and Monica signed below the fee reduction and signed the contract. Nicky looked at me wide-eyed. Then Hector reached across the table and shook my hand. Monica reached across the table and took my hand in both of hers. She pinned me with dark, soulful eyes. I loved this woman. A jury would love this woman. This was a good plaintiff.

Sylvia said something that sounded like "Coo."

Next, Hector gave me a short description of how Monica had spent four days at Overlake after the bowel resection on IV antibiotics to cure the gangrene in her bloodstream. On the fourth day, they finally verified that Monica's bowel was not obstructed. She farted. The surgeon and the nurses cheered.

I couldn't wait to get started on this one. I'd order the medical records through my service and compare them with the copy Hector and Monica had given me. Often, the copies were different. When a legal medical records service showed up, often medical providers changed the chart before they copied it.

Also, I couldn't wait to hear what that motherfucker would say about the discount. Before I made him a large pile of money.

CHAPTER SEVEN—GETTING HOMETOWNED

I rounded up the medical records in Monica Fernandez's case through our medical records service. I remembered what Duvonda had told me about "med mal."

You get the client to get his or her own medical records. Then, you order a set yourself from a legal medical records retrieval company. Then you get them page-numbered, and you compare. It's amazing how often they don't match. In med mal, the defendants often "fix up" the medical records before sending them to the patient's lawyer.

So, I had both sets page-numbered and reviewed them. They actually matched. No form for counting sponges and sharps in the operating room in either set.

Then I got a big mocha with lots of whipped cream for Duvonda and went to huddle. We sat down facing each other across her glass-topped coffee table in matching leather armchairs. We both took off our shoes and put them up on the coffee table. Our ritual. That day, she wore a cream-colored skirted suit, and her nails were dark pink. She wore faint lilac perfume. I wore my unvarying uniform—dark gray wool suit, white shirt, blue paisley tie, black lace-up shoes.

She wiggled her toes at me. This was how we expressed delight to each other.

First, she asked me about her case, where she had a great judge and wanted to prevent an Affidavit of Prejudice being filed by defense counsel. Any attorney in a case can file an Affidavit of Prejudice and have the assigned judge automatically taken off the case. But it's only available if the judge hasn't made a discretionary ruling—a ruling requiring any exercise of judgment.

"Okay, I did this," I told her. "I filed a very weak motion to extend the discovery cutoff right at the start of the case, and the judge I liked denied it. Defense counsel opposed it because they were Outhouse Counsel and opposed everything. They won the Motion. But I really won because the judge had made a discretionary ruling and couldn't be removed from the case after that. Outhouse Counsel tried to dump her a few months later when they finally woke up. They failed to remove the judge. The judge was, shall we say, un-thrilled."

Duvonda smiled. "That is wicked. Nice." I had the feeling she'd already thought of that, and she was humoring me. Sometimes, she just threw me a softball and let me swing. "Now, how about your case?"

I filled her in on Monica Fernandez.

She leaned forward and glared at me. That was her Let's Attack the Defendant face. I liked that face—the face of an angry leopard. She pointed at me. "And you have the actual notebook she and the ER staff wrote in? About abdominal pain? And the radiology reports showing they only x-rayed her chest?"

"Yes."

She whistled. "Rodney Mammon's pricey TV commercials do bring in some True Disasters." She'd taught me this phrase.

I sipped my iced Americano. "So, should I send a demand letter or just file suit?"

Duvonda nodded. "Just the right question. Ordinarily, with med mal, you just file suit. The defendants are going to use your demand letter to prep to defend the case, so don't give them any warning." She sipped. "Son, the best trial is an ambush."

She finished her mocha. "But this is the Holy Grail of med mal cases—a retained foreign body with pretty bad injury. Word on the street is they offer good money to settle those without litigation because they're afraid of the publicity. So write a good demand, and give 'em thirty days. That's the word from your Aunt Duvonda." She was chuckling and wiggling her toes when I left.

I thanked her and walked out into the plaza. June had turned windy and sunny. In the plaza reclined a homeless guy with a shaved head wearing nothing but a torn orange pleather jumpsuit. Panhandling. His sign said, *Cash for Chemo*. I gave him nothing.

I'd learned as a prosecutor that almost everything panhandlers got in Seattle went straight to their liquor store or their drug dealer. Most of them were on food stamps, and Social Security Disability, or TANF (Temporary Assistance for Needy Families.) Many of them lived in group homes for psych patients or addicts. They could get anything from entitlement programs.

Except cigarettes, alcohol, and street drugs.

So I wrote a good demand letter. I stayed late. I liked the weird ambiance of the streetlights, throwing psychedelic shadows from the rustling trees outside.

The next day, I asked Nicky to proof it. She suggested two grammatical fixes. I emailed the whole thing off to Sisters of Mercy's Risk Management Department in PDF form with exhibits, and I also sent a hard copy by certified mail, return receipt requested. I waited thirty days.

On the twenty-ninth day, I got a faxed letter from their insurance carrier denying fault.

Rodney was livid. He'd probably already made plans for the fee he expected. "We're going to have to stomp these nimrods, bro," he said through gritted teeth. We. The royal we.

I called Mr. and Mrs. Fernandez. I filled in Mr. Fernandez, and there was a pause for him to sign. "Let's sue," he said.

I looked up the Local Rules for Rockingham County, a rural county southeast of Seattle, where Monica had gotten her C-section at Sisters of Mercy Hospital. The Local Rules had plenty of traps. They usually do. I made a copy, highlighted the nasty parts, and stuck it in the file. I highlighted the really nasty parts with an orange dot next to them. I believe I mentioned I have a touch of obsessive-compulsive disorder.

When the legal messenger came back with the filed Summons and Complaint with the case number, I calendared all the case schedule dates and launched the whole nine yards.

When I have a defendant who's completely at fault and has no excuses, I serve them with not just the Summons and Complaint but with Interrogatories, Requests for Production of Documents, and Requests for Admission. I start the clock running for the defendant to answer questions under oath, produce all documents related to the case, and admit facts that only a total Cro-Magnon would try to deny. I call that the whole nine yards. The phrase comes from World War II when American fighter planes had machine gun ammo belts that were nine yards long.

Silent Mike served the CEO as he was getting into his Mercedes. And two court days later, Defense Counsel J. Charm Smythe filed a Notice of Appearance and Emergency Motion for Order to Seal Court File. He wanted to bury every single fact in the court file behind a seal that required a judge's order to open.

It was specially set for oral argument in a week. Oh, goody.

I cobbled together an Opposition and cited some cases. Secrecy in the courts is disfavored in the law. Most of the great cases had been fought by attorneys for newspapers. But there's an old saying—*a good lawyer knows the law; a great lawyer knows the judge.*

J. Charm Smythe's building was right across the public square from the courthouse. It was the semi-big firm in a small county with only three judges. I was starting to smell something.

I contacted The Ghost in our special way and then went to see her. "Could you tell me every single thing about Sisters of Mercy Hospital in Stonington, down in Rockingham County?" I told her why the hospital was a waste of oxygen.

She frowned. "I need to fill you in on a strange feature of medical malpractice," she said. "When a doctor or hospital in the US pays out on a medical malpractice claim, whether through a settlement or after a trial, they have to report it to the National Practitioners' Data Bank."

I looked at her unusually shiny blonde hair, her black cocktail dress. Was she having a non-vanilla date later? "I've never heard of it. Can the public see it?"

She wagged her finger at me. "No way, Vanilla Boy. The only people who can see it are doctors and hospitals, medical malpractice insurers, government officials, and of course med mal defense lawyers."

I gaped. "So my opposing counsel may know that Doctor X has killed twelve patients, and I would never find out?"

She nodded. She was kind of enjoying schooling me. "Yes. It's against the law for anybody with access to ever reveal the contents to non-authorized personnel. One side of a med mal lawsuit knows the defendant's history, and the other side can never find out."

I sighed. "So I can never find out?"

She put her hand on mine. "It's possible I have a…well, a playmate who could find out something."

I hugged her at the door.

"We really could have had fun," she murmured, into my shoulder.

I kissed her hair. It smelled like cardamom. "If only I wasn't Vanilla Boy."

***

On the hearing date, Rodney was in trial defending an accused rapist and couldn't go. "Kick some A," he told me. I took Nicky. I wanted her to understand how important her work had become.

On the freeway heading south, I noticed even more homeless tents in the right of way than last time I came this way. Now there were about fifty per mile in the first few miles. "Man, look at 'em," I said quietly.

Nicky looked at her hands in her lap. She'd dressed well for court, in a black turtleneck, black blazer, and cheerful blue paisley skirt. "If only they'd get their neurochemistry straight," she said, clenching her jaw.

I was pleased and surprised. "What do you mean?"

She whirled in her seat. "Anybody with the IQ of an amoeba knows that everybody in those tents is either an untreated addict or an untreated mentally ill person. If they'd just nut up and get treatment, they could get jobs and not live like that."

I looked at her. She was quietly angry. "I'm guessing this is personal for you," I said.

We drove for ten minutes in silence.

"My mother is bipolar," she said. "I'm an only kid. My dad was a mining engineer, a big bald guy, and he left when I was two. He never came back. The child support arrived like clockwork. That let my mother live the way she wanted to."

"How did she want to live?"

"Until I was ten she worked managing a gym. She took her Lithium. Life was okay, you know? But then she decided that Big Pharma just wanted her to conform like all the other Westernized linear people, and she wanted to explore her unique spiritual self. So she stopped the Lithium, and started visiting a spiritual healer who does energy work."

I reminded myself not to laugh. This was funny only from a distance. "What kind of energy? Volts? Kilowatts?"

Nicky shook her head and kept looking at her hands. She started talking in a singsong, Valley girl voice: "You know, like, I mean, energy," she said. "Like every sentient being is surrounded by this halo of, like, I mean energy and it suffuses everything, man, and when your energy gets off center or it turns black instead of healthy blue or pink then you need, like, energy work."

I'd lost my parents when I was seven. What right did Nicky's mother have to fuck up her daughter's life by going off her meds when she was lucky enough to be there for her daughter's life?

"So how did that play out?" I asked.

"My mom—I have to call her Esmerelda—she went to live with her guru in a yurt for a year, and I was in foster care. That's when I started playing piano." She flexed her fingers and looked at them fondly. "When she came back, she got on Social Security Disability because she does have bipolar disorder. Dad's checks kept coming in. For three years, she switched between manic episodes where she would shoplift and bring home random dudes for sex, and depressive episodes where she would binge-watch *Cops* for two weeks. She used me as her emotional punching bag. She could yell at me all evening, and the next morning be sobbing and begging for forgiveness. I just wanted her to vanish. I still do." She bit he lip. "When she was manic, she would call me Icky."

I shuddered. "That's really bad, my friend. I'm so sorry."

"But then she found the Nacreous Pearl Center for Spiritual Healing. She got a doctoral degree on very fancy paper, and everything. It took a rigorous online training course that lasted two weeks. And then she sublet an office in a, like, alternative healing space and started working. When she could. She even started sometimes taking Lithium again, so she could function as Priestess Esmerelda in her Temple."

Now I realized why I thought I understood something about Nicky. Because I did. We'd both had mothers who were, to get clinical, batshit crazy.

I probed. "So what kind of work does she do?"

Nicky pulled out her phone and looked up a website. "I might as well just read it to you. With some people, the worst thing you can do to them is quote them directly."

She tapped her phone twice. "Priestess Esmerelda's Temple of Healing Shamanic Soul Retrieval," she read, in a monotone. "Sometimes you may have a feeling of being off or stuck. That's because a portion of your soul has gotten trapped on the astral plane and you are not fully integrated into one spiritual being. When this happens, come see Priestess Esmerelda for soul retrieval." She tapped again. "Procedure: Arrive on time and place the Kindness Offering of $1,000 on the sacred pedestal by the door. Remember to bring one pound of fine-ground cornmeal. Disrobe completely and lie down on your back in the center of the wood floor. Priestess Esmerelda will then enter the Temple Space. She will sprinkle an outline of cornmeal around your body, invoking goddesses and presences as she does so. Then she will perform the Actual Soul Retrieval itself, fetching that portion of your soul which is severed and stored on the astral plane. The entire procedure requires complete concentration and takes roughly ninety minutes. Priestess Esmerelda is available for repeat therapeutic procedures. The cost is merely three hundred dollars." Nicky's monotone had become truly leaden.

I shook my head. "I'll bet she is available for repeat therapeutic procedures," I said.

Nicky looked out the window. "My mother is vicious, and crazy, and a fraud. I just hate her."

I knew better than to say the usual things. People often say you can't hate your mother, or your father, or your foster family. But if they do despicable things to you, the only healthy thing to do is to hate them. And then leave them. And then forget them.

I wasn't doing so hot on that last part. Neither was Nicky.

"My boyfriend Fred says she's a few beers short of a six pack," Nicky said. Fred—the preppy guy in the picture in her cubicle. "But I think it's worse than that. She thinks her clients are stupid. She thinks almost everybody is stupid. My father was stupid for leaving her. I was stupid for studying piano, and becoming a paralegal, and also leaving her. Everybody but her is stupid."

I nodded. "So that's why you're on board when I caution potential clients not to see chiropractors and naturopaths."

"Exactly! You tell them and tell them that they won't heal as quickly. You tell them their personal injury protection benefits will get used up and they'll still be in pain. You tell them these so-called healers will have the money that should have cured them. But they don't listen. Because they *like, you know, believe* in that stuff." Nicky frowned. "New Age fruitcakes are morons."

I burst out laughing. "Behind your serious face is a serious mind." I looked at her, and our eyes locked. "I'd say Fred is a lucky guy."

She looked away. I thought I knew why.

One thing kept bugging me. "So why does Priestess Esmerelda use cornmeal? Is the soul gluten intolerant?"

We both cracked up. With that we drove into Stonington.

***

We hurried across the lush courthouse lawn. On the courthouse roof, a group of crows traded cynical asides. I stopped to look at the tremendous khaki-painted howitzer pointing at the sky like a middle finger. "I guess they brought out the big guns," Nicky said, trying to jolly me along.

In Judge Pluffington's courtroom we were ten minutes early but J. Charm Smythe was already set up. He was a rotund tall man in his sixties wearing a three-piece pinstriped suit and a brown comb-over smeared down with Brylcreem. "J. Charm Smythe," he said, shaking my hand.

"Sam Strait," I said. "And this is my paralegal Nicky Schwartz."

J. Charm ignored Nicky. "So I take it you're a straight shooter," he asked, chuckling.

I opened the litigation case, pulled out the pleadings file and my argument outline, and tested my new highlighter. I fidgeted as always before a showdown in court.

The bailiff, a uniformed sheriff's deputy, came in from chambers. "All rise," he bellowed. "Superior Court for Rockingham County is now in session."

Fhsn Judge Pluffington swept onto the bench. He was a tense wiry white man of around fifty with a shock of gray hair, steel-gray eyes, and an expression like a furious deacon in a furious small church. "Be seated," he snapped.

We all sat. Judge Pluffington skewered me with his eyes. "Counselor, give me one good reason why the file in this case should not be sealed as Mr. Smythe suggests," he said.

I stood. "Your Honor, the Washington State Constitution and the cases cited in my brief show that civil litigation is to be carried out in public courts, except in cases where one or more parties is a minor or is alleging sexual abuse or rape."

He scowled. "The ruling in those cases does not rule out sealing a file in a case of unproven medical malpractice which threatens the major employer in Rockingham County," he said.

I nodded. I needed to find some way to agree with him about something. "Fair point, Your Honor. But the malpractice can only be proven after we go to trial and get a jury verdict," I said. "Until then I submit that the public has a right to know what happens in its courthouse."

He squinted at me. He clearly thought I couldn't do the math. When he mentioned that Sisters of Mercy was the major employer in the county, it should have been obvious.

"Your Honor, if you will," said J. Charm, struggling to his feet. His paunch was the size of a forty-pound pumpkin and just as round.

"Proceed," said Judge Pluffington.

"Your Honor, you hit the nail on the head. Let's not tear up our meal ticket here. Let's not throw out the baby with the bathwater."

Three cliches in three sentences. I almost admired his low-brow argument.

"Agreed," Judge Pluffington said. "The motion to seal the file is granted. Counsel will hand up his proposed order."

I was so shocked I nearly handed up my proposed order. For a specially set oral argument, this was the shortest one I'd ever been to. But handing up the proposed order is for winners.

J. Charm handed up his order and Judge Pluffington scribbled his signature with unnecessary force. He glared at me again. "Govern yourself accordingly, Counselor," he said. "We'll be in recess." He swept off the bench. The gentle Asian court reporter looked at me with pity in her eyes as she typed a docket entry. Then she made copies for J. Charm and me. I darted a glance at Nicky. She was covering her mouth with wide eyes.

"I hope we'll be able to cooperatively resolve this contentious matter," J. Charm drawled, again shaking my hand.

"If the insurance company didn't deny liability on this slam-dunk case, we would already have resolved this contentious issue cooperatively," I said. I was gritting my teeth.

"Be that as it may," he said mildly.

As I walked with Nicky across the courthouse lawn, I again looked at the howitzer. Yup, it was definitely a symbolic middle finger pointed at the sky. Nicky didn't mention bringing out the big guns again. She just looked at the ground.

When you're a personal injury attorney handling big-damages cases, you get stomped surprisingly often. It was all due to "Strait's Theorem"—the more zeros are at stake, the more shenanigans you will run into.

This was a pretty big case where I was big-city counsel in a small county. It was called "getting hometowned"—when the local lawyer and the local judge crush you because you're Not From Around Here. In Washington State, judges are elected. In the small counties the biggest lawyers are usually their biggest donors. Conflict of interest? Um, yes. But not the kind that ever got punished by the Bar Association or the Commission on Judicial Misconduct.

As I started my Subaru I remembered a T-shirt that Suzanne had given me, our first year at University of Washington School of Law. It said: *A Good Lawyer Knows The Law. A Great Lawyer Knows The Judge.* J. Charm was a great lawyer in Rockingham County.

As I drove north, Nicky said some comforting things that I couldn't focus on. I'd lost in court quite a few times. I'd lost when I deserved to win quite a few times. But I'd never gotten hometowned so hard and so quickly before.

"What about some music," Nicky said, fiddling with the sound system. I smelled her rose scent.

I turned on Jack FM, my favorite '80s station in Seattle. They were finishing up a commercial for a local casino. "*Why not roll the dice?*" the jingle caroled.

Then the DJ came in and said, "Okay Rodney, so who should call Mammon & Associates?"

Rodney said, "Anybody who's been injured in an accident, and it was not your fault, please call. We just got a big case where a surgeon left a sponge inside a patient at Sisters of Mercy Hospital down in Stonington, and we're going to make those dudes pay big-time, broski."

I almost swerved into another lane, and a semi honked at me. "What the actual fuck," I said under my breath.

I knew Rodney advertised a lot on Jack FM. I'd heard him do these live Q&A bits with the DJ before. But the Fernandez case was still in litigation. That was new.

"Judge Pluffington is going to hit the ceiling," I said.

Nicky opened my litigation case and read through the signed Order Sealing File. "He probably will, Sam, but look." I was so flummoxed I almost looked, and I swerved, and the semi honked again. "It says the file is sealed, and evidence, depositions, and discovery materials may not be disclosed to the public. But it doesn't prohibit pretrial publicity. Also we just got this order, and Rodney hasn't seen it yet. So maybe the judge can't punish you."

I nodded. "But does Pluffington strike you as the kind to care about the legal niceties?"

Nicky tapped the Order. "There's something else to consider, Sam," she said. "Maybe there's going to be some publicity about this. Maybe Rodney actually did you and the clients a favor. Besides, the media hates getting shut out of a case."

I was grateful to her for putting a brave face on it. "Nicky," I said, taking a risk. "Since you shared your hated nickname, I should tell you mine. I was orphaned at seven, and me and my twin sister grew up in foster care. My older foster brother used to call me Same Old—it's a takeoff on Sam. Whenever I lose something big, I can almost hear it in my ears—Same Old, Same Old. I thought you should know."

She put the Order back in the litigation case and turned away. "Maybe this time, it won't be Same Old, Same Old."

When we got back to the office, Kandy the stripper-receptionist waved to us. "Don't go see Rodney," she said. "His rape trial pled out during a recess. He's having a private meeting with a reporter from the *Seattle Times*."

Wow. Rodney had jumped on this. It was often said that the most dangerous place in Seattle was between Rodney and a reporter.

"What's up," I asked her.

She rolled her tongue stud around in her mouth. "He said it's about a sponge. Do you think he means a contraceptive sponge?"

Nicky snickered. "I doubt it," I said.

We walked down the hall to the Innocent Peoples' Department. I had to call Monica Fernandez, but maybe I'd have a ray of sunshine to offer.

***

The next day I noticed that Kandy the stripper receptionist had copied the demand package and given it to Rodney. I wondered if that was necessarily positive. Also I had an email from the judge with a cc to J. Charm. *I expect you to appear at a teleconference in seven days' time at 10:00 AM to show cause why you should not be sanctioned for violating the clear meaning of this court's Order Sealing File by engaging in pretrial publicity*, it said.

Gulp. I'd never been fined by a judge before. Not once. I wondered if Rodney would pay it. Yeah, right. I hadn't violated the Order, and Rodney hadn't either, but an angry judge is not a cautious judge.

The next morning, Nicky came in with a copy of the *Seattle Times*. "You might like this," she said, sliding it across my desk. She perched primly on my guest chair to watch my reaction.

The story was front page, above the fold. *Local Hospital Left Sponge Inside Surgical Patient. Special Report by Annika Frey.* All the basics were there, all right. There was a graphic showing the Pathology Report identifying the *retained foreign body, surgical sponge, enmeshed with six feet of gangrenous small bowel.* It promised a follow-up tomorrow.

Quick response.

The next day was the kicker. The follow-up story had a screen shot of the Sisters of Mercy Hospital history from the National Practitioners' Data Bank.

Quite a record. They'd killed a woman in trauma surgery by transfusing the wrong type of blood. They'd fatally injured an elderly man getting hip replacement surgery, by giving him saline solution that turned out to be a caustic cleaning fluid, because they were stored in identical containers in the OR. They'd removed the wrong lung from a lung cancer patient with one good lung, and one bad lung. Specifically, they'd removed the good lung, and left the bad one. Those were just the highlights.

The Ghost had somehow gotten this truckload of dynamite and shared it with Annika Frey. Kaboom. I couldn't stop smiling.

Nicky was watching as I read the story. I jumped to my feet. "Let us give thanks to The Ghost," I said cryptically, looking up at the ceiling. Nicky was puzzled and I didn't explain.

The next day, I was five days out from Judge Pluffington's teleconference where J. Charm would be polite and the judge would hammer me.

But the third story from the Seattle Times came out that day too. *Department of Health Acts on Sisters of Mercy Hospital*, said that headline. Annika Frey again.

The Department of Health had access to the National Practitioners' Data Bank, remember? They'd known what was going on. But when the public found out what was going on too, the DOH acted in self-preservation. Which is the signature move of government bureaucrats.

The Secretary of Health had held a press conference, and revoked the Certificate of Need and the business license for Sisters of Mercy. State troopers chained and locked the doors. They said it was temporary.

Sisters of Mercy, represented by J. Charm of course, promised to appeal these decisions. The Department of Health announced they could rush through the appeal process in a year or so. Hah! Sisters of Mercy was as dead as many of their poor patients.

That night I had a Scrabble game with The Ghost. She wore jeans and a gray cardigan and seemed muted. I filled her in even though I bet she knew everything already. "So where did the *Seattle Times* get that screen shot from the National Practitioner Data Bank?" I asked her. "Rodney couldn't get it. I couldn't get it. The reporter couldn't get it."

The Ghost smiled and played the word ONUS. "I suspect they had a confidential source," she said, with a lopsided smile. June rain rattled against the windows next to us, sending drops down the glass which reflected the café in each tiny spherical mirror. I was soaring inside.

I stared at the Scrabble board, and then put a B in front of her word, spelling BONUS. "They had a fucking marvelous confidential source," I said. "Did I ever tell you that I love you?"

She winked. "You did, Vanilla Boy. But only as a friend. And I like to be loved in more unconventional ways, as you recall."

***

The next day I got an email from Judge Pluffington striking the sanctions hearing, and another from J. Charm Smythe proposing mediation.

A mediation is a type of settlement conference where a mediator, usually a veteran lawyer or retired judge, shuttles between the parties in separate rooms relaying arguments and offers. It often succeeds because both parties are willing to pay for the mediator's expensive time. Usually they have exchanged offers already. I never went to mediation without an offer from a defendant. Until now.

We agreed to use Judge Amy Waltham, one of my favorites. She'd retired after twenty years on the Superior Court bench, and she was willing to put actual pressure on the parties, rather than just going back and forth exchanging pleasantries. Many mediators in Seattle were passive because many people of all kinds in Seattle were passive. Maybe it was the cloudy weather nine months out of the year. But Judge Waltham would use a little muscle. Back when I was a prosecutor I'd been thrilled to have her on the bench in my cases.

I went with Hector and Monica Fernandez, and Nicky. And Sylvia. By now I thought little Sylvia was a good luck charm. Thank God Rodney was in trial defending a Vehicular Assault—a case where a drunk driver had severely injured somebody.

At the start we had what's called a "meet and greet," where Judge Waltham brought J. Charm and the claims adjuster to our room to shake hands. The claims adjuster was five-two, two hundred pounds, fiftyish, dead-fish white face. She looked like somebody had just murdered her beagle. In front of her. To have settlement authority on this big a med mal case she'd have thirty years' experience and a checkbook of a million, minimum. She smelled like Avon products and terminal obedience. She wore a potato sack dress over a potato sack body.

"Nice to meet you," I said to her calmly, shaking hands. "So you're the adjuster who said that a retained surgical sponge is not a clear liability event." The adjuster squinted at me.

Judge Waltham looked sharply at me. She flashed a hint of a smile. Then we separated for our caucuses.

We volleyed back and forth for about an hour and a half, and eventually the insurer came to a good figure. It would pay for all of Monica's medical treatment, and over a hundred thousand dollars for her four weeks of pain and suffering. Because her bowel resection surgery had worked beautifully, and her infection was gone, Monica was perfectly healthy now. She could eat and digest normally. Her surgeon had said in the post-op report that she would have normal digestion. Monica was fine. But she would always be wary of doctors. Understandable.

It was a good result. It wasn't a huge result, but it was a good result. We wouldn't have to spend fifty to a hundred grand flying in an out-of-state surgical expert to testify about the obvious. We wouldn't have to do depositions to prove the obvious. We eliminated a ton of costs and at least a year of delay.

If the insurance company had negotiated before I filed suit, they could have had this settlement then. But then Sisters of Mercy would still be operating. Perversely I was glad the insurance company had denied liability and forced the issue. Now their insured hospital was padlocked and the insurance company wasn't getting premiums anymore. As hipsters would say around Seattle: "Sucks to be you."

We had one snag when the insurer insisted on a confidentiality clause. Med mal insurers always try that. Doctors and hospitals love to bury their mistakes behind a wall of secrecy. Even though they have the secrecy of the National Practitioner Data Bank, they want plaintiffs sworn to secrecy too. I said, "I don't think my clients would agree to that."

Hector interpreted for Monica. She signed back, furiously. "Monica says, the insurance company doesn't have enough money to buy that from us. Nothing would buy our silence."

I handed Judge Waltham some copies. "Judge," I said, "here are the *Seattle Times* articles about Sisters of Mercy. The second one has the printout from the National Practitioner Data Bank showing their screwups. Please tell them a nondisclosure would be like locking the barn after the horse has escaped."

I figured if J. Charm wanted to speak in cliches, I would try to use his language. "It won't cost them anything more," I said, "but they can't buy our silence."

Judge Waltham furrowed her brow and brushed back her steel-gray curls. I recognized that gesture from once when she sentenced a robber I was prosecuting. It meant this was getting juicy and she liked it. "I'll see what they say," she said.

She came back five minutes later, with a Memorandum of Settlement, signed by J. Charm and the insurance adjuster, with a faxed signature from the Chief Medical Officer of Sisters of Mercy Hospital, who'd been waiting at J. Charm's office in Stonington. There was no nondisclosure clause. Judge Waltham had specifically added, *This is not a confidential settlement* in graceful handwriting. Reading between the lines, I realized she did not like this defendant one bit.

Monica signed in small handwriting. She was blushing, and I could tell she was happy. Hector signed, in bigger letters. I signed. When Judge Waltham brought back copies, Sylvia said, "Cool." I would swear she said it, even though she was only a few months old.

"J. Charm would like to have a private word before you leave," Judge Waltham said.

"I'm fine with talking with him," I said. "But nothing in this case happens behind my clients' backs."

J. Charm came in. Behind him I could see the bitter insurance adjuster waddling down the hall. "I'd like to have a word about your deportment in this case," J. Charm said, unctuously. "Wouldn't it be better to make this a private conversation?"

Hector was signing quickly, and Monica was signing quickly too.

"Nope," I said. "Proceed."

I stood. I was a little shorter than him, but I felt a lot taller.

He cleared his throat. "Judge Pluffington and I have had some concerns about your deportment," he said, carefully using that flaccid word again.

"I see," I said, inching toward him. "So you've had illegal ex parte contact with Judge Pluffington regarding this case, while it is still pending in his court. That's a gross violation of the Rules of Professional Conduct for you, and of the Canon of Judicial Ethics, for him. Go on."

He looked down. A bead of sweat came down his forehead from his comb-over. "It is possible to resolve civil matters without engaging in any rancor," he said, using his orotund bass voice.

I took a step toward him. "I have never raised my voice with either of you. I have never used any obscene language. I have never been anything but polite. But your clown car of a hospital has killed four people, and injured sixteen, over the last four years, according to the National Practitioner Data Bank. I didn't have access to that. I'm a plaintiff's attorney, so I can't see it. But you did."

I took a step toward him. "I will bet my left nut that you settled every one of those cases with a nondisclosure agreement. This would have gone on if the reporter hadn't gotten that incredible screenshot from an anonymous source. Yes, I've provided zealous advocacy. The Rules of Professional Conduct say that I should." I paused. I was nose to nose with him. "I caught your client killing and injuring people, multiple times. Making the most stupid possible medical mistakes. Covering them up. And that makes me the bad guy?"

I wasn't shouting. I wasn't furious. I was ice cold. And by now I was backing him out the door.

J. Charm took a step back, then another. "The Bar Association might be interested in this case," he said, trying his final lever.

"They might," I said, looking over at Hector and Monica, who were conversing quickly in sign language. "But not because of me. Because of you and your favorite judge. So bring it on, Counselor."

"Oh, real professional," he muttered, rolling his eyes and sidling away.

I turned to look at Monica and Hector. "Monica," I said. "I don't know any sign language. Could you teach me to say thank you in ASL?"

She carefully made a gesture. I repeated it.

Then she hugged me. God help me, I cried on her shoulder.

This case was personal for me.

Because all of them were personal for me.

I'll explain why. But that'll have to come later. I'm not ready to tell you about that yet.

CHAPTER EIGHT—IMAGINARY CHILDREN

The next weekend I visited Catherine. We sat out by the paddock on the bench near the watering trough while a rare June sun blazed on the green grass and leaves, soaking into our upturned faces. Seattle is the gloomiest city in the US and the most introverted. These things are definitely related. It also has the highest suicide rate per capita. Go figure.

I told Catherine all about the Fernandez case against Sisters of Mercy Hospital, as she plucked a blade of grass and cupped her hands and blew. It honked. Jenny the retired racehorse turned around, her ears raised. Horses raise their ears and point them forward when they're happy or curious. They flatten their ears back when they're mad or scared. Horses are easy to read. Because of the scar where my earlobe got shot off, I'm easy to read too.

"You need to teach me how to do that," I said.

Catherine tilted her head and gave me her amused look. "So how's the ongoing mission?"

I told her all about the Fernandez case against Sisters of Mercy. All except for the super-secret stuff The Ghost had done. I wanted to show off for her. I hadn't had a girlfriend since Suzanne six years ago, and I didn't know Nicky Schwartz very well yet. I could only brag to Catherine.

"Sam, I'm glad you shut them down," Catherine said, leaning forward so her hair made a curtain.

"But?"

"But when your highs over your victories are this high, it means your next low is going to be very, very low."

I picked up a piece of grass, cupped it in my hands, and tried to make it honk. Nothing, as always.

I ducked my head. "Okay. So how can I get on a more even keel?" We'd had this conversation before, too, but I knew she was right. At last I was willing to take some good advice.

Cat reached into the pocket of her barn coat and pulled out a card. "This guy is simply the best. I've seen him. Terry has seen him. He's the therapist's therapist. He does hypnotherapy and EMDR and regular therapy too. He's the best sounding board I've ever found."

Cat had been my own sounding board since I was seven years old. This sounded promising. Swallows swooped over the paddock, singing tiny cries as they scooped up invisible insects, then climbing into the uncertain sun.

I looked at the name: Abe Aschmann, Logotherapy.

"What is logotherapy?"

"It was invented by Victor Frankl, a survivor of Auschwitz. Logotherapy helps us get our heads straight by clarifying our purpose in life."

"But I have a purpose in life."

Cat laid a restraining hand on mine. "You have one purpose in life. But maybe you'd do better if you had another one too."

I nodded and smiled. Even though I knew nothing about horses, I'd been a one-trick pony since that awful day in the camp dining hall when I found out our parents were dead. "Maybe," I said.

"Seriously, Sam. Do it before you take another punch on the chin. I've seen you when that happens. You always get more injured than you have to." She blew the grass again. Honk.

Jenny started ambling over toward us. Catherine took my hand in her work-roughened hand. "I don't remember who said it, but it's true—we are more often frightened than hurt."

I thought of how scared I'd been when I thought Judge Pluffington was going to sanction me. I'd catastrophized the whole thing, thinking the Fernandez case would be dismissed, and I'd let Monica and Hector Fernandez down, and I'd get fired by Rodney, and I'd even get disbarred.

See how that sentence spirals down rapidly? I'd always been vulnerable to spiraling down rapidly.

I did have only one purpose. My life was based only on whether or not I helped innocent people who'd been hurt. I didn't have anything else.

I didn't think I deserved anything else.

"Okay," I said. "I will call him within thirty days."

Cat sat up and patted me on the shoulder. "You should call him sooner. But when you see him, it's probably going to be a huge relief."

"For you or for me?"

She smiled. "We're still kind of one egg, remember?"

I remembered. Since that awful day in the dining hall we'd reminded each other we were still kind of one egg. Even though we were fraternal twins, we'd always said that.

Next, I went on TopFliteSingles.com and sent out some emails. HL Mencken once said, "Second marriages are the triumph of hope over experience." Maybe that wasn't true of second marriages, but given my history, it was completely true of online dating.

A little background. Research showed Seattle was the loneliest city in the US, as well as the gloomiest and the most introverted. It was all one ball of "leave me alone." I wasn't exactly a ninja at dating, either. But I was ready to spin the roulette wheel again. Maybe the next date wouldn't be a prostitute.

I decided I would tweak my profile to specify that I was looking for a woman who was open to marriage and children. No more Ferrari ladies for me. Then I ran a search and found several women who sounded promising.

I decided to break my pattern and only email one woman. She had pretty auburn hair, a mid-level job in tech, and she liked spicy food.

She actually replied. I had a response ratio of about two percent, so this was good. We booked dinner at a Thai place near her, northeast of Seattle in a suburb called Bothell. I shaved carefully, put on my best black blazer, and dabbed a little cologne on the back of my neck and my hands.

I got seated at Thai One On ten minutes early. The smell of ginger and sesame oil wafted through, and spiky Thai music twinkled from the kitchen.

She came in at five minutes after the agreed time. Anything less than fifteen minutes late was on time in the online dating world for the woman.

Well hello. She stood about five-two, wearing a sun dress and a pink cardigan. She sat and extended her hand. Clear nail polish. Good omen. "I'm Amber," she said.

I shook her hand. Some fizz in her grip. "My hand is a little moist because I'm kind of yellow," I said, trying a feeble pun.

She threw back her head and laughed. Splendid. For me, intelligence and humor were mandatory. I was looking for a needle in a haystack, but I only wanted to find one needle.

We got pad thai, three stars, and spring rolls. For once, I had an easy time with the give-and-take of a first date.

I picked up the check.

"So, would you like to see my place?" she asked.

"Sure," I said.

I thought I'd see where this goes. When you're a bachelor, you always have to see where this goes. It's an unwritten law.

I followed her to her place, a neat townhouse. She showed me around. I started to get a certain vibe. It was decorated like an expensive hotel room—reasonably good taste, but nothing personal at all about the place.

"Would you like to see my bedroom?"

"Okay," I said. My antennae were up. It was an almost universal truth that my online dates threw a curveball traveling about eighty-five miles per hour, and I saw it only when it crossed the plate and smacked me on the nose. Unlike baseball, that didn't mean you got to walk to first base. It meant you got to walk to your car. Without delay.

She led me by the hand into her bedroom, and snapped on the lights. She had a king-size four-poster bed with Spanish ironwork.

It was covered with small stuffed animals. Beanie Babies.

She walked to the bed and picked up a giraffe. "Hi, my name is Gerald, and I'm a giraffe," she said in a high squeaky voice. "I am a Pisces, and I like skateboarding."

My jaw dropped.

She put that one down and picked up a turtle. "Hello, my name is Tommy, and I am a tortoise. I like salt water taffy and swimming and Justin Bieber." This one had a slightly different, high, squeaky voice. This one was a Taurus. This one was vegan.

She got through two more before I could get my operating system to start working again. "Excuse me, but I have to use the bathroom," I stammered.

I fled.

Five minutes later I was on the freeway going seventy in the trusty Outback. "Fuck no, fuck no," I kept muttering. I slowed down to sixty. I felt as if my balls were trying to crawl up into my abdomen and hide there for protection.

Then I burst out laughing.

I'd said I wanted a woman who was open to the possibility of having children, didn't I?

The Online Dating Gods had evidently decided, "Hold my beer. I'll give you a woman who wants children, all right."

This one was so desperate to reproduce she'd made her stuffed animals into imaginary children and given them imaginary personalities.

I remembered a dark, ancient Chinese curse: May You Get What You Want.

I shook my head, smiling. The Sam Strait curse was still alive and well. At least I had a wonderfully weird and sad story to tell when I finally met Suzanne the Second.

If I ever did. There was no guarantee of that.

The brutal thing about "finding another purpose" through finding a mate?

It's the whole finding the right mate part.

CHAPTER NINE—A KENTUCKY ASS-WHIPPING

The Fernandez case against Sisters of Mercy Hospital brought us a lot of publicity and a lot of med mal potential cases.

One morning, I found Rodney standing in the lobby leaning on Kandy, the stripper-receptionist's desk, his blond gel-stiffened porcupine hair gleaming. He turned to Nicky and commanded: "Honey bunch, I want you to set up a med mal Intake Clinic pronto with at least ten potentials in it. Then, next week, do another. If we get another case like that Sisters of Mercy case, we're going to make enough dough to choke a rhino."

Nicky nodded. Kandy stared, fascinated at Rodney's dominant manner.

I came up behind Rodney and said, "Copy that, Boss."

Rodney whirled. "And you sign any med mal with enough vitality to fog a mirror."

I'd told him that approximately eighty-five percent of med mal trials in Washington led to a defense verdict. But Rodney heard only what he wanted to hear. Which was the sound of his own raspy voice.

Rodney clapped me on the back. He'd been a second-string quarterback in college, and he knew the faux-brotherhood gestures. "Nut up, bro," he declared.

When Rodney smelled money, he turned from a man into a… mechanism.

Nicky set up the Intake Clinic, and we soldiered on. But amid all the unwinnable dross, I found one that might be a winner.

Rachel Vandermicx slouched in her chair, her eyes with dark circles under them scrutinizing me. Her dull blonde hair was pulled back into a magenta scrunchie, so tight it stretched her forehead, her doughy arms crossed across her chest. Defensive gesture. "My mother died because her home healthcare aide gave her too much fentanyl," she said. Then she slid her documents across the table. I grabbed them. Great potentials always bring documents.

That smell again. The smell of True Disaster, like cinnamon and spice and everything nice. Another chance to justify my existence. Nicky leaned forward and clenched her pen, her knuckles white. Nicky smelled it, too.

I flipped through the documents, pretending to be objective. She had a Medic One report showing the decedent, Martha Vandermicx, had been *found deceased in bed, with rigor* showing she'd died several hours before. The medical examiner's toxicology screening noted *remarkable screen for twice the normal lethal dose of fentanyl.*

Fentanyl—a powerful opioid used for pain arising from cancer or other critical conditions. It was considered one hundred times as potent as heroin, gram for gram. (By the way, heroin had originally been a prescription drug, too. The German scientist who invented it named it "heroin" as in heroine, a female hero.) Fentanyl in Seattle had become a common street drug, causing more fatal overdoses than all other street drugs. Combined. Doctors generally prescribed fentanyl only as the last-ditch painkiller. There was a possibility the doctor shouldn't have prescribed it to Martha.

The medical examiner's Investigator Narrative stated: *Home healthcare aide Belinda Santorino states she administered to patient her usual meds. After performing some chores, she returned. Decedent was unresponsive. Skin was warm. Breathing was labored. She then called decedent's daughter and told daughter she could not wake her. Daughter asked aide to call 911 and get paramedics. Aide said sometimes patient was "sometimes sleepy after her meds" and declined to call 911. Daughter drove to the home—daughter lives 90 minutes away. When daughter reached the patient's home, patient's skin was cold, and she had no pulse or breath sounds. Daughter called 911. County Fire responded with Engine 31 and Medic One. Medic One was unable to revive patient and transported her to ER, where physician pronounced her deceased.*

Hmm.

Home healthcare aides were licensed by the State of Washington and often paid by the state, too, often through Medicaid. The only requirements were a super-simple certification, a clean criminal background check, and CPR training.

Home healthcare aides were not allowed to administer medication— not any kind of medication. Not even baby aspirin. According to the medical examiner, the aide had violated this rule.

I nodded. "What do you know about Belinda Santorino?" I asked.

Rachel slid another document across the table; it was a background report from InstantCheckmate.com. Dated three days after Martha's death. Santorini had convictions for misdemeanor assault (Assault Four—Domestic Violence), two counts of Violation of Antiharassment Order, and five for Misdemeanor Theft/Shoplifting. She was convicted on all of these counts before the date of death.

Santorino had disqualifying criminal history. She had administered medication illegally. And she had refused to call 911. On paper, this one looked like a real beauty.

"Okay, you've got yourself a lawyer," I said, shaking Rachel's hand.

"I just feel so guilty that I wasn't there," Rachel said. "I should have called 911 from my house instead of coming up there. I should have done more."

I nodded. I always ran into this dynamic. "The good people are always over-responsible," I said quietly. "It's the rotten people who don't take the blame even when they do something bad."

Rachel sniffled into a balled-up handkerchief. She'd been beating herself up, and she would continue to. I knew the defendant would allege comparative fault because Martha had not refused the medication.

They could try. But the Deadman Statute said a defendant could not allege fault of a dead person. Because the dead person was not able to contradict the defendant. Sensible rule. I would warn Rachel about the comparative fault angle. But not now.

"You trusted the trained medical professional who was on the scene," I said. "That person turned out to be as dumb as a bag of hammers. Of course, defendants will say it's anybody else's fault. They always do. But I think we've got a live one here."

I referred her to a probate attorney, a friend of Duvonda's named Bonus Malone. "We need to get a probate of your mom's estate opened right away. Did your mom have a husband, or any other kids?"

"No, there was just me."

"Okay. The probate attorney will ask if she had a will. Did your mom have a will?"

Martha sniffed again. "No. I looked through everything. She had bad arthritis, and she spent most of her time in bed. But she was only sixty-two. She didn't have anything except her Social Security Disability check, a subsidized apartment, and a parrot named Buster."

Fentanyl for arthritis? Treating arthritic pain with fentanyl sounded like opening an egg with a hammer. And a parrot named Buster. Hmm.

"Who has Buster now?"

"I've got him. He talks a bit. He likes to say, 'Well dog my cats,' which is something Mom used to say."

I remembered a weird case in law school where a parrot had actually been quoted in an arrest warrant. The defense moved to suppress on grounds of hearsay, and the court, making a really bold ruling, denied the motion. The court said in that one weird reported opinion that police could rely on statements from a parrot in seeking an arrest warrant. There was a one-percent chance I could quote a parrot in this case if the parrot could say anything other than "well, dog, my cats."

I shivered. It was not the air conditioning. The home healthcare aide refused to call 911. I couldn't think of any excuse for that.

"Okay, we'll get probate opened and get Letters Testamentary issued to you. Then we'll sign the contract and the authorization allowing us to get medical records. But I need Letters Testamentary first. That's the hunting license for your mom's case."

I looked at Nicky. She still leaned forward. She darted a look at me, her deep brown eyes urging me on. I was coming to think of Nicky as a mock juror, the kind of person who could give me a read on what the general public would think. I always looked at personal injury cases with my own set of lenses. I knew they were distorted. I needed a read from somebody without my…unusual personal history.

Rachel took out her keys and set them on the table as she shouldered her purse. I spotted the Jeep key fob with a photo of a big orange Jeep Rubicon on it. "Is that your Jeep?"

"Yes. When my husband dumped me a few years back because I couldn't get pregnant, I bought it. I call it Mad Bastard. I go off-roading with my friends because getting out on forest roads and churning some mud sets me free. My mom started calling me every morning after that. We'd read Dear Abby together. She'd tell me her advice. If I came up with something else, she'd say, 'Well, dog, my cats.'" Rachel met my eyes. "Now I'm the Mad Bastard. Nail that home healthcare aide. Please?"

"I'll do my best." We plaintiffs' attorneys aren't allowed to guarantee a result. It's for our own protection. But I was itching to pull out my sword and charge the enemy lines, singing "Battle Hymn of the Republic."

I escorted Rachel to the front door. Rodney was leaning over Kandy's desk, looking at her abundant cleavage. "Take care," I told Rachel. Rodney glanced at Rachel and found her un-checkoutable.

So I got the Letters Testamentary, and ordered the medical records from Martha's previous year of primary care treatment. I did public disclosure requests for Santorino's files and her criminal charges.

All the while, Abe Aschmann's card sat in my pocket. I didn't procrastinate when I was working for other people. But when my own peace of mind was on the line, I found excuses not to act.

When I got everything together, I stayed late one evening to read it all. Outside, the trees were rattling in an early summer wind. The fickle Seattle summer was beginning, and outside, a fingernail moon shone like some unreadable omen.

Every single thing Rachel had said checked out. I wrote a Notice of Tort Claim directed to the Department of Social and Health Services and a demand letter alleging that DSHS had negligently trained and supervised Santorino.

Why didn't I include negligent licensing? When Santorino had criminal history, disqualifying her from working as a home healthcare aide?

Because the Washington Supreme Court had ruled several years before that DSHS could not be held responsible for negligent licensing. They could have licensed Charles Manson, and if he murdered his patients, DSHS would have no liability.

But I was pretty sure I could get them on negligent supervision and training. Santorino had done CPR training. Doubtless, it told her when the patient has no pulse, you call 911. Doubtless.

Adequate supervision and training would have probably prevented Santorino from giving a big dose of fentanyl when she wasn't allowed to give any medication. And refusing to call 911 when her patient passed out.

Your average chimp was smart enough to call 911 when a person was given lots of drugs and then passed out. It didn't take much time. It didn't cost any money. It was a free phone call. This defendant was starting to piss me off.

I remembered Catherine telling me I needed to see Abe Aschmann and reminding me of how low I could get. In one ear and out the other.

So, I got the Letters Testamentary and signed the contract with Rachel. She said, "Do we have a good shot?"

"No guarantees, but we have a good shot."

***

I went down to Rachel's house to meet the parrot named Buster. I tried talking to him and whistling to him. I fed him some almonds, and Rachel did, too.

All Buster ever said was, "Well, dog, my cats."

I drove home feeling bemused. It had been a ridiculous long shot. But Rachel was glad to see me. I liked the parrot—a saucy fellow with a black tongue, bold yellow vest, bright green wings, and cynical eyes.

DSHS did not respond to the Notice of Tort Claim. The state almost never did. The Revised Code of Washington said we had to present the Notice of Tort Claim, basically a form with a demand letter and exhibits, and serve it on the at-fault agency. The agency had sixty days to respond. They used this interval, like good little bureaucrats, to prepare to cover their well-upholstered asses. Duvonda sarcastically called it "informal discovery." It meant they got a bunch of evidence, and then they could pretty up their records before litigation got rolling.

Here's another wrinkle—because I was suing the state, I had to file suit in Thurston County, home of the state capitol in Olympia. Thurston County had a jury pool flooded with state employees. The government got a sweet home court advantage in any lawsuit.

I launched service with Silent Mike and included Interrogatories, Requests for Production, and Requests for Admission. When I delivered the package to him, I walked over to Duvonda's office in the brilliant summer sun. In the plaza at her building, a white guy with dreadlocks clad in a fleece camo jumpsuit reclined on an Army blanket with a sign that said, *I Need To Get Really Drunk*. As I strolled past, he yelled, "Hey, bro! Don't leave Street Monkey hanging!"

Duvonda was in his office with her shoes off and her feet up. She was drinking a mocha, and she looked too tired for mid-morning. I knew she was in the middle of a hideous case where a daycare had turned into a pedophile ring. Unlike many of these storied cases, this one had DNA evidence and criminal charges pending.

"Any last advice about my DSHS case?" I asked her.

She looked at me and winked. "You're suing DSHS in Thurston County? Not a very friendly forum. But you got no choice."

I nodded.

She winked at me. "Fight like you're the third monkey to board the Ark, and it just started to rain."

***

DSHS appeared via an assistant attorney general. I had to file a Motion for Default to get their answer. I had to set a discovery conference to get their discovery. They answered the Requests for Admission on time and refused to admit or deny anything, saying for each one: "OBJECTION. This calls for admissions of facts for which proof is reserved for trial," citing the Reid Sand and Gravel case that didn't apply. But defense attorneys often did that anyway. They had the home-court advantage. Winning a Motion to Compel Discovery wasn't exactly in the cards. I did get skimpy responses to Interrogatories and Requests for Production of documents. I had all the documents already from my Public Records Act requests.

So, I noted the deposition of a DSHS employee under Civil Rule 30(b)(6).

This is a great rule. You know how people who work for big organizations love to say, "That's not my department," right? CR 30(b)(6) lets a litigator drill through that. It requires the organization to identify an employee to testify on specific subjects named by the attorney deposing the witness. Bureaucrats and organizational drones hated it. Which was exactly why I loved it.

I noted the CR 30(b)(6) deposition of DSHS's employee to be named to testify regarding "the training and supervision of co-defendant Santorino."

The deposition was set at DSHS headquarters in Olympia, a forlorn early-1960s building that looked like the headquarters of the world's saddest public school system. I noted it as a video deposition and booked my favorite court reporter, Fabulous Hal. Fabulous Hal was another one of my imaginary jurors, like Nicky. He was a gay Asian guy who dressed in checked suits with ascots and overdid it on flamboyance. He had a military-grade bullshit detector, like Duvonda and The Ghost. Best court reporter I'd ever had.

Since Duvonda introduced us, I'd brought in Fabulous Hal for every deposition, and he brought his own videographer, a slender morose guy with green hair and facial piercings he called "Romeo." And that was his real name—Romeo Pursuit. He'd legally changed it. Who the hell knew why?

So, I met Fabulous Hal and Romeo Pursuit at DSHS Headquarters. They were already set up, even though I was half an hour early. That was another thing I loved about Fabulous Hal. He was always on time. He recorded every deposition on a digital recorder and emailed me the sound file right afterward. There was a lot to like about Fabulous Hal.

As you've figured out, I was impulsive. But I had a marvelous group of friends backing me up, even when I was charging across No Man's Land with no weapon except a dull plastic spoon.

I set up in the conference room at a fake marble table with fake flowers in plastic vases at the center. The room reeked of Glade Potpourri. On the wall was a motivational poster in a gold frame showing a cyclist in the Tour de France, sweating as he climbed a hill. The caption read: *Whether you think you can or you think you can't, you're right. Henry Ford.* DSHS décor.

Romeo Pursuit already had his video camera set up on a tripod, at the far end of the table, pointed at the chair at my end where the witness would sit. He'd put collar-mikes with coils in front of that chair, my chair, and the defense counsel's chair. I looked around again. Glade Potpourri. If kitsch was a defense, DSHS was overdoing it.

Fabulous Hal set up his transcription machine and put his digital recorder in front of him, set to voice activation. I dropped a pen on the table to test it, and the red light winked. Hal cracked his knuckles and smiled at me. "Spooky place," he whispered.

"True dat," said Romeo Pursuit.

"True dat," I repeated.

I had all the exhibits copied and tabbed with Post-Its. The highlighted copies on top of each bundle were for me. I had a script keyed to them. I arranged my pen, my highlighter, and my book of the civil rules, opened to Civil Rule 30, "Conduct of Depositions." I'd had to read the rule into the record more than once.

Depositions are where defense attorneys are most likely to misbehave. They are court proceedings, but no judge is present to referee disputes. Putting them on video doesn't necessarily improve behavior. In this case I didn't even bother to bring the phone number of the assigned judge, as I usually did. I wasn't going to ask the assigned judge to make any rulings on the phone against DSHS. In Thurston County, that would be like asking a Siberian tiger to turn vegan.

The door opened. "I'm Tommy Split," the defense attorney said, shaking my hand. He was bald and skinny and tense, like an Iron Man runner with no love life. He was the typical government defense lawyer. Wound too tight. Nervous about offending the bureaucracy. He was competent, but in his job, competence didn't necessarily get you a promotion or even let you keep your job.

For that, you needed pull.

The door opened, and a coiffed, drab brunette in her fifties took the witness chair. "I'm Tammy Barnett," she said, shaking my hand. I met her totally false smile with one of my own.

Then, four more people came in and sat around the table. They weren't introduced—call them Baldy, Spinster, Super Fat Bowler Guy, and Nobody Lady.

I asked Tommy Split, "Who are these fine people?"

"Observers from DSHS," he said. Well, they were employees of the defendant, so I couldn't exclude them.

The organizational table of DSHS was a lasagna of layers. DSHS was a jobs program for state bureaucrats. They were all paid pretty well. None of them ever got fired, even when they made the most gruesome mistakes.

Fighting DSHS was like fighting a beanbag chair. It had no vital organs and no bones. You couldn't really hurt it. If you won, the taxpayers paid, and the bureaucrats stayed. You could just tire yourself out punching the beanbag chair.

Tammy Barnett was sworn in by Fabulous Hal. Romeo Pursuit did his video read-in. I gave my standard instructions about Tammy answering to the best of her knowledge and answering any question before taking a break, etcetera. Then I started drilling down.

"Did you review any documents in preparation for your deposition today?"

"Why yes, I certainly did."

"Did you review the discovery documents Mr. Split provided to me?"

"Oh yes." She smiled like the cat that ate the canary. I again smelled the Glade Potpourri. And something else.

I began to get the idea she had actually eaten an actual canary. The hairs on the back of my neck stood up. I suspected this was an ambush. Duvonda liked to say: "The best battle is an ambush."

"Did you review any documents other than the discovery documents in preparation for the deposition today?"

"I certainly did."

"Do you have them with you?"

"All righty then," she said, grinning as she reached into her massive needlepoint shoulder bag. I studied the needlepoint—a big orchid with a legend that said *A Smile Is Just A Frown Turned Upside Down*. She pulled out a single document, two pages, stapled.

"May I see it?"

"Certainly. I brought extra copies, too." A stir went up among the four droids that DSHS had sent to observe. Super Fat Bowler Guy snickered.

The document? A subsection of the Washington Administrative Code, entitled *Responsibility for Acts or Omissions of DSHS-Licensed Home Healthcare Aides*. It said, *Pursuant to the authority given the director by RCW XX.XXX.XX, the director finds that imposing civil liability on the*

Department for any acts or omissions of any licensed home healthcare aides would impose an unreasonable burden on Department finances. Therefore, the Department bears no civil liability whatsoever for any acts or omissions of any kind attributable to a home healthcare aide licensed by the Department.

Son of a bitch.

"Is this a true copy of the WAC section?" I asked her.

"Why yes, it is."

I opened the browser on my laptop. I looked up the RCW. Sure enough, it gave the director of DSHS virtually unlimited authority to adopt rules in the WAC for the *efficient and affordable administration of DSHS responsibilities.*

I looked up the WAC. It was correct. It had been adopted two years before.

I did a quickie search of Washington cases, looking for the specific WAC number. This was a great search term. With this one search, I could verify whether the WAC had ever been overruled, or limited, or interpreted by any court issuing a reported appellate decision. Unreported appellate decisions could not be cited as legal authority. Woe to the lawyer who tried that; that was a landmine.

Zilch. Never interpreted.

I re-read the WAC. I remembered H.L. Mencken's saying: "No matter how cynical you get, it's impossible to keep up."

I said quietly, "I think I need to go outside and throw up."

Hall arched an eyebrow at me. "Is that off the record?"

"Yes," I said, blushing.

"NO, it is not," declared Tommy Split, performing like a circus Chihuahua for the DSHS droids. "I am ordering this deposition, and I demand a copy of the digital audio file."

I stared across the table at Tommy. "Are you seriously arguing that there is something wrong with me being nauseated at the state immunizing itself in such a…shall we say bold manner?"

"YES," he yelled. Home court advantage. Faux outrage. The guy knew how to play his cards.

Tommy had struck gold. He would do his career a lot of good today. The DSHS observers looked at each other and, smiled, and shook their heads. Super Fat Bowler Guy snickered. They felt very, very, very represented right now.

I asked the witness, "Is it the state's contention that this WAC bars any legal liability for the wrongful death of my client due to the actions of Ms. Santorino?"

Tommy didn't object, saying "calls for a legal conclusion," as I invited him to. I was looking for stray threads to pull out. But DSHS wore a suit of armor.

"It certainly is," Tammy caroled, smirking as she returned her copy of the WAC to her needlepoint shoulder bag.

A Smile Is Just A Frown Turned Upside Down, remember?

Tommy leaned forward, his emaciated face lit up by some covert fever. "You can expect our Motion for Summary Judgment of Dismissal within seven days' time."

I swallowed hard. "I am recessing this deposition with leave to recall the witness depending on the outcome of the Motion to Dismiss. I would also like to order the transcript, the audio file, and the video from Mr. Pursuit."

The enemy filed out. Super Fat Bowler guy seemed to be in charge— he grabbed Tommy's elbow and started murmuring to him, darting a look at me. The door swung shut. Wafts of Glade Potpourri. Fuck me, pink.

Hal and Romeo packed up their gear, carefully not looking at me. They knew I was totally hosed. As was the daughter mourning my dead, very dead client.

I walked out with them, as always. I wheeled one of Romeo's carts, as always. They liked it that I always helped them with their gear.

"So, what do you guys think of this case?" I asked them.

Romeo flipped back his green forelock. "It looks pretty bad, Sam." He pulled out his vape and took a puff, sending cherry steam floating away. "Pretty bad."

Hall nodded sadly. "It smells like fish that's been dead for five days."

"Thanks, gentlemen," I said, shaking their hands. "You're right. There's a one-percent chance I don't get kicked in the balls. I'd hate to explain that to Rachel, the Personal Representative. But that's what's coming."

Fabulous Hal patted me on the shoulder and straightened my tie. He only did this when I was losing.

Because I was losing.

***

Tommy Split didn't waste any time. When I got back to the office after the seventy-mile drive from Olympia, his Motion for Summary Judgment had come off the fax, with hard copy to follow by messenger. Nicky was reading it. "Hey, Sam," she said faintly.

"Hey, Nick," I said. "I'm going to start working on my response. Please make me a working copy of this whole thing. Also, please tell me if you see even the slightest weakness in their argument. I'm going to need your good eyes on this."

I went into the office and sat down, sighing. My iced Americano from this morning was still cold. A lot had changed since I set it there at eight o'clock.

Nicky brought in the copies. "Let me know if you need anything," she said. "I read it before you got back. Defendant's Motion looks tight." All my friends were being nice to me today. At least when I took a big kick in the nuts, my friends tried to make it better.

"All I need, Nicky, is a goddamned legal miracle," I said. She nodded. "Please just put me on do not disturb for the rest of the day." To emphasize this, I unplugged my phone. "And please don't interrupt me unless the building is on fire and you've seen the flames yourself." I smiled at her.

I emailed Duvonda asking for her briefing on statutory interpretation and the "nondelegation doctrine." The nondelegation doctrine states that Congress and state legislatures cannot delegate to the bureaucracy the making of actual laws.

Like a lot of the law, it was a nice-sounding principle. In state court, it was as good a weapon as a handful of wet spaghetti. Ninety percent of federal law is made by the bureaucracies each year, grinding out mountains of minutiae to add to the Code of Federal Regulations. Under Washington law, the nondelegation doctrine was even weaker. Everybody cited the doctrine. Everybody knew that regulations hadn't been struck down under it, in Washington law, for decades.

I had words to put on paper. But I was going to fight with wet spaghetti.

I filed a good brief, considering I had squat to argue with. I argued in Thurston. I got my ass kicked. The Motion To Dismiss was granted.

The next day, the home healthcare aide filed for bankruptcy. I couldn't prove "willful and malicious conduct" against her, so she wouldn't have to pay a dime.

Afterward, Rodney raged at me. "I want you to file a Notice of Appeal right now! We're going to decapitate those cocksuckers and shit down their necks!"

I said, "All right, Rodney. I can file a Notice of Appeal and get an appeal heard in Division Two. In Thurston County. Just down the block from DSHS. That would be totally pointless. I hate losing. But they boned us fair and square."

He slammed his fist on my desk. "Just do it!"

I squinted at him. I remembered that for Rodney, money turned him from a man into a…mechanism. "Where's my profit sharing, Rodney? I'm making you a lot. You deserve it. But where is my cut?"

Rodney fumed at me, his eyes bulging. He loosened his Hermes tie, a floral pattern of irises. He had saliva at the corners of his mouth. "Just do it!"

He slammed the door.

He knew I wasn't going to file the Notice of Appeal. I was going to call Rachel and explain everything. I was going to ask her permission to file a Notice of Voluntary Dismissal, a so-called "nonsuit," because nothing else could be done.

Then I'd go for a five-mile run. Running cures misery. There's a Sam Strait generalization for you. Then Scrabble with the Ghost.

Who knew? Maybe I'd even go see Abe Aschmann and try fixing myself.

Two days after I filed the nonsuit I got Tommy Split's Bar Complaint. There was no downside for him. If he won, he was the Asskicking Hero of DSHS. If he didn't, he hadn't lost anything. Super Fat Bowler Guy would approve either way.

Tommy Split filed the audio file from the deposition with it.

I researched cases interpreting the applicable Rule of Professional Conduct, the one requiring "civility."

Civility is etiquette. Civility is what you have when right and wrong mean fuck-all.

The cases showing discipline for "incivility" were worse than mine. I hadn't yelled—only Tommy had yelled. I hadn't used profane language. I hadn't hit any furniture or broken anything. I would probably skate.

Isn't that messed up? I was nauseated because my client was getting screwed after her mom got killed by a moron paid by the state. I said I was nauseated. Now, I could be punished for saying I was nauseated. Because of "incivility."

After I knew what I was looking at, I called Duvonda. I asked her how the preschool case was going.

"They're deliberating," she said. Man. The jury was back in their private room. The hardest moments of a trial lawyer's life are when the jury is back in their private room.

"How do you think it's going?" I asked.

Duvonda laughed. "You know better than to ask me that. What do I tell you about verdicts, Sam?"

I laughed. "You don't know before you know."

"Exactly. Just wish I could get my mind off it. I brought a legal thriller to read, but it's one of the mainstream cookie-cutter ones. It's garbage."

"I know what you mean," I said. "I once read one where the prosecutor called the criminal defendant as a witness! And that author went to law school! It's time somebody besides Scott Turow and Michael Connelly started writing good legal thrillers."

Duvonda zeroed in. "So what's got your panties in a twist?" She had intuition, all right.

I filled her in.

"Son, you've just gotten a Kentucky Ass-Whipping," she said.

"What's that?"

"Where I come from, near Louisville, they say a Kentucky Ass-Whipping is when the guy beating on you has already won, but he just can't make himself stop. He might end up in prison for life because he doesn't have an off button. That's a Kentucky Ass-Whipping." She sighed. "But you didn't get sanctioned. And the Bar Association won't do anything because you said you want to go outside and throw up. It's not severe enough for discipline. You just need to shake it off. Be good to your client. See an old friend. Hell, get laid."

I laughed. Duvonda knew about my pointless online dates. "It's all on the menu except the last one. I don't know why I can't find a good woman, Duvonda."

"What's Fabulous Hal say?" Duvonda used Fabulous Hal as her court reporter, too.

"He says I need to find a good man instead."

"He would." Duvonda said, "Oh hell and lordy, they're back in. Gotta go."

She hung up. I'd need to find out the verdict. Duvonda's trial tales fascinated me.

So now I knew what a Kentucky Ass-Whipping was. I'd confirmed that my friends were backing me up. My client Rachel understood; she was less upset than I was. There must be something halfway worthwhile in me. I needed to see The Ghost and play Scrabble.

The Bar Association notified me that I did not need to respond to the complaint because it was being dismissed. I sent Tommy Split an email saying. *It has been a true pleasure to work with you, Counselor*, knowing the sarcasm would be obvious only to him and to me.

Then, I found Abe Aschmann's card. Maybe I needed to do some routine maintenance after all.

CHAPTER TEN—NIGHT TIME IN THE SWITCHING YARD

I wrote a draft email on the Gmail account I shared with The Ghost after my Kentucky ass-whipping. I said, *Let's go out on the town. You pick the place. I'll show you a swell time.*

She responded quickly. *Swell? Don't tease me, Vanilla Boy.* She said she'd tell me where we were going when I picked her up that night. She said *Dress as if you were cool.*

That night, I put on black jeans, a black turtleneck, my Doc Martens, and a black leather bomber jacket. I even put a handful of gel in my hair. Best I could do. I dabbed on a little English Leather cologne, even though that could not possibly be cool.

I reached The Ghost's place at eight. When she opened the door, she was wearing a red crushed-velvet evening gown hemmed very high—way above the knee. And a white feather boa. And black fishnet stockings. Her flyaway blonde hair? Up in a French braid held in place by a red lacquered chopstick.

On a scale of one to ten, she was a seventy-three. "What have we here," she said, turning me around with one finger. "Heavens to Betsy."

"Meow," said Guinevere, her tuxedo cat.

"Meow yourself," I said, scratching her behind the ears. She arched her back and purred. I stroked her cheek, and she stretched her neck, blinking as happy cats do.

As I walked to my battered Outback, I walked behind The Ghost—she looked like a red velvet cupcake with Magic Frosting. I asked, "Okay, so where are we going? I'm expecting something memorable."

She smiled and checked her dark red lipstick in her compact. "Fasten your seatbelt, Sam."

"It's already on."

"It's a metaphor, dummy. I'm taking you to The Switching Yard."

I'd heard rumors about The Switching Yard. An "alternative lifestyles nightclub." Not gay. Just alternative in the universe of sexual variations that Seattlites seemed to flock to.

We parked south of downtown in the warehouse district known as SoDo. The Switching Yard was identified only by a railroad crossing sign mounted over the black steel doors. The sign was spotlit and rusty.

When we got out, a ship blew its horn in the harbor. Perfect July night in Seattle. Cool. Clear. You could barely smell the urine from the homeless camp about an acre big down the dark street.

"Now, when we go in, just stick with me for a few minutes, and I'll give you a little narration," The Ghost said.

"Okay. I'm fine with weirdness. Just as a spectator, not a participant."

I paid the cover charge of forty bucks each. The bouncer wore a pastel blue polyester leisure suit, a top hat, eye shadow, fake eyelashes. "Have a fabulous time, kids," he said in falsetto. He swung the door open, and '80s dance music gushed out.

Holy smoke.

A tall and broad industrial space painted entirely black. Up on a small pink stage, a drag queen. A drag queen decked out like Marilyn

Monroe—perfect platinum blonde wig, perfect makeup—wearing a pink skirted suit and pink pillbox hat. With large fake boobs.

The drag queen was spinning Dead or Alive "You Spin Me Round." Excellent. I had a useless encyclopedic knowledge of '80s dance music and mondo CDs in my anonymous condo. I could actually dance to '80s music and couldn't actually dance to anything else.

From this point onward, remember all dialogue was yelled over great music.

The smell of hash and weed and perfume and cologne and sweat and funk and whatnot filled the place the way helium fills a balloon—it nearly stretched out the walls and ceiling.

The dance floor was mobbed with…patrons. Shirtless men in black leather chaps and nothing else, on leashes, being led around by dominatrixes with haughty expressions and vintage 1940s dresses. More drag queens. The majority? Dancing couples, both gay and straight, wearing vintage tuxedos and evening gowns and dinner jackets and cocktail dresses. The dancing couples seemed to be…switching partners. Duh. The Switching Yard. I hadn't gotten the idea until now.

"Let's go meet them," I said into The Ghost's ear, pointing at the couples. In for a penny, in for a pound. I'd bet my left testicle that eight or more of these people had been her playmates.

The Ghost cut through the crowd, touching this one, kissing that one, hugging another couple. One shaved-headed Black woman stuck out her pierced tongue.

We edged into a circle of the couples in vintage evening wear. "Nice jacket," I said to a woman wearing a white dinner jacket with black satin lapels, leather jeans, and nothing else.

"I'm Tabitha," she said, shaking hands. She ran her middle finger up the middle of my palm, widened her green eyes, and giggled. She leaned over and talked into my ear: "I'm a poly sub-switch, and my life partner

Trevor and I are looking for a tertiary sub switch to play with on alternate Thursdays."

I blushed. Even though the place was dark except for the spotlit disco ball, I know she noticed. She was messing with me. But that finger trailing up the center of my palm? Yeah, I felt that all right. "That's fascinating," I replied. "I'm just here with my friend." I nodded at The Ghost, who winked at me.

I went over to The Ghost. "I need a stiff drink."

"I need a stiff something else," she wisecracked, poking me in the ribs.

I shook my head, laughing. She never missed a trick. "Okay, but can I buy you a drink anyway?"

"Sure. Campari and soda. No ice. Ice is for vanillas, honey."

I edged over toward the bar. Behind the bar? A massive dude, long red sideburns, wearing striped overalls and a John Deere hat and nothing else. He was dressed ironically.

In Seattle, the cool people expressed irony. Never sincerity.

Sincerity was just not done. This was reason number 458 why I would never be cool in Seattle.

"Hey," I said. "I'd like a Campari and soda, no ice, and two shots of Johnny Walker, neat."

He nodded and spun around, whipping up the drinks. The service here was worlds better than most Seattle bars.

"Hey there, you tall drink of water," said a high voice somewhere down near my beltline.

I looked down. A bald, bearded dwarf with V-shaped lines on his forehead and black eager eyes. Wearing a green evening gown and stiletto heels.

He leered at me. "Haven't seen you in here before, tough guy," the dwarf ventured in a high voice.

"I haven't been here before," I said. I could tell he also wanted to embarrass me. It seemed the theme of the night.

The dwarf said, "So what's your sign, big fella?"

The bartender slid the drinks over and took my card.

"My sign is I'm not at all interested in you," I replied with a shrug.

The dwarf recoiled. "Hmmph!" he said, clomping away on his stilettos.

The bartender gave me my card, and I signed the receipt. I motioned him closer and said into his ear: "That dwarf was really short with me."

The bartender threw back his head and laughed. "Okay, that's brutal," he said, grinning. He reached forward and crumpled up my charge slip. "This one is on the house." He high-fived me.

I was still laughing when I made my way back to The Ghost, cutting through a cloud of hash smoke and clove essential oil from somewhere, conquering all other scents. Probably the ventilation system. They were probably even "curating" the smell in The Switching Yard.

The Ghost closed her clasp purse. She'd snagged a phone number. Or two or three. The superpower and tragic flaw of The Ghost? She was irresistible. I wasn't the only moth drawn to her flame.

"I need to sit down," she said into my ear. "My left leg's kind of weak. The MS is acting up." We went to a booth.

The drag queen DJ kept spinning awesome tunes. Dead or Alive followed by The Tom Tom Club, followed by The Cure remixed, followed by Joy Division, followed by Belouis Some.

"Would you like to dance?" I asked The Ghost.

She took a deep pull on her Campari and soda and licked her lips. She shook her head. "My balance isn't so hot tonight. But you go ahead."

"Will you be here when I get back?"

She shrugged and winked at me. "Perhaps. If not you'll know I got dragged off and ravaged by Tabitha and Trevor and their party gang of dominant-submissive poly switch players."

I got on the dance floor. She was just my friend. Even though that word seemed laughable in this place. Friendship? Sincerity? Not comprehended by Seattle cool people.

I danced with a luscious, tall brunette with blue eyes, lavish curves, just a hint of sadness in her eyes. She wore only Saran Wrap and, clear plastic sandals and a tiara with LED lights that flashed blue and red. Nothing under the Saran Wrap. It clung to all the right places.

We danced for four songs. "Would you like a smoke?" she asked as Blancmange faded out.

"Sure, if it's only a cigarette," I said.

She crooked a finger and we went out the back door into the alley. Seattle had harsh anti-smoking laws. Not weed or hash—there were lots of people "sparking up" in The Switching Yard. But tobacco? Even though Seattle seldom arrested people for shooting heroin in public or selling meth in front of the courthouse, smoking tobacco in a bar could get the bar's license pulled right quick. There might be a Liquor Control agent dressed as whatever lurking here.

When the door swung shut, the music was chopped off to a rhythmic thud.

The Saran Wrap brunette and I huddled by the dumpsters with two submissive guys on leashes being guarded by their "Doms," two middle-aged couples in vintage evening wear, and a man in a sailor outfit whose stoned red eyes nearly glowed in the dark. I might as well have been wearing a sandwich board that said Vanilla Boy.

The Saran Wrap brunette gave me a Kool Extra Long and lit me up.

I explained that The Ghost had taken me to her favorite club, to mess with me, but we were just friends. She cocked her head at me as if to ask: *For real?* "Yes, for real," I said.

"That one is hotter than a three-dollar pistol," she said. "I'm Julie, by the way."

"Sam. And yes, she is hotter than a three-dollar pistol. But she likes bisexuality and S&M and sometimes degradation. That's not my brand of vodka, so to speak."

Julie arched her swan neck and blew smoke rings up at the stars.

Perfect July night. Another ship hooted from the harbor. Julie's dark pink nipples poked, erect, against the Saran Wrap like little fingertips. Taut. Proud. These women turned me on. I'd had a steel erection since we walked in. But I wouldn't pursue this desire. Some desires can confuse you. Some desires can even kill you.

Julie licked my ear and whispered: "I'm guessing you're quite vanilla."

I laughed. I took a drag. "I am quite vanilla."

"So let me tell you how all this works." She blew another string of smoke rings. "In poly culture, especially with a BDSM flavor, the important thing is consent. Let's say I'm your life partner."

I said, "Okay, just for laughs, let's."

She raised a cautionary finger. "If I'm your life partner, neither of us swings without prior consent from the other. Permission is key. But with permission, it is all okay. Have you ever read a book called *The Ethical Slut*?"

"Let's presume I have not read *The Ethical Slut*."

"*The Ethical Slut* teaches us that everything between consenting adults is all right. But we need to get buy-in from our partners first. So your life partner, or your primary as we call it, has to agree before you play outside the relationship. Anybody other than your primary is called a secondary. Or maybe even a tertiary, if they are very occasional. Everything is negotiable. Bisexuality, orgies, switching, and BDSM."

"Ah," I said. "That's why they call it The Switching Yard. You can switch partners. With consent."

Julie reached in and bit my ear. My right ear. "Care to disclose how you lost your earlobe, Vanilla Sam?"

"I'd rather not say," I said. I wanted to hear all her weirdness. Not share my own.

Julie ran her tongue around the inside of my ear. Then she stepped back and studied me. "Some primaries only want you to play with others that they play with too. Some say it's okay to play with others, without their participation, but they have to meet them first. There are ground rules, like condoms are required, only on Tuesday, ordinary stuff like that."

"Ordinary stuff like that. I can dig it." Wince. Why did I say something as archaic as *I can dig it*? I was hopeless with this crowd, even as a mere observer.

"Then there's BDSM, which gives it a different flavor. You know what BDSM is?"

I remembered one of The Ghost's mini-lectures over Scrabble. "Bondage, discipline, sadism, and masochism."

"Right. In BDSM, the parties agree beforehand on a safe word that anybody can use to say that's enough. I'm tapping out. It has to be something you would never say when you're doing a scene. Especially a scene involving physical restraint, physical pain, or extreme play. Something like giraffe. My safe word is giraffe." Julie took another drag. She was halfway playing with me and, halfway, recruiting me and halfway seducing me.

When I have an erection that hard, there can be three halves.

Hell, I was just playing cultural anthropologist. I told myself a personal injury lawyer has to know a little about everything people do. Because a client could come from any conceivable background.

After all, they all bleed red.

That reminded me of something. "So what's this blood play thing I've heard about?"

She gave me a playful jab with her elbow. "My word, Mister. You've been holding out on me."

I held up my hand. "No, no. I don't do this stuff. I've just heard about it. I'm wondering what that is."

She tossed her cigarette butt. I put mine out in a puddle, then tossed it in the dumpster. She pulled out two more Kools and lit us both up.

Julie resumed. It was faintly comical to be getting a kink etiquette lesson from a woman wearing nothing but Saran Wrap, who littered.

"Blood play, or blood sport, is considered an extreme variant. But some people like it. I've done it, but I much prefer chain restraint and vigorous pegging with a strap-on dildo."

She looked at me. I wasn't blushing. I had a good poker face at times. "In blood play, one partner feeds the other blood. Sometimes, his or her own blood. Sometimes they smear it on the body, writing words with it, stuff like that. I've heard of women making their male slaves suck their used tampons. Some people say nothing beats it. If that's your flavor."

I swallowed. Hard. Used tampons. I was on the dark side of the moon.

I shook my head, smiling and looking down at my Doc Martens.

I knew why The Ghost had brought me here—to normalize herself. Maybe The Ghost was trying to make me into the man she needed.

It's a little-known fact that when a woman is attracted to a man she often tries to…remodel him. Into the man she likes more.

Julie reached up and flipped a switch on her tiara. The lights changed patterns, zooming around her head, spangling the dumpsters. She said, "The important thing about all of this, polyamory, bondage, blood play, and scat—that is shit—is that there has to be prior consent, worked out clearly before any clothes come off. Nobody gets going until the limits are set."

I nodded. Given my somewhat-dark childhood, I wasn't going to dip a toe in these waters. But I wanted to learn about The Ghost. So I'd just listen and absorb.

I knew about stuff happening without consent.

"Anyway, end of lesson," Julie said. "Let's go inside. Now that you know the rules. Also I need to check in with Tabitha, because I came with her and Trevor."

"I bet you did," I jibed.

She elbowed me, and stuck her tongue in my ear again. "We could have fun, Sam. I could show you another world."

I nodded. My erection nodded too.

Julie gave me a playful elbow again, and we walked back inside.

Kink apparently had more rules than you'd need building a nuclear power plant in California. On an earthquake fault. In a wildlife sanctuary. It didn't matter if I approved. But I guessed the rules prevented rape. Or even murder.

I followed her back in and went to the booth. The Ghost sat primly nursing another Campari and soda. She smiled faintly. She'd wanted to let The Switching Yard work on me. Bend me a little. She was going to evaluate the results. Vanilla Boy might turn into a decent fixer-upper worth remodeling.

Then Rodney Mammon sat down next to her, sliding into the booth.

His blond gel-stiffened porcupine hair sparkled as the disco ball twirled and Elvis Costello yodeled about "What's So Funny 'Bout Peace, Love And Understanding."

Rodney darted a glance at me. His eyes wide. Then he leaned into The Ghost. The song ended just then, sudden silence.

Rodney asked The Ghost: "Are you a model? You have really stunning eyes."

The Ghost regarded him. Half amused, and half interested.

"Hey babe," I said to The Ghost. "This is Rodney. My boss." Rodney glared at me.

The Ghost looked over at me, delighted. "Get out of town."

"Seriously. Rodney Mammon & Associates. Mondo TV commercials."

The Ghost snapped her fingers and pointed at Rodney. "That's it! I knew I recognized you." She made air quotes: "Get Your Money Justice."

Rodney flinched. I'd never seen him off balance before.

I liked that.

The Ghost leaned toward me. "So, are we ready to make like a baby and head out?"

"Absolutely," I said, helping her to her feet.

The Ghost leaned on me. At first I thought she was tipsy, but then I remembered. Her MS was acting up. Her balance was off and her left leg was weak.

Rodney leaned back and scrutinized all this. Her leaning on my arm. Her white feather boa, her red crushed velvet evening gown.

Rodney squinted at me. He almost spoke. For the first time, Rodney didn't understand me. I liked that.

I waved goodbye to the bartender, who waved back. Julie raised her glass to me. Tabitha blew a kiss to The Ghost. The drag queen DJ started the extended remix version of Blondie's "Rapture."

When the door clicked shut behind us, The Ghost burst out laughing.

"Okay, what's the joke?" I asked.

"That cheeseball is your boss? I mean, he's somewhat yummy, but actually, he is your actual boss?"

"Yup. He runs the Guilty Peoples' Department, doing criminal defense with all the other lawyers. I run the Innocent Peoples' Department, doing personal injury. That's the setup."

She laughed harder, leaning on me. "How in the world did you wind up with him?"

"It's a long story," I told her. "Just like my childhood."

The Ghost had heard the story of my childhood. The entire story. Other than Catherine, nobody else ever had. But I promise you will. Eventually.

We drove back to her place in silence. At her door, she said, "Why don't you come in for a cup of tea?"

She unwound her feather boa and put it over the back of a chair at her kitchen table. I took off my black leather jacket. She put the kettle on.

Then she went back into the living room. "Puss puss," she called. "Puss puss."

Silence.

The Ghost screamed.

I ran into the living room. Guinevere was on the couch, her legs stretched out as far as they would go, her eyes open and sightless.

The Ghost picked her up and cradled her. "Oh baby, my baby," she crooned. I touched one of Guinevere's paws. It was cold.

The Ghost cried and stroked Guinevere's head. I stroked The Ghost's shoulders and held one of Guinevere's cold paws, touching the perfect pink pads. "I mean, she's fifteen years old," The Ghost said, leaning forward. "That's old in cat years. But she's never been sick. I hand-feed her salmon and calamari, and I take her to the vet. Sorry. Make all that past tense." Her voice was shaky at first. But it evened out.

Suddenly, being The Ghost's friend didn't seem so useless after all.

The Ghost went to her entertainment center, and slipped a catch I couldn't see. She brought out a tablet computer and turned it on. It was hard-wired back to the entertainment center. "My security camera," she said.

She brought up the footage. "So, where is the camera?" I asked.

"It's a pinhole cam in the wall. It's motion-activated and sound-activated. So if nothing is happening, no recording is made."

"Not connected to the web?"

"Certainly not," she said, glancing sharply at me. "No web access and no Wi-Fi connection. I'm security conscious. You know that. That's why all my playdates happen in this room."

She brought up the footage from tonight. It was time and date stamped in the lower right corner, with very sensitive sound and accurate color. It could be switched to infrared but it was set on normal viewing. The resolution was remarkable for a camera smaller than a nail head.

We watched as Guinevere took a run around the living room, up over the back of the couch, back down toward the litterbox.

Then she stopped. She had a seizure. She stood shuddering, for about a minute. She twitched. One leg kicked over and over. Then she leaped onto the couch. She fell, and her limbs stretched out in a rictus of agony. She twitched a couple of times. Then she froze and said, "Meow."

The footage stopped. Because the motion and the sound had stopped. It happened about three hours ago.

"Dammit," I said. I really had liked Guinevere.

The Ghost stroked Guinevere, and I stroked The Ghost.

She needed listening. That was all I had.

"Do you think she had a good life?" The Ghost asked, in a forlorn voice I'd never heard before from her.

I stroked The Ghost on the back of her head, gentling her blonde flyaway hair. "Yes. You worked at home. So she had your constant companionship. You fed her the best seafood no matter what the cost. You got her great vet care. You played with her. The fishing rod with the feather bunch on it? I've seen you tease her for an hour with that, and she never got tired of it."

The Ghost shuddered. "I let you use the laser pointer too. She couldn't understand how a red dot cannot be physically grappled."

"And the wind-up mouse. That wind-up mouse infuriated Guinevere. In a good way." I kept stroking The Ghost's shoulders. "Honey? She followed you around the house. Even when you just went from the bedroom to the kitchen. She loved you. She was a happy cat."

The Ghost looked at me with her dark eyes rimmed with red. She wanted to know if I was bullshitting her. The Ghost had a military-grade bullshit detector. She nodded. I wasn't bullshitting her.

"If I were a cat," I murmured, "I would want to be your cat."

And then she kissed me. At first just a peck, then nipping my lower lip, then turning her head and opening the pink wonderland of her mouth to me. Our tongues played a duet. I felt my blood turning to champagne.

I hadn't felt like this since Suzanne left.

You've seen a snow globe, right? You shake it, and the snow whirls around the little scene inside and takes a minute or two to settle?

My head was a snow globe most of the time. Lists and plans and anxieties whirling around in Brownian motion. Me trying to herd them all. Like an air traffic controller directing spastic planes on radar.

At this moment my snow all…settled to the ground. All this in stillness. The tiny sounds of our kissing mattered more than all philosophy falling.

The Ghost gently pushed me away. She held up a cautionary finger. "Let's go to bed, Sam," she said, measuring me.

I watched her.

The Ghost took a deep breath. "But first, I need you to tell me I'm a whore."

I smiled at her sadly. "Baby, I grew up in a swimming pool of degradation. I was humiliated. Every day. You know."

She nodded sadly. She knew, all right.

"So I can't call you a whore. Because I love you," I said.

She tilted her head. Measuring her effect.

I plunged ahead. "I'm so aroused right now I probably couldn't even stand up. Every cell of me wants you. But I can't love you the way you want. It makes me want to tear out my hair that this is how it will be." I paused. "But that is how it will be."

She nodded and put her head down. I kissed the top of her head. I wanted to give her my benediction, right now. Not my unnecessary but informative erection.

"All right, you," she joshed, playfully pushing me in the chest. She walked me to the door. She embraced me.

I thought she was better off without sex tonight. Sometimes, affection is better than sex.

That crowd at The Switching Yard would never understand this.

Maybe that's why they needed weirder and weirder sex variations to feel something. Because they didn't feel anything.

When I got back to my condo, I showered for a long time. I haven't told you about my condo until now. Why?

My condo in Northgate was an ordinary one-bedroom with blonde oak trim, furnished in Danish modern, with no distinguishing features other than a big portrait of Catherine over the gas fireplace, and multiple CD racks holding over a thousand '80s albums. And two bookcases stuffed with great fiction—Hemingway, Steinbeck, Margaret Atwood, Turow, Connelly, Helprin. Stuff as good as I would write. If I could write anything other than legal stuff.

The blue light from the pool below my balcony flickered on the ceiling.

My condo was an anonymous bankers box that I filed myself in every night. But I was always grateful that it was all mine, and it had a deadbolt on the door.

At the Malletts' Therapeutic Foster Home I hadn't had a lock on my door.

Then, when I aged out and joined the Coast Guard, I didn't have my own room at all, but I really liked my buddies and the work—picking up people from sinking yachts doing safety inspections. And doing drug interdiction—including hostile boardings.

I didn't tell anybody in my circle I'd been shot at and had shot others. I didn't want to be the center of attention. But the Coast Guard rebuilt me in just a couple of years, and I got a bachelor's out of the deal, too.

When I got my Honorable Discharge as an E-4 I took my GI Bill benefits for law school. I'd lived alone ever since, except for the three years in law school with Suzanne.

You know how many people talk about The One? How there's only one person in the world you can love, and if you don't stay with that one, you will never love again?

I think it's one of the most destructive myths on earth—the mirror image of the casual sex at The Switching Yard.

But I halfway believed it.

My condo was empty. My heart was empty. It was time to call Abe Aschmann.

CHAPTER ELEVEN—JUMBO SHRIMP

After I ran into Rodney at The Switching Yard, I fretted. He had met The Ghost. What if they decided to "play together"?

I wondered again if I should have just tried calling her mean names and taking her to bed. But I couldn't possibly have called her mean names and taken her to bed.

A few days later, Rodney invited Nicky and me out to lunch at Rattan, the trendy upscale Thai place near the office. We got seated, and he ordered the jumbo shrimp appetizer. Then we looked at menus.

Rodney asked: "I'll bet you two are wondering why I ordered jumbo shrimp."

I looked at Nicky, and she shrugged. Under the frosted skylight shining July sun, she looked more than ever like a petite swan.

"I've been thinking, team," Rodney said, smoothing down his turquoise silk tie. "We bring in a fuck-ton of cases with my marketing. And I'm going to be bringing in a fuck-ton more because I just signed us up with Collision Comrades."

"You didn't," I said despite myself.

Attorneys aren't allowed to contact potential clients. That's called ambulance chasing.

But Collision Comrades was a clever work-around. They got copies of all Traffic Collision Reports in the Seattle area. They cold-called everybody on the reports except Driver 1, the driver that the police said caused the collision. Then they set up these people with "diagnostic chiropractic appointments" so the non-liable people could start chiropractic. That would typically go on until the personal injury protection (PIP) benefits on the auto policy were exhausted. Once the patients were firmly committed to chiropractic, the chiropractors would refer them to lawyers who were signed up with Collision Comrades. The more the lawyers had paid, the more referrals they got from the chiropractors. Because they were paying Collision Comrades, but the chiropractors were making the referrals. Cute, huh?

"So what level of sponsorship did you get with Collision Comrades?" I asked, even though I had a sickening feeling I already knew.

"What do you think, Einstein? Number one. Numero uno. We're about to be up to our asses in shrimps."

Rodney called meritorious but small cases "shrimps." He wasn't the only personal injury lawyer who did this. If the client was modestly injured in a clear-liability collision—say they just needed five to ten grand of physical therapy or chiro—some lawyers called those clients shrimps.

After the treatment was done, they could have a paralegal round up the records and bills, do a low-quality quickie demand package, and walk away with a fee of somewhere between five and twenty grand. People who called these clients "shrimps" never litigated. They did a quick shakedown and moved on. The settlement mill firms—low quality and high volume—loved shrimps. Want to know who are the settlement mills in your town? Everybody with TV commercials.

I believed that any case I took on should be litigated if necessary. I also believed chiropractic was fake medicine.

The problem with doing a high volume of shrimp cases, however, was that the insurance companies had gotten the memo, too. They had databases of which law firms did a high volume of low-value cases. Especially if they never went to trial. These databases were organized by tax ID number. That's why the adjuster on a small case often asked for the tax ID number of the firm right at the outset. They wanted to look up the lawyer and see if he or she was a "paper tiger"—a lawyer that seldom filed suit and never went to trial. They would make lowball offers to paper tigers. The paper tigers would settle rather than sue.

The chiropractors made money. The lawyers made money. The clients typically got lousy treatment and lame settlements. It was the grimy underside of personal injury law.

I'd always hated it. I thought of myself as a crusader. I thought of high-volume lawyers doing Collision Comrades cases as shakedown artists. I'd done low-value cases, plenty of them, particularly at my last firm. But I read the medical records myself. I wrote the demand letters myself. I did all the negotiations myself, talking to adjusters who were faintly astonished they were talking to a lawyer, not a "case manager" with two hundred cases on his or her caseload.

If necessary, I filed suit on any case where the insurance company wouldn't offer what considered fair value. If I'd have had my own tax ID number, I would have come up with a skull and crossbones on the adjusters' database. If only.

The insurance companies didn't like my style. They preferred high-volume lawyers with ten or twenty paralegals per attorney. Ever-present TV commercials. Lavish Google marketing. Collision Comrades contracts. They sometimes called me a "true believer."

"You're damn right I am," I always replied. I considered it high praise.

All this flew through my head as Rodney was plowing into his jumbo shrimp. Rodney's forehead got sweaty when he devised a new money-making scheme. He'd been looking at new Maseratis lately. His current one was five years old, after all.

Rodney took out his turquoise handkerchief to wipe his forehead. I noticed something fell out of it. He said, "I've got to piss like a racehorse," and went to the bathroom.

I bent down to tie my shoelace and to see what he'd dropped. It was a little oval green pill with a line down the middle and some numbers. A prescription pill. Curious, I put it in my shirt pocket. I wondered precisely what drug Rodney was taking.

When I sat up, Nicky was a little swan with her hands over her face. "So he's going to quadruple our workload and not give us a raise," she said through her hands.

I clenched my teeth. "Not if I have anything to say about it."

She dropped her hands and stared at me, her deep brown eyes questioning, her black eyebrows arched.

I tipped my hand to her. "Remember how he's not paying me my profit sharing? That's leverage for you and me. I'll tell him he needs to start paying it, or I won't allow you or me to do an increased caseload. He'll yell at me, of course. He does that. But in the end, after the primate display of dominance behavior, he'll probably just set up a boiler room full of case managers. Like the other settlement mills in town. He'll have this separate operation handle all the shrimps. God, now he's even got me saying it."

Nicky knew I didn't like calling any client a shrimp. "That's the problem with sleaze, Sam," she said, drinking her iced tea. "Sleaze leaves a gummy residue on anybody who touches it."

I marveled at her. At first I'd taken Nicky to be a shy woman with a lot of brains. But she was gutsy. Also she had a military-grade bullshit detector. Just like The Ghost. I remembered when we were driving south on Interstate 5, on our way to get hometowned in Rockingham County. She'd looked at the homeless tents and said, "If they'd just get their neurochemistry straightened out, they wouldn't live like this." Nicky could do the math.

It occurred to me for the first time that Nicky could become a friend on the same level as The Ghost and Duvonda and Silent Mike. She was an ally. It was pure serendipity that Rodney had hired her. In The Guilty Peoples' Department, the lawyers and paralegals all looked like models. They were as intellectually complex as a tube of Cheez Whiz.

Rodney came back, and our curries arrived. We ate with focus. Rodney knew I was mulling it over, and I knew he knew.

Then we had the exact argument I'd told Nicky we would have.

I pulled the latest printout from my suit coat pocket, showing the profit sharing he owed me, and handed it over.

He crumpled it up and threw it on the floor. Lots of his stuff was winding up on the floor at this lunch. "Bro, are you trying to get fired?" he asked me, his glassy eyes bulging as his gel-stiffened blond porcupine hair quivered.

"No," I said. "I'm standing my ground. Nicky and I can keep handling the majors, the cases with crippling injuries or death, and big dollars at stake. We're making you a fuck-ton of money, as you'd put it. But you'll have to hand the hundreds of shrimps over to a separate crew of case managers. Just remember, bro. Pigs who become hogs get slaughtered."

He burst out laughing. Rodney was capable of these radical changes in direction. I had certain questions about his psychological stability. "You should consider yourself lucky to have this job, Sam," he said, wiping his eyes.

I regarded him. "I do, Rodney. I think you're missing out on the best part of your own practice. It's a damned shame."

"The money," he said, putting down his napkin.

"Money's great," I said. "I love money. I think everybody does." I looked at Nicky, and she nodded. "But the best part of the practice is the clients. You should have been there, the day we got hometowned. Even though I got punched out, quickly and efficiently, I walked out of that courthouse feeling ten feet tall." I thought about how to put it in Rodney terms. Football terms. "Remember, we took their knees out at the end."

Rodney raised a finger. "Yeah, thanks to my chops at working with the press."

"You're right." I knew Rodney had to feel he'd won or I'd wind up with hundreds of shrimps, and Nicky would just quit. She could do better somewhere else.

So we walked out with Rodney picking up the check, feeling smug, and Nicky looking at me with sympathy. I'd risked my neck. But the shrimps would go to the new boiler room. Nicky and I would keep focusing on the majors. Rodney would get a newer Maserati. It was a workable trade-off.

When I got home to the condo that night, I went to my fire safe concealed inside a bankers box inside my closet. Notice I had a locked box inside the locked box of my condo. They say every person's home is a model of their personality. Mine was locked compartments within other locked compartments.

I put the pill inside an envelope from Rodney's office. I sealed it and signed across the seal. Then I wrote "recovered from Rodney Mammon," with the date.

I wondered just what the hell he was taking.

CHAPTER TWELVE—DOES THIS SOUP TASTE FUNNY TO YOU?

The day after the jumbo shrimp lunch, Rodney struck a deal to rent the empty suite next door for the Boiler Room. The next morning, carpenters cut a hole through to the lobby and started banging and sawing. Fortunately the Boiler Room would be on the far side of the Guilty Peoples' Department, far from the Innocent Peoples' Department. We'd deal with the Boiler Room only when they stumbled over a potential True Disaster and sent it to us.

Kandy, the stripper receptionist, stumbled in late, looking very hung over. The pink stripe in her hair hung down into her cleavage. She'd forgotten to put in her large tongue stud. "My head really hurts," she said. I got her a glass of water. "I went out clubbing with Rodney to celebrate the new marketing push," she said. "We really tied one on. I woke up in my bed at four in the morning, and I didn't know how I got there."

I leaned over to her. "I'm probably just snooping, but are you two sleeping together?"

She squinted at me. "A lady never tells."

Not that I would ever make a move on Kandy. Blonde strippers with pink streaks in their hair, tongue studs, partial tattoo sleeves, and breast implants? Not my type.

On the other hand, I doubted there was any woman for me in Seattle. It probably wasn't just my attachment disorder—it was the culture.

I was starting therapy with Dr. Aschmann soon. I decided to test this theory. So I went on TopFliteSingles.com and sent out another search. I tried to tune my criteria a little so I wouldn't get a woman who wanted a baby tomorrow morning, like the Imaginary Children lady. Also, I added an asterisk at the bottom of my profile that said, *No escorts, please* to screen out women like the Ferrari lady.

I got a ton of hits. Apparently tall lawyers with a decent income and no ex-wives or child support were popular. As far as that went. Again defying the odds, I sent an email to only one woman—Kaylee, a "highly trained healthcare professional." She had shiny brown hair, a dreamy face, and a long straight nose. I'd been told long noses indicate intelligence.

So I emailed Kaylee and then went back to work screening intake sheets from Nicky for the next Intake Clinic. From across the lobby, the hammering and sawing continued. The sweet smell of sawdust wafted over.

Nicky had gotten good at filtering out the Barking Dogs before we met them. We'd developed a single-page phone screening form. We'd learned these questions the hard way:

1) Date of Injury—if it was more than two and a half years ago, hard pass. The statute of limitations for negligence was three years in Washington. We never signed anything within six months of the statute running. Those cases were just potential malpractice claims ripening on the vine. Also, clients who procrastinated about hiring a lawyer for two and a half years were likely to procrastinate in cooperating with us. Life was too short to sign those people.

2) What SPECIFICALLY Did The Defendant Do That Was Wrong—they had to be able to tell us why somebody else was at fault. If they couldn't tell us, then I damn sure couldn't tell a jury.

3) Were You Getting Any Treatment Immediately Before Your Accident/Injury—it was amazing how many people were getting

alternative healthcare like chiro or naturopathic before their car crash and kept getting the same treatment after their car crash. (And most potentials were car crash clients. We almost never even did an intake on a med mal or slip/trip and fall case anymore. The odds on those were slim.)

These were people who "like, believed in alternative healthcare." Most were dumb as a bag of hammers. They couldn't understand how they didn't have a case, just because the treatment didn't change from before the crash to after the crash. Again, life was too short to try to reason with them. "My mom Esmerelda would love those wing nuts," Nicky said. As I said before, she'd developed a military-grade bullshit detector.

So I reviewed about twenty of these sheets, putting a diagonal slash across anybody who didn't sound promising. If somebody had a gleam of a possible small case, I put an L on the sheet. That stood for King County Bar Lawyer Referral Service, the place we sent too-small but possibly worthwhile cases. Once Rodney got his Boiler Room up and running, these cases would go there.

There were only three left. One was summarized as a "fatality slip and fall." I put a star on that one, meaning Nicky should book a private one-hour intake.

I just had to hear this. It could be a Nothingburger or a very juicy Somethingburger.

Working in personal injury required intuition and curiosity. Each case was a gamble. I was basically playing poker at a professional level. Occasionally, a likely Barking Dog metamorphosized into a True Disaster. As I'd learned in the Kentucky Ass-Whipping case, a True Disaster could also transform quickly into a Barking Dog.

I went on TopFliteSingles.com again and checked for messages. Would wonders never cease? Kaylee wanted to meet for drinks that night at Einstein's Brew Pub up on Queen Anne Hill at six. I liked Einstein's: They made a hoppy IPA on the premises and had succulent bar food. And I liked Queen Anne Hill, an upscale neighborhood just north of downtown. Ferrari Lady had lived on Queen Anne Hill, but I was playing the odds that most single women in that neck of the woods were not escorts.

I'd put in ridiculous amounts of overtime the past few months, so I didn't feel guilty about shoving off at three and going home for a brief nap, a long shower, and choosing my wardrobe. I settled on tan corduroy slacks, a black turtleneck, and the trusty blue blazer. Summer be damned; I needed to dress up. No shorts and flip flops for this date.

I put a dab of pheromone cologne on the back of my neck. Some people thought pheromone cologne gave an unfair advantage. I'd noticed wearing just a tiny drop made pretty women stand closer to me, look longer into my eyes, and touch me more. In the interest of testing my "attachment disorder," I decided to take any edge I could get.

I drove to Queen Anne from Northgate in the brassy July sun over the Aurora Bridge. The Aurora Bridge was Seattle's most popular place for a suicide jump. The "community" was having a "deliberative process" about whether an anti-suicide fence would "ruin the aesthetic of this classic structure." The "deliberative process" had been going on for four years. Still no fence.

***

I got to Einstein's at five-thirty. The place smelled of piquant beer, frying food, and, subconsciously, excitement. In my head, anyway.

A waiter with a braided beard and pierced nose appeared. He drawled: "My name is Trevor. Our special tonight is Manhattan-style clam chowder."

"Do you like it yourself?"

Trevor drew himself up to full height and stroked his braided beard. "I don't eat anything with a face." This was a standard vegan line.

"But clams don't have faces," I jibed, handing back the menu. "Anyhow, I'd like to try that."

Trevor sniffed and walked back to the kitchen. For unjustified superiority, vegans were champs.

The Manhattan-style clam chowder was really great. "This is really great," I told Trevor. Sincerity with cool people? Useless.

"I'm totally glad," he said, rolling his eyes.

Right at that moment, the front door opened, and breeze flowed through the pub. A woman standing there…shiny brown hair dark gray sundress, scanning the room. I waved, and she wove through the crowd. Nice. She walked like she had something special, and she knew it. She stood about five-six, high-heeled black leather boots curves in all the right places.

One thing that makes me Vanilla Boy? I am a gentleman. I always arrive early for a date. I stand when a lady joins me. I always pick up the check on the first date. I liked to send signals that a lady who appreciated these things might appreciate me. It could happen, right?

"I'm Kaylee," she said, offering me her hand. Nice—short nails, no polish. She had somewhat dazzling hazel eyes.

"I'm Sam."

She sat down without lowering her eyes. Actresses do this. It's nifty.

Trevor, the waiter, appeared. "Dirty martini, two olives," she said. He nodded without comment. Olives don't have faces.

Kaylee and I did the obligatory five-minute dance: Met anybody good online? Any exes or kids I should know about?

I did not have a military-grade bullshit detector. So, I asked the best questions I knew.

Number one. "What do you like to read?" I asked her.

She winced. "Mostly magazines and blogs," she said. "My work doesn't leave me much time for the longer stuff."

If I haven't told you already, I'm a book addict. That's why I'm writing this. Every worthwhile person I knew liked to read books.

So, I asked my second-best question. I'd found the answers to these two would almost certainly give a good picture. Like an X-ray of her personality. If not, there was the third, the primo question—what kind of future would you like?

I ate another spoonful of Manhattan chowder. Yum—tomato savor, juicy clams, creamy stock. "Would you like to try this?"

Kaylee stretched. Nice. "No thanks. I had a late lunch." Apparently, she had picked up on the pheromone cologne. She was tracing small circles with her fingertip on the tabletop, the universal signal for, *at some point, I want you to touch me.* Cool.

I lobbed question two into this natural opening. "So what kind of work do you do?"

Her dirty martini came with two olives. She speared an olive and ate it. Hmm. Nice dark pink lips. She drank half of it in one gulp.

"I'm a doula," she said.

I decided to play dumb. "What is a doula?" I asked.

She tossed back the rest of the martini and raised her hand for another round. The waiter nodded.

"A doula is a birthing coach who assists the mother during labor. Our demanding training typically consists of twenty-eight hours of classwork, attending two to five births as an understudy, and sometimes additional coursework to be a post-delivery doula. I've been doing it two years, so I have some major experience. Doula is from the Greek meaning *woman who serves.*"

Super. If a doula was a "highly trained healthcare worker" then a McDonald's fry cook was employed in haute cuisine. I'd seen "grade inflation" on TopFliteSingles.com. But this was a whole new kettle of fish.

Speaking of fish, I was liking this chowder. "Are you sure you won't have some?" I asked again.

"Oh no. Late lunch and all that. I assisted today at a birthing. Afterward, I met with the members of our Womyn's-Only Doula Spirit Circle." By the way she pronounced womyn's, I knew it was with the Y. Like the vegan waiter, she was establishing her alternative bona fides early.

In the summer of 2007, Seattle was full of "non-judgmental people" who were extremely judgmental.

They would toss out their self-branded lifestyle variants and then sniff for any hint of disapproval so they could pronounce you "judgmental." While they were judging you. Isn't it odd that the most judgmental people loved calling other people judgmental? It was a Möbius strip of manipulation.

This was why I was toying with the idea of writing *no New Age fruitcakes* at the bottom of my profile on TopFliteSingles.com. Even though it would eliminate many women on the site. "New Age" people could not be "fruitcakes" in Seattle. The concept was "offensive."

I kept probing. "So what happens at your Womyn's-Only Doula Spirit Circle?"

She got her second martini and again speared an olive. "Usually, we just cast the sacred circle, do some chanting, perhaps get naked, and give each other full body massages and salt scrubs. The usual."

"The usual," I said. The remnants of the Manhattan chowder sat there cooling.

"But today, I assisted at bedside with a woman who is very enlightened. I don't usually have patients who deeply comprehend alternative spirituality."

"Go on," I said, taking a drink of ice water. I was glad I hadn't had any alcohol. It would interfere with my diagnosis.

"So, on this particular occasion, she gave me permission to take the placenta and use it in our ritual. We only get to do this every couple of months." She gulped the rest of her second martini.

I drank more ice water. "If you don't mind me asking, what happens when you use the placenta in your ritual?"

She regarded me, looking for the slightest sign of judgment so she could judge me for being judgmental. If you think I'm exaggerating, you've never lived on the West Coast.

"In this particular ritual, we make placenta soup and eat it."

I didn't flinch. I nodded as if this were a totally reasonable statement.

But then I looked down at my unfinished Manhattan clam chowder, the kind with tomato juice in it, the red kind. A thin skin formed over the surface as it cooled.

A hideous joke popped up in my head like a jack in the box: Does this soup taste funny to you?

I got dizzy. My mouth flooded with saliva. Uh oh.

"Would you excuse me for a minute, Kaylee," I asked.

I walked quickly back to the men's room. I took the handicapped stall. My mouth was leaking a trickle of slobber now. Uh oh.

I fell to my knees and vomited explosively into the toilet. Placenta soup. Manhattan clam chowder.

I was abstractly thrilled I got all the vomit into the toilet. My stomach tried to turn itself inside out.

I vomited and vomited all my loneliness up. My nose burned with the acid stench. I stayed there for five minutes until I was sure I had nothing left to unload.

I put cold water on my face and checked myself in the mirror. I didn't have any vomit on me. Minor miracle. I drank several handfuls of cold water. Right now, my breath would knock a buzzard off a shit-wagon, I thought.

I washed my hands and ducked out of the men's room. I was looking for Trevor, the vegan waiter. I caught him as he was ambling back into the kitchen.

"Excuse me, Trevor," I said. "I've gotten an emergency call and I'll have to leave. Here's fifty bucks. Please convey my apologies to Kaylee, the young lady at my table."

He glared at me. "The dirty martinis alone are twenty apiece."

"Okay, here's another twenty," I said. "The chowder was quite good. Mind if I duck out the back?"

Trevor mused. He wanted to impose some obstacle, but I didn't care.

Without waiting for an answer, I darted through the kitchen, through the back door, and into the blameless Seattle summer evening. Brassy light. Passersby strolling and laughing.

I looked forward to seeing Abe Aschmann. For once, I thought maybe I was single because the single women I was meeting in Seattle were all totally bent. Placenta soup? God, that was cannibalism. The one variant I had not even suspected existed here.

When I got back to my battered Outback, I shook myself like a wet dog. I thought I'd vomited my loneliness up, but I was wrong. I still bulged with an ocean of lonely, dark, sad water sloshing around in my chest.

I felt no regret about ditching Kaylee. After all, if you eat afterbirth, you must anticipate some attrition in your possible romantic partners.

I drove home with all the windows down, letting the balmy wind scour away that experience. At home, I needed another long shower. "Does this soup taste funny to you," I asked myself.

I burst out laughing. Maybe it was time to cancel my membership at TopFliteSingles.com.

CHAPTER THIRTEEN— BULLETPROOF GLASS PART ONE

The afternoon I went to my intake with Abe Aschmann, I got a parking space right in front of his building, a Spanish-style structure resembling an undamaged Alamo. A crow on the roofline said, "Caw caw caw."

"Hey, buddy," I replied. The crow cocked its head at me, then flew away. It was so quiet on this golden August evening I heard the wings flapping.

Dr. Aschmann led me back to his office and gave me an intake clipboard. Hmm. So this was what it was like to be a client.

Abe Aschmann was about fifty with horn-rimmed glasses, ginger hair, overgrown eyebrows and crow's feet beside his pale blue eyes. He leaned back and sighed. "Make yourself comfortable, Sam," he said. "You can call me Abe." Low voice, slow intonation.

Everything here told me it was okay to slow down. Bookshelves lined his walls jammed with texts—cognitive-behavioral books, philosophy books, trauma books, even self-help books. I checked out his diplomas. A BA in Psychology from Stanford. MA and Ph.D. in Psychology from NYU. Certifications in Hypnotherapy, EMDR, something called

Contract Therapy, and even Marriage and Family Therapy. Apparently, he would use anything useful.

"So Sam, can you give me the five-minute summary of your life?" Abe asked. He bent forward.

My bullshit detector wasn't always accurate, but I sensed Abe was perceptive and trustworthy. Catherine had sat in this exact chair and probably told him some of the same ancient horrors.

So this is what it's like going to one of my Intake Clinics, I thought.

I filled him in on the basics. Mom and Dad died in a natural gas leak when Catherine and I were seven. We got "foster care," loosely defined, at the Malletts' Therapeutic Foster Home and aged out at eighteen. Then, I joined the Coast Guard and developed my rescuer complex while receiving a BA in Criminology. After discharge I got my law degree at the University of Washington. There I met and lost Suzanne, the love of my life. I wondered if I would be alone forever. I'd prosecuted and loved it, but management didn't love me back. Now, I loved my job because I got to show up at people's worst moments and sort things out so they got understanding and, compensation, and a sense of payback.

Abe didn't just listen, he absorbed.

When I got to the death of my parents, his bristling eyebrows rose. When I talked about the Coast Guard, he leaned forward showing a modest paunch. When I described my law practice he cocked his head, examining me. He was not running the clock to cash in, the way my court-ordered therapist in foster care had.

"Okay, so that's the thumbnail sketch," he said. "Now let me tell you about what I do. My favorite modes of therapy are three—cognitive behavioral therapy, logotherapy, and EMDR. Cognitive behavioral therapy seeks to straighten out your reasoning so you can make better and more free decisions in life. When it works, clients report an increased sense of agency—basically, they feel free to make changes without undue distress. That helps them change their behaviors. Logotherapy helps clients refine their sense of purpose. There's a saying in logotherapy—'he who has a why to live can endure almost anything.' It was developed by Viktor Frankl, arising from his survival of Auschwitz."

"I read *Man's Search for Meaning*," I said. "If he could distill out something useful from that, I take it seriously."

"Just so," Abe said. "We are on this earth to accomplish our purposes. We don't need to eliminate stress. A stress-free life is a useless life. We don't need to revisit our past, or even achieve insights, so much as we need to clarify our reasoning and get on with accomplishing our purpose."

I smiled. "That doesn't sound like ten years of talking about my childhood," I mused.

"Exactly. I am not a psychoanalyst. I sometimes think extensive discussion of childhood just strengthens flawed cognitions, rather than changing them. I have a saying—those who vent a lot just develop bigger vents."

I laughed. The last thing I'd expected. Not wallowing, but climbing out of the wallow instead.

"But I do want to revisit the most pivotal traumatic events in your life," Abe said. "Not to strengthen what you already feel or ingrain what you already remember. To reframe it. In EMDR, we revisit these things, not to strengthen them, but to weaken them."

He took a big drink of his tea. I could smell it from where I sat in a snug beige leather chair. Market spice.

He leaned forward. "Most lives tend to pivot on a small number of crises when our old relationships and behaviors are shattered. With EMDR, we drain the residual anxiety from these events. It's often used with combat veterans and police officers involved in combat events. Anxiety is not just a psychological thing. It is physical. The amygdala in the brain produces the neurotransmitters associated with anxiety. Often, it's simply overactive. EMDR can help pull out the residual memories that over-activate the amygdala. Otherwise, the amygdala is like a smoke detector that never stops going off."

"Catherine said the exact same thing."

Abe nodded. "I'm not allowed to discuss what she said in our sessions. But it sounds like your mother had an overactive amygdala. Sometimes, there is a genetic component. Sometimes, children of anxious parents inherit a physical predisposition to anxiety. But often, very often, it's simply a behavior learned from a parent."

I liked that Abe was teaching me. He knew I was a diligent student, a guy with two college degrees who compulsively sought to understand stuff. He knew the way into my head, all right. The way in was by offering my brain the food it wanted to taste.

"So on your intake form, I asked you to list the three biggest crises in your life," Abe said. "Let me see if I understand these. First, when your parents died when you and Catherine were seven."

"I felt I was alone in the middle of the ocean with no life preserver."

"Second, something that happened between you and your foster brother, and you wound up on a locked ward at a psych hospital when you were twelve."

"Yes." I bit the word off. It wasn't going to be a cakewalk to describe that.

"Third, the death of your foster brother."

"Yes. It's really related to the second one, but yes."

Abe looked behind my head. All good therapists have a big clock on the wall behind the client's chair so they can check the time remaining without seeming to. I gathered I was almost out of time.

Then he regarded me for a moment. I heard buses go by outside, moaning into the gathering August dusk. The silence coagulated. He surprised me.

"Sam, are you willing to let me go into the darkness with you?"

That was a challenge. As you've figured out by now, I don't trust very many people.

"Yes, let's give it a try," I said.

"Fair enough." He shook my hand, and the session was over.

I drove home in my battered Outback to my anonymous condo where my books and CDs and silence waited. I wondered if he knew how deep and black the darkness was. But he'd counseled Catherine. Also, I had a feeling in his book-lined office that he'd uncovered and… reframed…terrible things. Abe had hooked me with knowledge. I was hungry for it.

***

At the next session, Abe set up a funny device next to his chair facing me. Mounted on a tripod, it was a black metal bar, about two feet wide, with cords running out of it.

"This is my old friend, the EMDR light bar," Abe said. "Now, in EMDR therapy, we revisit the traumatic event in as much detail as possible. Then I lead you through it again, in intervals, using the light bar to shift your visual focus from left to right, repeatedly, to get these traumatic recollections housed, or seated, on both sides of the brain. This helps diminish their power over you. Sometimes, I will also use headphones that sound tones alternately in the right and left ear. We'll play it by ear and then see if we need to play it by ear." He chuckled.

I loved wise teachers.

I'm not going to try to fully describe or explain EMDR here. The purpose is just to show you my three crises in detail before Abe applied EMDR to them.

"Let me get you some decaf market spice tea," Abe said. "I've found going straight into the darkness can be easier with market spice tea. Maybe it's the cinnamon and cloves."

He fussed at his wet bar in the back of the office, then handed me a thick handmade mug of tea. I had a feeling this pause was mainly to get me used to looking at the light bar.

I took a big drink. That smell. Cinnamon and cloves and spices, like the smell of a sunny Mediterranean port on a crisp day.

Abe said, "Now, I want you to close your eyes." I did.

"You are just about to find out that your parents have died. I want you to put yourself entirely inside your body at that moment. I want you to be seven-year-old Sam in that exact place and time. Let me know when you're ready to go."

I breathed deeply. My mind hopped around, looking for some distraction, and then stopped hopping like an exhausted puppy.

"I am seven, wearing blue camp shorts and T-shirt with a half-eaten Milky Way in my pocket next to my Swiss Army knife. Catherine and I are at Camp Skykomish, a YMCA camp high up in the Cascade Mountains. I'm small—all elbows and knees. When I get called in by the camp director, I'm afraid I've been busted for writing graffiti with toothpaste on the cabin wall."

"Continue," Abe murmured.

My heart sped up a little. "I've been in my cabin reading *The Martian Chronicles* by Ray Bradbury during Super Free Time right after lunch. My counselor, Zed, tells me I have to go to the dining hall. The camp director wants to see me." I sighed. "I'm going to get in trouble even though I almost never get in trouble. We walk to the dining hall under the pines, and people are playing softball—hey, batter batter, swing! We get to the dining hall and climb up the concrete steps into this big screened-in porch, where we all eat. and there are bangs and smells from the kitchen, and it smells like bug juice which is what we call fruit punch.

Two flies buzz around me. The camp director is waiting—a severe bald, tanned guy wearing sunglasses with his ever-present clipboard. He keeps clicking his pen. There's a state trooper in his pale blue uniform and Smoky Bear hat. Catherine is there too. Catherine didn't get in trouble, not ever, so maybe I won't get in trouble either. So what's going on?"

My heart sped up more.

"So the camp director says he has unfortunate news. Then he just looks at the state trooper. The trooper takes off his Smokey Bear hat and turns it in his hands. The trooper said I'm sorry, kids, but there has been an accident, and something happened to your parents. He feeds it to us in bites. Catherine demands to know what kind of accident. The trooper says there was a natural gas leak at your house. Unfortunately, neither of your parents has survived. They are deceased. In the background, somebody hits a home run in the softball game. Cheers. The flies still buzz around my head the way thoughts are buzzing inside my head, too fast to catch."

My heart sped up more.

"I knew what he was saying. But I couldn't know what he was saying. Our parents hadn't even been separated from us for a week before Camp Skykomish, our first sleepaway camp. A fish doesn't know it's wet, you know? Mom is at home in her apron with cabbage roses on it, wringing her hands just like always, and Dad is putting together some real estate deal with a highlighter and four different colored Post-It pads just like always. It had to be just like always."

The ventilation system turned on.

"The trooper told us he would drive us back to Kirkland, where our parents' house was, and our counselors had packed up our camp stuff, and our bags were outside. I thought like an idiot. *Well, at least they didn't find out about the toothpaste graffiti* and the trooper put our bags in the trunk, and we sat in the back seat. There weren't any door handles in the back seat. I didn't believe the trooper about our parents, but I wasn't going to sass him, and maybe it was just a prank because I really had written some bad words with my toothpaste on the walls of the cabin, you know, the F word and the S word, so maybe some kind of scared straight thing?

"It's hot and humid driving in the car with no door handles in back, and the sky is dead white like a fish stomach, and everything far away looks light gray, and Catherine and I keep quiet and keep looking at each then away because we can read each other's minds which isn't so good right now. The trooper's radio buzzes like the flies buzzing around my head in the dining hall, and he pulls into our driveway at our yellow house with the horse plywood cutout on the garage door, which is normal, but the windows and the doors in our house are all wide open with big fans in them, and there's this smell like rotten eggs and roadkill; you can never forget that smell anyway I can never forget that smell anyway. Rotten eggs, I guess because of the natural gas and roadkill because, oh shit, excuse me, that has to be my mom and dad cuz they died inside in August with no air conditioning, and oh shit, that smell is them.

"The rotten eggs and roadkill stench gushes out like an open fire hydrant would gush water, and there's yellow plastic tape at the front door, but now the door's open, so the tape is hanging, and there's a gray van in the driveway, and the trooper who's named Bo Jorgenson says some motherfucker didn't get the memo because the medical examiner people were supposed to be gone already and that smell must be my mom and dad.

"So then two men in gray pajamas-clothes push a metal wheeled stretcher thing out the front door, one pajama man in the front, one pajama man in the back, and one back wheel keeps flopping around, and the pajama man in the back kicks it, and then keeps pushing, and it squeaks like a cartoon mouse, and there's a black vinyl bag on it and from the pushing it must be heavy. The pajama men pull the van doors open, and there's another heavy black vinyl bag in there. and Bo Jorgenson helps the gray pajama guys grab the handles on the bag on the stretcher, and they grunt and say one, two lift, and they stow it in there and close the doors carefully as if they'd wake up the vinyl bags, but that can't be right of course. But there are no handles on the back doors where me and Catherine are, and Catherine starts screaming.

"Catherine goes nuts and she wants to get out but there is no door handle and there is this cage in the space over the front seat and she starts banging her head against the window trying to break it and her pink barrette flies off and Trooper Bo Jorgenson comes over and yanks her out by an arm and says oh baby I'm sorry you had to see this little miss and then he put his jacket over her head because she needs that and Catherine stops screaming and hugs Trooper Bo Jorgenson and he takes the jacket off her head and she leaves these shiny trails of snot on his shirt reflecting the dead white sky and the van drives away and I bury my face in Trooper Bo Jorgenson's shirt also but I don't know how to cry or even move until Catherine shows me how because I'm just frozen.

"I still take two showers a day because of that smell and I still need Catherine around because what if I freeze up again? Only she can tell me what to do if I freeze up again, but there's no goddamned way I'll ever freeze up again in danger. I'm just going to move when stuff goes sideways, but in foster care, I keep freezing again and again, which I am very embarrassed about.

"Trooper Bo Jorgenson takes us inside with garbage bags to get some clothes, and the smell is like swimming underwater in sewage, and then he takes us to IHOP, and the frumpy social worker gives us pancakes and takes us to the Malletts' Therapeutic Foster Home, and stuff happens where I freeze again, but I'm not ready to talk about the stuff yet."

I shut up. The ventilation stopped.

"Just breathe a bit," Abe Aschmann said in his low and slow voice. He pushed his sleeves up.

Then he worked me through this, in steps, with the light bar. Now I understood why he'd booked a two-hour session. I repeated it in chunks, and he worked the light bar after each one.

"Now I want to have you close your eyes and put yourself back in your front yard, at your parents' house in Kirkland, looking at the gray van. Got it?"

I nodded.

"Do you have a very vivid picture of your front yard and the gray van on that day?"

"Yes."

Abe lowered his voice. "Now I want you to see a thick plate of bulletproof glass, tinted light blue, lowering in front of this scene. The scene is still there. But it's tinted blue, and you're shielded from it by the bulletproof glass."

He guided me out of the visualization and told me to open my eyes.

"So that's why I can't let myself get separated from Catherine," I mused. "I've always told myself it's so I can protect her. But it's so she can make sure I don't freeze when there's danger."

Abe nodded. "Perhaps. But one great thing about cognitive therapy? It teaches us that sometimes both things are true. She protects you when you freeze. You protect her by always standing by for her. No one-sided relationship can ever be strong. When a relationship is two ropes winding around each other, each strengthening the other, then it's a cable that can bear immense weight."

I was sweating now. But my heart was no longer kicking at the insides of my ears.

When I left the undamaged Alamo building, I noticed three crows sitting on the roof line staring at me, and they all tilted their heads at me. "Caw caw caw," they all said in unison. Funny how you can imagine an animal approves of you when you need to do exactly that.

It almost seemed plausible that I do this with the subject of the Malletts' Therapeutic Foster Home.

CHAPTER FOURTEEN—THE SLIPPERY SLOPE

The next day, Nicky and I did Intake Clinic. A fatality slip and fall? You never know what'll walk in the door. This was either the ultimate Barking Dog or a True Disaster which would be a brawl from the start.

Insurance companies thought all slip-and-fall cases were garbage. Almost always, they were right.

Personal injury cases were divided by insurance companies and lawyers into just a few categories—med mal, vehicle crashes, product liability, and slip/trip and fall—also called "premises liability" cases. Premises case mostly involved slip/trip and fall injuries but could include injuries on trampolines or swimming pools or any other injury on somebody's property. Some of the trampoline and swimming pool cases were clear liability and very gruesome—but all "premises liability" cases got pigeonholed as garbage by insurance companies.

Most premises cases were unwinnable. The "watch where you're going" defense almost always worked with juries. Most plaintiffs' attorneys wouldn't even do an intake on a premises case and certainly wouldn't file suit on one.

The insurance companies never made a settlement offer on a premises case until the plaintiff filed suit, got some good depositions, and probably defeated a defendant's Motion for Summary Judgment of Dismissal.

The funny thing? A tiny fraction of premises cases were winnable and worthwhile. I'd never even seen one that was a True Disaster. But I was willing to be surprised. The Kentucky Ass-Whipping case had looked like a sure thing until I ran into the brick wall of governmental immunity. Maybe something that sounded like a Barking Dog could turn out to be a True Disaster.

Kandy, the stripper receptionist, showed in the family a spare Asian man, his even thinner Asian wife, and a bemused six-year-old boy. The man looked calm and severe, fortyish, in blazer and slacks. The woman? Chin up, brave, composed in a rose-colored pantsuit.

She walked like a broken egg holding itself together.

The little boy? Dark blue suit with clip-on tie, confused by something. Six-year-old boys, right? Surprised when life punches them in the mouth. The Dangs looked dressed for church, and I'd bet they went to church.

Nicky and I nodded to each other. That smell. This case was not a Barking Dog.

I stood and shook their hands, including the little boy's hand.

"I am Phuc Dang," the man declared. Proud of his wife and son. "This is my wife Binh Dang and my son Pham Dang. We are here about the death of Pham's twin brother, Cao Dang."

I nodded. "Please be seated. I'm sorry for your loss. Please tell me how it happened." I spotted Kandy loitering in the doorway. "Kandy, please make sure we are not interrupted." Nicky nodded emphatically. That was code for please make sure Rodney doesn't show up and ruin the vibe. Kandy winked at me and closed the door.

Phuc Dang began. "I am a pharmacist, doctorate level. My wife is a registered nurse. We are legal immigrants from Vietnam."

I kept my head down, taking notes. Some people could talk about intense stuff only if you didn't look at them. I created a big vacuum that they could fill. I was learning from Abe Aschmann.

"We rented an apartment at Glen Lochs, from the Bitterroot Apartment Company. It's about a year ago, this time. We tell them we have children, the twin boys age six. They are identical twins."

Mrs. Dang put her hand to her forehead. "They were."

Phuc nodded and adjusted his tie. "They were." He paused. He took papers out of his briefcase, a classic displacement activity. He focused on the papers because he didn't like what he had to say. "So about three weeks ago I am home asleep because I work graveyard shift at hospital. My wife in kitchen cooking. The boys wore the same clothes that day. Sometimes they like to be identical, and sometimes very different, because they are six, you know?"

"They did," Mrs. Dang said, her face stamped with sorrow. "So I see boy running back and forth down hallway, he singing, he sliding on his sock feet. It was Pham, but I thought it was both of them. Pham make enough noise for both of them truly."

I nodded. It was getting cold in here. I was about to mentally go to The Scene.

Mrs. Dang plunged ahead. "Both boy told strictly you never go outside without permission. There is reason. At Glen Lochs there is duck pond and little canal connecting to other apartment and condominium in The Lochs complex, very big complex. Duck pond is deep, artificial, cement sides. It just vertical wall inside the water. There is slope with grass around duck pond and company run sprinklers all the time in summer to make grass green. All time I and the neighbors tell kids you stay away from pond, it not safe."

Then she just stopped. Dr. Dang took her hand, and she squeezed it so hard her knuckles turned white.

Dr. Dang—really Dr. Dang—took up the thread. Their English regressed. "So I sleeping, and my wife yelling now. I wake up and say what, what is matter? She ask Pham where is Cao and Pham say Cao he outside he want to feed ducks even though that against all our rules. I run outside grass very wet from sprinkler. I run around pool fence and look at duck pond and there is muddy drag mark leading down to pond and there Cao floating in the water. I run down to water. My wife yelling for help. I tell wife you call 911 right now okay? I pull him out, he not heavy, I start CPR. Pharmacist know CPR, right? So I start CPR. I force water out lungs but cannot get a pulse. I clear airway, pull tongue aside, push a breath in and his little chest rise so he have airway but I cannot get him breathing. My wife come back she say fire department on the way, is he breathing, is he breathing, and so I keep doing CPR, and then my wife she just freeze until fire engine come. It only about three minutes to fire engine come, and then Medic One come, and the EMT take over."

He'd rushed through this because otherwise he wouldn't get through it at all. Nicky's eyes shone, shiny brown jewels.

True Disaster all right. I hadn't known it was a fatality slip and fall of a…child.

Mrs. Dang squeezed Dr. Dang's hand very hard and she froze. She wouldn't cry in front of strangers but she was a broken egg holding herself together, trying to keep the jagged pieces pressed together.

Dr. Dang concluded, "The EMTs and Medics cannot save my boy. His brother still ask when Cao come home? He cannot understand Cao cannot come home."

I looked at the surviving twin boy, Pham Dang. He stared at me demanding I do something because I was supposed to. He seemed to think I had some kind of answer. I did have an answer, but I didn't have what he needed. A magic wand.

I decided to give Dr. Dang the gift of displacement activity again. "I'm very interested. Do you have any documents?"

Dr. Dang pulled out the Certificate of Death, the medical examiner's Scene Investigation, and the Autopsy Report. He also had the fire department's Run Report and CAD dispatch log. Putting these documents into the roaring void helped a tiny bit.

I read the Certificate of Death: *Cause of Death: Asphyxiation By Drowning. Manner of Death: Accident.*

The Scene Investigation confirmed everything the Dangs had said to the letter, as did the Run Report. The CAD log showed that the fire department had sent two engines as well as a Medic One. The reports confirmed the grassy slope by the pond was overwatered and slippery.

There's a wise saying—depression is anger turned inward.

I couldn't bandage their emotions yet. But I could give them a little Band-Aid. Because somebody else had screwed up and caused this. Certainly, the prospective defendant had some liability with the right jury, maybe even sole liability.

That's the crazy thing about life—the good people are over-responsible, and the bad people are under-responsible.

Good people think they need to take responsibility for everything that happens to them and their families. Bad people deny responsibility for their obvious crimes and undeniable screwups. Just about everybody leans one way or the other. This tilt defines the basic structure of their character. The Greek philosopher Heraclitus once said: "Character is destiny."

"Was there a fence around the pond?" I asked, but I knew the answer.

"No," said Mrs. Dang, quietly. She glared at me. "No fence around pond. There is fence around pool, but no fence around pond just fifty feet away."

Dr. Dang nodded. "That why we here. We want an answer. Was there supposed to be a fence around this pond?"

I nodded. "Yes, there was. Were your children on the lease?" Dr. Dang slid the lease over to me. Man, he was prepared. Man, these people were deserving and hurt and deserving. I flipped through the lease. Under the paragraph headed "tenants," all four were listed. Pham and Cao were noted as six years old.

Bang.

"So they knew they were renting to families with children," I said, staring down at the lease. Again I wasn't looking at them so they could be as bold as they liked. "There was no fence around the pond. *Degel v. Majestic Mobile Manor*."

Nicky caught my eye, her eyebrows raised.

I turned to Dr. Dang. "Degel says if a landlord knows he's renting to a family with children, the landlord has to fence off any adjacent bodies of water. This landlord violated the rule in *Degel v. Majestic Mobile Manor*. Also, there's a section in the Restatement of Tort Second regarding dangers in rental housing, and there's the Landlord-Tenant Act. But the real silver bullet is *Degel v. Majestic Mobile Manor*. In that case, a couple with a young child rented a mobile home next to a ravine with a creek, and the landlord didn't fence off the ravine. The child drowned. The landlord lost at trial and lost the appeal, too. It's on all fours—sorry, that's lawyer-speak, for the important facts are the same as your case. In your case, the defendant worsened the hazard by overwatering the grassy slope adjacent to the pond. I'd like to take this case if I may." I paused. "We will not charge a legal fee unless we get damages for you. We will pay all costs and won't ask for reimbursement unless we win or settle. My firm takes the risk."

Mrs. Dang interjected. "You make them fence that pond! We move out last week. We not there anymore, but there dozens of kids on that property! That property is not safe place! That place need to be fixed!"

I nodded. "I will try to force them to fence it. I can ask the court to order it. It's called a request for injunctive relief. I will also sue for damages. Is this landlord a big company?"

Dr. Dang nodded. "Thirty-seven thousand unit in Washington, Oregon, California. Landlord owner is big guy who have private jet. Big company. Nothing wrong with that. In America is okay to get rich. But no fence. There should have been a fence."

"And a slippery slope next to the pond because they overwatered it," I said. In the law there's a catchphrase—slippery slope. It means once the court or legislature starts down a path they cannot stop, and it's meant to caution against taking any action at all. But this fatality was a literal slippery slope case. Fatality slip and fall causing death of a child.

This one would be a brawl. I couldn't wait.

Nicky slid the contract and authorization over to Mr. and Mrs. Dang, and they signed. "Please don't date anything," Nicky said. "We need to get a probate opened. That's where the court gives you permission to handle your poor son's estate. Once you get the Letters of Administration, I'll date the contract and authorization. Then we can start." She looked over at me with a faint smile. "He likes to call the Letters of Administration his hunting license."

They signed. Mrs. Dang looked at me after she signed. She looked like a skinny tiger. She had some fight, all right. That was the best sign. It was possible the anger could be turned outward. That would help them survive.

I signed too. Nicky went to make copies.

"I have a goal for this case," I said. "Of course I want to get the fence put up. Another child could die there. Of course I want to get damages for you. But I want to get enough for you that you can buy a house outright, no mortgage, and you will never have to deal with a landlord again. You should never have to deal with a landlord, not ever, after this. Does that sound like a decent goal to you?"

I was taking a very presumptuous leap, trying to get them to imagine a house, and no landlord, and possibly some kind of future that could be halfway acceptable. But I thought I saw a little spark start glowing in

Mrs. Dang's eye. She wanted to be done with landlords for good. She had another little boy to protect. And like almost every hard-working person in the world, she wanted her own property.

Nicky came back with the copies. "How much longer do you have on your lease?" I asked them.

Mrs. Dang said, "Landlord say he will let us out of lease on first of month, end of next week. He return security deposit. Such generous company." She glared at me again. I liked her tiger look. I liked that these people would fight. There was an American military saying from the Vietnam War—we had to destroy the village to save it. I wanted to save this family by hammering the idiot who destroyed it. I could tell Nicky this, but I would never breathe a word of it to Rodney.

Talking to Rodney about loyalty was like talking to a dog about calculus. His eyes might focus on you, but he would never get it.

"Can you meet me at the property tomorrow?" I asked.

"Sure," Dr. Dang said. "What purpose?"

"I need to bring an investigator to take video and pictures. And I need to see everything for myself. Also, may I borrow your documents and give you copies tomorrow? I need to read everything."

"What about cost of probate?" Mrs. Dang wanted to nail down every corner.

I pulled the contract over to me and hand wrote, *Probate fees to be paid by attorney without reimbursement from Client.* I initialed it, and the Dangs initialed it. Rodney would flip. Screw him.

I paused. "I need to warn you both about something, too." They had started to stand, and they sat back down. "This is what's called a premises liability case. There are categories of cases. Defendants and insurance companies treat them differently. If your son had died in a school bus crash, they would take us seriously. But premises liability cases get treated as if they are all worthless. The defendants never offer to settle without a lawsuit. They fight dirty and they fight every step of the way. I will not file suit until I have every scrap of evidence I can get. Until then, I will be invisible. Please don't tell anybody you hired me. But understand that they will fight all the way."

Mrs. Dang reached over and shook my hand, and she squeezed it. She had dry, calloused nurse's hands. She also had a fierce grip. "You tell that Mr. Big we got plenty fight too."

***

I booked Silent Mike to meet me at the scene. The Ghost never did scene investigations.

It turned out Glen Loch Apartments was part of a bigger development called The Lochs Community, arranged around a series of artificial ponds and canals.

Glen Loch was a cluster of three-story buildings with balconies and patios facing the duck pond. There was a pool, securely fenced with a locked gate, a tennis court, securely fenced, and a two-acre duck pond, totally unfenced. The grass beside the pond was still squishy in the hot August sun from overwatering.

It wasn't a trade secret that landlords had to fence off bodies of water. *Degel v. Majestic Mobile Manor* had been decided over ten years ago.

Silent Mike arrived ten minutes early with his digital camera and an array of lenses. He climbed out of his black Yukon and sauntered over to my battered Subaru. Duvonda had chosen her boyfriend well—he was huge, strong, confident, a man of hidden talents. Years working for Seattle Police, many of them leading a SWAT team. I felt confident just standing next to Silent Mike.

"Hey," Silent Mike said to Nicky. They shook hands. Her hand was a quarter the size of his.

Dr. Dang pulled up in a minivan. When he got out, I remembered he worked graveyard shift as a hospital pharmacist most nights. He looked exhausted, but game.

"I'm glad you still have a few days on your lease," I said to him. "You're still a tenant. We have the legal right to be here. So show me your apartment, the patio, and the duck pond. My investigator here will take video and photos as we go. Then I'll have him round up some documents from the King County Recorder so we can learn everything about the legal ownership of the pond."

Dr. Dang nodded. He strode quickly across the wet grass, past the pool and pool house and turned to Silent Mike, who started the video camera. "This is pool, and it fenced," he said grimly. Silent Mike handed the video camera to Nicky and snapped about a dozen photos. The pool gate was on an automatic spring, the latch at the top, five feet high. Pretty child-proof. Dr. Dang demonstrated it. "See this sign?"

The sign on the gate said, *Caution—to prevent drowning do not prop open gate or let unattended children inside enclosure.*

Brutal irony. Dr. Dang let the gate slam shut on its strong automatic spring. *Clang.* On top of the pool house two crows observed.

"Here is lawn and our patio," he said, walking to the building next to the pool house. Only one patio was empty. "This was ours," he said, pointing at it. Silent Mike took video and photos.

"Now you see the scene," he said. I gulped. The Scene was where your client got killed. Silent Mike held the video camera and centered Dr. Dang.

Just fifty feet from the back of the Dangs' patio, the short and lush grass sloped down to the duck pond. I followed him to the start of the slope. Mushy grass again. Then I froze.

On the slope leading down to the duck pond? Muddy skid marks.

Next to them there was a single blue disposable glove left by the medics.

Floating in the pond, near where Cao Dang had drowned, there were several plastic toys—a Barbie, a Ken, and a Transformer. Another kid would drown unless I nailed this.

"Mike, get this," I said, pointing to the skid marks, the glove, and the toys, but he was already all over it. Video and photos.

This case was as rare as an albino rhino. A slip-and-fall True Disaster. The law required the landlords to fence the pond. The victim was a six-year-old boy. Children of six were too young to have any comparative fault. *Price v. Kitsap Transit.*

Defendants had only one out—a variant on the "watch where you're going" defense. They would blame the mother for not watching her son. They knew this was a good defense, because it was legally plausible and also because it would cause maximum pain to the parents, amplifying the blame they already felt.

But Mrs. Dang had a novel and ferocious response. She had seen one of her identical twins, who was dressed the same as the other on that day, and she thought she had seen both of them. This had legs. Defendants probably wouldn't even imagine that defense before I smacked them with it.

There was another strong and stealthy argument in this case. Poor Cao Dang had a surviving identical twin, Pham Dang. Pham was going to turn seven in a few weeks, long before trial.

The most tragic thing I'd heard during the intake? Little Pham wondering when his brother was coming back.

If it electrified me, it would electrify the jury.

When Pham turned seven, he could be qualified as a witness as long as he understood the difference between right and wrong, and knew it was wrong to lie. But why would I want him on the stand?

Multiple reasons. The overt reasons were to have him describe how he was wearing identical clothes, so he got mistaken for his brother, and also to show how he still missed his brother, to prove lost consortium—destruction of the sibling relationship.

But I had a covert reason in my back pocket. It was so spicy, so inside-out, that I didn't want to tell anybody. I wouldn't tell anybody unless we went to trial. Not the Dangs. Not even Nicky.

I wanted to put Pham on the stand as the ghost of his brother. I wanted the jury to see this bright little boy. I wanted to tell the jury there should be two of these bright little boys. I wanted them to imagine what Mr. and Mrs. Dang felt as they looked at Pham every day at the breakfast table, knowing there should be two of them.

No parent can forget a dead child's face. But for a parent to see the dead little boy's identical twin every day? Torture.

It was so inside-out that it was definitely right.

I was going to put a ghost on the stand.

"Sam, look," Nicky said, touching my elbow.

Dr. Dang was pointing at the patios all around the duck pond while Silent Mike shot video. "See? There is Big Wheel. Over there, tricycle. Over there skateboard. All kids play on wet mushy lawn all the time. No fence around pond!" He threw up his hands. "It going to happen again."

Silent Mike shot me a ferocious look. He was an ex-cop and he knew when to get mad. I met his eyes.

"Maybe it won't," I said. "We're going to hammer these people until they put up a fence. When I have them served with the lawsuit I'll include a Motion for Injunctive Relief. Let's see if I can make these people move. Even if they do have twenty-seven thousand units and a private jet."

***

I didn't bother sending a demand letter to Bitterroot's insurer. They'd just put this case in the category of a slip and fall and consider it a frivolous case. I sued them. Sometimes you start your war with an exchange of nice diplomatic notes. Sometimes you just punch them in the mouth.

I included a set of requests for admission, asking to admit the basic facts establishing fault. I knew they would deny everything. But if I proved all of my RFAs, as we called them, I had a chance at a whopping fee award. Requests for Admission are intended to make defendants admit things that they can't reasonably dispute. Arrogant defendants often get in trouble by disputing them anyway. I'll show you just a couple so you can see what they look like:

REQUEST FOR ADMISSION NO. 1: Admit that Defendant Bitterroot knew that it was renting to Plaintiffs with actual knowledge that Plaintiffs would be occupying their unit with two six-year-old children.

_______________ADMIT_______________DENY

REQUEST FOR ADMISSION NO. 2: Admit that prior to the date of Plaintiff's decedent Cao Dang's death, Defendant Bitterroot did not fence off the pond adjacent to the Glen Loch Apartment Complex.

_______________ADMIT_______________DENY

If defendants admitted both of these RFAs, we were ninety percent of the way toward proving fault. Therefore they would deny them. However the lease showed they knew they were renting to a family with two six-year-old boys. Also the pond wasn't fenced and we had video and photos proving it. So when they denied them, they would be putting their heads in the noose. I liked that.

The only way the noose could fail to pull tight was if the judge chickened out on enforcing Civil Rule 36, the Requests for Admission rule. That was always the joker in the deck.

Many Seattle judges, too many, thought that enforcing the rules as written wasn't "nice." It was the dark side of practicing in the Seattle area. Battling this idea that justice and rule-following was somehow not "nice."

I sent Silent Mike out to stake out the Bitterroot headquarters building and asked him to personally serve the CEO, Hank Bitterroot, a former airline pilot who had parlayed a sterling credit rating and some strategic friendships with bank loan officers into an empire. I admired the CEO's business. I thought it was great that he'd used his ingenious mind to build a big business. Also I knew that founders of thriving businesses often cared more about doing the right thing than their lackeys did. I wanted to make sure this didn't get buried on the desk of some sycophantic risk manager who would send it to the insurance company for defense without telling the boss what was up.

Mike gave me the video of the service he'd taken on his button camera. "He looked surprised," Mike said. "He hadn't even heard about this claim."

"That's what I expected," I said. "I'm going to depose him on video. He's less likely to be a liar than any of his employees. My gut tells me so."

"My gut tells me it's time to get enchiladas with Duvonda," Mike said, fist-bumping me. "I'll tell her that her favorite upstart is at it again."

Then I told Kandy that if anybody called about the Dang case, she should put the call right through to me, nobody else.

"Dang," she said. "Funny name."

"Honored Vietnamese name," I corrected her. "These beautiful people lost their six-year-old boy. He drowned. We're going to be seeing a lot of the Dangs. You'll probably like them. Nicky thinks they are stars."

Kandy winked at me and wrote down their names. She'd had her pink streaks re-done in her blonde hair. I felt vaguely sorry for her that she seemed to be mixed up with Rodney. It had been a hard sell getting Rodney to agree I could take the case and file suit immediately. I gave him a copy of *Degel vs. Majestic Mobile Manor* and told him, "This is probably worth big bucks, bro." He liked it when people called him bro. Who knew? Maybe he even read the Degel case. It could have happened.

I expected to hear quickly from defense counsel and I wasn't disappointed. The next day I got a call from a well-known but widely disliked defense attorney at a big firm. His name was Bob Sauer. His detractors called him Call Me Bob or Sour Bob Sauer.

The next morning he called. "Sam, Bob Sauer here. Call me Bob. What the hell is up with you serving the CEO of the company as well as the registered agent? Was that necessary?"

"Well, Bob," I said, "when a six-year-old boy dies because of Bitterroot's negligence, I think maybe the CEO should hear about it."

"Hold your horses, Sam. It's a long way to establishing negligence."

"It is, but we'll get there." I wanted Call Me Bob to get his back up and resist everything. That would make the noose work. I needed him to be arrogant until it was too late.

"I hear you're a straight shooter. How about giving me a two-month extension on answering the Requests for Admission, Interrogatories, and Requests for Production."

I said, "No." Then I waited. This was getting good.

"Okay, how about an Agreed Protective Order stating that no facts disclosed in discovery may be revealed to anybody other than the judge and jury?"

"Again, no. You can file a motion. But I'm not going to give that away."

He snorted. "Okey doke. You're going to lose, and I'm going to bill some sweet hours."

"I'm counting on it."

He politely said goodbye.

There was the thing about Outhouse Counsel—the kind who were paid hourly by the insurance company. They tended to file elaborate and often worthless motions that stretched the judge's patience. Also the adjusters often got what I called "billing fatigue," when they got tired of writing big checks to defense counsel.

It's a popular myth that insurance companies don't like paying claims.

Most insurance companies don't like paying anybody. Their own retained attorneys included. They paid their Outhouse Counsel a reduced hourly rate, and the Outhouse Counsel responded by padding their bills.

Right at the start I was trying to set up friction between all the players on the opposite side—the defense attorney, the client, and the insurance company. In many of the big cases, the most crucial arguments were those I would never hear…the arguments between the various players on the other side of the case. There's a great saying about this: when lions fight, jackals come into their own.

Call Me Bob filed a Motion for Protective Order, asking that all evidence be held confidential, and asking for a fee award because the discovery requests were "overbroad." I countered that "overbroadness" is nowhere in Civil Rule 26 governing protective orders, and they had failed to meet the test.

This was juicy. When my opponent demanded a fee award right out of the gate, and started rhetorically pounding the table? That made it more likely that I would eventually get a fee award. Especially if I didn't pound the table. After a couple of bruising experiences in court as a rookie, I'd learned that blowhards tended to get punished. I had a great juvenile argument: "All this bickering about attorney fees? They started it." Usually a winner.

I wondered if Bob had a reason to be overconfident. I researched him, and researched the judge, but couldn't find even a single tie. They'd never worked for the same firm. They didn't go to the same law school. There was something cooking underneath. Remember, even paranoids sometimes have enemies.

Judge Schifter denied the motion. She had been one of my favorites through the years. She was a former personal injury litigator, the rare one who went on the bench. Most judges were former public defenders or prosecutors, and some of them took a while to learn about civil litigation. Judge Schifter was smart and a little cynical and good at cutting to the chase.

She also denied the request for attorneys' fees, without comment. Priceless. I was going to put Call Me Bob's demand for fees in my back pocket. Later on I'd pull it out at the right time and see if I could make it pay.

Next, as I promised Mr. and Mrs. Dang, I filed a Motion for Preliminary Injunction, asking Judge Schifter to order Bitterroot Apartments LLC to fence the pond at Glen Loch or pay a fine of five hundred dollars per day. I spiced it up with scene photos, an autopsy photo of Cao Dang on the table at the medical examiner's office, and the *Degel v. Majestic Mobile Manor* case showing that the defendant was required to fence off the pond. I lost.

Not surprising, although it did hurt. Motions for Preliminary Injunctions are almost never granted. The injunction is called an "extraordinary remedy" and the test to win is much tougher than just winning a civil trial. But Judge Schister had seen little Cao Dang lying dead on that stainless steel table in the medical examiner's autopsy suite. There was no way she could unsee that. As litigators say, "You can't un-ring the bell."

Then I started requesting deposition dates. I wanted to start with two—the Civil Rule 30(b)(6) deposition of Bitterroot's "employee in charge of safety at the Glen Loch Apartments," and after that, the CEO. I thought the 30(b)(6) guy would toe the party line and stonewall and mock us. Then perhaps the CEO would walk it back, and I could use that difference in their testimony.

To my surprise, Call Me Bob didn't request the depositions of Mr. and Mrs. Dang right away. Usually major cases are riddled with tit for tat.

Defense attorneys have a playbook. I could write big sections of it myself. Sooner or later Call Me Bob would get around to the "why didn't you watch where you're going" defense that always appeared in premises cases. But this time it would be "why weren't you watching your own children?" Maybe he was letting the case simmer, in hopes that in time, the Dangs would either blame each other, or blame themselves.

When a child dies, very often the parents turn on each other. Most married couples who lose a child don't stay married, looking ten years out. I wasn't the only one who could get conflicts cooking on the other side of the case. But then I remembered the Dangs. These people were welded together. I'd bet they would stick.

I finally got my CR 30(b)(6) deposition date for the safety person at Bitterroot designated to supervise the Glen Loch Apartments. I called Mrs. Dang and asked her about this guy, Erik Smalls. "We never met him," she said. "He not at complex. Only time we hear from him is when he let us out of the lease. He from headquarters."

He wasn't at the complex. Perfect. I wanted a drone from headquarters who didn't know the scene very well. Maybe he would get overconfident.

But here's the biggest lesson I learned in personal injury litigation—if you're certain you're going to win, you're in trouble. As Duvonda said: "The best battle is an ambush." Overconfident people got ambushed hard.

Never be certain you are going to win. Do everything right, eat some Tums, do it again, and doubt. Charge like a bastard, but always doubt. The law is a labyrinth. You remember what lives in the labyrinth, right?

***

I set the Civil Rule 30(b)(6) deposition of Erik Smalls at Bob Sauer's firm. I wanted Bob to feel confident. On the elevator, I told Nicky: "If you think I let the witness get away without answering, or you see anything interesting, please write me a note. I could use a second set of eyes on this." She nodded. She wore a black turtleneck and blue paisley skirt and looked more nervous than I was.

The dep was set up in a huge boardroom with thirty leather chairs around a granite conference table that must have been fifty feet long. Fabulous Hal and Romeo Pursuit were already set up. Bob Sauer and Erik Smalls hadn't come in yet. At the head of the table Romeo had set up his gray background screen, and his camera was at the opposite end. Romeo had added peacock blue highlights to his green hair. "How close do you want the focus, Sam?" he asked.

"Very close," I said. "Nothing showing but head and shoulders. Can you send me an audio file that is separate from the video file?"

"Please," he said, smiling. Romeo could give it to me backward in Sanskrit if I asked him to.

I huddled with Fabulous Hal, who was resplendent in a three-piece white and black checked suit with a lemon-yellow bow tie. "Hal, this may turn into a brawl," I said. "Please don't stop the audio recording no matter what. Please don't go off the record unless I specifically agree we are off the record. Is that okay?"

"Please," Hal said. "Don't you worry, dear heart. We'll debrief afterward and I can give you my totally objective impression."

Then I sat down next to the head of the table, across from Hal, and set up. Before every deposition I made an outline with bullet points, keyed to every conceivable exhibit. I brought three copies of every conceivable exhibit. As I said before, depositions were where opposing counsel misbehaves the most. I could use that. In a hostile deposition I liked to keep my voice level, never shout or swear, and keep drilling down on the same question until I got a responsive answer. I liked to have documents to back up every conceivable point.

The stuff I most wanted to learn was what the defense counsel most wanted to keep me from learning. Litigation is an alternative to war. In depositions, the analogy is obvious.

Bob Sauer came in. He was a gnarled gnome of a guy with overgrown gray hair and a brindled mustache over little rat teeth. He introduced Erik Smalls, a wiry, tall man with a shaved head who looked like he played handball when he wasn't running marathons.

After Smalls was sworn and Romeo did the video deposition read-in, I lobbed Mr. Smalls the customary softballs. Name, business address, education. I did more of this than most lawyers to get the witness in the habit of answering. Then I started drilling.

"Do you recognize this exhibit?" I said, sliding the Notice of Deposition over to Hal to mark it as an exhibit. Then Hal handed it to Smalls.

Smalls squinted at it through his Eurostyle glasses. "Yes."

"You are the Bitterroot employee in charge of safety at the Glen Loch Apartments?"

"Yes I am."

"Is there a pond on the premises?"

Sauer said, "Objection, calls for a legal conclusion. Mr. Smalls is not a surveyor and does not know the legal description of the premises."

I looked at Mr. Smalls. It's important to ignore the defense counsel when he or she is disrupting. "Mr. Smalls, your answer?"

Smalls picked up on his cue. "I'm not sure of the physical dimensions of the property."

Okay, it was going to be a brawl. And I wasn't going to play. I was going to drill.

"Mr. Smalls, have you been to the apartment formerly occupied by my clients, the Dang family?"

"Yes I have."

"When was the last time you were there?"

"I was there two weeks ago to make sure they'd left the apartment in good condition, so we could give them a refund of the damage deposit without deducting anything other than the usual cleaning fee." He smirked. Both he and Bob Sauer thought they were being clever.

Delicious.

"On your visits to the Dangs' former apartment, have you noted that there is a pond within sight of the apartment?"

"Yes," Smalls said.

"Objection," Sauer snarled again. "Question is vague. Within sight of the apartment doesn't take into account that this witness wears glasses."

I kept looking down at my outline. "Reporter, please read back the last question and the last answer." Hal did. I had this point pinned down.

"Mr. Smalls, this case involves the death of a little boy, do you understand that?"

"OBJECTION," Sauer shouted. "The phrase death of a little boy is inflammatory and prejudicial and it has not been established at this early time in the case."

I looked at Mr. Smalls. "Mr. Smalls, what is your answer?"

"Same objection," Sauer said. He was in fine form that morning. It's illegal obstruction to repeat an objection to the exact same question. Maybe Bob should have switched to decaf.

"Mr. Smalls, what is your answer?" I said again.

"I do not understand that a little boy has died," Smalls said, "and I vehemently deny that Bitterroot Apartments LLC has anything to do with this supposed death." Now Smalls was heating up. Both of them were hot under the collar.

I was not. Excellent.

I took out another exhibit and slid it over to Hal for marking as Exhibit 2. Hal handed it to Smalls.

"Mr. Smalls, the reporter has handed you Exhibit 2, Certificate of Death. This states that Cao Dang died at the Glen Loch Apartments of drowning, and he was a six-year-old boy. Does this not establish to you that this case involves a dead little boy?"

"Objection," Sauer interrupted. "We're going off the record."

I kept my head down, staring at the Certificate of Death. "No, we are not going off the record. If counsel is advising this witness not to answer, I will take this up with Judge Schifter and obtain an Order Compelling Discovery and an award of attorney's fees." I decided to back off a little, to make Smalls overconfident. "Mr. Smalls, this Certificate of Death states that Cao Dang was six years old when he died, is that not true?"

Smalls smirked again. "The document speaks for itself." Man, he'd really been coached.

"And you have no contrary knowledge?"

"Nope."

"The Certificate of Death states the death occurred at the Glen Loch Apartments, doesn't it?"

"Again the document speaks for itself. I didn't prepare this document. You'd have to talk to the medical examiner."

"Have no fear, we will," I said quietly.

"Objection, counsel is testifying," Sauer interrupted.

Bob Sauer was turning handsprings to keep me from gathering evidence. While video and audio recording was running. I remembered Napoleon's adage—never interrupt your enemy when he is making a mistake.

I looked at Smalls again. "The Certificate of Death states that the cause of death was drowning, isn't that correct?"

Smalls smiled broadly. "Again, the document speaks for itself."

"But you have no contrary knowledge? You have no knowledge that Cao Dang died of any cause other than drowning?"

"I do not."

"You have no knowledge that Cao Dang died anywhere other than the Glen Loch Apartments?"

"I do not."

"And the Glen Loch Apartments is owned by Bitterroot Apartments LLC, is it not?"

"It is. We have twenty-seven thousand doors, or units in layman's terms, and that is one of our complexes."

Smalls couldn't contradict any facts on the Certificate of Death. On to the next.

"Mr. Smalls, can you list for me all the documents you reviewed in preparation for today's deposition?"

Sauer piped up: "Objection, calls for attorney-client privileged communication."

I kept looking down at my script. The more I bowed my head, the more Sauer shouted at my bowed head.

I liked this. "Counsel, it's my impression that any communications between you and Mr. Smalls are privileged. However I'm just asking what documents he reviewed, not for anything you and he discussed. Are you instructing him not to answer?"

Sauer said, "Oh heck, I guess not. Go ahead, Erik."

Smalls listed a bunch of documents. I only cared about one of them.

I pulled out copies of the Dangs' lease. I slid one over to Hal for marking. "One of the documents you listed was the Dangs' lease at the Glen Loch Apartments, was it not?"

"It was."

"I'd like you to turn to page two and read aloud the names of the tenants who were listed on that lease."

Smalls squinted at the lease. "Phuc Dang, Binh Dang, and Pham Dan and Cao Dang, children aged six. Wow, sounds like a whole bunch of Dangs."

I kept my face neutral. The judge and jury would not be…amused.

"So the lease states that Bitterroot knew it was renting to parents of two six-year-old boys, does it not?"

"I don't know whether Pham and Cao are boys' names. I don't know what kind of names those are."

I looked at him. He was leaning back in his chair, his eyes twinkling through his Eurostyle glasses. "They are Vietnamese names, are they not?"

"Search me," Smalls said.

"But Bitterroot knew it was renting to parents of six-year-old children, isn't that correct?"

"The document speaks for itself," Smalls said, retreating.

"Fair enough, Mr. Smalls, but you did review the lease in preparation for your deposition today. Since you reviewed the lease, can you state yes or no, under penalty of perjury, the lease shows Bitterroot knew it was renting to parents of six-year-old children?"

"Yes, I suppose," he said. I wondered at Sauer's silence. He must be boiling over there.

Nicky tapped my elbow. She wrote, *Sauer's face is red and he keeps flexing his hands.*

I nodded. Never looking at Sauer was crucial. The more I ignored him, the hotter he would boil.

All this was on video and audio too. Eventually a jury was going to see this. Again I wondered what was up with Sauer. Did he have an in with Judge Schifter? Did he have some special relationship with Bitterroot? Was he just trying to impress the insurance company so they would send him more cases that he could over-bill on? What was up?

"Mr. Smalls," I continued, "concerning the pond at Glen Loch that we were discussing, has it ever been fenced off?"

"Objection," Sauer said. "Calls for a legal conclusion. The term 'fenced off' is a term of art and implies a legal obligation that is certainly not present in this case, and therefore the question is grossly improper."

"Hal, please read that question back," I said. Hal read it in his high clear voice. Sometimes witnesses were more likely to answer when they heard the reporter read the question and they realized they were stepping in quicksand.

I looked at Smalls again. "Sir, your answer."

"I'm not aware of any fence adjacent to the pond, at any time," Smalls said. "But if certain people would watch their children it would be a moot point anyhow. This kid slid down the slope into the pond because he wasn't being supervised."

There. Blaming the victim. I liked this. This wouldn't look good at trial for this POS—which is not a legal term of art.

Sauer said, "Off the record."

I said loudly, "NO, we are not going off the record."

I looked at Hal. He nodded.

Sauer jested: "I guess this case involves a slippery slope."

I looked at Sauer for the first time. "Excuse me?"

Sauer was smiling under his brindled mustache, showing his little rat teeth. "I did two tours in Vietnam. It's an inside joke."

I nodded. I kept my voice level. Now I was on to something. "I see, Counsel. Slope being the term that some American soldiers used for Vietnamese people during the Vietnam War."

Sauer spread his hands, the soul of reason. "Hell, it's better than calling them gooks. And this is all off the record."

I regarded him. "As the transcript will show, I never agreed to go off the record. And I never agreed to stop using the term 'dead little boy.' This case involves a little boy who is in fact dead and he was Vietnamese, not a slope." I stared straight into Sauer's face for the first time and I imagined ripping off his head and he knew it. But I stayed quiet and polite.

Sauer stammered. "I'm going to file a motion in limine to prohibit you from using the term 'dead little boy' at trial," he said.

"Bring it on," I said. I let the silence grow. I made a show of looking through my exhibits, just to let it sink in with Sauer and Smalls how far over the line they had gone.

"No further questions," I concluded. "Hal, I need the transcript and audio file. Romeo, please send me the video."

"Wait, what?" asked Smalls.

"You are excused," I said. "Unless Mr. Sauer here wants to ask you any questions."

Sauer looked flummoxed. "No questions. I need a copy. E-transcript and digital file of the video. It's crucial for my motion in limine."

The silence grew in the room. The place was drenched in pheromones—rage and fear.

Smalls gathered his things and left. Nicky tapped my elbow, and I looked at her note: *Did that actually just happen? Holy moly.*

I nodded at her. I loved taking depositions in a flat voice. I loved looking down at my script and exhibits, patiently drilling. I loved it when I stayed calm and the other side got hotter and hotter.

But slippery slope? Holy crap.

I took Nicky, Hal, and Romeo out for coffee afterward. "Okay, my mock jury, what do you think?"

Hal weighed in first. He'd taken countless depositions and had seen some awful attorney behavior. "Bob is overconfident," he said. "Either the fix is in, or he is succumbing to hubris."

"You read my mind, Hal," I said.

"Don't mention it, dear heart."

I turned to Romeo. "Okay Romeo, you're a professional at doing depositions too. What do you think?"

Romeo took out his vape and took a long pull. A question mark of cherry steam wafted away. "Dude, I can't imagine that Sauer doesn't have an ace of spades up his sleeve. Otherwise he wouldn't be pulling this shit."

"Thanks, Romeo, I agree," I said. "There's an ace of spades up his sleeve. I'm wracking my brain, trying to guess what it is. Nicky?"

Nicky stirred her latte, avoiding my eyes. "The best thing about this is you never lost your temper."

"Thanks," I said. "It was hard. My blood pressure nearly made my eyes pop out a couple of times. I can't say dead little boy—when the case is about a dead little boy? And slippery slope? Jesus H. Christ."

Nicky smiled at me. "In the Spanish Civil War, the guerrillas used to say fortify and hold and you will win."

There were many levels to this woman. Her boyfriend Fred was a lucky man.

***

Next I deposed Mr. Bitterroot, the founder and owner. Again it was on video, and again I did it at Sauer's office. Bitterroot Apartments LLC had a huge policy, and I'd gotten it through discovery. The policy required Bitterroot's consent to settle. So I wanted to go straight to the CEO and soften him up.

Mr. Bitterroot turned out to be a tall and trim gentleman in his early sixties, with a silver beard and bushy eyebrows. He dressed in a check shirt and chinos and a down vest. He looked smart and unpretentious. After the usual softball introduction, I got down to the gist. I had the lease marked as Exhibit 1 and asked him to turn to page two.

"Mr. Bitterroot, did your company know when it rented an apartment to the Dangs that they had two six-year-old children?"

"Objection," Sauer snarled. "Calls for a legal conclusion. Notice is a legal requirement in a premises case such as this, and Mr. Strait, you have no right to ask questions establishing that Bitterroot deserves to lose this lawsuit."

I didn't look at Sauer.

But Mr. Bitterroot did. "Relax, Bob," he said. "You already passed the audition."

Aha. Maybe Sauer was hoping to get hired by Bitterroot as in-house counsel. Lots of big firm lawyers dreamed of leaving the world of backstabbing partners and billing extreme hours, and going in-house at a corporation where they would be part of the management team. Where they could stop struggling. Where they could relax and coast. It was a one-way ticket—once you left a big firm and the billable-hours treadmill, you could never come back. But maybe Sauer was angling for that.

I looked at Hal. "Hal, could you read that question back?"

Hal looked down at the screen on his machine. "Mr. Bitterroot, did your company know when it rented an apartment to the Dangs that they had two six-year-old children?"

I looked at Mr. Bitterroot. "Your answer, sir?"

He raised a hand to silence Sauer. "Yes, we knew these tenants had six-year-old children," he said.

"And at any time before Cao Dang's death, was the pond fenced off?"

Again, Mr. Bitterroot raised his hand to silence Sauer. "No, it was not."

Checkmate. That was all I needed to win the case, if the judge wasn't biased or chicken. Also if the jury didn't agree with Smalls that some people just need to watch their children more closely.

We went off the record, and I started packing up. Mr. Bitterroot shook my hand, a friendly gesture. I liked the cut of his jib, actually.

Beside me, Nicky wrote, *Short and sweet.*

There were wheels within wheels here. Maybe Mr. Bitterroot was just being refreshingly honest. Maybe he was throwing his insurance company under the bus so he could wrap up this lawsuit, which had to be hurting his ability to borrow money to buy more property. Lenders hated lending to people in litigation. They never knew how it would turn out.

Maybe it was both. Maybe Mr. Bitterroot was an honest man, and he wanted his insurance company to make this go away so he could borrow without having a cloud over his company's name. The increased interest rates he was paying on loans were probably higher than the premium increase he'd pay if his insurance company made a reasonable settlement.

Also, it looked like he knew Sauer was acting the tough, bitter defense lawyer in hopes of getting a job with him. He had Sauer pegged. He could silence him with a simple gesture.

But why did Sauer seem to think he had an ace of spades up his sleeve?

***

Then I deposed the medical examiner, who confirmed the cause of death and said, "Without fencing, that pond is a death trap." Sauer bellowed about that, but it was on video and in the transcript. Next I deposed the defendant's property management expert witness, who said it wasn't a breach of the standard of care for an owner or property manager to refuse to fence the pond. I didn't mention *Degel v. Majestic Mobile Manor*, which said the owner and property manager were unquestionably required to fence the pond.

Expert witnesses were paid well. Almost every time they said whatever the attorney hiring them wanted them to say. True believers like Don Meissner were unusual.

Then Sauer deposed my property management expert, who said a reasonable owner or manager who knew he had tenant children was definitely required to fence the pond. I'd prepped him well. He also didn't mention *Degel v. Majestic Mobile Manor*.

Then I pulled a fast one.

A Motion for Summary Judgment is a motion filed by either the plaintiff's or defendant's attorney asking the judge to resolve some part, or all, of the case before trial. When there's no "genuine issue of material fact"—no question about what actually happened—summary judgment is authorized, to prevent useless trials over an issue, or even over the whole case.

Either the defendant or the plaintiff can file a Motion for Summary Judgment. But there's law, and then there's custom. Plaintiffs almost never filed the first Motion for Summary Judgment. It was just weird to do that.

I liked weird.

I liked to file a Motion for Summary Judgment of Liability whenever I had a clear shot at proving fault without trial. Defense attorneys sometimes yelled at me for doing that. Cool. The more upset they were, the more I knew I was on to something.

So I filed a Motion for Summary Judgment of Liability. I cited Degel. I used the lease, the Certificate of Death, and excerpts from Mr. Bitterroot's deposition. I argued that Bitterroot knew it was renting to a family with children. I argued that they did not fence off the pond. I argued that this caused the death of Cao Dang.

I kept something in my back pocket—the documents from the King County Recorder that Silent Mike had gotten for me. I suspected Sauer would nitpick about the legal ownership of the pond. I wasn't going to use these documents until my Reply—the final pleading I filed before the hearing. I needed a Sunday punch that Sauer couldn't answer in a pleading.

I always liked having a Sunday punch. Defense attorneys sometimes yelled at me about that, too. But Sauer hadn't asked for discovery of any documents I had concerning property ownership or control. So he'd see it only when it was late in the game.

Sauer filed a Motion to Continue Summary Judgment Hearing, citing Civil Rule 56(f), arguing that he needed more time to "properly address the novel and curious allegations in Plaintiff's Motion." His motion to continue was granted.

Then, when it was twenty-eight days before the new hearing date, he filed a Cross Motion for Summary Judgment of Dismissal.

He had backpedaled so he could sandbag me. This did not shock me.

Sauer argued that we hadn't shown the legal ownership of the pond and therefore we couldn't establish that it was "adjacent to Glen Loch Apartments."

I filed my Reply and a Declaration. The Declaration included the plat map that Silent Bob had gotten for me. It showed that Glen Loch was part of the Lochs Homeowners' Association, which was a separate corporation that owned this pond, and the other canals and ponds. It showed that the pond really was "adjacent"—it was right next to the apartments, with nothing at all in between. Duh. Adjacent.

Then Sauer filed a Motion to Strike, to exclude the plat map claiming it hadn't been disclosed in discovery. I responded with Defendants' Requests for Production showing they'd never asked for my property ownership documents so nothing had been withheld.

This thing was a brawl. I knew what Sauer was doing. He wanted to talk about anything except the dead little boy, and why the little boy was dead.

Then Sauer filed a Motion to Expedite Trial asking for a trial date in thirty days. I huddled with Dr. Dang and Mrs. Dang and filed a Response Agreeing to Expedited Trial Date.

My Spidey-sense told me Sauer was shitting bricks when he got that.

At the hearing Judge Schifter came on the bench after Sauer and I had been waiting nervously for ten minutes. "Mr. Strait, I need to make a disclosure to you," she said, fixing me with her bright gaze. "Mr. Sauer was the chairman of my fundraising committee the last time I ran for re-election. This raises the appearance of a conflict of interest. I need to ask you if you want me to recuse myself from this case."

Fuck.

There was the ace of spades up Sauer's sleeve. He had an in with the judge.

When a judge offers to recuse herself, at least in King County, it's a no-win situation. If I asked her to recuse herself I was basically accusing her of being unfair. The new judge would hear all about it and get mad. I would get booted all over the courtroom by the new judge.

If I didn't ask her to recuse herself I was taking a big gamble that she wasn't biased. But it looked better than the alternative considering I really did like Judge Schifter and I'd had positive interactions with her as a prosecutor.

"I'm sure Your Honor will be fair," I said. "I am not asking you to recuse yourself."

She smiled and nodded. Then Bob Sauer grabbed the initiative and started monologuing.

I watched my watch. Each party had twenty minutes for argument. Almost every lawyer I'd ever met thought he or she had a holy duty to use all their time.

I'd found that less is more. I tried to write taut and meaty briefs, then hit the high points in a couple of minutes of argument…and then shut up and sit down. Judges were astonished and pleased when a lawyer didn't use all the time granted. Their jobs consisted mostly of listening to lots of arm-waving and hyperbole. I never knew how they didn't die of sheer boredom. My simple style made me seem better than I was.

Once Bob had been haranguing for twenty minutes, I said, "Time, Your Honor."

Bob said, "And there's another really crucial policy issue here…"

Judge Schifter raised her hand. "Time, Mr. Sauer."

Seemed like lots of people were raising their hands to get Bob Sauer to shut up. I again remembered Napoleon—never interrupt your opponent when he is making a mistake.

"Mr. Strait," Judge Schifter said, turning to me.

"Thanks, Your Honor. First, the parties concur that setting this case for trial soon is appropriate if the court can find a window for us."

"I concur. My bailiff will be in touch."

"Second, there's no factual dispute that the defendant is liable for negligence. The defendant knew it was renting to tenants with six-year-old children. Their names and ages are on the lease. Defendant's CEO and risk manager both admit that the defendant did not fence off pond adjacent to the apartment complex. The medical examiner's report and Certificate of Death show that this was the only cause of Cao Dang's death, a.k.a. accidental drowning. The defendant is liable as a matter of law. I respectfully suggest that summary judgment for Plaintiff is proper. I cede the rest of my time to the talkative Mr. Sauer."

Then I sat down and took a deep breath. Huh?

Judge Schifter was laughing. "Counselor, that was the shortest and least bloated argument I think I've ever heard," she said, smiling down at the proposed order. "You get points for originality. I'm going to take this under advisement and send my Order by email later this week. I'll include a new trial date. Thanks for a juicy discussion today."

Judge Schifter stood. "All rise!" called her bailiff, a tough sheriff's deputy with a crooked nose. Judge Schifter vanished through her private door in a whirl of black robe.

Sauer was thrusting things into his briefcase. Now I'd seen two aces from his sleeve. He was fighting like a maniac in hopes of getting hired by Bitterroot. He thought he had the edge because he'd been the chair of Judge Schifter's fundraising committee. I wondered what other aces he had.

Then I realized the big one—defensive attribution.

Most people and most jurors like to say they are empathetic. But empathy is overwhelmed by another phenomenon that nobody talks about.

Defensive attribution.

Let's say a man gets mugged and pistol whipped. His friends will make all the right noises, oh man, tough luck dude. But feeling empathy means feeling what the other person actually feels. Empathizing with a victim of violence means you feel the same thing. That's when defensive attribution takes over, to make you feel better. You start thinking, *Man he was stupid going to that neighborhood after dark*, or *How could he not be carrying mace, at least?*

You start creating reasons why this bad thing could never happen to you. This makes you feel safe. This makes you feel better. It ends up with the feeling "sucks to be you."

Not everybody embraces defensive attribution. But in a case with a dead child, some jurors would. Especially parents.

When a child dies, other parents really don't want to know what that is like. So they blame the parents. I was going to focus group the case, but I knew some of what I'd hear already. "Third World parents don't supervise their children," or "Why wasn't the mother keeping a better eye on them?" or even "Why did they rent an apartment at that place to begin with?"

When it is uncomfortable to believe something? Many people just… won't…believe it.

I had a saying that I had shared with The Ghost: "Most people don't want to hear what they don't want to hear." It took a strong person to consider any information that made them uncomfortable. Many people believed obvious absurdities rather than grapple with troubling truths.

Defensive attribution. No matter what aces I flushed out of Bob Sauer's sleeves, that was one I knew was lurking. It was lurking in every courtroom where a personal injury case was tried.

Three days later Judge Schifter denied both Summary Judgment Motions and gave us a trial date just a few weeks away. Well both parties had requested it right?

***

Next came the final flurry of depositions. Mr. and Mrs. Dang held up well. The plaintiff's property management expert testified that the defendant was obligated to fence the pond. The defendant's expert disagreed, but when I confronted him with *Degel v. Majestic Mobile Manor*, he lamely replied, "That's just one case."

"It's the definitive case," I said.

"Objection, objection, objection," Bob Sauer chanted with a dark pink face.

In other words, the experts said what they were paid to say. They almost always do. If you pay an "expert witness" enough, he or she will testify that the moon's made of green cheese, and it is yummy.

Our economist testified that Cao was likely to become either a doctor or physician assistant, and he calculated lifetime lost accumulations—earnings minus expenses—of half a million, assuming he topped out as a physician assistant in a primary care practice. He'd have four times that much if he became a primary care physician. Just for laughs, he also gave figures for if he'd become a radiologist. Radiologists make crazy money. It was approximately a bazillion dollars. To use a term of art.

The defendant's economist assumed he'd top out as an assistant manager at a fast food restaurant, etcetera, etcetera.

Then we went to mediation.

The defendants hadn't offered a nickel. I thought mediation was useless. But the King County Local Rules required attending a mediation. I booked a four-hour session—the minimum—with Will Szalak, an eighty-year-old retired plaintiffs' lawyer that I'd had good luck with before. Bob Sauer agreed to split the fee fifty-fifty.

The defendant didn't make an offer before mediation, so I didn't either. I'd had a long talk with the Dangs over tea at their new apartment. I had my authority to settle. I finally talked them up—not down—to two million. My research on Jury Verdicts Northwest showed that was a good but not great verdict for a death of a six-year-old boy from a productive family with minimal comparative fault attributed to the parents.

We also agreed that we would discount this up to two hundred thousand dollars if Bitterroot would simply fence the damn pond.

Will Szalak worked with the big and glamorous mediation firm. He had the initial huddle with me and the Dangs, without Bob or the adjuster present. "This is an odd one, Sam," he said, leafing through my mediation statement. "I don't usually see a death case with no pre-mediation offer from the defense. And you haven't made an opening demand either."

"Will, it's a fatality slip and fall," I said. "There's been some pretty serious misconduct by the other side. But we'll make an opening offer." I paused and looked at the Dangs. "We'll accept $4,800,000. That's our opener. We'll offer a discount if they fence the pond with a six-foot-high chain link fence within thirty days."

Will scribbled furiously. "It's a start," he said. "The adjuster wants a meet and greet. I like the fence idea. Trying to fix the problem, huh? Okay, let's shake hands."

"Fine," I said.

He left and came back with Bob Sauer and the adjuster, an obese woman with dark circles under her eyes wearing a frumpy brown polyester suit. Where did they get these adjusters? They all looked like they came from a factory labeled as Depressed Worthless Functionaries. The adjuster said hi to the Dangs and shook their hands. "I'm deeply sorry for your loss," she said, with patent insincerity.

"Meet and greet adjourned," I said, ushering them out. Bob flashed me a snide smile, showing his rat teeth.

"Okay," said Will, returning. "Now I give them your opener. Can I give a hint about how much room to move you have?"

"Sorry, no," I said. "They have to put some amount of money on the table first."

He was gone for an hour. It's usual gamesmanship for the defendant to burn a lot of time before responding to the plaintiff's opener. I wasn't concerned. I'd bet we were going to trial.

After an hour, Will returned. "I need to see you alone, in the defendants' room," he told me. Mrs. Dang nodded. Outside the door, Will said, "Whatever you do, don't get mad." His wintery blue eyes gleamed under his shock of snow-white hair.

"I won't get mad, Will," I said. "Because nothing these people do could surprise me."

I was wrong.

The adjuster was playing with her laptop and she didn't look up. Her brown suit fell in wrinkles around her sweaty folds of fat. Bob motioned me to sit.

"Your opener," I said to Bob.

He sneered. "Your case sucks," he said. "I'll offer you my Superman #51 comic book in mint condition. It's got to be worth a couple grand."

I looked at Will Szalak. He nodded. That's what Bob had said to him too.

What the actual fuck.

"See you in court, Mr. Sauer," I said in a quiet tone. I went back to the Dangs.

By 11:45 AM, with fifteen minutes left, they were up to twenty thousand, offered by the adjuster, after Bob Sauer told Will Szalak that he would not participate in giving any money for such a frivolous case.

Will called me into his office, alone. I hate to do anything outside of the clients' sight, but Will Szalak was good people. "What can I do for you?" I asked him. I'd have liked to be Will Szalak's associate, rather than Rodney Mammon's associate.

"I never said this, and this conversation never happened," Will said to me with his wintry half smile.

"Agreed."

"Hammer them."

***

After the mediation I sent what I call a "punch through" letter to the adjuster, and to Bob Sauer to submit to Bitterroot. I said that Bob had offered a comic book to settle this death of a child case. I said Bob was forcing me to obtain a judgment against Bitterroot. I said it was legal malpractice and insurance bad faith to do this. I told Bob in the cover letter that he must provide it to Bitterroot or he would be violating the Rules of Professional Conduct, and would be committing legal malpractice.

Wonder of wonders, he did send it onward to Bitterroot Apartments LLC.

Five days after I sent the punch through letter, I got a Notice of Association from Bitterroot's VP for Legal Affairs, Mel Bitterroot. I looked him up. He was a current member of the Bar, and a former insurance defense attorney. He was also the brother of Hank Bitterroot, the CEO.

I started sending everything to Mel Bitterroot that I sent to Bob Sauer.

A crack had appeared in the defense team's facade. I wanted to jam my best arguments into that crack and split it open.

I huddled with Duvonda and we worked over my trial script. "There's a likelihood of a defense verdict," she said, finishing her mocha. She got a droplet on her leopard print top and brushed it away. She looked troubled. I felt damn lucky to have a friend like this.

"I know," I said, with my head in my hands. "But do you remember *To Kill A Mockingbird*?" She nodded. "Atticus Finch said when he took the Tom Robinson case that every lawyer gets a case in his lifetime that he can't turn down, or he will never be able to look at himself in the mirror or correct his children. This one is mine."

She carefully set down her cup. "You call me if you're getting your ass kicked," she growled. "I'll feed you a pocket brief or a new line of questioning if you need it."

"The water's getting awful deep," I said. "I hope I don't let these people down."

She regarded me. "Sam, we can't guarantee we win. We can only guarantee we deserve to win. Be the most honest person in the courtroom. Then you deserve to win."

I promised. When I left her building and was walking across the courtyard, I noticed that Street Monkey, the homeless junkie with dreadlocks in the orange jumpsuit, had a new sign—*I Need To Get Really High*. I laughed. "That makes two of us, buddy," I said, smiling at him.

***

At trial our first battle was about jury instructions. I got a custom instruction restating the rule in *Degel v. Majestic Mobile Manor*: *Where a landlord knows it is renting to tenants with children, the landlord is required to fence off adjoining bodies of water so the children do not drown. Failure to do so is negligence.*

Bob Sauer threw everything but his lunch into the argument. Judge Schifter was not amused, and she silenced him.

But on the comparative fault instruction, I lost. She approved an instruction stating that where parents fail to supervise their children, they bear comparative fault for injuries sustained by them.

I threw everything but my lunch into stopping that, and Judge Schifter silenced me too. In all honesty I deserved to lose that. The jury was entitled to consider fault of the parents.

Bob Sauer actually did file a motion in limine prohibiting me from using the phrase "dead little boy."

Judge Schifter looked at me. "Counsel?"

"Your Honor, this case involves a six-year-old male, who is deceased. Therefore it does involve a dead little boy. Evidentiary rulings are vested in the sound discretion of the trial judge and will only be overturned for abuse of discretion. But granting this motion actually would be an abuse of discretion."

"I agree," she said, as Bob spluttered. "Motion denied."

***

Mel Bitterroot turned out to be a tall, very thin man in his early seventies with a shaved head and an eagle eye. He reminded me of Will Szalak. He'd seen a thing or two, and he hadn't forgotten any of it.

He attended the whole trial. So did the adjuster, wearing a different frumpy suit to conceal her beanbag-chair-shaped body each day. They never spoke. I sensed tension between them.

Duvonda had reminded me, "When you're picking your jury, pick your foreperson of the jury. Try to get somebody on the panel who's your kind of person and also a natural leader."

My foreperson was a woman in her early forties with dazzling green eyes and a sassy brunette bob who supervised a group of therapeutic foster homes for The Halsey Foundation. I'd heard great things about their foster homes. They were better than the one I grew up in, for certain.

A two-week wrongful death trial is a war. It would take a whole other book to tell you about the trial of *Estate of Dang v. Bitterroot Apartments LLC*. I'll just give you the moments that still shine so many years later:

Hank Bitterroot on the stand, wearing a plaid wool shirt, saying to the Dangs, "I really am sorry you lost your little boy."

The defendant's economist, a pencil-necked accountant in a bow tie, testifying, "Yes, Cao Dang's parents are healthcare professionals. He's a pharmacist and she is a registered nurse. But Cao likely would have topped out as the equivalent to a middle manager at a fast-food restaurant." And I replied, "And that's based on the size of the check you received from Defendant's counsel?" And the jury laughing.

Mrs. Dang saying on the witness stand, "I think I watching both boys, but I was only watching one boy and they wearing same clothing." She paused, and almost started crying, which was earthshaking, given her iron self-control. She gulped. "But they should have fenced the pond. The law say that." I looked over at the jury, and my imaginary foreperson nodded, her brown bob shining under the fluorescent lights.

Then I put Pham Dang on the witness stand. Bob and I had a furious argument over that in recess, as Judge Schifter watched. Bottom line? If Pham could tell the difference between the truth and a lie, and describe why lying was bad, he would be qualified to testify.

Judge Schifter allowed Pham to testify about the threshold questions regarding whether he qualified as a witness with the jury present. This could be reversible error. By this point I suspected she wanted a different chairman for her fundraising committee next time she ran for re-election.

Pham qualified to testify.

"Do you remember your brother Cao?" I asked him.

"I still remember him. I am saving my favorite toys, some toys, for when he comes back," Pham said, tugging at his little clip-on tie. "But I know he's not coming back."

There was a rustle from the jury box. You don't look at the jury when you're getting this amazing stuff. You listen, instead.

"What was the biggest difference between you two?" I asked. I was trying a simple bank shot, as Duvonda, an avid pool player, would say. The jury sometimes suspected that what lawyers presented was the opposite of the truth. I was planting in their heads that these were identical twins. There once were two of them, and now there was only one.

I was putting a ghost on the stand.

Duvonda had loved this idea. "But it's risky, Sam," she'd said. "A cynical juror will think they still have one of these boys. But decent jurors will realize there should be two."

Pham tugged at his little tie again. "Pham, if you like, you can take off your tie," I said. "Your Honor?"

"I'll allow it," Judge Schifter said. She was engrossed, too.

Pham handed me his little tie, and I put it in my pocket. "I'll give it back to you later when we go for chocolate milk," I told him.

"Objection," said Bob Sauer. "Is there a question in here somewhere?"

It was a technically valid objection. From a tactical perspective, it was stupid. I noticed Mel Bitterroot looking down and scowling. Bob had hoped to replace Mel. I guessed that was off the table now.

Judge Schifter overruled the objection. Apparently, chocolate milk was not objectionable.

"So, what was the biggest difference between you and your brother, Pham?"

Pham unbuttoned his collar. He looked tiny on the stand, in that big oak chair, surrounded by the big oak lower bench. "He liked stories and poems. He liked exploring. I like science and math. I want to know if something is true. Not if something is interesting, like he did."

My God.

I'd done a simple prep with him. But I hadn't heard this stuff before.

I most remember one thing I said in closing argument. "There should be two of these boys," I told the jury, focusing on my imaginary foreperson. "But there is only one. You've heard from Pham. I wish you could hear from Cao. You can't. But I ask that the defendant hear from you."

I most remember Bob Sauer's one argument. "This is a tragedy, but the Phams should have been watching their children, and no amount of money will make up for the harm they themselves caused. To themselves." He was going for an outright defense verdict, all right.

The jury deliberated for four days. I was useless at the office. Nicky put papers under my nose, and I signed them after a glance. Most of the time I chewed antacids and stared out the window at the trees as the yellow and orange autumn leaves whipped away in the wind. It was past Halloween and I'd done nothing but this case for three months. Because we'd gotten an insanely early trial date it was all over but the torture of waiting for the verdict.

The jury awarded five million dollars, reduced by five percent for the comparative negligence of the parents. It turned out my imaginary foreperson was the real foreperson. When I talked to her after the verdict was read, she said, "We had one stick in the mud. So we had to give him something."

When I walked out of the courthouse into the usual crowd of homeless drug addicts, I was filled with exultation. "Well, you can't beat that with a stick," I said loudly.

"True dat, brother," the fat woman wearing the filthy Pepsi Challenge T-shirt said, showing her few and bad teeth. The junkies laughed and puffed on their roll-your-own cigarettes.

I patted the verdict form in my pocket and walked back to the office. When I got back, Nicky scrutinized me. "So, how did it go?"

I didn't say anything. Because I couldn't say anything.

I walked into my office, stood in the window, and did The Crane.

Nicky said over my shoulder. "Good news?"

Still balanced on one foot, I handed her the verdict form.

"That's what I'm TALKING about," she cried, running off to Rodney's office.

Bitterroot had a ten-million-dollar general liability policy. Unless the defendant got this overturned on appeal, the verdict would be paid in full from insurance. And I would have earned Rodney $1,600,000. Which was twenty years of my base salary. I still wasn't getting my promised profit sharing.

I wasn't going to let Rodney weasel out of profit sharing any longer.

My door opened, and I smelled Rodney's sandalwood cologne behind me. Still doing The Crane, I looked at him over my shoulder. "Bro, you just won the Super Bowl," Rodney said, nodding with his gel-stiffened porcupine hair.

"I want my profit sharing, Rodney," I said. "I want to start receiving it within thirty days. I could get a better job now. I'm a profit center, and you should keep me."

Rodney's eyes glazed over. "Be that as it may," he said.

***

Bob Sauer filed a Notice of Appeal, of course. But then the worm really turned.

I noted up a Hearing On Fee Request, asking for attorney fees from Bob Sauer and his firm on several grounds. First, Bob had denied a bunch of Requests for Admission, and I'd spent many hours disproving these denials. Bitterroot didn't sign the denials and did not know about them. Second, Bob had violated Civil Rule 11, by engaging in frivolous litigation, multiple times. A motion in limine saying I couldn't say "dead little boy?" That was just sad. Third, I just had to throw in my Declaration Regarding Counsel Misconduct. That's where I described his "slippery slope" joke, his offer of a Superman comic to settle this death of a child case, and his other hijinks. That shit was napalm.

Judge Schifter awarded me $680,000 to be paid solely by Bob Sauer personally. At the hearing, Bob Sauer grimaced, showing his little rat teeth.

After some invisible fighting between Bitterroot and the insurance company, which I sensed but never got involved with, the insurance company offered us $4,500,000 to settle. Plus, payment of my entire fee award. The Dangs approved if Bitterroot would finally fence the damned pond. I conveyed that. Bitterroot refused. How stupid. They could protect themselves from another lawsuit, and it was necessary. Blind stubbornness, that's all.

The Dangs and I had a serious discussion. I countered that we would take $100,000 less if we got written permission to fence the pond ourselves. Again, Bitterroot refused. By this time, I was grinding my teeth to stumps.

Finally, the Dangs directed me to accept the money. I'd done everything but the Hula to get the pond fenced. I had struck out. What an idiotic defendant. Probably another kid had a date with the pond.

There was one condition which I was delighted to agree to. "Plaintiff's counsel will render all material assistance to Bitterroot and Insurer in pursuing the legal malpractice case against Robert Sauer and his law firm."

Done and done.

I got an award from the Trial Lawyers' Association. That stuff embarrassed me. I gave a very short speech at one of the self-congratulatory awards luncheons they gave. I said, "I want to thank my clients and my friends. None of us in court ever goes in there alone."

Then I sat down. I hated long-windedness. Judges liked that. Audiences liked that. Nobody needed to be drowned in rhetoric when they were trying to simply understand something.

Afterward, I mingled and collected a lot of cards. I suspected Rodney would never pay me my profit sharing unless I left his firm, and I sued him, and I won. I was thinking about doing just that.

But it was very unlikely that a firm would hire me and Nicky both. Do you see the symmetry here? I had to behave myself at the Malletts' Therapeutic Foster Home to stay with Catherine. Now I had to accept Rodney cheating me of a fortune to stay with Nicky. I was vulnerable to hostage-taking—both times.

Did that mean I thought of Nicky as my sister? Oh no. I thought of her as the one worthwhile single woman that I'd met in Seattle since my law school girlfriend, Suzanne. But Nicky wasn't single. Her boyfriend Fred was a lucky man.

Still, I didn't want to abandon Nicky.

***

The Dangs bought a modest house outright with their recovery. No mortgage. It was a well-kept split level in Lynnwood, just north of Seattle. They invited me to see it one Sunday afternoon.

I took them a badminton set. "When I was young, I loved badminton," I explained. Pham drilled me with questions about the rules as I set up the net. Then we played three games. Pham was agile and fast. I didn't let him win. But he won one of the three games.

As I was getting into my car, his mother whispered in Pham's ear, and he came up to me. "Mr. Strait, my mother says I should give this to you," Pham said, looking down, suddenly shy.

He held out his hands. It was a Hot Wheels car—The Batmobile.

"Thank you, Pham," I said. "This is very kind of you."

"It was Cao's favorite car," Pham said, bravely looking at me.

"I will keep it on my desk from now until the end of my career," I said.

I have. It's here right now. No sane person gets rid of The Batmobile.

As I started my car, I looked at the Phams on their front porch, waving. Nothing could give them a happy ending. But I'd gotten them as close as any lawyer ever could. They would never have a landlord again. Also, they had put the balance of the money into a mutual fund account for Pham. He was excellent at math, testing four grades above his age.

They planned for him to be a doctor. Probably someday, he would resuscitate a drowned little boy. Circle of life.

I looked at myself in the rearview mirror. I was just some dude. I was nobody special. But I'd been part of a special thing.

In my best gravelly voice, I said, "I'm Batman." Then I drove home, drenched with some emotion I can't name even now. Call it All The Emotions Combined.

Was there a Heaven where Cao Dang and Pham Dang could play Hot Wheels again? I had no idea. I hoped so…but hope is not a strategy.

You couldn't pay me enough to change careers. I was born to be a plaintiffs' personal injury lawyer. I still am one today. This is what I was made for.

Maybe it was time to see Abe Aschmann and see about installing another layer of bulletproof glass. Maybe it was time to go on TopFliteSingles.com and see if my luck had changed.

CHAPTER FIFTEEN—THE MEAT OF THE TOMATO

During the Slippery Slope case, Abe Aschmann emailed me to set the next session. I had to tell him I was immersed in a True Disaster. Then he sent an email with a curious assignment: *Write down the three most ugly beliefs you have about yourself and your life. It doesn't matter if they are objectively true or even intellectually plausible. Just pick the ugly ones. We're going to get into the meat of the tomato.*

For three months until the end of the Slippery Slope case, this simmered in the back of my mind. When I got the verdict and then the settlement, it was late fall. Halloween had come and gone; Thanksgiving was coming up. Fallen brown leaves swirled like little brown hands in vortexes of cold wind. Canadian geese trumpeted regrets as they fled south.

One night, I drove the battered Outback home under velvet-blue sky; the forecast called for mid-twenties and light snow. When I got home I poured a shot of Jack Daniels and wrote my list. I had lots of dumb and ugly beliefs about myself, but I narrowed it down to three.

1) If I'd done something different, my parents wouldn't have died. Their deaths were my fault.

2) Nobody would be my friend if they really knew me.

3) I'm not married or in a relationship because I don't want to poison a woman with too much of myself.

Each time I read one of these aloud, my stomach hurt. Hypothesis confirmed. I took a long hot shower, curled up in new flannel sheets with blue polar bears on them, and let the Jack Daniels take me into the Land of Nod.

I have vivid dreams every night, and I usually remember them. But next morning, all I remembered was my childhood home smelling like rotten eggs and roadkill, my parents' tombstones engraved with IT's SAM's FAULT, and my friends giving me a lie detector test and then turning away. In disgust. All of them—The Ghost, Duvonda, Silent Mike, Fabulous Hal, Nicky, even Romeo Pursuit.

I had my three ugly beliefs.

That morning, we got about an inch of snow. Seattle turned crisp and white and black and scintillating. I loved breathing air so cold it almost hurt. I loved icy air on my skin, outlining what was me and excluding what was not me. Late in the afternoon, an ice moon capsized over the Olympic Mountains as I ran up the steps of the undamaged Alamo and reached Abe Aschmann's office. Best advice I ever got when I was in the Coast Guard?

Embrace the suck.

If you have to confront something difficult, speed up and hit it full force. Flinching makes it worse.

I hoped we were going to put something behind bulletproof glass. I was wrong.

Abe handed me a matching homemade mug full of decaf market spice and I smelled cloves and cinnamon and maybe the bazaar of Marrakech. Abe said: "Tonight we're going to get into the meat of the tomato." He sat and pushed up the sleeves on his sweater. This gesture meant he was ready to grapple with something. As an orphan I was always ready to have a pseudo-dad, a pseudo-mom, any nonrelated family members who might offer nourishment. The flip side of my rescuer complex?

I was needy. I was ashamed of it. Still am, in fact.

Abe asked: "Remember that we agreed to do some cognitive behavioral therapy, in addition to the EMDR?"

"Sure." The clock behind my head ticked like a metronome.

"Okay. When I was getting my Psy.D., my faculty advisor liked to talk about getting into the meat of the tomato. He was the best cognitive guy I ever knew. He had known Albert Ellis the cognitive pioneer, and also Victor Frankl, the author of *Man's Search for Meaning* and founder of logotherapy. Remember when I assigned you that book, early on? Well my advisor occasionally tried something called extreme cognitive therapy. That's what we're going to do tonight."

"I brought the list," I said.

"Fair enough. But first, please tell me about this red-hot case you were obsessed with the past few months."

I gave him the two-dollar summary of the Slippery Slope case.

He winced at several points. When Abe listened there was body language to it.

"As you say, that was a True Disaster."

"It was," I said.

"So now you're at a good point to get into the meat of the tomato. What's your first ugly belief? Read it loud and proud."

I cleared my throat. "If I'd done something different, my parents wouldn't have died. Their deaths were my fault."

He nodded. It sounded like an indictment.

"Nobody would be my friend if they really knew me," I said.

Again he nodded. I looked in his eyes, and I could see him combining things at impossible speed.

"I don't have a long-term relationship because I never wanted to poison a woman with too much of myself," I concluded.

His eyes met mine. Diagnosis confirmed. "Do these statements torment you when you read them aloud?"

"Yes," I said. I took a big swig of market spice tea.

Abe leaned forward with his elbows on his knees, sitting the way I was sitting. I knew he was mirroring my body language to tighten the bond. Mirroring worked even when you noticed it. I sometimes did it in depositions.

"Now we're getting somewhere. Let's take number one, your parents' deaths. Do you believe that it's factually, literally true that your parents deaths are your fault?"

"I know it's not true," I murmured, "but I am convinced that it's true."

"Aha," Abe said. "Nicely done. You have identified a belief that you are convinced of, even though your cerebral cortex denies that. That's the meat of the tomato—the irrational conviction. Let's unpack that one a little bit. Have you ever heard of defensive attribution?"

I nodded. "Totally. Defensive attribution is when jurors, or anybody, blames the victim of a tragedy. So they can reassure themselves that the tragedy couldn't have happened to them. It's a form of cognitive distancing. If empathy makes you feel sad or endangered then you don't indulge empathy. My mentor Duvonda calls it the Sucks To Be You Syndrome."

"Full marks," Abe said. "Have you ever considered that you are also engaging in defensive attribution?"

Weird. "I'm sorry but I don't see that yet."

Abe leaned farther forward. "Psychoanalysts and psychodynamic therapists would turn aside right here. But with cognitive therapy, we try to actively assist our clients. That's one reason why, to toot my own horn, it's faster and more effective. You believe that if you had done something differently, your parents would still be alive. You said their deaths were your fault."

"I did." I drank more of my tea while my mind scrambled to get this like a dog trying to run on ice.

"I want you to lean back and close your eyes."

I did. Stronger smell of cloves. Louder ticking from the metronome clock.

"I want to put you back in Trooper Jorgensen's car. Catherine is screaming. She is trying to get out, but there are no door handles. You are frozen."

I was right there. The smell of rotten eggs and roadkill. Even though Abe had put me through EMDR in this scene, I could still replay it like a film. But now I didn't get flooded.

Abe said, "Deep down…in the marrow of your bones…as you are in this situation… Do you believe you are actually in control of this situation?"

I sat bolt upright and opened my eyes. "No! That's what's so horrible about it! I'm helpless!"

"There it is," Abe said, pointing. "You were helpless. But your belief says that it was your fault." He waited. I felt a weird shiver. "You believe you caused it because acknowledging your powerlessness feels worse. But that's the bedrock truth. You were helpless. It wasn't your fault."

He paused, letting this sink in. "You are spending a significant amount of effort in your life to avoid ever being powerless again. That's fine. That's what healthy adults do. So just let yourself admit that you were powerless when your parents died. Sit back again and close your eyes again."

I complied.

"You are in Trooper Jorgensen's patrol car. Catherine has begun banging her head against the window, screaming for Trooper Jorgensen to let her out. You're frozen. But it doesn't matter whether you've frozen, or not. You can't get out of the car. There are no door handles in the back seat. You are a seven-year-old orphan. The world can wallop you without any warning. Do you see how that applies to your life now?"

My jaw dropped. "My whole career is showing up for people who got walloped without any warning. Helpless people." I was breathing hard. "I keep rescuing Catherine and myself, again and again. God damn. This is what Freudians call a repetition compulsion, isn't it?"

I opened my eyes. Abe was smiling at me. He was an active therapist—he coaxed, he prodded, and he smiled too. "Your parents' death just wasn't your fault, Sam," he murmured. The clock said tick. Tick.

But the stupid conviction in my skull writhed like a dying snake. I'd rather accept blame for my parents' death than admit I'd been helpless. Tick. Tick.

"It wasn't your fault," Abe repeated.

The snake kept writhing. It thrashed around every time Abe said that.

"It wasn't your fault," Abe said. Again the snake.

"It wasn't your fault," Abe said.

Suddenly I was doubled over, gasping for breath, crying a little. The dying snake writhed inside my skull.

I remembered in an early session I'd told Abe: "If I let myself start crying, I might never stop."

He had said, "You will stop. It's physically impossible to cry for more than an hour. The body has a self-correcting mechanism, Sam, like the keel on a sailboat. When it tips over too far, it brings itself level again."

I sat up.

And now? I sat back as quiet inside as Abe's office with the metronome clock and the smell of cloves. Damn. The snake had died and nothing remained. Tick. Tick.

Abe handed me a box of tissues. "Class dismissed," he said, grinning. "Keep that list. We'll tackle the other two beliefs another time. Killing one of these snakes is enough for one evening."

"That's just what it felt like," I said. "Like a snake writhing around thrashing inside my skull each time you told me it wasn't my fault. How the hell did you know it felt like a dying snake?"

He patted me on the shoulder. "I had my own snakes to kill, Sam."

I blushed. How dumb could I get? Of course he'd been down this road. That's how he knew the way out.

At the door, Abe said, "Sam, we're getting there."

On the street my battered Outback had a half inch of fresh snow, and more swirled and spun in the streetlight. Magnificent. I'd never seen such…intricate snow before. When I turned on the Outback I noticed frost flowers on the windshield. Each different, sharp-edged, intricate. I could see better without that snake in my head.

As I made progress, I was going to learn what the world actually looked like.

Now I understood why Catherine had recommended him.

I was glad I'd done everything necessary to stay with Catherine at the Malletts' Therapeutic Foster Home.

We'll get to that soon.

CHAPTER SIXTEEN—UNBEFITTING

After my breakthrough with Abe Aschmann, with my new clear vision, I decided to give TopFliteSingles.com one last try. Maybe I'd meet somebody good. Maybe I'd just discover a new kind of weirdness.

After my law school girlfriend Suzanne went back to New Jersey I felt like somebody had ripped off my arm. For weeks I limped around saying nothing to anybody about any possible thing. Staying mute can work, short term. Then I cut my hair shorter, started running longer distances, and used my career as general anesthesia. Work was great—when you do the right stuff, you'll probably get a reward. Romance for me was a minefield—don't step on the invisible explodey things and you might possibly get through it. The cost-benefit analysis leaned far in the direction of workaholism.

But it'd been years and years. Now that I had clear cognitive vision, maybe it would be all different.

I'd gotten good advice about how to meet good women from Duvonda and from The Ghost. They told me to take a partner dancing class, join Meetup.com, even take a writing class. They knew I loved smart women who liked books, who liked dancing, who could make actual friends with actual face-to-face interactions. That's a lot of actuals, isn't it?

I did precisely none of those things. Maybe once Abe Aschmann and I got past the Malletts' Therapeutic Foster Home I'd start doing what the smartest women I knew actually recommended.

Ergo, one last online date.

This time I matched with a WASPy brunette with horn-rimmed glasses named Margaret. She'd been to Harvard and had an MBA from Wharton. She sounded like she'd had an actual rigorous education. It was clear she was smart. All that remained was to see if she was compatible.

Yeah, right.

So we planned to meet at the inevitable Boring Green Coffee chain café on First Hill.

First Hill was called "Pill Hill" because it was the hospital district.

That night was windy and cold, the last autumn leaves fleeing. I parked close by under a streetlight, by four tents and a tarp and an RV with *Ice Ice Baby* spray-painted on the side. Not promising.

The café had precisely zero customers. Just five baristas in Boring Green Coffee aprons behind the counter. Not even mood music. My last online date would take place before a live barista audience.

At 7:01 Margaret breezed in wearing a black trench coat over a fire-engine-red skirted suit, her brunette hair wind-tousled. Punctuality. Nice. I always left if an online date was more than fifteen minutes late. That kind of manipulation signaled nothing good about the woman.

I stood and shook her hand. Firm grip. Again nice. "I'm Margaret," she said. Husky alto voice, like a shot of good whiskey.

"Sam Strait," I said.

She cocked her head. "Straight? Glad we got that out of the way." Pleasant laugh, a low ripple.

She sat down and smiled faintly at me. "So what's your occupation, Sam Strait?"

I glanced at the idle baristas. "Can I get you a drink?"

"Let's play it out," she said. Brisk. Efficient. This one turned into a "job interview date" right away. "What kind of work do you do?"

"I'm a personal injury litigator."

"Ah. Lawyer. I'm a management consultant. Who do you work for?"

"I'm the personal injury litigator for Rodney Mammon's firm."

Margaret flinched. "Rodney Mammon? I met him. Through TopFliteSingles.com."

"Care to share?"

She looked over both shoulders. I sensed the baristas listening. "Sam? Rodney Mammon is a freakazoid. Probable psychopath. Into club drugs. I wouldn't leave my drink unattended around that guy. And the gel in the hair? And the Maserati? I think not."

Freakazoid. Good word for what I already knew.

"Well I'm not like that," I stammered.

Margaret examined me, her red nails drumming on the table top. "So you aren't into club drugs too? And you're not a freakazoid?"

"Definitely not. My drug of choice is victory," I said evenly.

"Hah! Nicely said. So where do you see yourself in five years?"

Job interview date, all right. But it was a good question. "Well I'll definitely still be suing people who hurt other people. But I'll probably have opened my own practice by then. I just got a pretty big verdict."

She clicked her nails again. I noticed she was wearing a Harvard signet ring. Well of course she was.

I cleared my throat. "How about you? What do you do for a living?"

"I rationalize workflow processes for Fortune 500 companies to cut overhead and plump up the bottom line." Efficient woman, all right.

"So where do you see yourself in five years, Margaret?"

Again with the crab fingernails. "I'm going to make partner. By then I will have married an alpha male and we'll probably be expecting our first child." I hypothesized she already had an Excel spreadsheet for all of this.

She scowled. She stuck out her hand. I shook hands with her again.

"Sam, I don't sense a fit," she said.

Then she walked out.

Rude? Yes, but I was relieved. She had all the charm of a surgical scalpel. I would never have kissed this woman, because I would be afraid of losing my tongue.

As I always thought after a TopFliteSingles.com date, I thought I was better off alone than with this particular specimen of female.

I realized I was avoiding romance with online dating.

Once, Duvonda said something very Zen to me: "The problem with a placeholder is it holds a place." Now I got it. I had to allow the vacuum to hurt. Then I'd find a way to actually fill it with an actual worthwhile woman.

I'd been sitting with my head in my hands. I looked up at the counter. All five baristas in their green aprons were staring at me. "Dude, that was ice cold," said the huge barista with the neck beard.

I asked. "Could you give me a free water? I need something to put out these flames."

They laughed. I laughed.

I wondered which "club drugs" Rodney was taking. What was that pill he'd dropped—which now sat in my safe?

I put two dollars in the tip jar, and the lead barista winked at me and said, "Thanks for the unintentional entertainment."

I started my battered Outback and turned on the defroster. I'd gotten one thing out of this dismissive non-date. I'd decided to start my own law practice.

CHAPTER SEVENTEEN—THE TRUTH WILL OUT

A few days later I called Rachel Vandermixz to find out how she was doing in the aftermath of the Kentucky Ass-Whipping case. "So how are you holding up?" I wondered.

"For the first couple of weeks I just moped around the house. But then I took Mad Bastard out off-roading. You should try off-roading sometime."

"You know what? I will."

"But Buster just sits there looking bedraggled. Hey Sam—would you like to adopt a slightly used parrot?"

"Hell yes," I blurted out. The idea tickled me—coming home to my anonymous condo with an actual life form in it. Maybe I could teach him to say something other than "well dog my cats."

"Then come on down this Saturday. He kinda reminds me of Mom, you know? You'll appreciate him more than I do."

I drove down the next Saturday under a cloud layer and drizzle. "Rain changing to showers," the radio meteorologist said.

"That's not a change," I muttered. We'd just entered the eight-month gloom period that hits Seattle every October or early November. We got two or three sunny days a month and everybody put on sunglasses, went for long strolls on Alki Beach or around Green Lake. We all thought *This isn't so bad.* Then the gloom came down for another several weeks. Our optimism was as misplaced as Charlie Brown trying to kick the football while Lucy held it.

When I got to Rachel's house she welcomed me with a brief hug. I was ashamed—if she could shake off losing her Mom, I could shake off losing her Mom's case.

Rachel said, "Now here's the big cage with all the toys and water and food and the ropes of seeds. Here's extra food. Here's the cover for the cage—you have to cover it at night so he knows it's time to sleep. Otherwise he caws and squawks in the night. And here's Buster in his travel cage."

I knelt by the travel cage and Buster cocked his head at me. "I'm going to adopt you, buddy," I said. "I'm going to feed you great food and teach you cuss words."

Buster said, "Well, dog, my cats," showing his black tongue, then preened his yellow vest and stretched his emerald-green wings.

"He's probably got another eighty years to live," Rachel said. "I'm glad he's getting a good home." We loaded everything into my battered Outback. Rachel held me at arm's length and said: "My mom taught me this—if you never surrender, you're never defeated."

"That's good advice," I said.

As I drove north in the drizzle, Buster kept meeting my eyes from the travel cage in the rearview mirror. "Hey Buster," I said. "Today is the first day of the rest of your life."

"Yack," Buster replied. Valid criticism, actually.

***

The next day I took Duvonda out for Indian food to thank her for basically everything. "Sam, if that Slippery Slope fee was yours it would support you for years," she said. "Your Auntie Duvonda thinks it's time to set up your own practice." I knew she was right but I needed a boot in the butt from life first.

When I got back to Mammon & Associates I heard raised voices coming from the Innocent Peoples' Department. As I walked back, a wave of gardenia perfume hit me, making my eyes water.

A fiftyish woman with long black hair, wearing a green velvet robe, was leaning over Nicky's desk. "You don't understand! The entire Soul Retrieval industry is experiencing a seasonal recession," she declared, waving her hands. Her hands with costume-jewelry rings on all ten talon-like fingers.

Nicky said, "I'm at work, Mother." She saw me behind Priestess Esmerelda and blushed.

Priestess Esmerelda whirled and looked me up and down, her pupils pinpoint-sized. I wondered if she was off her Lithium. She crossed her arms and said, "You must be Sam Strait the ambulance-chaser who runs my daughter ragged."

I squinted at her. "You must be Nicky's emotionally abusive mother," I said. I saw Nicky clap a hand over her mouth so she wouldn't laugh.

Priestess Esmerelda chortled. "Nicky's never too busy to see her mother. She only has one mother. I just swung by to ask her to spot me a couple hundred."

I glanced at Nicky. She kept blushing. I said, "If I read Nicky's body language correctly she doesn't want to spot you a couple hundred. And you're not a client or an invited guest. So I'll walk you out." I nearly choked on the cloud of gardenia perfume; my eyes watered.

Priestess Esmerelda said, "She did not speak. Did you, Icky?"

I went nose to nose with Priestess Esmerelda; the gardenia perfume nearly choked me. "Madam, you are not to call my beloved assistant Icky. If you don't walk out with me, right now, I'll call the police. And they will walk you out in matching stainless-steel bracelets."

She flinched. Priestess Esmerelda flinched. I wondered if Nicky had seen that before.

I stared Priestess Esmerelda down.

"You are both very unenlightened," she murmured. I followed her all the way out to the reception desk, following her gardenia stench. Kandy the stripper receptionist gawked at her. "Hmmph!" exclaimed Priestess Esmerelda, closing the door behind her.

Kandy brightened. "Okay, who was that fruitcake?"

I covered for Nicky. "A potential client that I wouldn't think of signing. Don't let her past you again, okay?"

Kandy snickered. "With that hella dose of perfume, she couldn't sneak up on anybody."

I walked back to Nicky's desk. Nicky was making herself busy, putting papers on top of other papers. She was still very pink. "I know I shouldn't let her distract me," she said.

I knelt down by her chair. "We all have parents," I said. "I won't let her bug you again."

Nicky looked at me, confused. "We all have parents, I guess. But wait. You don't. There's a rumor around the firm that yours both died when you were seven."

I nodded. "Yup. I guess I don't really know what it's like to have parents. But no parent should embarrass their kid at work. Especially when they're scamming for money."

Nicky looked away. "I think she's off her meds," she said.

I looked away too, to give her some space. "She's out of her mind to mistreat her only child," I said. "Personally, I don't understand how you turned out so well. The breaking point for me was when she used that vile nickname."

Nicky turned to me, pleading. "Please don't tell anybody here about that nickname. The Guilty Peoples' Department and the Boiler Room Crew can be really mean."

I nodded. "As far as I'm concerned, I never heard that nickname, and that woman was never here. I told Kandy she's a potential client who I'm not going to sign."

Nicky laughed. "Can you imagine? If she brought in a case, it would be about somebody turning her aura black or getting her chakras out of alignment."

I laughed too. "Now that would be a real Barking Dog. Hey, I adopted Rachel Vandermixz's parrot Buster. I may bring him to work. So maybe you'll start thinking I'm weird too."

Nicky leaned closer. I smelled talcum powder, an innocent scent after that tsunami of gardenia perfume. "If anybody squawks, I'll say Buster is your emotional support animal."

I smiled. "Hopefully, if anybody squawks, it'll be Buster. I'm going to teach him how to make objections."

Nicky pointed to a *New Yorker* cartoon in her cubicle, showing a pair of hillbillies sitting in lawn chairs in front of a trailer home. The man was saying, "I coulda been a lawyer. Shoot, I object to almost everything."

"Seriously," I said, turning to her. "Everybody's got a nemesis. For you it's your mother. A nemesis is somebody who you feel powerless and miserable around. The powerless feeling is the key. Everybody's got one. That's what friends are for—to help repel the nemesis."

"What about you? Is Rodney your nemesis?"

I laughed. "God no. Sure, he yells at me, he threatens to fire me. But I don't feel powerless around him."

Nicky pressed. "So who is your nemesis?"

I met her eyes and smiled. "My nemesis died years ago."

***

I wrote a draft email on Vanillaboy6969, and heard back from The Ghost. I was long overdue to play Scrabble with her. Also I needed to give her a warning. We settled in at our favorite Scrabble café. She pumped me about the Slippery Slope case, and I gave her the short version. "So who's doing your process serving now, Sam?"

I told her Silent Mike's real name. I will not reveal it here. Like The Ghost, Silent Mike is too good a resource to disclose. "The regular process servers are cheaper, and usually just as fast," I said. "But they make a lot of mistakes. I've had them serve the wrong person. At the wrong address. I've had them serve a dog walker who doesn't live at the house. If something can go wrong with service of process, it will go wrong."

She nodded, her blonde flyaway hair glistening in the orange lights. "Then you don't have jurisdiction over the defendant. If the statute of limitations expires before you get valid service, you are SOL."

I laughed. "At my first firm, we used to say SOL means shit outta luck. I don't ever take a chance with the SOL. I never let it get closer than a year away before I file and get service with Silent Mike. I give him a background check and some photos from online if I can get them, and the Traffic Collision Report too. He uses a button cam and emails me the video. I'm a very careful guy."

She played HARM. "So how's the love life?"

"There isn't one. I'm just about done with TopFliteSingles.com. And you know I don't exactly belong with the crowd at The Switching Yard."

She sighed. "I guess." She still had hopes that we could have her kind of relationship. But I knew I would never be her kind of guy.

"Hey, a word of warning," I said. She looked up, eyes bright. "One of my online dates told me she met Rodney Mammon through the site. She said he's into 'club drugs.' Do you know anything about that?"

"I see him at The Switching Yard now and again, but no, I don't know anything about Rodney and drugs."

"The reason is, when Nicky and I went to lunch with him once, he dropped a little green pill. It looked like a prescription pill. Also sometimes his pupils are really small, and he's salivating a lot, and he rants. Sometimes he yells at me and hits the desk. There is something not right with that guy. I wanted to warn you."

She shook her head. "Aw Sam. Are we getting jealous?"

"No," I said. I played a C, to form the word CHARM. "I'm worried you might get tangled up with that guy. There's something wrong with his neurochemistry." I was proud of using Nicky's word.

"That's sweet. But how do you know what the pill is? Maybe it's a vitamin."

"It's a prescription pill. It has a number on it. He didn't notice when he dropped it, so I took it home and put it in an envelope. If anything blows up with Rodney, I want to know what he's on." I reshuffled my Scrabble tiles. I had a Q that wasn't going to go anywhere. "I just don't want that something that blows up to be you."

She patted my hand like a maiden aunt. "That's adorable. I consider myself warned."

"That reminds me. Once when I was seven, right before my parents died, my mom wanted my dad to spank me for not coming home before the street lights came on. How could I know when they were going to come on before they came on? I didn't even have a watch! Anyway, he came into my room, and told me what Mom was freaking about, and then he did something brilliant. He took his belt and doubled it up. 'When I hit the desk chair, each time, I need you to yell,' he said. Then he swatted the seat of my desk chair six times, and I yelped. It was a fun game. After that, he said, 'Consider yourself spanked.' That's one of the best memories I have of him."

She patted my hand again. "I hadn't heard that story before. I heard about your foster home, but not that one."

I winked at her. I smacked the table, twice. "Consider yourself spanked," I said.

She laughed. "Guess that's the closest Vanilla Boy is going to get to fulfilling my kink," she said.

"Afraid so. But consider this, my dear. Our friendship has lasted longer than all but one of my relationships. Probably longer than most of yours too."

She counted on her fingers. "Longer by a long shot."

"So let's make a deal. I'll dance at your wedding, if you ever have one."

"Deal. And you'll dance at mine. Even if I'm marrying a bunch of people."

I looked at my Q tile again. It wasn't going to fit anywhere. I couldn't play QUESTION or even QUEST. "Deal. After all, how many married couples have as good conversations as we have?"

She wrinkled her nose, one of her most charming gestures. "Not very many."

***

A few days later, after work, I met with Catherine at her paddock again. The drizzle stopped for half an hour, and a scrap of blue showed through the clouds—what local weathermen called a "sun break." We sat on adjoining hay bales. Jenny, the retired racehorse, watched us with raised ears from across the paddock.

I looked at her. "I need to do EMDR on the Malletts' Therapeutic Foster Home."

Catherine looked down, her hair curtaining her face. "I don't like this at all." Then she turned to me. "But I recommended you see Abe. So I guess I should encourage you to see it through."

I shrugged. "Since Suzanne I can't get a relationship started. I want what you and Jerry have. I want to get married and buy a house. I even adopted a parrot."

"Get out of town! A parrot?"

"Dead client's parrot. His name is Buster. I want to teach him to cuss."

"Well that'll bring the ladies running."

"Catherine, I need to go all the way into the darkness with Abe. I need some antivenom for all the…events. But I wanted to give you veto power first."

Catherine leaned her head on my shoulder. "I told you to get your work done. So okay, get it done." She picked up a blade of grass, cupped her hands around, and blew. It squawked. I could never get the hang of that. Jenny the retired racehorse took a couple of steps toward us. "Maybe it's time to rip off the scab and see if there's healthy pink skin underneath."

I shrugged again. "There's only one way to find out. When I'm waiting for a verdict, and my clients ask how it went? I always say you don't know until you know."

This book probably should be called *You Don't Know Until You Know.*

CHAPTER EIGHTEEN—THE MALLETTS' THERAPEUTIC FOSTER HOME

(In November 2007 Abe Aschmann brought me in for four two-hour EMDR sessions to help me put the Malletts' Therapeutic Foster Home behind bulletproof glass. I hadn't told anybody but The Ghost this story before. Why? Because I'd frozen for years rather than fighting back. I was still disgusted with myself. Here's the whole story.)

About three hours after Catherine and I got picked up at camp and learned from Trooper Bo Jorgensen that our parents were dead, we sat at the Kirkland IHOP with a garbage bag full of clothes apiece. A fiftyish woman with a silver crew cut, a teal polyester pantsuit, and a permanent scowl stared at us across our pancakes. "I am Ms. Concrete, your assigned caseworker," she said in a monotone.

She always spoke in a monotone. "I have a therapeutic foster home for you. It's the only one that will accept seven-year-old twins. Placing multiple minors is complex. If this therapeutic foster home doesn't work out for you? You will be separated. So make everything easy peasy. Fair enough?"

Three hours after I lost my parents, I might lose Catherine?

I met her eyes. I didn't know what easy peasy meant but I'd do whatever I was told. Three hours earlier I'd seen Catherine bashing her head against Trooper Bo Jorgensen's window trying to get out of his patrol car. I'd give them easy peasy all day long.

I glanced at Catherine, and we nodded. Ms. Concrete clearly knew already we didn't want to be separated. She was applying leverage to make us comply with whatever came next.

She drove us to Ballard and pulled into a driveway behind a gold VW Bus with a bumper sticker on it that said: *You Can't Hug Your Child with Nuclear Arms.* Beyond it? An early-1900s Craftsman bungalow painted minty green with moss on the roof and bedsheet curtains. Beyond that? A sandy bluff showing railroad tracks and Puget Sound, gleaming blue in the August humidity and punctuated with heeling sailboats.

Ms. Concrete put a hand on the small of my back and told me to ring the bell. "Easy peasy," she repeated.

A fat woman with a face full of brown freckles and frizzy orange hair opened the door, drying her hands on a green-and-pink calico apron. Her eyebrows soared. "THIS is just what I visualized," she said over her shoulder. "Come in."

I shrugged at Catherine and we picked up our garbage bags full of clothes.

Apparently, we were "this," which she had visualized.

Ms. Concrete met our eyes. "Easy peasy," she warned, then trudged back to her state-issued Taurus.

"I'm Glucinda Mallet," the orange-frizzy-headed woman caroled. Her voice climbed and swooped always, the opposite of Ms. Concrete's monotone. She said over her shoulder, "Hector, they're HERE."

Glucinda sat us down at a picnic table in the dining room and poured us almond milk in jelly jar glasses. The house smelled from a crock pot burbling in the kitchen cooking lentils and onions. The rooms were lined with handmade lumber book cases crammed full—*Das Kapital*, *The Theory of the Leisure Class*, *Bougeois Entitlement and Its Discontents*, and tracts and tracts and tracts.

A tall fat man with frizzy orange hair lumbered in, his hands jammed in the pockets of blue coveralls with *Hector* in a patch on the left breast. "Hi youngsters," he said, settling his bulk at the picnic table. The picnic table groaned in protest and our almond milk sloshed in the jelly jar glasses. "I'm Hector, Glucinda's husband, even though the whole concept of husband and wife is a mere bourgeois construct. I'll fill you in on the standard operating procedure." His left eye wandered, and his right eye stayed with us, twitching.

Hector took a jelly jar full of almond milk and cleared his throat, his neck beard bristling. "Our standard operating procedure is based firmly on equity. You will do all homework on time. You will do chores on the chore wheel and when accomplished you will receive weekly allowance of two dollars. You will drink Glucinda's spirulina each Monday evening for colon health. When you are old enough we'll give you instruction on how Late Stage Capitalism is a systemically racist structure built on the backs of the workers. You will also get along in all respects with your foster brother Benny Mixon. He's your older brother now and he knows the standard operating procedure better than you."

We nodded. We would have nodded no matter what. Here's a Sam Strait generalization—never give up your leverage. But seven-year-old orphans in foster care possess exactly zero leverage.

Hector Mallett was actually Dr. Mallett, a Ph.D.-level professor of sociology at the University of Washington, with tenure. Glucinda Mallett was actually the other Dr. Mallett, a Ph.D-level anthropology professor at the University of Washington, also with tenure.

Not exactly real doctors.

Why was it called the Malletts' Therapeutic Foster Home? So they could charge the taxpayers more. That's why.

There were locks on the cupboards that held the food. We got our clothes at Value Village. The first new clothes I got after my parents died were my Coast Guard uniforms.

The Malletts were licensed for four foster kids but only had one other than Catherine and me. The fourth bedroom stayed empty the whole eleven years we were there until we "aged out" at eighteen. I wondered why since they were getting paid by the kid. But I didn't find out why until long afterward. All will be revealed.

A skinny, redheaded twelve-year-old guy slouched in and sat down and accepted a jelly jar of almond milk.

What I noticed first? His stench of rancid sweat and nicotine. His yellow-toothed grin with one snaggle-toothed incisor. His red-gold body fur showing in tufts from his unraveling white tank top. His yellow horny toenails in red flip-flops.

The smell of rotten eggs and roadkill from our house got elbowed aside by Benny's stench of rancid sweat and nicotine.

Benny smiled at us with yellow teeth. But not with his pale hurt eyes. "What up homies," he said. Then his smoker's cough. At twelve Benny was already a heavy smoker.

Hector said: "Benny here will get his allowance for looking after you on weekday afternoons. Glucinda and I are stuck at the university until about five laboring in the salt mines." He gave a short crack of laughter. His eyes didn't match his laugh either.

We figured out the standard operating procedure quickly. Lentil stew with onions most nights, punctuated with homemade yogurt. Spirulina on Monday nights. Trotsky Discussion Group on Sunday afternoon in place of "bourgeois church," but we weren't invited—we had to play quietly while the shaggy Trotskyites bickered about miniscule differences. Benny looking after us on weekday afternoons.

We did get separate bedrooms. The first two nights Catherine snuck into my room and we slept together, a ball of twins. But Glucinda yelled at us and we stopped that.

Easy peasy? No. But mandatory.

Our first Tuesday afternoon Benny told us to sit on the back porch. School was out until Labor Day, about three weeks away but Dr. Mallett and the other Dr. Mallett were at the university.

Benny sat down in his frayed pink fabric lawn chair. Out here the stench of rancid sweat and nicotine blew away in guiltless wind. He rolled a Bull Durham cigarette and licked the edge with his whitish tongue.

"Let's play a game," Benny said. "It's called the Punk Test."

"What exactly is a punk test?" I asked.

"It's a test to find out if you're a punk, faggot. See, I take a dull jack knife and I scrape on the inside of your forearm. I keep scraping. If you start crying, you're a punk. If you never start crying, then you're never a punk. You'll start bleeding eventually, but it's better than being a punk."

"When do you stop scraping?"

Benny laughed, showing his yellow snaggle tooth. "That's the beauty part! I never stop scraping until you admit you are a punk. That's why it's a cool game!"

I looked down. "I don't want to play that game," I said. I had been living with my parents, or at camp, until eight days ago. I wasn't a scared boy yet.

"Okay, but this game is special," Benny said. "See you have two options, and you get a choice between the options. That's fair, right?" He gestured with his cigarette. "Nothing could be more fair than giving you a choice."

I regarded him. "What's the other choice?"

Benny squinted. "I beat the shit out of you."

I was confused. I had two options but both led to pain. I didn't want to choose. That was Benny's art—he gave me two options, every time. Both of them were bad. Then he enjoyed my indecision before he enjoyed my pain.

At least the game didn't involve Catherine.

"Okay, punk test," I said.

Benny took out his jack knife, came over, and knelt in front of me. He made it a ceremony. I breathed through my mouth, avoiding the stench of rancid sweat and nicotine. He opened the knife, ran his finger down the blade to show how dull it was. "See? Totally dull. Don't be a pussy." Then he began scraping.

It didn't hurt until he'd been at it for five minutes or so. The anticipation was awful for me. Therefore the anticipation was wonderful for him.

Later, I explained to Mrs. Mallett that I'd scraped my arm playing down by the train tracks. "Well then don't play down by the train tracks," she said, pouring me a yummy jelly jar of almond milk.

Next, Benny started offering me hard candy if he could throw it at me as hard as he could. Catherine always had to watch. The alternative was always the same—he could beat the shit out of me. But I had a choice! Nothing could be more fair.

About this time he started in with my new nickname. When he offered a new game he'd say, "Same old, same old. Right, Sam old, Sam old?" Then he'd mess up my hair to show what a regular guy he was.

Once I told him he couldn't throw hard candy at me. So he backhanded me with his fist and broke my nose. That night when Glucinda interrogated us Benny said, "He went down the bluff like you told him not to and he fell and he broke his stupid nose because he's hella clumsy."

I said, "Benny hit me when I told him he couldn't throw hard candy at me."

Glucinda glared at me. "I told you to obey your older brother. He knows the standard operating procedure. I should have told you that standard operating procedure forbids lying."

She took me to the hospital and a serious Black doctor x-rayed my nose, gloved up, and said, "This is going to hurt, little man." Then he manipulated my nose until it was reasonably straight and put a metal brace over it and secured it with medical tape. I bled all over the pale blue towel in my lap. My eyes watered. But I did not cry. After all I was a liar and it wasn't easy peasy. I did have to stay with Catherine because I did believe Ms. Concrete that twins were hard to "place" together.

The serious Black doctor shook hands. "You're a brave patient, kiddo," he said.

Thus did I learn what "beating the shit out of me" was.

Once, when we'd been at the Malletts' for three years, it snowed and school was canceled. But the university did not close. So Benny had us to himself all day. He told me I could run around the block, naked and barefoot, or he supposed he could just beat the shit out of me. For a bonus? He could beat the shit out of Catherine too because he totally hadn't forgotten about her.

Benny got in lots of fights at school, and he usually won. He'd been suspended three times, once for…breaking the other kid's nose.

Catherine had to watch. She always had to watch.

That day I finally realized that Catherine suffered watching as Benny extorted me with his dilemmas.

After my naked run around the block through the snow, some neighbors called the Malletts, and they called Ms. Concrete.

Ms. Concrete declined almond milk in a jelly jar and sat me down at the picnic table in front of Hector and Glucinda and Benny and Catherine. "You are forbidden to engage in any more sexual acting out," she told me. "If you do anything like this again, you will be placed separately from Catherine."

I was now a proven liar who was guilty of "sexual acting out." Apparently I'd become quite a little bastard.

Benny learned from that. He never drew attention from the neighbors again.

As Benny grew into his teens he developed a new game. Catherine and I had to watch as he locked his door and pulled out a *Penthouse* with the pages stuck together and watched him masturbate, his pale penis bucking in his hands while he smoked. Yes he did smoke when he masturbated.

Or, he offered, he could just beat the shit out of Catherine and make me watch.

He'd learned where our levers were—each of us suffered more watching the other suffer than from suffering ourselves. He weaponized our empathy.

When Catherine and I were twelve, Benny turned seventeen. He was close to "aging out." He now stood five foot ten. His red-gold body fur had thickened. His rancid stench of sweat and nicotine? On a scale of one to ten, it was fifty-six.

Benny had been arrested and thrown in Juvenile Hall for Assault 2 for breaking a kid's arm at high school because the kid called him "dildo." After Benny first called him "skanky pussy."

Benny Mixon's arc on a chart would be pretty obvious.

Twice, he gave me "swirlies." A swirly is where the bully puts your head in the toilet and flushes it. The second one was a "lemon swirly." That meant he had pissed in the toilet first.

Twice more he "beat the shit out of me." I was careful to defy him periodically to keep him distracted from Catherine. Once he broke my left little finger and ring finger and I told Glucinda I fell off my bike and Benny told her I fell off *his* bike and I lost my $2.00 a week allowance for two months. For lying. The second time he kicked me in the balls to make me hold still and then shaved my head with the Malletts' Deluxe Home Barber Kit and then told the Malletts I was a neo-Nazi. I said

Benny kicked me in the balls and shaved my head. I lost my $2.00 a week allowance for four months. I needed to stop lying.

Where was my head all this time? I was trying not to be present. I was escaping into intellect.

I got two or three books a week from the library so I could find a better world. Catherine and I traded them. We didn't discuss the books. We just dove into them and swam around. Jules Verne. Edgar Allan Poe. Joseph Conrad. Dickens. Tolstoy. John Irving—my personal favorite. Maya Angelou. Joan Didion. Margaret Atwood.

Also, I saved up my allowance and went to the Ballard Army Surplus Depot and bought a

Gerber Mark II commando knife with 6.5-inch double-edged serrated blade and rubber grip. I removed the heating vent cover in my room and duct-taped it to the inside of the top of the heating vent. I liked knowing it was hidden there.

Also I started playing lots of chess on the Malletts' elderly PC. They approved of chess because the Soviet Union approved of chess and the Trotsky Discussion Group approved of chess. I became president of my middle school chess team and went to regionals, where I placed a respectable second. The chess team advisor said: "Sam, you should seriously consider becoming a lawyer. You can do logic, kiddo." Just like the serious Black doctor, the advisor—a bald Jewish guy in his early sixties—saw something redeeming in me.

I hung on to these scraps of approval the way a Middle Ages pope would hang onto alleged remnants of the One True Cross.

I got frequent severe headaches. I got frequent severe nosebleeds. But I was managing to distract Benny from Catherine whenever I could sense—and I could sense it—his pale hurt eyes turning toward her.

Benny had x-rayed my personality. I'd rather get the "shit beaten out of me" than let him hurt Catherine. But Catherine hurt more watching all this than if Benny had simply hurt her.

They say depression is "anger turned inward." I was stuffed with repressed rage. Ergo, headaches and nosebleeds.

Then came the day when Benny came into my bedroom. I'd just finished *Twenty Thousand Leagues Under the Sea* and gave it to Catherine. She'd given me *All Creatures Great and Small*. We lay on my bed with the blinds halfway open and gold stripes across my plaid bedspread.

Benny closed the door and locked it. It was three thirty on a weekday. Hector and Glucinda wouldn't be home for an hour and a half.

Benny pulled out my desk chair and turned it around, then folded his arms over the back, his red-gold body fur showing around the apertures in his tank top. He sat next to my desk with the globe with the steel stand I'd bought with my allowance. Two dollars a week could buy a used globe if you saved up for a couple months, which was okay if you hadn't lied about something that was the truth and had your allowance taken away for lying.

In the distance a freight train hooted.

Benny pointed at me and lit a cigarette. "I have an exciting new game, Same Old. You will play this game willingly. Or else I'll say Catherine stripped and said 'Oh Benny I need to get fucked doggy style' and then Catherine will get placed in another foster home. Everybody believed you were sexually acting out that day you decided to run around naked in the snow and Catherine is your twin so everybody will believe she was sexually acting out and then she'll go to a special Sex Therapy Foster Home and you two won't get to live together. Pretty nifty plan, huh?"

Benny's pale hurt eyes drilled into me. I recoiled from his rancid stench of sweat and nicotine.

The freight train hooted.

"Or what, Benny?" I asked. "There's always an alternative. And it's always gross."

"Or Catherine sucks my cock until I shoot my hot yummy spooge in her mouth. Genius, right? She has to have sex with me or I'll accuse her of wanting to have sex with me and then she goes away, so it really sounds like she's going to have sex with me. Pucker up, Sis," Benny said. "It's not so bad. All the girls do it. In prison most of the boys do it too."

The freight train hooted. Closer.

Benny unbuckled his cargo shorts and dropped his Twisted Sister logo briefs. His pale erection nodded like a conductor's baton.

I felt my nose start bleeding and pat-pat-pat the drops fell on my lap.

Either Catherine? Or Catherine?

I was twelve; I'd started masturbating. No problem. But Benny and Catherine? Or else Benny and Catherine?

The train yelled nearby, "Hoot." My blood went pat-pat-pat on my lap.

Benny yelled over the train: "You don't want Catherine to feel left out, do you?" His pale penis nodded.

Catherine caught my eye, her fist jammed into her mouth, tears running down her face.

I smelled rotten eggs and roadkill and rancid sweat and nicotine.

And the room turned red.

HOOT.

Benny sat between me and the heating vent cover. But right next to the globe on my desk.

I jumped up and grabbed the antique globe and smashed Benny over the head with it then hit him forehand and backhand across the face with the steel stand then I jumped over him as he fell and I leapt to the heating vent and reached in and my ripped Gerber Mark II commando knife with 6.5-inch double-edged serrated blade and rubber grip free from the duct tape and then I jumped on top of Benny and stabbed him in the belly as hard as I could and then Catherine threw herself on me and wrapped her arms around my head yelling, "DON'T KILL HIM,

DON'T KILL HIM," and then her yelling was loud because the train was gone.

***

The paramedics came. The police came. I was handcuffed and taken to Juvenile Hall. I was interviewed by a social worker much like Ms. Concrete, and a public defender. Then I was put in a Juvenile Hall Custody Pod with four other twelve year old boys. They were gang bangers and I was an undersized nerd.

The pod warden told the gang bangers, "You just leave Sammy here alone. He nearly killed his foster brother with a commando knife. The foster brother is in surgery right now. Sammy is one mean little fucker."

I never got a chance to thank the pod warden. The gang bangers whispered to each other and stayed away from me. When people know you can go berserk on them, they usually keep away. Berserk shifts the balance of power.

Somewhere in there the Juvenile Hall Medical Staff held me down and gave me a big shot of Haldol because I was deemed "a danger to myself or others." Then they escorted me to a Juvenile Court hearing upstairs that mystified me because the Haldol turned my brain to Styrofoam.

Then, I spent three weeks on the locked children's ward at a psych hospital.

Then I was discharged. I hadn't spoken in weeks. Even with a Styrofoam brain from the Haldol I knew if I told the truth everybody would know I was a liar and I'd get separated from Catherine.

So I shut up and let everybody conclude I was insane.

Ms. Concrete picked me up. "The Mallett Therapeutic Foster Home has decided to give you another chance," she said. "Benny Mixon has made a full recovery after bowel resection surgery. You're going home."

I wasn't going home. I hadn't had a home since my parents died.

But Catherine was there. And Benny Mixon hadn't gotten to ejaculate in her mouth.

The Haldol was wearing off. Colors and sounds started to…inch forward into vividness. I wasn't going to juvenile prison because I was insane and medicated but now I wasn't having to be medicated and I was going home even though it wasn't home but at least no Styrofoam brain and Catherine still didn't have semen in her mouth and, and. And.

The Malletts were oddly glad to see me. I had no idea why. Benny was oddly glad to see me. I had no idea why. Catherine gave me a short hug and a short smile. I knew why she was holding herself back. She didn't want Benny to know she still trusted me.

Never feed information to your enemy.

I was allowed to return to the Malletts' Therapeutic Foster Home only if I went to weekly counseling.

The counselor, a jittery balding bear with a pasted-on grin diagnosed me with "attachment disorder." He said, "Call Me Carter." He scraped away at me for months, one session a week. I told him I missed my parents and I would be good and stop lying and never act out again. Carter and Ms. Concrete and Dr. Mallett and the other Dr. Mallett put all bad behavior under the circus tent of "acting out." Nobody ever told me—acting out of what?

Bob's reports went to the Malletts and to Ms. Concrete but he never showed them to me because I was an incompetent minor with a personality disorder called "attachment disorder." I walked a tightrope and apparently kept my feet on the invisible rope because I got to stay at the Malletts' Therapeutic Foster Home and nobody made me take Haldol or other stuff Carter called "meds."

Okay, now the home stretch. How did Benny change after I stabbed him?

Benny decided that I was his little friend. I swear I am not making this up.

Benny didn't propose any gross dilemmas anymore. Conclusion? He respected me because I'd tried to kill him.

When the Haldol cleared out of my system, and I was actually smart again, I started considering the endgame. Chess teaches you to always visualize the endgame.

The funny thing about Benny? Benny could not refuse a dare. No matter how stupid a dare, Benny could not refuse a dare.

I didn't even tell Catherine the next part. I never have. Only Abe Aschmann and The Ghost ever learned this next part.

I had hit Benny over the head with the globe. But now I would use the whole world to hurt him. He couldn't refuse a dare. The whole world would be my weapon.

Many people preach forgiveness under all circumstances. I do not.

If those "radical compassion" people see their twelve-year-old sister about to be mouth-raped, and they can still forgive the rapist, hooray for them. I cannot.

Forgiveness without recompense is injustice. There's a Sam Strait generalization for you.

The next day, I told Benny: "You know what would be a good prank? See what's the most expensive thing you can steal from Bartell Drugs. I'll wait outside and we'll check the price tag on what you got."

Benny's face lit up. "Totally, homeboy. Like Mr. Mallett says, property is theft."

Benny sauntered into Bartell Drugs, and he was caught on video and he was arrested. He'd stolen a Bulova watch and a pack of gum. The watch made it felony theft. He got probation. He thought it was "a really good prank."

Then, the newspaper I delivered on my paper route mentioned that Veterans Day was coming up. The American Legion would be putting flags on all the veterans' graves at a nearby graveyard. I told Benny: "You know what would be a great prank? You see how many tombstones you can push over up at the graveyard in the veterans' section. They'll all have flags on them and everything. The more tombstones you tip over, the higher the score."

Benny lit up again. "That's fucking awesome. I'm on that like white on rice. Let's ride our bikes up there tonight."

"Okay," I said, "but this is your prank. I just keep score."

"Totally. You're such a little bitch, you couldn't push over a gravestone anyway."

I waited outside, of course.

Turns out the graveyard had infrared video cameras, and he got arrested again. This time, he spent two weeks in Juvenile Hall. When Benny came back, he said, "Dude, I got hella knowledge in juvie." He was "stoked." He congratulated me on my inventiveness.

Christmas Eve dawned sunny and frosty. Seagulls cried over Puget Sound as they swooped and flapped, picking delicious rotten bits from the surf. Benny came to my room. "Homeboy, we haven't done pranks for weeks. What's your new prank?"

I remembered the day he attempted to mouth-rape Catherine. Hoot. I remembered the freight train thundering past.

"I dare you to hop a freight train and ride it to Tacoma," I said.

"Fuck yeah! That's epic, bro!" He still called me, bro.

I hate it when anybody calls me "bro."

Benny and I walked down the bluff to the train tracks as seagulls swooped and dove overhead in the pale sun. Frost shot tiny prisms into my eyes, and the stony beach sparkled. Offshore, a sea lion yelped.

Omens flooded my blood.

All the houses uphill except the Malletts' house had Christmas lights. The Malletts condemned Christmas lights as "indicators of late-stage capitalism amplifying a Hallmark holiday." Well, naturally, they said that. Everybody in the Trotsky Discussion Group had agreed about that.

Up north, I heard it. Hoot.

"Dude, you always have killer ideas," Benny said, cuffing my head then lighting his latest hand-rolled cigarette.

Benny thought we were friends. Such a good prank.

Hoot. The train just a mile north now.

Benny raised his voice. "Dude, what we ought to do after this one for the next prank? We need to gather up our pennies and go to a strip club! It's time you got ahold of some boobies!"

"Excellent," I yelled with a fake smile. "But first, you do this, chicken."

He punched me on the shoulder with fellowship. "Nobody calls me chicken, you skanky pussy."

Hoot.

The train approached. Benny spun around and squinted at it.

HOOT.

The engines passed, rumbling and thundering and shaking everything on the frosted scene as they throbbed like gigantic hearts.

Next, the freight cars rattling and jittering, one with a squealing brake. Some with locked doors. Some tank cars. But look! Here came a red and gold freight car labeled *Mississippi Central Consol-PC* with open door black as an open mouth and Benny pointed and laughed showing his yellow nicotine teeth.

Benny crouched. Then he sprinted across the nearer empty tracks, then sprinted up to the open door, and he leaped and caught a frosted grab rail beside the open door, and he turned and yelled, "NOW YOU DO IT."

I shook my head. This prank was all his.

"NOW YOU DO IT HOMEBOY," he said, waving wildly.

Then his hand slipped on the frosty grab rail and he fell and bounced off a signal box and ricocheted back and the train ran him over, cutting him in half.

I was yelling and even today I don't know what I was yelling.

Benny's pale intestines writhed like pale worms under the train and pink mist fumed out and for the first time I realized it's possible for a plan to work too well but no it's not too well if it's the right plan.

***

The police investigation showed that Benny ran toward the car and jumped the train alone. The car he jumped was only ten cars ahead of the caboose. The brakeman in the caboose cupola saw the whole thing.

I was a hundred feet away when it all happened. Nobody called me a liar.

The medical examiner ruled it: *Cause of death: misadventure on train tracks. Manner of death: accident.*

I'm still disgusted with myself that I froze when Benny started in on Catherine and me. I didn't start fighting until much too late. But?

But it worked.

Then Catherine and I aged out of the Malletts' Therapeutic Foster Home. We each got a hundred dollars and a garbage bag to put our clothes in. Symmetric, right? Garbage bag full of clothes when we left, just like when we arrived.

Catherine had become a skilled riding instructor by then. She worked her way through her psychology training by giving lessons to rich people who wanted to take tall jumps with perfect form.

I joined the Coast Guard and did hostile boardings out in the Gulf of Mexico. True confession? Sometimes we boarded drug-smuggling boats and they shot at us. True confession? I shot and killed more than one of them. True confession? I am not sorry.

Play stupid games? Win stupid prizes.

I seldom told anybody about the hostile boardings. In Seattle in 2007 you were supposed to show compassion even to shitty violent people. I have exactly zero compassion for shitty violent people. So I evaded the issue.

While in the Coast Guard, I got my BA in Criminal Justice, then got an Honorable Discharge (with some medals that I won't enumerate), took my GI Bill benefits, and went to law school.

Except for the three years with Suzanne, I always lived alone. No woman, no pets, no house plants. Alone with my books and my '80s music.

A couple of years after Catherine and I aged out, the Malletts' Therapeutic Foster Home made headlines in the *Seattle Times*. Dr. Mallett and Dr. Mallett got arrested and charged with felony theft and fraud.

I learned why the fourth bedroom had always been empty.

Before Catherine and I were "placed" there, the Malletts had a five-year-old foster boy named Timmy Simms. Timmy Simms had been murdered on a home visit by his mother who was psychotic because of the street drugs she was taking.

Street drugs, or "club drugs," can drive people insane.

After Timmy Simms died, the Malletts kept getting paid for his "foster care." The Mallets got four thousand dollars per kid, per month, because it was "therapeutic" foster care. That was $192,000 per year. As icing on the cake, they kept getting paid for Benny even after he died, and even after he would have "aged out."

Evidently Dr. Mallett and Dr. Mallett did not believe property was theft. They believed theft was property.

Before the *Seattle Times* revealed all this, the Department of Social and Health Services hadn't noticed, or maybe hadn't cared, that it was paying for two dead foster kids.

After the scoop, the Malletts pled guilty and got three years in prison apiece, because the enraged public applied actual heat to the nerveless beanbag chair that is the Department of Social and Health Services. The Malletts both lost their tenure at the University of Washington. Apparently felony theft and fraud violated some professorial code of conduct.

Ms. Concrete got immunity in exchange for turning state's evidence. She even kept her job.

Ms. Concrete had been the "assigned caseworker" for all the Malletts' kids. She had to have known about the payments for the dead kids. After all, she gave periodic "progress reports" about them. Even after Timmy Simms and Benny Mixon died. Even though Timmy Simms and Benny Mixon weren't "progressing" at anything. Except decomposition.

As HL Mencken once wrote, *No matter how cynical you get, it is impossible to keep up.*

Now I sue people who hurt innocent people. Heraclitus, one of the ancient Romans, once said, "Character is destiny." But sometimes destiny creates character, too.

I found a weird alchemy. I took my blackened past and harnessed it into useful energy.

I'd grown a ball of rage as big as a skyscraper inside me. I'd crushed it down until it was only the size of a golf ball. Then it started to glow. Then I used it to power me on my mission—the way a golf ball of enriched nuclear fuel powers a submarine, across the oceans of the world.

I don't get ferocious headaches or sudden nosebleeds anymore. I don't have any anger turned inward anymore.

I'm not full of rage anymore. I'm full of determination.

I'm simple, really. My personality only has about three moving parts.

Abe Aschmann led me through EMDR about all this and didn't show any emotion, but one time he had to blow his nose and I thought he might have teared up.

I hang onto this scrap of paternal approval too. Like a Middle Ages pope treasuring a fragment of the One True Cross.

CHAPTER NINETEEN— BULLETPROOF GLASS PART TWO

After our EMDR marathon, Abe Aschmann set an ordinary counseling session.

"So I want to talk with you about your diagnosis," Abe said.

I nodded. "Attachment disorder."

Abe leaned forward like a basketball coach. "What do you know about attachment disorder?"

I sighed. I'd read the DSM-IV about it. "It's a personality disorder that prevents the patient from ever forming a mutually beneficial relationship with anyone, ever. It's not considered very treatable. Some clinicians report that after years of therapy, some signs of improvement may be noted." I sighed again. I was incurable.

Abe half-smiled. "That's almost word for word from the DSM. So that is what you understand about it?"

I nodded. "That's why I've never been in love, except for the three years with Suzanne. That's why I'll probably never be in love again."

This time, Abe sighed. He took off his glasses, pulled out his shirttail, and cleaned the glasses on it. He put them back on. "You don't have it," he said simply.

"What? But I was diagnosed. I went to years of counseling. I'm still alone. I've got to have it."

Abe shook his head, smiling. "You don't have it. You never did. Know how I can tell?" I shook my head. "You've had mutually beneficial relationships all along. Look at your sister Catherine. Look at your friends—Duvonda, Silent Mike, Nicky, even this character you call The Ghost. These are good friendships. People with attachment disorder don't have good friendships. Because they can't."

"But I had years of counseling for it."

He looked down and smiled again. "Why did you get sent to counseling? Because you defended yourself…and your sister. Who ordered you sent to counseling? DSHS, and the Malletts. Why did you go for years? Because it's considered untreatable unless you get years of therapy. The therapist got paid for counseling you—the more counseling you got, the more he made. I'll bet my bottom dollar the Malletts got paid more because they were providing foster care to such a 'disturbed' kid."

Abe kept smiling at me. "Mark Twain once said, it is easier to fool people than to convince them they have been fooled."

"That's disgusting," I said. "Who would do that to a kid?" Then I shut up. The same people who would rip off the taxpayers for "caring" for two dead foster kids.

"Okay, you're mad, and that's healthy," Abe said. "But look one level deeper. What is underneath your anger?"

I took a big swig of the market spice tea. I inhaled the smell of cloves and cinnamon. I was disoriented.

There. Underneath the anger.

Joy! I was healthy! Not only was I cured, I'd never been truly sick in the first place.

It was easier to fool me than it was to convince me I'd been fooled. I'd been an easy mark. Kids usually are an easy mark. That's why they need parents to protect them from becoming easy marks.

I was healthy!

A yellow glow, bright as the sun, filled me. I was flooded with happiness. I felt I could light up the world.

"Now he gets it," Abe said, looking up. "Now. Grab that feeling. Remember that feeling. This is why I had you in several nights running. I thought we were close to breaking through. Now we have."

I grinned. "Holy moly."

"Indeed," he said. "You may return if you want to, or need to. But Sam, you've reached your breakthrough. You don't need counseling any more. I went the extra mile for you because you go the extra mile for your friends and your clients. Who knows? Maybe I'll dance at your wedding someday."

I laughed. The Ghost had said that, too. Maybe it was possible for me to even have a theoretical wedding.

I was still grinning when I stepped out onto the sidewalk. December wind gushed across the front of the undamaged Alamo, smelling of snowfields and maybe even the future.

I noticed a shaggy homeless guy in an Army blanket huddled inside the nearby bus shelter, only his reddish face and black beard protruding. He squinted at me. "Dude, you look hella happy," he said. He didn't even ask for money.

"I am hella happy," I said, even though I never use the word hella, because it's a word used by drugged-out slackers. "Hella." I laughed and did a little jig.

I was still smiling when I started up the trusty Subaru Outback. I was going to teach Buster that word. Hella. Suddenly it was a hilarious word.

CHAPTER TWENTY—A HARD RAIN

I started bringing Buster to the office in his travel cage. Nicky would sit by his cage on her breaks, feeding him pecans and murmuring catchphrases to him. She said, "He's the Innocent Peoples' Department Mascot."

The Guilty Peoples' Department staff didn't like him. Sometimes, I would walk around the office with Buster on my shoulder because that made me feel like a pirate. Buster never pooped on me and never tried to escape.

Once, I was standing in the lobby with Buster on my shoulder, talking to Rob Monarch, the self-proclaimed Second-Ranking Stud in the Criminal Defense Department. (Rodney had dubbed himself the Top-Ranking Stud, of course. That week, Rodney was at a Radical Centeredness Silent Hot Yoga Retreat™ in Big Sur, California.) The bros and babes of the Guilty Peoples' Department stared at Buster.

Rob said, "Bro, doesn't your parrot crap on you?"

I reached up and stroked Buster's cheek. "He's very civilized. He only craps on criminals."

"Hang 'em high," Buster said out of nowhere.

Rob rolled his eyes. "I guess our resident ambulance-chaser taught his bird some prosecutor talk." The ex-cheerleaders and ex-football players high-fived.

"You have the right to remain silent," I told them.

"Well, dog, my cats," said Buster.

"Not you, my buddy," I said, giving him a treat.

Rob persisted. "Didn't I do a DUI against you out in Northeast District Court when you were an intern prosecutor?"

"Yes, but I don't think you want to go into that."

Rob snickered. "Why? Did I stomp your ass?"

I smiled. "Kind of the opposite thing. He blew a 3.6 BAC and got hammered because it was his third DUI. Pretty good day for me."

"You must be kinda petty if you're still hanging on to that," Rob Monarch said, and the bros and babes high-fived again.

Nicky stood beside me, whispering to Buster. "You have the right to remain silent," Buster yowled.

The bros and babes of the Guilty Peoples' Department cackled as Rob Monarch turned red. Those people didn't like each other any more than they liked me.

Here's a Sam Strait generalization—if a person doesn't have anybody in life that they actually respect? Then that person sucks. Good people can feel and show respect. I learned that from a certain deceased foster brother.

Kandy kept taking phone calls, mostly criminal defendants. She'd replaced the pink streak in her blonde hair with a blue streak. Which fit perfectly because Buster had started talking a blue streak.

Nicky and, Buster, and I went over to Kandy's desk. Kandy had dark circles under her eyes—apparently, some late nights at the strip club.

"So, how's it going with the other job?" I asked her.

She inspected her nails, which were painted turquoise. "The money is great."

I asked, "Do you like it? Do you like stripping?" I really wondered. Now that I'd put the Malletts' Therapeutic Foster Home behind bulletproof glass, I was much more curious about other people.

Kandy considered. "I do," she said. "I've gotten hired at a high-roller place called Reincarnation. When a new high-roller comes in, the bouncer asks him have you ever been here before? If the high-roller says, I kind of feel like I have, he gets a free Diet Pepsi."

Nicky and I walked back into the Innocent Peoples' Department. I put Buster in his cage, where he promptly crapped. I gave him a treat. He climbed onto his pink-and-green rope and rang all the bells.

Nicky murmured to me: "Something's wrong with Kandy. I don't like the look of those dark circles."

I shrugged. "She's old enough to take care of herself. If I'm having a good day, I can take care of the clients and Buster. I can't really do much for Kandy."

"But still…there's a bad look about Kandy," Nicky said.

Nicky seemed worried in general. I wondered if Fred, the preppy boyfriend in the photo in her cubicle, was giving her trouble. Or Priestess Esmerelda.

"So, how's your Mom?" I asked her. Is she still pestering you?"

"Maybe it was you. Maybe she's on her meds. Maybe business has picked up in the booming business of soul retrieval." She smiled. "It's funny about West Coast cities. Lots of people out here will believe just about any nonsense that can cram itself under the umbrella of New Age Thought."

I nodded. "Which is a contradiction in terms."

We had another Intake Clinic coming up soon. After the Slippery Slope case, we needed more clients, and the trial had generated some publicity, too.

***

Nicky and I had trained the Boiler Room people how to spot a True Disaster and how to weed out the Barking Dogs. She told me the next Intake Clinic might even have multiple True Disasters.

Before the Intake Clinic the next day, Rodney pulled me into his office and sat me down on the red-striped couch. He sat people on the red-striped couch when he was going to try to play them. The desk chairs were for overt business conversations.

"I've given some consideration to your future with my firm," he said, fixing me with his flat, glazed eyes.

"All right."

"It occurs to me that there might be an avenue toward considering your profit sharing," he intoned. Again, the flat, glazed eyes.

I thought about telling him he'd already signed a contract, which was the only avenue I needed. But with my newfound mellowness, I decided to let it play out. "Okay, what avenue is that?"

He looked at his professionally manicured nails. He wore a beautifully tailored houndstooth suit with a purple tie. His gel-stiffened porcupine hair gleamed.

"It's come to my attention that you've become too dependent on Nicky, and she is hampering your advancement as a lawyer," he murmured.

Straight up reversification.

Reversification is a primitive tactic—calling something the exact opposite of what it actually is. It's meant to confuse people so they can be tricked. The true mark of the manipulator.

When somebody's trying to play you, ask yourself—is the truth the exact opposite of what this person says it is?

If so, you've decoded the reversification. For example, if somebody says they love you? But their actions show they hate you? You've spotted reversification.

Nicky was my good right arm. I was twice as good with her as I would be without her.

Rodney was making a play, all right. And it certainly wasn't for an agreement on profit sharing.

"So what's the connection with profit sharing?" I asked.

Rodney opened his glazed eyes wide. "I can see my way toward considering your profit sharing if you agree that your dependency on Nicky is pathological, so I have your okay to let her go."

There it was. The false, painful dilemma.

Rodney could fire Nicky anytime he wanted. However, he suspected that I would follow her right out the door with my middle finger raised. He was dangling the obviously false promise of profit sharing in front of me to get my agreement to betray Nicky.

Once I'd betrayed Nicky, my true-believer status would be broken. I would be just another shyster like him and the other people in the Guilty Peoples' Department.

For the first time, I realized he was a lot like my late foster brother Benny. He gave me a choice to try to torment me. Accepting either choice would torment me. The only way to play this game was to flip the game board and send the pieces flying.

Rodney was actually pretty stupid. I was making him a fortune because I was a true believer. If I was just another oleaginous sleaze monster like him, I couldn't charge up San Juan Hill with a saber in one hand and a Bible in the other, singing "Battle Hymn of the Republic." My compressed rage, which I'd turned into determination, was my secret sauce.

"Okay, Rodney," I said evenly. "The day you fire Nicky, I quit. I'm making you a ton of money. I'm guessing you want me to keep making you a ton of money. "

His eyes widened. He didn't expect me to overturn the game board.

I continued. "I've asked around about your prior personal injury litigators. They were a pretty sad bunch. I'm making you eight times as much money per month as the best previous personal injury lawyer in his best month. That's right—I can run a revenue report from the case management software, too." I decided to try a cliche, a technique I'd learned from J. Charm. "So let's not throw out the baby with the bathwater, okay?"

Rodney nodded, confirming something for himself. I'd known since the beginning that I had something Rodney lacked. It puzzled him.

Rodney smiled. "You really are a Boy Scout, aren't you? Faithful, loyal, clean, and reverent."

I laughed. It was a fake laugh, but Rodney couldn't tell the difference. "I'm loyal anyway. You really had me going there for a second," I joshed. I acted as if he were kidding. Just the way I'd handled Benny once I decoded his cross-wired brain.

Pretend everything is a play with these people. Watch carefully. Prepare for the crucial moment.

"Okay tiger," he said, walking me to the door and clapping me on the back. "Go make me some money."

***

This Intake Clinic was one for the ages.

First up—*Park v. USOnTime*. An elderly Korean man crossing the street in a marked crosswalk had been hit by a parcel delivery truck which was evidently speeding. Genevieve Park, one of the five daughters, came in with her mother, an elderly woman dressed in black looking terminally confused.

"Genevieve Park, sir," she said. "I'm in Naval Intelligence up at Whisby Air Stations. I'm a lieutenant senior grade."

I liked her brisk handshake. "I was an enlisted guy in the Coast Guard. I think we're going to get along fine."

We sat, and I studied her—about five foot six, short black hair, direct gaze, decked out in blue camouflage. Since the Coast Guard, I intuitively tested clients, asking myself: *Is this someone I want to go into battle with?*

In Genevieve's case, the answer was hell yes.

Poor Mr. Park had died two days ago after a week at the Harborview Medical Center Neurosurgery ICU, spiraling down into decorticate posturing and multiple organ failure.

Genevieve had the Traffic Collision Report and I studied it. Because this had been reported as a likely fatality collision on a state route, the Washington State Patrol had rolled their major collision team and had done a total station data survey of the scene, mapping it. WSP wouldn't release the full report for weeks, because of course there was a possibility the driver would be charged with vehicular homicide, if he was intoxicated or driving with "extreme indifference to human life." But reading between the lines, I could tell the state patrol wanted to nail this guy.

The clincher? WSP had carefully mapped how one of Mr. Park's shoes had landed 160 feet from the point of impact in the crosswalk. They had carefully noted that his phone flew ninety feet. They established the point of impact with "headlight lens material" in the crosswalk, and "blood spatter" in the crosswalk.

The crosswalk was newly painted and announced with two warning signs—one a hundred feet up the road, and one right at the crosswalk, with an arrow pointing down at the crosswalk. They noted the time of impact was 11:36 AM, and the weather was clear and sunny.

"I want this one," I said, nodding to Nicky. I explained I couldn't be hired until Genevieve was named personal representative of the estate and she had Letters Testamentary—the "hunting license." I referred Genevieve to Bonus Malone—a moon-faced trustworthy guy who did probate litigation. Genevieve said she would hire him. I shook her hand. "Don't worry about paying Bonus. We'll pay him as a client cost of the case. I'm optimistic about this one. I want to roll up my sleeves and jump all over this," I said.

"Copy that, sir," she said, leading her broken mother out.

I liked having military people and police officers as clients. They understood the necessary and strategic application of force. They typically participated more than most other clients.

I told Nicky: "Get Don Meissner to go pull the airbag control module data from that truck. Also could you walk Genevieve over to Bonus's office and probate rolling?"

"Of course," Nicky murmured. That was what I loved about Nicky. She was the only paralegal I'd ever worked with who cared about the clients as much as I did.

As the Parks filed out, Genevieve murmuring with Nicky, Kandy showed in the next potential. Nicky's training with the Boiler Room people was really working. She'd given them a two-page form to sniff out the True Disasters and weed out the Barking Dogs. She even had two boxes at the top, to mark with a check if the Boiler Room supervisor thought a case was a True Disaster or a Barking Dog. I couldn't get the supervisor paid more for accurately categorizing the cases. Yet. But I'd told her I would push for it.

It was funny. I wanted to get Nicky a raise and wanted to get the supervisor a raise. All to reward good people who actually helped me work. I was postponing the inevitable confrontation with Rodney over my unpaid profit sharing, as leverage, to get better terms for my people, and to get better service for my clients.

Boy Scout? I'd never been a Boy Scout. But I was trying to be faithful, loyal, and clean. Reverent, maybe someday.

The next one was a puzzler. A fortyish woman walked in with her evident daughter, a brown-eyed waif of a girl in a hoody. The fortyish woman said, "I'm Rikki Lawson and this is my daughter Linda Lou Lawson."

"Pleased to meet you," I said, shaking hands with both. Linda Lou was hiding in her hoodie—skinny girl of maybe fourteen, standing five foot nothing, weighing maybe eighty-five pounds soaking wet. She had high cheekbones and dark brown eyes which looked everywhere except at me.

Rikki said, "Linda Lou was removed from my care by DSHS. While she was at the ReachKids group home a staff member sexually defiled her. The police did investigate. I'm here to assert my rights as her mother."

I studied Rikki—a pudgy blonde wearing lots of makeup and a maroon halter dress.

"I work as a hostess at the casino," she said. "DSHS said I wasn't caring for Linda Lou and the four younger ones. So they took them all and cut off my state benefits. Now look."

Linda Lou cringed at every word her mother said.

Linda Lou would need a litigation guardian, but I didn't tell Rikki that.

I took a family history. Rikki had five kids from different fathers, and was on Social Security Disability for "multiple personality disorder" in addition to her state welfare payments for taking care of the kids. She had to be working "under the table" at the casino as a hostess—paid in cash with the government none the wiser.

I put Rikki under a little stress to see if she would "switch personalities." You know—different voice, different mannerisms, the whole bit?

Not even a twitch. This was a high-intensity situation for Rikki—she leaned forward, clicking her polished fingernails with inset rhinestones on the table, wanting my "wild ass guess" about how much she "could net from this awful thing."

Rikki didn't switch personalities—no different voice, stance, accent, demeanor. She didn't have multiple personality disorder; she was simply a scammer. I wouldn't go into battle with this one. But since Linda Lou wasn't in her custody and needed a litigation guardian ad litem, Rikki would have exactly zero control over anything.

From the way Linda Lou flinched when her mother talked, I'd bet I could bond with Linda Lou if I could tell her confidentially that I would ace Rikki out of the picture.

Rikki concluded that she'd been "unfairly targeted by the police" while selling PCP, also known as "Angel Dust," and her kids had been removed from her home and placed at one of DSHS's wonderful licensed facilities around the Seattle area. I knew a bit about that myself.

"How about if we hear from Linda Lou," I prompted.

Rikki asked me about a civil rights suit against the police and DSHS for wrongful termination of custody. "Not a chance," I said. "They have governmental immunity."

I had a brainwave. "Rikki? Could you go to Starbucks and get me a triple iced Americano? I'm starting to fade. Here's a twenty. That would be a big help."

Hypothesis confirmed. Rikki's eyes zeroed in on my twenty-dollar bill. She left.

"Cool," I told Linda Lou. "I wanted to give you some privacy."

Linda Lou pulled her hoodie an inch above her dark eyes, looking a little less like a terrified chipmunk.

She told her story in a quiet voice. As doctors would say, she seemed like a "reliable historian."

Linda Lou had been vaginally raped by a large male group home staffer who subsequently turned out to be a convicted felon, who shouldn't have been working with kids. But DSHS hadn't run his criminal background check, allowing him to work "provisionally" with kids until they could "rush it through."

DSHS hadn't "rushed it through" for eleven months after he was hired. Then Linda Lou was raped. On her birthday.

"Oh hell," I said, wincing and covering my eyes. That was a psychological kick in the balls for me.

Linda Lou resumed her story, a little louder. She ran away from the ReachKids group home after the rape, went to a minimart, and found an actual payphone. She called 911 and got Seattle Police dispatched. The patrol officer quickly called the Sexual Assault Unit. They asked if Linda Lou had bathed or changed clothes. "I told them I hadn't done either," Linda Lou said, meeting my eyes for the first time. I scribbled notes as quickly as I could so she didn't have to look at me.

The SAU detectives transported Linda Lou to Harborview's Sexual Assault Center where they did a rape kit and then the detectives bagged her clothes, giving her a scrub suit in exchange. Linda Lou knew what would come next—another "placement" in another "fine DSHS-licensed facility." She fled and found shelter with a friend. She still had an active Run Report and would be arrested if the police contacted her.

In her little backpack with the Backstreet Boys stenciled on it, Linda Lou pulled out a manila folder. She had the entire police report. Also the defendant's Statement of Defendant Upon Plea of Guilty. Also the defendant's transcribed confession describing Linda Lou as a "hottie who been sending all them signals." Also the Judgment and Sentence. He'd pled out in exchange for a slightly-reduced sentence.

I would go to war with Linda Lou. I trusted this kid; she was a parentified child taking care of the younger kids, and resourceful, and intuitive.

Linda Lou had somehow even gotten part of the DSHS investigation report in which they said the abuse allegation was "founded." But only after the rapist pled out, of course.

I got Kandy to copy everything. I told Linda Lou, "I want you to keep all these documents. I'm impressed with you for rounding up this stuff. Now let me tell you what comes next."

"Shouldn't you wait for Rikki to come back?"

I leaned forward. "Rikki doesn't have custody. If you want me to sue ReachKids, I'd like to do that. If you hire me I'll hire a litigation guardian ad litem to stand in—in loco parentis—in court."

Linda Lou squinted at me. "In loco parentis? Inside a crazy parent?"

We both laughed. "That's fresh," I said. "No, the litigation guardian acts as your parent or guardian for purposes of the lawsuit only. I know somebody great—Bonus Malone. He drew up my will and he does this stuff all the time. You can proceed with this case without your mother. If you want to proceed."

Linda Lou's eyes went wide. She was imagining something actually being finally being actually under her control, finally.

"I want to proceed," she said. "If I can do it without Rikki butting in."

"I can arrange that," I said.

Here was where I took off my lawyer hat and put on my ex-foster-kid hat. "So Linda Lou," I asked, "where are you staying?"

She blushed, still looking down. Where had I seen that gesture recently? "I'm couch surfing with friends," she said. "Remember DSHS issued a Run Report and technically I could be arrested if any police contact me. So I'm keeping my head low. That's why I wear a hoodie and cover my head whenever I go out."

"Fair enough. But can I get an email address and cell phone number for you?" I slid my legal pad and pen across the table.

Linda Lou looked down and wrote. Girlish round letters. Excellent—both cell and email.

I said, "I won't bug you about where you're staying. But do you have enough clothes?"

"Oh no. Three pairs of jeans. Three hoodies."

I said, "I'd like to give you a Walmart gift card so you can get some better clothes. It bugs me that you had to leave your stuff behind. Does that sound like a good idea?"

Linda Lou squinted at me. "Yeah, I guess."

She wondered if I was sidling up to her with some nasty agenda in mind. I'd have to be formal and distant and not chummy with her. God knows what kind of random felons had been traipsing in and out of Rikki's house.

"Okay, I'm going to get you the Walmart gift card, and meet up with you to hand it off," I said. "Can your mother be trusted?"

Linda Lou rolled her eyes. "Seriously?"

"Okay, she can't. Just checking that out."

"My mother won't bring you change from the coffee place. Just watch."

"I don't expect her to. I gave her the twenty so we could talk alone. My Spidey-sense says not very good things about Rikki."

Linda Lou smiled faintly. "Spidey-sense. Ha."

"I suggest you not tell your mother anything about your case."

"No doubt."

I thought. "I am very optimistic that I can win your case. After that? Well you sure don't want to go back to some DSHS placement. I'm guessing you don't want to live with Rikki again. So how would you like to be an emancipated minor?"

Linda Lou darted a glance at me. "What's that?"

"If you can hold a job and take care of yourself, the Juvenile Court can give you an Order stating you're a legal adult and you're allowed to live where you want and do everything with no adult supervision."

Linda Lou gaped. "Seriously? Can you do that? That would be dope!"

"I'll sure as hell try. You strike me as more trustworthy than the people who've been saying they were taking care of you."

Linda Lou took out a pink Post-It from her backpack and a glittery pen. She wrote *emancipated minor* on it. Then she put them in her wallet. "I'd better Google this."

I said, "We lawyers aren't supposed to promise results—but it's just us two here. A judge wouldn't emancipate you yet because you don't have any money behind you. Do you have a job?"

"My roommate offered me one. Minimum wage, coffee shop."

"I prosecuted in juvie once upon a time. That wouldn't cut it. But if I can get you a settlement or a judgment from ReachKids, you'll have serious money and I'll bet my bottom dollar I can get you emancipated."

Linda Lou grinned, suddenly just a regular kid. "Okey dokey artichoky."

Just then Rikki burst in. She had the smallest iced Americano. No change. Good use of twenty bucks.

I gave Rikki a contract and authorization to sign for "our case," so Rikki got the mistaken impression she was in charge.

Rikki's signature would be nullified once the litigation guardian was appointed by the court, and he or she signed the contract and authorization. Her signature might not even be valid now, because her kids had all been removed from her custody due to her selling PCP.

PCP? What the actual fuck?

But I wanted Rikki to think she had hired me so she wouldn't interfere until I had Bonus Malone in place as litigation guardian.

Two True Disasters in a row? The moon was in the house of weird.

***

That intake had been a long one. Nicky came back from Bonus's office. "The Parks are all set up to get the probate opened," she said, her voice low. "But there's something you need to see."

I grabbed the Linda Lou intake papers and followed her back into the Innocent Peoples' Department. She went into my office, picked up a little yellow box next to Buster's cage and rattled it at me.

I squinted at it. In the little yellow box was a window showing blue pellets. "What on earth?"

Nicky handed it to me. "Rat poison. Somebody put a box of rat poison next to Buster's cage while we were in the Park intake."

I walked over to Buster's cage and examined the floor and the food tray. No little blue pellets. Buster nodded at me. "Well dog my cats," he said.

"He didn't eat any," Nicky said, her voice trembling. "But somebody's trying to send you a message."

I froze. A big ball of white-hot rage swelled inside me, like a balloon ten times the size of my body. I just stood there breathing through it for a few moments.

Then I held out my open hands, and slowly closed them, and crushed it down.

Now it was part of my golf-ball-sized nugget of radioactive determination. Now it would power me toward what I had to do.

Apparently, I had a new nemesis.

"All right," I told Nicky. "I'm taking Buster home tonight. He'll never come here again. If you want to visit him, you'll have to come to my place." I turned away from her and looked at Buster again, even though he hadn't eaten any of the poison. "If that's all right with Fred," I said.

"It will be all right," Nicky said. "There is one more intake."

"I didn't have the time to read the fact sheet on this one," I said. "Can you line it out for me?"

"It's a fatality car crash. The potential defendant is the mayor of Stonington, down in Rockingham County. He is already represented by J. Charm."

Rockingham County again. J. Charm. The hits just kept on coming.

"You're kidding," I said.

"Nope."

"Okay, let's go get 'em," I said.

The client was a very overweight backwoods woman with red nose and eyes from days of crying. "I'm Marjorie Gamble," she said, her voice shaking. The poor woman looked like a sack of potatoes wearing a potato sack.

I started furiously taking notes while she gave her story. She was a single mom who supported her four boys by running a minimart down in Rockingham County. The father was "not in the picture."

Her youngest, the victim, was named Stone Gamble. Stone had been playing paintball with his friends. On their way back home, two blocks from the house, the friend driving turned left in front of a distant oncoming crew cab pickup. The pickup was going about warp factor 8. It slammed into the Camry right where Stone was sitting in the back seat, cutting the Camry almost in half, throwing the Stone onto the pavement, where he hit his head, coughed once, and died.

Stone had just been accepted to West Point. He was going to be the first member of his family ever to go to college. National Honor Society. Varsity track. The whole bit.

The defendant's name was Ron Porcine. Well of course it was. He was the mayor of Stonington. Rockingham County again. I gave Marjorie the spiel about being named personal representative, then signing her. Nicky said she'd take care of everything, and made a call to Bonus Malone's office to make an appointment.

Three True Disasters from one Intake Clinic. If there were three of me, they would have been very busy.

CHAPTER TWENTY-ONE— MR. UNCLE

I took Buster home that night and put on Jack FM in the background. I told him: "I can't take you to work anymore, buddy, but maybe we can sing some Talking Heads together." Buster nodded with a cynical smile.

Buster was the first pet I'd ever had. Now, when I returned to my anonymous condo every night, it wasn't just like filing myself away, alone, in a bankers box.

Given Rodney's attempt to manipulate me into betraying Nicky, I knew he'd been behind the implicit threat with the rat poison. In his upside-down mind, these things showed he considered me useful enough to manipulate.

I checked my email. I sent a draft gmail to The Ghost, because I would need her to run down all the assets on Ron Porcine, the mayor of Stonington. Also I was overdue to play Scrabble with her. Maybe I could bring Buster to our café. I could call him my "emotional support parrot."

Nobody loved pets more than The Ghost. She had adopted a cat because she wanted a "little creature" at home. But she hated that term "emotional support animal." She said: "That's just a pimped-out term for pets. They are pets."

I had new matches from TopFliteSingles.com. Since I'd told Abe about the Malletts' Therapeutic Foster Home, I hadn't been tempted to try another online date. Online dates were guaranteed disappointment. Did I want more guaranteed disappointment?

I logged into TopFliteSingles.com and deleted my account. And smiled.

Online dating had been a placeholder for a real romantic life. Here's one of Duvonda's epigrams: "The bad thing about a placeholder is—it holds the place."

I took off my customary gray single-breasted suit with a subtle pinstripe and laid out another for tomorrow. I had an even dozen of these, all bought at Nordstrom Rack at big discounts. That was my uniform—gray suit, white shirt, blue paisley tie. Black leather shoes, belt, and briefcase. Pewter tie clip, even though that was retro. Hell…my whole personality was retro.

I showered and ate. Buster was swaying a little to the B-52's singing "Cosmic Thing."

I looked at my racks with hundreds of CDs of '80s music, mostly new wave, some Euro synthpop, more than a little punk.

Music had been my life preserver since Suzanne left. But maybe I would find dry land someday soon.

Next, I drove to Walmart and, got a gift card, and put two hundred dollars on it. Once I was back in the battered Outback, I called Linda Lou.

"Hello?" she asked in her small voice.

"This is Sam Strait. I got the Walmart gift card. Could I maybe meet you somewhere and give it to you?"

She pondered. "Okay. There's a café in the University District called Has Beans. Meet me there in thirty."

"Gotcha," I said.

Has Beans turned out to be the archetype of the Seattle coffeehouse that had led to a certain chain spreading across the world. It had chipped granite-topped tables, firehouse chairs, a red cement floor, and The Pixies playing on the overhead, not too loud. Redolent with symphonic aromas of good coffee varietals—Blue Mountains Jamaican, Yirgacheffe, others I couldn't name.

A hipster barista, mandatory goatee and nose ring and ski hat, stood behind the espresso machine.

"I'd like a decaf venti iced Americano," I said.

He smirked. "We don't call them venti here. We call them huge. What varietal?"

"Yirgacheffe. I love Ethiopian coffee. Make it huge."

He pointed a finger at me like a pistol. "Coming right up," he said.

For somebody who had no patience with the homeless addicts who swarmed Seattle, I was pretty addicted myself. The difference? My drug made me smarter—not dumber.

I sat at a window table and tried the Yirgacheffe Americano—deep, rich, complex layers. I was a coffee snob for sure. Has Beans had a great roaster. Maybe they roasted their own.

In Seattle in 2007 people actually cared about this stuff.

Linda Lou sidled in five minutes later, her hoodie hiding her face. The way she hid her face reminded me of Catherine's curtains of hair. I wondered—what must it be like to have the police out there, ready to arrest you and take you to one of DSHS's wonderful "care facilities," after you'd been raped in one?

"Hey," she said, sitting down. Looking down. Still making herself small. She kept her hood up, concealing most of her face.

"Can I get you anything? It's on me. It's even a deductible business expense."

"Okay," she murmured, looking from side to side. "Big old mocha with lots of whipped cream." Just like Duvonda.

"Decaf or caf?"

"Decaf. I've been having trouble sleeping."

I got it and watched her spoon up the whipped cream. She still had her hood over her head, shading her deep brown eyes. Dark circles under her eyes.

I handed her the gift card. "Don't tell Rikki," I said. "I don't want her burning up your gift card."

"Seriously? I won't tell my mom." She tucked it into her hoodie pocket.

I drank again. "I know what it's like," I said.

She darted a glance at me. "What do you mean?"

I took a deep breath. I wanted her to see that somebody with a rotten "DSHS care facility" story could bounce back, eventually. "When I was seven, my parents both died on the same day. My twin sister and I were put in foster care. We were given fifteen minutes inside the house we grew up in to throw some clothes in a garbage bag. Then we were put in so-called therapeutic foster care. That's where I grew up."

I looked up to see how she took that. She nodded. She lifted her eyes for the first time. "But there's more."

"Unfortunately," I admitted. "My older foster brother abused Catherine and me. Sexually."

She leaned forward, her eyes wide. "What happened next?"

"I stabbed him. I wound up on a locked psych ward for weeks, so full of Haldol I felt like I was stuffed with Styrofoam. Then I went back to the foster home. It was the only one that would take Catherine and me together. I didn't want them to split us up. The foster brother was still there. Nobody even considered charging him with a crime. But after that, he acted buddy-buddy with me. He called it 'those games I used to play with you two.'"

Linda Lou drilled down. She'd told me her story; now I owed her my own. "How did it end up?"

I took a drink from my splendid Americano. It was delaying behavior, I knew. In depositions, very often the best admissions came right after the witness took a drink. "Well, he ended up dead."

Her eyes went wide again. She nodded. "Let me ask this the right way. Were you, shall we say…involved?"

"My fingerprints weren't on it. But yes. I didn't kill him. But I kind of engineered it."

I almost laughed. Engineered it? For him to get hit by a train? For some reason, so many years after, it struck me as hilarious. Every day I was glad that Benny was dead. The world was better off without him.

She smiled, looking down. "I get that. So you were protecting your sister?"

"She was all the family I had left. We're still very close. She does therapy with teenagers. She introduces them to her horses. Would you like to maybe meet her horses sometime?"

She dropped her eyes and pulled her hoodie down lower. Defensive posture.

"Hey," I said. "I want to be super clear about something. I will never hit on you. It's disgusting when people with power hit on underaged kids. You're my client. But I kind of think of you like my niece."

She looked at me with guarded eyes. This would take some persuading. Reading between the lines, I suspected that Rikki had tried to pimp her out. "Okay, I guess I'll call you Mr. Uncle."

I liked that. Mr. Uncle. "Great. Don't tell me where you're staying. If I don't know, then I can't tell, even by mistake."

She bit her lower lip. "So what happens next with our case?"

Our case. Excellent. "Next I'll order public disclosure from DSHS about everything to do with the ReachKids group home. Licensing. Personnel list. Criminal background check information carefully hidden in the middle of the list. DSHS will probably produce a bankers box of paper. That's what they do best—generate documents. They can't be sued because they're immune under state law for negligent licensing of the group home, the staff, blah, blah. So they'll give me what they call a 'document dump.'"

She stifled a laugh. Dump. Of course.

"How many pages in a bankers box?" she asked.

"Typically about five thousand pages. I can review a hundred pages an hour. Sometimes two hundred, when I'm wading through the meaningless stuff. I have the whole thing electronically page numbered. Then I print it all from the CD or flash drive they give me. As I go through, when I find something good, I type the page number, the date, and a summary of what I found. So when I'm preparing depositions it goes much faster."

She considered. "Five thousand pages. Fifty hours or so."

"Typically. Then I sue ReachKids, and I demand all their documents regarding you, and the rapist staffer, and their employee screening stuff. I'll already have the public disclosure, so I'll have a good idea if ReachKids is hiding something."

She smiled. "So you're kind of dealing from the bottom of the deck." Yup, she was equipped to be a poker player, all right.

"That's right. I never lie, and I never break the rules. But I want to ambush these bastards." Another Duvonda epigram? The best kind of battle is an ambush.

She applauded softly, like a golf clap. Somewhat ironic. Linda Lou wasn't comfortable with enthusiasm. She reached into her pocket. I could tell she was touching the Walmart gift card, making sure it was still there.

I told her goodnight and left. I hoped she'd be pleased when she found out how much was on the gift card, how many clothes she could buy. She was a teenaged girl. And she was as wary as a feral cat.

I wanted to storm ReachKids's headquarters with a battle axe and demolish the place. I wanted to get her a bazillion dollars. I wanted to make her an emancipated minor so she didn't have to be under the greasy thumb of DSHS any longer.

I wanted to deserve to be called Mr. Uncle.

This was what the more cynical personal injury lawyers never experienced—the joy of the clients. The joy of the work itself.

When I drove home to my anonymous condo, Buster would be there. Maybe he had even learned a song.

CHAPTER TWENTY-TWO— THE DISTINCT SMELL OF ROCKINGHAM COUNTY

A few days later, as I was loading up to go down to Rockingham County on the Stone Gamble case, Nicky came into my office. Bonus Malone had gotten me Letters of Administration for both the Gamble fatality and the Park fatality. I had two hunting licenses. Nicky set them down on my desk. I got a whiff of her faint rose perfume.

I asked, "Could we huddle for a minute?" I shut the door.

"What's up?" she asked, sitting and folding her hands in her lap.

"I'm thinking about that little incident where somebody put a box of rat poison next to Buster's cage."

Nicky flared. "Incident? That was a threat."

"I agree." Then I filled her in on that weird conversation with Rodney where he'd offered to "consider profit sharing" if I agreed Nicky should be fired.

"You told him no, right?" Nicky asked, wringing her hands.

"I told him you were my right arm. I told him the day he fired you, I would quit."

She blushed. She'd been doing a lot of that lately.

"Nicky, if I leave this place, will you come with me?"

She looked down at her lap.

"I've been saving," I said. "I don't spend much. Except on Americanos and parrot food."

That got a faint smile.

"I can offer you the same pay, the same benefits. The time will come when I need to jump ship. I've already got a life raft in the water. Question is, will you come with me? If it's all right with Fred?"

She met my gaze, her deep brown eyes shining. "If you leave, I will come with you."

A warm glow spread all over me. I was always surprised when somebody believed in me. "Awesome," I said. "I'll let you know when the time is drawing near. I guess I'd better get down to Stonington now and see what our good friends in Rockingham County have been up to."

She slid one more document across the desk. "I got the Traffic Collision Report. The tow yard confirms that the police hold on the vehicles has been lifted."

I read through the TCR quickly. "Investigation by Stonington City Police. They investigated their own mayor. Everything about Rockingham County exudes a certain scent, you know?"

She winked. "A fetid miasma," she said.

I burst out laughing, and we high-fived.

"I want you to come with me," I said. "This field trip is going to be pretty interesting."

***

On the freeway, I talked with Don Meissner, who confirmed he'd meet me at the tow yard after lunch. Then we drove to Mrs. Gamble's house. It was one of those prefab log cabins you could build from a kit. I gathered her husband had built it before he left her with all those sons to raise alone.

As I parked in the driveway, I took a deep breath.

Grief has a bad smell. I was going to be drenched in it, and absorb it, so I could understand this case. If you don't feel it, you can't advocate for it. Sometimes I struggled with that. But hell, disaster and I were on a first-name basis.

Mrs. Gamble restrained three boisterous pit bulls that took turns sniffing me and gamboling around the living room, giving yips of delight, jumping over the plaid couches, their hair swirling in the sunlight. Nicky shrank from them. Then Mrs. Gamble led us to Stone's room, which he'd shared with the next-oldest brother.

Stone's side of the room was clean. His bed was made with hospital corners and an Army blanket pulled taut and straight. He had marksmanship awards on the wall and a framed letter of acceptance from West Point. "He's the only one of the family done ever got into college," she said faintly. "My other boys don't have the head for it."

The other side of the room was a mess of gym clothes, an unmade bed with Star Wars sheets, and posters of bikini models on the walls. The other side of the room, like everywhere else in the house, was thickly adorned with dog hair. I looked at Nicky. She wrinkled her nose. She was smelling the grief too.

I needed to get Mrs. Gamble into action. Grief can be a paralytic poison, like the curare surgeons used way back when.

I nodded at Nicky, who started taking notes. I told Mrs. Gamble: "I need you to gather all of the photos, yearbooks, shooting awards, and a copy of the letter from West Point accepting his application," I said. "I need to tell his story."

Mrs. Gamble began weeping again. I'd learned that a mother's grief for a child was the worst grief. I could smell it. I was drenched in it.

"Okay," she said, dabbing at her red-rimmed eyes.

"When you've got it together, call Nicky, and she'll send a messenger," I said. "Once we've copied everything, we'll get the originals back to you. I know these things are important to you," I said, putting a hand on her shoulder.

She flung her arms around me, and we hugged. Sobs shook her. "He was a good boy," she whispered. "Why did this happen to my good boy?"

There was no answer. I was here because of a monstrous wrong.

There's a cynical saying in personal injury law: the worse it is, the better it is. But the reverse is true. Any True Disaster hurts to work on. Pain is money. The trick is to turn the awful feelings into terse and merciless litigation.

I gave her the number of the local twenty-four-hour crisis hotline. After I'd left the Coast Guard, I volunteered there for several years. I also promised to find a grief counselor for her. She was going to need somebody to talk to. If Abe hadn't been so far away, he'd have been my first choice.

Mrs. Gamble saw us out. The three pit bulls sat in a row, their tongues lolling, staring at me. They'd picked up her grief too. Many dogs have a sense of smell ten thousand times as sensitive as the human nose. They knew, all right.

As I left, I saw Mrs. Gamble pick up the phone.

"Look Sam," Nicky said with excitement. "She's calling."

"Thank God," I said.

***

We got lunch at the McDonald's drive-through and parked facing the courthouse square. I looked at the huge khaki howitzer facing the sky, like a raised middle finger. Maybe I would be able to answer it with my own middle finger very soon.

We met Don Meissner at the tow yard, a place called Brownie's Tow and Salvage. It was a small lot that apparently did towing and scrap both. We went into the office.

Malcolm Brownie proved to be a tough and wiry guy in his early thirties with a graying goatee, wearing blue coveralls. He stood and wiped his hands on a rag. "What can I do you for?"

I said, "My name is Sam Strait. I was wondering if I could have a look at the Toyota with the major damage in the back."

He said, "Major damage? Damn, that car is nearly torn in half. But we need legal permission from the car owner to let you back there."

I slid out a copy of the authorization from Stone Gamble's friend Jordan that Nicky had gotten. "Here's the permission. It says Sam Strait may inspect and measure and photograph the vehicle, with his collision expert."

He read through it. "Wait a minute. Sam Strait? You're that guy?"

"Guilty as charged."

Brownie smacked the counter. "My auntie was the lady who died at Sisters of Mercy Hospital after they injected her with cleaning fluid during an operation. It was kept in the identical type of containers as the saline solution." He squinted at me. "Took her weeks to die. She dissolved from the inside out." He took a deep breath. "You done settled their business. They're still closed, last I heard. I think I'm on your side, whatever side that is."

Brownie led us back into the salvage yard. Don Meissner elbowed me. "There's your wreck," he said.

The champagne Toyota Camry was indeed nearly torn in half. Ron Porcine's Dodge Ram crew cab pickup had crashed into the right side at high speed. It felt like the temperature dropped twenty degrees.

"This is the Toyota," Mr. Brownie said. "You can inspect all you want. Hey, can you guys keep a secret?"

I edged closer to him and lowered my voice. "Sure. What's up?"

Mr. Brownie looked around too, edged in closer, and whispered. "The Stonington Police released the investigation hold yesterday. Right after that, I got a call from some…person. The guy offered me ten thousand in cash for this wrecked Toyota if I would let him come pick it up from the yard, no calls to the owner, nothing. Just leave the gate open tonight, in the morning it would be gone. Report it as stolen. Easy peasy. Any idea why somebody would want to do that?"

I looked at Don Meissner. He stroked the ends of his walrus mustache. I'd never seen him angry before. Nothing gave it away but the cold glint in his blue eyes. "Somebody's tying up loose ends," he said.

I had to buy this Toyota and get it stowed away. Right now. "Can I use your phone?" I asked.

"Sure. Even if it ain't a local call."

I called Stone's friend Jordan, the Toyota owner. I said: "Eventually the insurance company is going to offer you four hundred for the car in salvage value. Could I buy it for a thousand, in cash, right now?"

Jordan said, "Sure. What's the rush?"

I told him about the anonymous offer to Brownie. "I need to preserve it to nail the bastard who killed Stone."

"I'll be right down. I'll bring the whole file with the title and stuff."

I told Don Meissner and Mr. Brownie, "I need to run to the bank to get cash. I'll be back in two shakes of a lamb's tail."

I drove to my bank and withdrew a thousand from my savings in $100 bills. Rodney would never reimburse me. I didn't give a shit. I had to get this car stashed away.

When I got back to Brownie's Towing, Mr. Brownie and Don Meissner were huddled, whispering—beside a Dodge Ram crew cab with impressive damage to the right front bumper and fender and grill. The driver's side door was open. That had to be Porcine's truck. It even had some paint transfer from the champagne-colored Toyota.

Mr. Brownie said, "I was just telling Mr. Meissner here that the owner came out last night, with buddy and a spare battery, and kept starting the truck. He started it, and turned it off, dozens of times. Unfortunately he left the driver's door open when he left. Strange, huh?"

Don patted his laptop case. "Since the vehicle was not secured, I plugged my laptop into the data port and downloaded the airbag control module. Surprise, surprise. It was wiped clean when the truck was started over one hundred times in the past twelve hours. So there's no data on how fast the Ram was going when it hit the Toyota."

Nicky gasped.

I said: "And the Toyota is too old to have a new-style airbag control module?"

"Shoot, it's a fossil," Mr. Brownie said. "No airbags and no airbag control module and no data."

Don glared at me. "The only way to prove the defendant's speed is the crush damage on the Toyota," he said. "Crush damage on the truck is minimized because…mass wins. I photographed the Toyota's crush damage and measured compartment intrusion, the whole bit. Let me show you."

I took a deep breath as we walked over to the Toyota. Stone Gamble had been in the back right seat, right where the Dodge Ram hit. His blood was splattered inside, in thick globs that looked like chocolate syrup but smelled like copper. Old blood smells like copper. The Toyota had been twisted so violently that all the windows exploded out. The car was shaped like a shallow V.

Don showed me the seatbelt in the right rear, where Stone had been sitting. He pointed to a scorched discoloration next to the adjustment clip on the seatbelt. "The poor kid got hit so hard that the seatbelt essentially burned as it was pulled through the clip. This detail alone shows the Dodge Ram was going well over forty. Seatbelts don't scorch when they're pulled through the clip unless the opposing vehicle is doing forty-plus."

Some cases gather force on their own. The more you dig, the more awful they get.

"Yo," called a handsome lanky blond kid, about six foot, wearing a Seahawks ball cap backward. Jordan. We all introduced ourselves. "So line up the forms and I'll sell you the Toyota," Jordan said, trying not to look at the Toyota. Trying not to smell it—the coppery smell of old blood.

Brownie said, "I'm a notary public. I do title transfers all the time. Come back in the office."

I gave Jordan the thousand dollars. Brownie made up a receipt for Jordan to sign. Then he did the title transfer documents.

Jordan shook hands with me. "But there's one more thing I want other than the money," he said, glancing at Nicky. Because he was a polite kid, and he was about to swear.

I gulped. "Okay."

"I want you to nail this motherfucker."

"I'll do my absolute best," I said. We shook on it. He met my eyes. When an honest young man makes me promise something? I fulfill the promise. They taught me that in the Coast Guard.

Brownie clapped Jordan on the back. They walked out together, talking about the Seahawks's chances of a playoff run.

The funny thing about a corrupt small town with a corrupt old boys network? Old boys make a lot of enemies. Those enemies accumulate. They gossip. And they never forget. In a small town, word gets around.

Don cleared his throat. "In the good old days, when I worked for the NTSB, we had federal warehouses to store wrecks. But where are we going to store this one?"

I hadn't gotten that far yet. I was the proud owner of a V-shaped Toyota in the very salvage yard where the anonymous caller had said it would be "stolen" after Brownie got ten thousand dollars for merely leaving the gate open.

I looked at Nicky. "Any ideas?"

Nicky said, "Just call Duvonda."

I called Duvonda on my cell. I was lucky; she was both in the office and kind of bored. I walked out into the front parking lot so we wouldn't be overheard.

I filled her in. "So here's the thing," I said. "Do you know anybody who has a warehouse or a barn on property that they protect with lots of dogs and lots of guns?"

She said, "Bet you didn't know that Silent Mike grew up on a farm, down in the South Sound, didja?"

"No way!"

"His uncle Chester Arthur raised him. Chester has sixty acres in strawberries and whatnot just east of Olympia. Chester is as honest as the day is long, but he can be as mean as a snake. I know you're down in Rockingham County, so I used those cliches just for you."

I laughed. Today was turning out well, even though it was going to be expensive. Because of course I was going to pay to transport the Toyota and rent Chester Arthur's building. "Does he have an empty barn that he might like to rent out?"

"He's got three barns. I bet he'll rent you one. He won't charge you much, so long as I call him and get him good and mad about this situation."

"Does he have watchdogs?"

"He has five Presa Canarios. He breeds them on the side."

Presa Canarios. A hundred pounds of carnivorous loyalty. Certain dictators used Presa Canarios exclusively because rumor had it they were the best guard dogs ever bred.

"Does he have guns?" I asked, pressing my luck.

"Silent Mike and I spend holidays with him. Before dinner we always do some shooting at his dirt berm out back. I've seen twelve of his guns. I bet he has more. He was a Green Beret in Vietnam. He says eternal vigilance is the price of liberty."

"Can you do me a huge favor and ask him for me if it's okay to rent his barn, and bring the car down today? I don't know him. It'll sound better coming from you. I know I owe you one."

Duvonda chuckled. "You owe me seventeen or eighteen. Sure I'll do it." She cleared her throat. "Sam, do you think Rodney is going to be Okay with this? Will he pay you for the car and towing and whatnot?"

I sighed. "He won't give me a dime. But a good kid died. It has to be done."

Duvonda said, "Sam, when are you going to leave that place? You don't belong alongside a bunch of DUI defense lawyers, working for a cobra like Rodney Mammon."

"I was just thinking the same thing. But I have to run this case to the ground first."

"My friend, there is always going to be a case to run to the ground. Just promise me you'll consider it. You know if you leave, your clients get the choice to come with you. No matter what it says in your contract, lawyers cannot agree to noncompete clauses. It's against the Rules of Professional Conduct. You could leave and take the clients with you if they want to stay with you. Just think it over."

"I'll think it over."

"Good. Now, you only owe me sixteen favors."

When I walked back into the office, the back door was open, and I could see back to the Toyota. Don Meissner was holding up something that looked like a quarter. Brownie was looking at it in disbelief. Nicky had her hand to her mouth.

I rejoined them. "What's that?" I asked.

Don glared at me. "This is a GPS transmitter. I found it in the front left wheel well of the Toyota. Apparently some interested party placed it there."

Brownie jumped in: "Ron Porcine was here last night with his buddy restarting the Dodge Ram over and over. His buddy had the spare truck battery if they needed it. I couldn't keep my eyes on them the whole time."

Don said, "You know this defendant is really starting to piss me off." He pocketed the GPS transmitter. "You know what I'm going to do? On my way home, I'll stop by the FedEx dispatch yard near my house. I'll plant it on one of their delivery vans. The Toyota will apparently be looping all over the Puget Sound area in the next couple of days, until the defendant figures it out."

I was moved. "Don, you're a genius," I said.

"I'm an expert witness," he corrected me. "But I'm just really getting pissed off."

He left.

My phone dinged. Duvonda had texted me the address for Chester Arthur and said he would be delighted to rent his barn.

"Okay, Mr. Brownie," I said. "I'm going to stick my neck way out here. Would you be willing to swear by God that, if I hire you to transport the Toyota, you won't tell anybody—not anybody—where we took it?"

Mr. Brownie stuck out his hand. I shook it. His grip was stronger than mine. "Listen, Sam. I just turned down ten thousand dollars to keep my gate open tonight. Why? Because some money is too dirty to take. Ron Porcine was on the board of Sisters of Mercy Hospital. He signed off on those secret payoff deals in the medical malpractice cases, like the one where they killed my auntie. My uncle was willing to take the money and shut up because he was just crushed. But damn all those people. I won't tell." He regarded me. "Ron Porcine really deserves to get himself stomped on."

Nicky hugged Brownie.

Mr. Brownie tarped up the Toyota, and then backed up his tilting-bed truck, the kind for transporting cars that were so smashed they couldn't be towed. He tilted the bed until it formed a ramp. I helped him fix cables to the front bumper of the Toyota. Then he activated the winches and dragged the Toyota up onto the bed. The Toyota groaned as it was loaded. Its frame was bent, probably broken in places. It shrieked with metal fatigue. It stuck out on both sides of Brownie's truck. Brownie stuck a "wide load" flag on the back and we were in business.

It turned out that Chester Arthur was definitely interested in our story. He said the rent for the barn would be one dollar a month. I paid him for a year out of my wallet. As we drove away down his gravel driveway, the Presa Canarios gamboling beside us, Nicky said, "Twelve dollars? You spend that in a day on Americanos!"

I smiled, sad and happy both. You know how you can be sad and happy at the same time? Complex feeling. "I know. This case wants to make itself into a winner. All you and I have to do is follow where it wants to go."

The funny thing about True Disasters? You can meet wonderful people while working on them. A True Disaster can call forth the best in people.

CHAPTER TWENTY-THREE—THE GHOST DID SOME DIGGING

Next, I set up a meeting with The Ghost to get her started on Ron Porcine's asset search. I needed to know everything he owned so I could consider filing for a Prejudgment Writ of Attachment. Since he'd wiped the airbag control module on his Ram, he knew he'd been speeding. He was what we called a "sophisticated defendant."

Okay, Vanilla Boy, The Ghost said. *Come by tonight at seven. I'll show you what I've got. And I can introduce you to my new kitty. I got a mackerel gray tabby named Pirate. He's a talkative little guy.*

I showed up at seven and met Pirate—he was leggy, almost fully grown, with icy green eyes. "Meow," he said.

"Meow in return," I said, scratching him behind the ears. He stretched out and purred.

"If you did that to me I would stretch out and purr too," The Ghost said with a wicked gleam in her eyes as she set up the Scrabble board. She wore horn-rimmed glasses tonight and had her flyaway blonde hair in a bun. She wore a slate-gray pantsuit. Hmm. Sultry librarian look. My favorite. But I'd never tell her that. I had the impression she'd had an epic playdate the night before.

"So, your pet," The Ghost said, scrambling the Scrabble tiles.

"He's the green parrot that my dead client owned. Remember the case against the home healthcare aide and DSHS? His name is Buster. He's learning some interesting phrases."

The Ghost smiled. It was rare for her to smile. "I'm glad you have some companionship at your anonymous condo, as you call it. So are you ready for me to wipe the floor with you?" In fairness, she did usually win.

We played only one game. The Ghost was not at her best, but she took an unbeatable lead when I played OVERT, and she made it into COVERT, landing the triple word score and cinching the win.

I gave her the Traffic Collision Report in the Stone Gamble case. "I need you to do an asset check and dig up some dirt on Ron Porcine, the mayor of Stonington, down in Rockingham County. Stonington City Police did the collision investigation, if you can call it that." I filled her in on how somebody working for Mr. Porcine had offered to buy the wrecked Toyota for ten thousand dollars and had put a GPS tracker on it at the salvage yard. I also told her about how Mr. Porcine had wiped the airbag control module on his Ram pickup.

"Okay, so this guy is officially a waste of oxygen," The Ghost said. "You've got a True Disaster. I'll get everything within a week and let you know. I assume you want to seize his assets?"

"If he doesn't have super-strong asset protection in place. My well-trained nose thinks he's been doing insider deals with the city while he's mayor, and he's probably concealing the profits with skill. This man is not stupid."

"My favorite flavor. Okay." She paused. "But Sam, I want to bring up something."

Uh oh. I wondered if she was in some kind of trouble.

"All right," I said, petting Pirate. He leaned into my hand. "What have you gotten into now?"

There was sadness in her eyes. "I've gotten into you," she said. "More specifically, your past."

This was unexpected. "What do you mean, my past? There's nothing important about my past."

She took a deep breath. "You know I am afflicted with excessive curiosity, right? I looked into your parents' deaths. I've found out something. But I want to know if you want to know. Some secrets are better left unshared."

I was rocked. My parents' deaths had been a closed issue for over twenty years. "They both died because of a natural gas leak. I don't think there's anything more to know."

"There is," she said, putting away the Scrabble board. "But only if you want to know it."

I was afflicted with morbid curiosity too. But why dig up that stuff? Did I really want to know?

Since I'd gotten my head straightened out with Abe, I actually did. "Okay, I want to know. What did you find?" The Ghost could find unfindable things.

"I got the medical examiner report. They did both die from natural gas inhalation, all right. But there's more to the story."

She took a document out of her purse and slid it over to me. It read *Medical Examiner's Report – Narrative Addendum.*

My blood turned cold. Suddenly I was at THE SCENE of my parents' death, in the cheerful yellow house I'd left when I was seven.

I smelled rotten eggs and roadkill.

Further investigation by police revealed additional facts regarding the deaths of RON STRAIT and PHYLLIS STRAIT. PHYLLIS STRAIT had pre-morbid generalized anxiety disorder, and was under a psychiatrist's care, but reportedly treatment was ineffective. On the night of the STRAITS' demise, RON STRAIT was out of town at a real estate seminar with his partner, RODNEY COMBE. RON STRAIT returned home early. He invited RODNEY COMBE in for a drink. When they entered the residence they heard PHYLLIS STRAIT upstairs in the residence, audibly crying. RON STRAIT told RODNEY COMBE his wife was distraught. This was not unusual. He said he would sleep on the couch, and told RODNEY COMBE to go home.

RON STRAIT and PHYLLIS STRAIT were discovered deceased the next morning by a neighbor who backed out when she smelled the strong odor of natural gas and called police. Police brought in Fire to ventilate the house so it was safe to work in.

I remembered the house that afternoon—all windows open, big fire department fans blowing in the windows, as my parents were brought out in black body bags and loaded into the gray medical examiner's van. The fans gushing the smell of rotten eggs and roadkill. I remembered Catherine going berserk while we were locked in the back of the state police car. I wondered if I should tell Catherine any of this.

Once the residence was adequately ventilated police discovered the following. PHYLLIS STRAIT was deceased in the upstairs master bedroom, well dressed, on her back, with no visible marks or signs of violence on her. Next to her on the bed was a note in red ink that read "I QUIT." The handwriting was determined to be hers, and her fingerprints were on the note. Downstairs on the couch, RON STRAIT was found deceased with no visible marks or signs of violence on him. In the basement, the natural gas supply pipe feeding the furnace had been detached from the furnace. An adjustable chrome wrench was located next to the detached natural gas supply pipe. A fingerprint technician bagged the chrome wrench and lifted latent prints. They were determined to be those of PHYLLIS STRAIT.

The causes of death for both decedents are retained as "inhalation injury, natural gas." The manners of death are amended. PHYLLIS STRAIT's manner of death is determined to be SUICIDE. Because RON STRAIT was not expected home and was evidently not observed when PHYLLIS STRAIT opened the natural gas supply line during the night, his manner of death is amended to ACCIDENT.

I remembered Rodney Combe, my dad's partner, saying "your dad was the dumbest smart man I ever knew." Now I knew what he meant. Dad was dumb because he had married Mom.

Mom meant to kill herself, thinking Dad was safely out of town, and Catherine and I were at camp. Dad came home early and didn't disturb Mom, so he slept on the couch. Mom didn't see him there when she opened the natural gas line.

Mom meant to kill herself. She killed Dad by accident.

We were orphaned because of a giant screwup.

"Christ," I said, with tears in my eyes.

The Ghost moved her chair over to mine, and put her arm across my shoulder. "Maybe I shouldn't have looked into this. Maybe I shouldn't have told you."

I shook myself. "No, I've always wanted to know the truth, even if it hurts. That's what my whole job is about, hey? It's just weird."

"What's weird," she murmured, stroking my hair.

"I feel so, so sorry for both of them. Those poor people." I took a deep breath. Pirate jumped up on my lap and blinked at me, the way cats will do. "Damn, they both suffered." I gave a hollow crack of laughter. "Catherine always says that our mom was like a smoke detector with messed-up wiring. You can be boiling broccoli and it keeps going off because it thinks there's a fire. But it's just steam. My mother had defective wiring."

The Ghost stroked my hair again. "So, does this change anything? In your life? In how you feel about me?"

I put my hand over hers. "No, of course not. You gave me the choice. I decided I wanted to know. Funny, it actually makes a lot of questions I had just dissolve." I gave a hollow crack of laughter again. "Just this afternoon I was down at the salvage yard in Stonington. I thought how I've always been on a first-name basis with disaster. Maybe that's why I do what I do."

The Ghost kissed the top of my head. "You do what you do because you are driven," she said. "That's why we understand each other."

She made me some herbal tea. We drank it in silence. Ever since I was a kid, I was comfortable being good friends with women, because of Catherine.

"So," she said, shooing me out, "I'll get you the dirt on Mr. Porcine as soon as I can. This is yours to keep," she said, tucking the Medical Examiner's Report – Narrative Addendum into my shirt pocket.

***

When I got home, I called Catherine and asked if I could come out and talk with her by the paddock. She said sure.

The next day was a Saturday, windy and sunny—rare for the Northwest in December. Crows cavorted in the wind. Catherine sat me down on a hay bale beside her paddock and took an adjoining hay bale. "Okay, you have no poker face whatsoever," she said. "What's up?"

"My investigator did a little extra-curricular digging and found out something about how Mom and Dad died. She asked me if I wanted to know, and I did. So now I'm wondering whether you want to know."

Catherine sighed. "Why would it make any difference now? I'm a trillion miles past all that."

I nodded. "I think I am too. What's bothering me is that it isn't bothering me. It seems like a 'so what' moment. But am I being pathological or something?"

Catherine shrugged. "I can't see that it would make any difference, at this point. Sometimes I can barely remember them." She picked up a broad blade of grass, cupped her hands around it and blew. Honk. Across the paddock, Jenny the retired racehorse pricked up her ears.

I got it. "Okay. I agree. Let's not pick at the scab."

Catherine honked again. "However, it is bothering you. It's bothering you that it doesn't bother you, which is truly neurotic. So if you want to bounce it off me, go ahead."

I handed her the Medical Examiner's Report – Narrative Addendum.

She read it with a frown. She shook her head when she was done and handed it back to me.

"You always had her number," I told her. "I was the one who tried to argue that Mom was somewhat normal. You always knew she was batshit crazy. That story about how we had to come home before the streetlights came on? But we couldn't know when they would come on until they actually did come on? You were the one who remembered that. There were dozens of stories like that."

I remembered Nicky talking about how people had to get their neurochemistry straight or they couldn't possibly live a good life. "She really was wired like a defective smoke detector that keeps going off when you're steaming broccoli, because it thinks steam is fire, because it just cannot stop alerting about every damn thing."

Catherine leaned forward, her hair curtaining her eyes. "Poor Dad," she said. "He went to sleep on the couch so he wouldn't intrude on her. That's what got him killed."

"I know," I said. "He did everything but stand on his head to make her stop freaking out. But nothing other than the right psychotropic drugs could do that. They hadn't even been invented yet."

She leaned forward more. "Remember what Dad's partner used to say? That Dad was the dumbest smart man he ever met? It's because he married Mom."

I plucked a long stalk of green grass. "And because he stayed with her."

Catherine sat up straight and looked at me. "I never told you this, but while we were living at the Malletts' place, I used to wish that Dad had just divorced her."

"It would have saved everything. Except Mom."

"Mom couldn't be saved. She was the *Titanic*. The only thing to do was get away from her before the undertow dragged you down. You. Me. Dad."

A thought hit me, hard. "You know the only thing that stuns me? Dad died because of a giant screwup. Yet my whole career is spent trying to fix giant screwups, fixing mistakes people make that get other people clobbered. Sometimes even screwups that get people killed. It's so weird. My crusade started when our parents died. And I didn't even know it until now."

Catherine put a hand on my shoulder.

A weird chill went through me. You know that feeling, when you squint at the world a little, and you can see the whole plot? It was like that.

"If God is a novelist," I said, "he's a very good one. He really knows how to put everything together so that, in an inside-out way, it fits together." I shivered. "I think I'll spend the rest of my life marveling at that."

We just sat there like that for about five minutes. A chill gust of wind whipped across the paddock. I felt like I was looking through a kaleidoscope, and I'd twisted the swiveling part just right, and finally, I saw a clear picture of my parents.

I saw it all, and I understood it all, and I forgave it all. My poor parents. They'd done the best they could, but my Mom's best wasn't good enough.

Now, I was finally ready to be a really good personal injury lawyer. Now that I'd been clobbered myself in a way I never saw coming.

Catherine stood up. "But. Here's the question I always ask my clients right before we start counseling." She squinted at me in the bright sun. "How is your life right now?"

Well that stopped me. I thought for a minute. Then I broke out into a smile. "You know what? It has never been better! I'm doing work I love. I have wonderful friends." I stood up and hugged her. "And I have a sister who is really loyal. Even if she won't show me how to make that duck sound with a blade of grass. And even if she does have an unfriendly horse."

Catherine sat down, and I did, too. "Okay. Here's how it works." She picked another long blade of grass and cupped it between her hands. I did the same. She opened her hands so there was a narrow oval between her thumbs. I did the same. "Now, just exhale with medium force, not too hard."

I did it. Honk.

Jenny pricked up her ears again, and turned around. "Don't look at her," Catherine murmured. "Reluctant horses, like reluctant people, only approach when they are being ignored."

I looked down. I honked again.

"She's coming," Catherine whispered. I heard a couple of muffled steps.

"Now open your palms and keep looking down," Catherine whispered. I did it.

Jenny put her stubbly lips in my hands and took the grass. I stroked her velvety nose.

"Try it again," Catherine said. I did.

"Now you can look at her."

I looked up at Jenny. Her huge brown eyes shone. I looked down again so I wouldn't overwhelm her.

"We can't do anything about the past," Catherine said. "So here's a thing. Because we can't do anything about it? It doesn't matter. All that matters is what we do from now on."

Such a simple formula! On the drive home, I felt a great big weight of…wreckage…just slide off and go away. I wasn't dragging it around anymore.

When I got home, I went out on the balcony and tore the medical examiner's report into tiny pieces. I waited. Then, a breath of wind came and took them away. "Goodbye, Mom and Dad," I said. "Rest in peace."

CHAPTER TWENTY-FOUR—KANDY

Next Monday, first thing in the morning, Rodney gathered us all in the lobby at the firm.

"I have some sad news," he said in a monotone. "Our friend Kandy died over the weekend. The cause of death is undetermined, but it wasn't something violent like a car crash. I'll be posting a schedule showing what support staff will be filling in at Reception until I hire her replacement."

Since it wasn't a car crash or something violent, I'd bet my lunch I knew the cause of death. Drug overdose.

Rodney droned on: "If there is a memorial service, I will post the details in the break room so we can all turn out to show our support to her family at this difficult time."

The former football players and cheerleaders in the Guilty Peoples' Department all started talking at once, demanding to know how she died, and when she died, and where she died. Rodney silenced them with an upraised hand. "I don't have any more information now. Let us go back to work and remember our good friend Kandy." Total monotone. He might have been reading the weather report.

Nicky and I traipsed back into the Innocent Peoples' Department. "What do you suppose the cause of death is?" I murmured to her.

Nicky turned to me. "Given her age? And her lifestyle? I'm thinking drugs." She looked down. "Maybe she just couldn't get her neurochemistry straightened out."

I leaned in and said, "I'm thinking drugs, too. The smart money says it was drugs."

I remembered Kandy describing stripping, saying that she only felt free when she felt exposed. Strip clubs and drugs went together like peanut butter and jelly. Poor kid.

"I'm guessing you'll have to fill in some at Reception," I told her. "Listen." I stepped closer to her. "You are the only one here that I trust even a little. If you hear something about Kandy will you let me know?"

"Of course. We're a nation of two back here."

I mulled that over. Nicky and I were already our own firm.

I sat in my office and watched the December winds lashing the trees. Christmas shoppers with their heads down hurried on the sidewalks. Now it came—the six months of gloom and rain that made Seattle the suicide capitol of the US. That was another reason I ran—to avoid the lethargy and low-grade depression the locals called seasonal affective disorder. Sometimes, I thought the addiction and despair and decadence and homelessness I saw around me was mostly due to the everlasting gloom.

Later that morning, Nicky buzzed me on the intercom. "Sam, you really want to see this," she said. There was a courier at her desk with a hand truck loaded with two bankers boxes.

I'd recently filed suit on Linda Lou's case and sent out Requests for Production of Documents. Apparently, ReachKids had decided to over-comply.

When you sue a big organization with a big insurance policy protected by a big firm and request documents, there are two types of responses. Sometimes, they claim you didn't ask for the right stuff in the right name, and they stonewall. More commonly they do a "document dump," where they produce mountains of sometimes-irrelevant stuff and hope to spoil your appetite.

Outhouse Counsel always pulls stuff like this. The beauty part? They bill the insurance company for reading it all. But usually, they don't read it all. Usually, then, flip through a few things, record a lot of hours, and pocket the difference.

I've found plenty of smoking guns that way.

Nicky glanced at the bankers boxes with alarm; she was worried I'd tell her to go through it all. She'd been a paralegal for five years, so this wasn't her first rodeo.

I pulled up a chair. "Okay, here's how I like to handle a document dump. First, I want you to get the legal copying service to Bates number all pages from Lawson 0001 onward. Then, I'm going to review everything in the next couple of weeks. Don't worry, I won't ask you to read anything except for the Easter eggs I find."

"Easter eggs?"

"In something of this size, there are bound to be some Easter eggs—stuff that is pure gold that defense counsel doesn't realize is there. So, while I'm indexing it, I'll just need you to hold my calls and never interrupt me unless the building is on fire. And you've seen the actual flames."

"So, how do you index something like this?"

I took a deep breath. I'd developed my system the hard way—by doing something else first and getting hammered. "As I review each page, I look to see if there's anything juicy. If there is, I enter it into my Word document, that I call an IDX file. For example, if I find an email where ReachKids decides not to do the criminal background check before letting Mr. Rapist work with Linda Lou, I'll type in *00097—date—ReachKids fails to get criminal background check*. Then I'll put in some asterisks—more depending on how good it is for proving liability. That email would rate ten asterisks, the maximum. Then, when I'm preparing the deposition of the president of ReachKids in a couple of months, I'll search the IDX file for entries with lots of asterisks—say three or more—and make those deposition exhibits in chronological order. When I'm deposing the president, I'll ask questions about the subject. When I have the answer, I'll lay down the document and point out contradictions, and get some embarrassed backpedaling. At the end, I have testimony and exhibits in chronological order explaining how ReachKids let the unscreened Mr. Rapist work alone with Linda Lou, which allowed him the opportunity to rape her. When I've got a few of these deps I'm ready to move for summary judgment. There is no dispute of fact because I'm relying solely on the defendants' documents and witnesses. Most witnesses won't deny the truth of a document they've never seen before with their name on it. It's laborious but pretty unstoppable. It often leads to what's basically a confession."

She clapped her hands and smiled. "I love it. But ten thousand pages?"

I nodded. "It's the brute force approach. But I've found it usually works. It's just hilarious when I confront the defense counsel with a document he gave to me and he doesn't know exists. It's common for them to make lots of objections and turn funny colors. That's why I do these deps on video. I want the judge or jury to see the defense trying to cover up after they've handed me the family jewels. But it only works because I'm willing to look at this giant pile of paper," I said, nodding at the two bankers boxes.

"How long will it take you to go through all that?" she said, following my gaze.

"If I'm totally caffeinated and not interrupted, I can go through about a hundred pages an hour. So that's a hundred hours. Given that we've got a couple of other big cases starting to cook, I can get it done in three weeks if I do lots of it at home. It feels like starting to cross the Atlantic in a rowboat. But crossing the Atlantic in a rowboat is the last thing the defendants expect. Most plaintiffs' lawyers have a paralegal read the stuff or hire an expert to read the stuff. Sometimes that works, granted. But when I throw myself totally into it, it hasn't failed yet."

"Okay," Nicky said. "I'll be up at Reception some of the time. But the rest of the time, I'll guard your privacy. And hey, I got you a little present recently. I thought you might want this after some of the exuberant criminal defense paralegals kept interrupting you to triumphantly announce the arrival of a fax." She opened her desk drawer. "It's a Do Not Disturb sign."

I smiled. "Thank you." She'd evidently stolen it from a Radisson.

This was what I liked best about Nicky. She cared as much about the mission as I did. I'd never worked with a paralegal like her before. Many law firm staff do as little as possible for as much as possible. I'd always gotten stuck with that kind before. Nicky really was my strong right arm.

***

So I put my nice Do Not Disturb sign on the door, got two large iced Americanos, and dug in. Twice that afternoon, the criminal defense paralegals interrupted me with routine faxes. Like all of the support staff besides Nicky, they looked like supermodels. Both times, I politely told them, "Please don't come in when the sign is on my door." After the second time, I put a box on the shelf in Nicky's cubicle with a sign on it that said, *Sam's Stuff.* Nicky promised she would head off any further interruptions. The supermodels didn't like that. They assumed everything they did was important and fascinating.

Document review is metaphysical for me. Just when I'm starting to get bored, I'll find something explosive. When I'm fully in the zone, I realize the evidence is whispering. I just have to listen closely.

I was three hundred pages in when I turned up my first Easter egg—a current list of home phone numbers, home addresses, and personal emails of all ReachKids staff. Not just at the group home where Linda Lou was raped—system-wide, across twenty-two foster homes, seven group homes, and three youth shelters. There was no way Outhouse Counsel knew they had given this to me. It strongly implied that they hadn't read the ten thousand pages in the document dump.

I put it through my desktop scanner and saved it in the file in Linda Lou's file, under the new folder Easter Eggs. It was a great start. While I was doing that, I checked my gmail account at Vanillaboy6969.

Yup, I had a draft email from The Ghost. Quick work. Apparently, she'd found something on Ron Porcine. I wrote my own draft email suggesting I come by at eight. *Bring a big flash drive*, she replied.

Big. Sweet.

So I got home at six, changed out of the obligatory gray suit and blue paisley tie, showered, and fed Buster and myself. "Hang 'em high," I said to Buster.

"Burn 'em to the waterlines," Buster said. New phrase. I nearly dropped my fork.

I got to The Ghost's condo at eight. Tonight, she was wearing a delectable maroon cocktail dress. She ushered me into her living room—the Playroom. The Toy Closet door was open about three inches. A lazy blue curl of sandalwood incense rose from the bar, where a Bose Wave played early Sinatra, turned down low. She was messing with me all right.

We sat at the kitchen table. "I have a playdate in an hour, so we'll have to keep this short," she said, seating me at her table. Pirate jumped into my lap, and I stroked his soft head. "Flash drive?"

I handed it to her. She plugged it into the USB port on her computer, and it started blinking as she transferred the folder.

I asked, "So, is Mr. Porcine a waste of oxygen?"

She pointed at me and winked. "Totally. Once the data transfer is done, I'll give you the overview." I took out my legal pad and pen. The drive blinked. The Ghost liked building my anticipation.

Finally, the flash drive stopped blinking, and she handed it back to me. "All right. Rockingham County. Stonington. There's an aroma."

I said, "Nicky calls it a fetid miasma."

The Ghost laughed, which was rare. "Splendid. A fetid miasma." She drank her tea. "Mr. Porcine was elected mayor of Stonington two years ago. Several years before that, he bought land zoned industrial adjacent to the existing city hall and police station. After he was elected, he hired a consultant to determine the city's need for public facilities over the coming decade. Wouldn't you just know it? They needed a new municipal center comprising a city hall and police station. The old facilities would be turned into a Community Center for Underserved Populations. Note my sarcasm. There was only one large piece of vacant land adjacent to the existing buildings, which was owned by Hamm LLC, which was owned by Hamm Inc., which had a registered agent named J. Charm whatever."

I gulped. J. Charm Smythe. That guy turned up in the middle of every mess down in Rockingham County.

"Hamm Inc. is owned by a bunch of people who live in Stonington. None of which is Ron Porcine. But they all happen to be his friends, and four of them are on the city council. Nobody protested when the city bought the land for about twice its assessed value. Except for one poor sap on the city council, who was ruled out of order. The vote was six to one."

"Just out of morbid curiosity, who was the one dissenter on the council?"

"Some guy who runs a towing yard named…" She shuffled papers.

"Brownie?"

"That's it, Brownie! I knew it was a name like that."

Brownie. What a guy. You find heroes in the weirdest ways when you do this kind of work. He could have had ten thousand dollars for a V-shaped wreck of a Toyota. He could have had a fat slice of something for going along with the inside deal about the new municipal center. But Sisters of Mercy had killed his auntie. J. Charm had defended Sisters of Mercy and swept it under the rug.

The funny thing about bad people? They can't seem to realize that good people can't be bought. They just can't see it. That's how they get blindsided. Call me simplistic. I call 'em as I see 'em.

I finished up with my notes and pocketed the flash drive. I looked The Ghost up and down. "You look as delicious as a hot fudge sundae," I murmured.

"Enough of that," she chided me, walking me to the door. Pirate trailed us. I bent down and again stroked his soft head. "I have a very alternative evening planned. I'm glad I could help. I'll provide you with my usual reasonable invoice in a few days. This playdate is going to be somewhat…extended."

I thought about asking. But I didn't. The Ghost valued her privacy more than anything. If I wasn't going to be her playmate, then I could not know anything about her playmates. That was okay. I wasn't wired the right way to be her playmate.

CHAPTER TWENTY-FIVE— ALCHEMY

When Don Meissner told me he'd pulled the airbag control module data from the delivery truck that hit Mr. Park in the crosswalk, I set a meeting with him and Genevieve Park.

"ONI Whidby," she said, answering the phone.

"Genevieve. My collision reconstructionist is coming in today at one to present his findings after he got the data from the black box in the truck. Would you like to be there?"

"Affirmative," she said. "I have a Change of Command ceremony at eleven and I can head down after that." She paused. "Thanks for the intel."

I felt a little lift. After I found out about my parents I would keep clients better informed.

I had a tactic I called "alchemy." If you're smart you can find a way to harness the frustration from a bad thing and use that energy to do good things.

That was how I'd squeezed my tower of rage into a little nuclear golf ball that powered me through my career. If you can harness the power of badness, you can sometimes create goodness from it. Alchemy.

In my office I ate at my desk, watching the wind-whipped trees, the silver rain crawling down the window, and the monochrome gray cityscape.

At one, Nicky showed Don into the conference room. He opened up his laptop and accepted a cup of black coffee. Then Genevieve Park showed up in her dress Navy uniform, deep blue with gleaming lieutenants' bars. Two rows of medal ribbons, the things the veterans called "fruit salad." Given her specialty, she probably had medals she wasn't allowed to wear. The Office of Naval Intelligence (ONI) was like that.

Don set down his coffee cup and I introduced everybody around. When he shook hands with Nicky and Genevieve, there was a twinkle in his eye. I guessed Don Meissner had cut quite a figure with the ladies back in the day.

"Okay ma'am, here's what we've got," he said. "I pulled airbag control module data from the delivery truck that hit your pop. The state patrol established he was hit in the crosswalk. Because this is a new commercial vehicle, the ACM is sensitive enough to pick up even fairly low-mass impacts. There's one right before the ACM shows him hitting the brakes. At the moment of impact he was traveling at fifty-two miles per hour. The speed limit at the scene is thirty. Driving conditions were optimal— broad daylight, straight and level road, well-marked and newly painted crosswalk. This driver will possibly be charged with vehicular homicide on the extreme indifference to life prong." He smoothed down the ends of his walrus mustache. Classic displacement behavior. He was gathering himself to say the next thing.

"There's one more disturbing element, ma'am. I've gotten a supplement to the narrative in the WSP report. The driver refused to get a blood draw for substance use after the impact. You may know it's standard operating procedure, when a commercial driver has a collision, to transport him or her to a local hospital ER and do a blood draw to look for alcohol or drugs in the blood. This driver refused."

Genevieve Park sat upright, rigid.

"Genevieve," I said. I waited until her eyes met mine. "There is no innocent reason to refuse a blood draw. We can use this evidence to create an inference that he knew he was intoxicated. Driving while intoxicated creates negligence per se. It means the driver is civilly responsible for the damage he caused. The facts of speeding, failure to yield to a pedestrian in a crosswalk, all of that is just the cherry on top of the sundae. This guy is cold-busted. But there is one catch."

Genevieve glared at me. "What is the catch, sir?"

I took a long pull on my Americano. That was my own displacement behavior. "When a civil defendant is facing criminal prosecution, we cannot conduct any discovery, like taking his deposition or making him answer Interrogatories, until the criminal prosecution is resolved. The relevant case in *Washington is King v. Olympic Pipeline*. The defendant has a right against self-incrimination, so we won't be able to force him to make any statements until his criminal prosecution is completed."

Nicky slid the file over to me, and I flipped through it. "He has hired criminal defense counsel." My heart sank for a moment. If the Guilty Peoples' Department had signed him as a client, we couldn't proceed. We might lose a multimillion dollar wrongful death case for the innocent person, so Rodney could get a ten-thousand-dollar retainer for the guilty person.

I hated working in the same firm as criminal defense lawyers. When I started my own practice—when, not if—I would not do any criminal defense. They weren't all guilty as charged. But almost all of them were.

I'd rather be a garbageman than defend criminals.

No, the defense lawyers weren't Rodney's crew of ex-football players and ex-cheerleaders. He was represented by a guy named Thomas Schlitt, a DUI defense specialist who drove a Jaguar with the vanity plate DUI BUX. When I'd been a prosecutor we'd referred to his clients as "pieces of Schlitt."

Genevieve cleared her throat. "So we're dead in the water?"

"Not dead in the water. But delayed. I'll sue him right now. I will allege negligence per se due to intoxicated driving, and negligence due to speed, hitting a person in a crosswalk in broad daylight, all of that. But we cannot force him to make statements, not yet. But there's a silver lining." I looked deeply into her eyes. "If he is convicted, or pleads guilty to any crime, there will be no defense regarding fault. None. Then all we need to prove is damages. The damages are enormous. I expect the police and the prosecutors will crush this guy for us, but we will have to wait for them to do it."

She nodded. "I understand, sir."

It sounded like a stupid question, but in my newly-altered state of mind, I had to ask it. "Genevieve, how do you feel right now?"

She glared at me again. "I am fucking angry. Sir."

Don nodded. Nicky nodded.

"I'm glad," I said. "This is not my first rodeo. I've done fatalities before. The clients who worry me are the clients who get quiet and morose. I once had one at my last job—a New Agey widow who 'forgave' the drunk driver who killed her husband, on the TV news, even before he was charged. She stopped eating. She refused to take antidepressants because she didn't want to 'play into the hype of Big Pharma.' She wound up cutting herself and getting involuntarily committed to the psych ward over at Harborview. So I'm glad that you're angry." I paused, thinking of my own history. I quoted The Clash. "Anger can be power. You know that you can use it."

Genevieve nodded. "I think I need to go run about five miles before I tell my mom about all this."

Don looked at her. "When I was working at the NTSB, I investigated hundreds of fatalities. The survivors who exercise do a lot better than those who don't. I admire your determination."

"I think I'd better head out," Genevieve said. She stood and turned to Don. "Will you be issuing a report, sir?"

"I'll email it to Sam tonight."

"I'll look forward to it. If you'll excuse me."

She left.

Have I remembered to tell you that grief has a smell? Mrs. Gamble's house was drenched with the smell of grief.

Rage has a smell, too, and the conference room was thick with it. It wasn't all Genevieve's.

Nicky looked at Don. "I appreciate how you told her about the NTSB, and the victims," she said. "I think Genevieve needs to normalize her feelings right about now."

Don nodded. "One of the worst things about loss is the person who lost a loved one can feel like they're going crazy. But they are not going crazy. It's a sane response to an insane situation. People need to sweat it out sometimes."

I finished my Americano. "I have a theory about all this." Don and Nicky smiled. They were indulgent about my wild-ass theories. "We humans have been civilized for about two or three thousand years. In evolutionary terms, that's the blink of an eye. Biologically we're still wild animals. When we're confronted with danger—and losing a loved one is a kind of danger—we need to fight or flee. The chemicals get altered in our bodies. We need to exercise hard to work off that response from the nervous system. That's why I go for a run every night. If I didn't I'd be climbing the walls."

"I didn't know you ran," Nicky said.

"Running is medicine," I said. "I'll never win any races. I only go two or three miles. But it works."

Nicky gave a faint smile. "That's how you keep your neurotransmitters straightened out."

"Precisely." I stood and shook hands with Don. "Thank you," I said. "Another reason I can sleep nights is because I have the best people helping me."

Don nodded at Nicky, who dimpled. "You sure do."

After he left, I asked Nicky, "So anything new come in from the Boiler Room? I think we have all the True Disasters we need right now. Our dance card is full."

"Nothing new," Nicky said. "But I got a Notice of Association of Counsel on the Linda Lou case."

"New co-counsel. Anybody I know?"

"Guess."

I thought. The only reason she would dare me to guess was that it was our old buddy. "Aloysius Miller."

"Bingo. He's got a new associate named Lorna Weiss. She's on the NOA. Apparently, Aloysius's office is expanding."

"And since he does rape defense, Lorna probably does too. So it's going to be a mud-slinging contest. I'll need to use the rape shield law at every turn."

"What's that?"

"The rape shield law prohibits introducing the victim's prior sexual behavior before the rape. It originally applied only in criminal cases, but it's been extended to civil cases now by the appellate courts. That kind of litigation is where the term 'blaming the victim' came from. Knowing Aloysius, he'll seek evidence that Linda Lou was not a virgin and therefore she was not truly raped; she's just a sexually advanced teenager."

Nicky gasped. "That's disgusting."

I nodded. I leaned closer. "Between you and me, criminal defense attorneys generally are disgusting. That's why we'll have to get out of this place one day."

She looked down. She was mulling it over, again. She'd said she would come with me, but the thought made her very nervous.

"Come on," I said. "I put together some Interrogatories last night in Linda Lou's case. Contention rogs. I'm going to ask them for all the facts, witnesses, and documents supporting their denial of liability and affirmative defenses."

"Did you finish reading the two bankers boxes?"

"Yes. I'll show you what I found. I'll bet you dollars to donuts that I know more about their case than they do."

Nicky said, "I'll have to refuse. I don't even like donuts."

I was overdue to see Linda Lou at Has Beans. I'd want to armor her for whatever filthy stuff the defense was going to pull. Before I took a client into a hostile deposition, I liked to outline a hostile deposition of my own and run them through it. I wanted to simulate everything they would experience beforehand. Hell, it worked for the Apollo astronauts. My clients were just as important.

Nicky paused in front of her cubicle. "Sam, there's something different about you the past few days. Care to tell me about it?"

I sighed. "Let's just say I found out more about how my parents died. I think I have more in common with our clients than I had ever realized. I'll tell you all about it someday."

CHAPTER TWENTY-SIX—LINDA LOU'S SONG

Two weeks before Christmas I finished reading ReachKids's ten thousand pages of documents in Linda Lou's case. I was talking with Nicky when the Innocent Peoples' Department fax spit out the defendants' Notice of Deposition for Linda Lou—a video-recorded deposition scheduled, without asking us for dates, at Aloysius Miller's office.

Aloysius Miller's henchwoman Lorna Weiss was signaling aggression. Nicky frowned at the Notice of Deposition and asked, "How do we respond to this?"

I said, "Note the video-recorded deposition of the president of ReachKids for one hour earlier, also at opposing counsel's office. Schedule Fabulous Hal and Romeo Pursuit to cover it. They're great mock jurors to debrief with. This time I don't want you there, Nicky. I might get distracted. Now that I've read the document dump? Game on."

Nicky fist-bumped me and started typing.

I wasn't going to flinch. I wasn't going to ask this Lorna Weiss character to reschedule or whine about her not cooperating with scheduling.

Some lawyers want all depositions to occur at their own offices. I prefer to do all of them at the enemy's offices. Give 'em a false sense of security, politely ask questions, then whip out the defendants' own documents exposing their lies.

Then, I would politely drill down until I got to the gooey rotten center of the facts.

Next I met Linda Lou at Has Beans to prep her. She'd gotten hired as a barista. She was working bar, haloed in steam, when I came in. She stood straight and met my eyes. She seemed confident at the espresso machine. She made me a big iced Americano, Yirgacheffe of course, and led me to the storeroom—a blank concrete box full of burlap sacks of coffee beans and delicious coffee scent.

I pulled up a sack, and Linda Lou pulled up another. It felt like meeting with Catherine out at the paddock and sitting on adjoining bales of hay.

Before every deposition of my clients, I put them through a "mock dep" that is designed to be as hostile as possible so they will be ready for horrible conduct by the other side.

I gave her my customary speech. "Okay. A deposition is a meeting where an attorney takes sworn testimony from a party or a witness. Party depositions are the place in civil litigation where attorneys often act like worst kinds of jackasses, because there's no judge to stop them. This will be a video deposition. That's meant to scare us, but it's really a gift. I love video depositions because I don't lose my cool and very often the other attorney forgets about the camera and pulls stupid shit."

Linda Lou pulled back her hoodie and shook out her fine black hair. "Okay, Mr. Uncle," she said. "Bring it on."

"I like to prep my clients by asking them the most awful questions I can think of," I said. "The purpose is to prep you for whatever hostile stuff they try. I want you to be so ready, so on your toes, that the defense lawyer can't shake you. Can you remember that I am still your friend? Because the next hour or so will be pretty gross."

"All right, Mr. Uncle." Faint smile.

That nickname. It always grabbed me. I knew she meant it half-sarcastically, but it grabbed me anyway.

I took out my list. "Remember, I'm the wicked defense attorney wearing a Nazi hat, and I'm trying to mess with your mind. But I'm just playing a part. I'm your coach, and this is training for the big game."

"Get on with it, Mr. Uncle," she said, smiling shyly.

I took a deep breath. I hated this part of my job. But it really worked.

"You weren't a virgin when Burris Smalls had sexual relations with you, right?"

She sat up straight. "That's none of your business." She didn't raise her voice but she looked right at me.

I gave her a thumbs up. "You didn't offer any physical resistance when Burris Smalls had sexual relations with you, did you?"

"He didn't have sexual relations with me. He raped me. He put me in a chokehold and told me what to do. I'm five-two and I weigh ninety-five pounds. I expect Burris Smalls is six-two and he has to weigh two-forty or more. So I obeyed because I didn't want him to kill me. By the way? It happened on my birthday."

I drilled down forty-five minutes. She hesitated a few times but she didn't lose her temper or cry or storm out.

Linda Lou could handle this because her family had been a horror show. She'd changed the diapers and fed the kids while her mother was hooking and drugging and gambling and "casino hostessing" and committing welfare fraud. I'd done my own investigation of the esteemed Mrs. Lawson.

Linda Lou was a parentified child. She wasn't only fit to be an emancipated minor; she was more grown up than her mother ever would be.

Finally I ran out of horrible questions. "That's it," I murmured. "Do you hate me? I was only trying to prepare you for whatever comes at you in there."

"I don't hate you," she said, trembling. "But I'd appreciate it if you'd take off the Nazi hat now."

I mimed it. "One thing that will make you feel better," I said. "I'm deposing the president of ReachKids right before your deposition. You're a party to the lawsuit. You'll be sitting right beside me. I'll get that on video too. You can watch it and see where we're going. I have more than one smoking gun for this lady."

Linda Lou perked up.

I said, "ReachKids dumped ten thousand pages of documents on me, right at the start, remember. It was meant to do two things—intimidate me, and let the hourly attorneys on the other side bill tons of hours for reading it all. But I suspect they haven't read it all. Lorna Weiss comes from a firm that does almost all criminal defense. Criminal defense lawyers love standing up in court and yakking. They hate reading. I love that. I've read everything, and I seriously suspect they have not."

"Do you have any of those smoking guns with you?"

I knew she would ask. I'd brought some of them. I opened my briefcase and handed her a sheaf of papers. Then I relaxed and inhaled the smell of good coffee.

Linda Lou leafed through them. She was a good reader. "God," she said, rolling her eyes at one. That would be the ReachKids policies about How Much They Really Care. "Holy smoke," she said. That would be something about ReachKids failing to do a pre-employment criminal background check on Burris Smalls.

The final one? She just winced. That one was Burris Smalls's pre-employment criminal history. Felony convictions. More than one. Even one disqualified him from working with kids.

Finally, she handed them back to me.

"Okay, Mr. Uncle. I'm all set." Then she unwrapped a piece of bubble gum, and read the little comic inside. I made a plan to pick her up the next day.

When I got back to my battered Outback, I needed to breathe for a bit, the way Abe had taught me. Something about how she opened the bubble gum and read the comic. It was easy to forget how young she was.

If I'd been her father, I would have been awfully proud of her.

(I later got that comic from her and put it in my client scrapbook next to a photo of her haloed in steam running the espresso machine at Has Beans. Every True Disaster has a page or two in the scrapbook. Even now, if I get discouraged I leaf through it. It's sitting on my desk right now.)

***

The next morning I picked Linda Lou up at Has Beans at nine. She was wearing black slacks and a tan pullover sweater with long sleeves under her customary hoodie. She pulled the hood over her head before she stepped outside, and looked both ways on the sidewalk. I reminded myself she was still the subject of a Run Report and there was still a warrant out for her arrest for leaving her "placement."

Aloysius Miller's office was in a two-story Victorian brick building just south of downtown which had been updated with track lighting and soft gray carpets and nauseating Muzak leaking from concealed speakers. We walked into the conference room next to the lobby and sat down. Fabulous Hal and Romeo Pursuit were all set up, and mikes with coiled wires were placed in front of each seat. I sat down next to Fabulous Hal. The empty witness chair was at the head of the table, and Romeo's video camera was at the foot of the table.

Across the table sat Lorna Weiss, a tense forty-year-old blonde with frown lines wearing a black suit with a peace sign button in the lapel. Yeah right. She had a big coffee cup, and I'd bet this was her second or third. She drummed her fingers on the table as we came in.

"What's all this?" she asked, pointing to Linda Lou.

"All this is my client, Linda Lou Lawson," I said.

"She can't be here. This is the deposition of the president of ReachKids."

"Yes she can. She is the plaintiff. Parties are always allowed to attend depositions."

"But she is a minor. The case is filed in the name of her litigation guardian ad litem, an attorney by the name of…" She shuffled her papers.

"Bonus Malone," I said, putting my West Court Rules book and my legal pad on the table.

Lorna glared at me. "Mr. Malone is the party. Linda Lou is not."

I flipped open my court rules book to a pink Post-It. Before depositions I always put pink Post-Its on the rules the other side was most likely to violate. I cited the Rule of Professional Conduct entitled "Client Under A Disability." (Being a minor was considered a disability under the law.)

I read aloud: "The attorney shall as far as possible maintain a normal attorney-client relationship with a client under a disability." Then I pulled out a court opinion holding that depositions are court proceedings, and court proceedings are open to the entire public, not just parties. I slid my spare copy across the table to Lorna Weiss.

"So unless you're prepared to reschedule both depositions and face sanctions, let's get started," I told Lorna.

She muttered, "What a cheap trick," and went to get the president of ReachKids. Fabulous Hal winked at Linda Lou. She gave him a shy smile. Romeo Pursuit looked like he already wanted a break so he could go vape. I introduced Linda Lou to both of them. "They will be your support team today," I murmured, "and afterward they'll tell me what they thought."

Lorna Weiss jerked open the conference room door and led in a tall, emaciated brunette in her fifties with shiny dyed brown hair. "Splenda O'Malley," Lorna said. Splenda O'Malley shook hands with me; her hand was icy. Splenda smelled like Chanel No. 5 and looked like money. I bet she spent most of her time fundraising with rich people and backscratching with DSHS bureaucrats.

I pulled out my four-inch-thick accordion of exhibits tabbed with color-coded Post-Its. My hand tingled as I touched it. Then I pulled out my script keyed to each exhibit.

We went on the record. I always warm up with softballs and try to get the defendant boasting a little. When people are lunging ahead with their self-congratulatory statements? That's when you can get them to run right off the cliff. Just like in the cartoons, they don't start to fall until they look down and see they're already over the edge.

Splenda had been in the Peace Corps in Africa. She had a master's in psychology and had been working with "underprivileged youth in roles of increasing responsibility" for thirty years. She was licensed as a marital and family therapist but spent most of her time on "administrative matters." Like raising money from rich people and backscratching with DSHS bureaucrats. And spending it on ReachKids's management salary and benefits, with a dribble going downstream to pay for services. As I said, I'd read a lot of stuff about ReachKids in their document dump. Also I'd found stuff on their website that was so ironic it was painful.

I wouldn't use all my ammo here—you never use up all your ammo at the start of a war. The self-congratulatory website printouts about ReachKids's "Care and Concern for At-Risk Youth," and all that related stuff? I'd save that for summary judgment or trial.

When you sue a bureaucracy, you get their policies and website statements talking about How Wonderful They Are. Then you use depositions and client records to prove they are not actually wonderful at all.

The contrast is what makes juries and judges get mad. When they get mad, magnificent stuff happens.

"So, turning to the employment of the rapist, Burris Smalls, can you fill me in on the pre-employment background check?" I murmured. I nudged my big accordion folder.

Splenda glanced at it nervously. "We verified previous employment and requested a criminal background check from the Department of Social and Health Services," she said.

I checked his date of hire. "You requested that before Burris Smalls started working?"

"Yes, that is correct. We're required to do that, and we always do."

They had. They had requested it. As I've mentioned before, DSHS is not legally responsible for almost anything they do, or do not do.

"When did the criminal background check come in?" I asked, casually. I knew the answer.

"I do not believe I know."

I pulled out my first exhibit—an email from Splenda to the DSHS screening person demanding the overdue criminal background check. Hal marked it and handed it to Splenda. "Would it surprise you to learn that it never came back before Linda Lou was raped?"

"Objection!" Lorna Weiss snarled, her face mottled red. Man, I was glad this was a video dep.

"Counsel," I said quietly, "are you instructing the witness not to answer?" I kept my eyes on Splenda. I was drilling right into her.

Lorna had a full head of steam. "This question assumes that Linda Lou was raped and the document in question has not even been authenticated!"

The rapist had pled guilty. But I wasn't going to start hair-splitting. That was a trap. Again I didn't look at Lorna. "Please look at the document, ma'am," I said to Splenda. "Is that your email address?"

"Yes."

"Did you send this email to the screening person at DSHS?"

"Yes." She verified the date.

"That is after the rape of Linda Lou, is it not?"

She dissembled. "I'm not sure."

She was sure, all right.

I took out the initial police report taken about Linda Lou's rape and gave it to Fabulous Hal to mark it. I read the date. "Does this refresh your recollection?"

"Yes, it does," she said.

"Objection," Lorna said. "This witness did not prepare this police report."

I kept looking at Splenda. A drop of sweat was wandering down from her hairline. "Counselor, she already answered the question," I said, not even looking at Lorna. "Therefore the objection is waived.

It seemed like Lorna was more used to criminal defense, where the attorneys trumpet objections in the courtroom, to depositions—where they are forbidden to make any objection except "objection due to privilege" and "objection to form."

It was strictly illegal to tell witnesses not to answer unless a privilege was invoked, like attorney-client privilege, doctor-patient privilege, or the spousal privilege.

I wondered if Lorna had even re-read Civil Rule 30 regarding depositions before showing up today.

I had. I even made a copy to use as an exhibit and to read into the record. This sounds stupid but it actually works. Judges hate it when lawyers violate Civil Rule 30. So I try to prove that they are doing exactly that.

"So taking your answers together," I said, "you did not receive the criminal background check results from DSHS before you permitted Burris Smalls to start working at the Wedgewood Birches Group Home operated by ReachKids," I said. "Is that correct?"

"Correct. But we have ninety days when our staffer can work before the criminal background check has to be done."

I handed a section of the Washington Administrative Code to Hal, who marked it and passed it to Splenda. Lorna Weiss took her copy and frowned at the sea of fine print. "I assume you are familiar with this?"

Splenda nodded.

"I'm sorry, I need a verbal answer," I said.

"Yes," she said. She was familiar with it. But she wasn't thrilled that I was. Her Chanel No. 5 wafted across the table. Because she was sweating.

"I'd like to draw your attention to paragraph (b) (12) of this section of the WAC," I said. "Could you review that and let me know when you've finished?"

She read it quickly. "Okay."

Lorna was still leaning over her own copy.

"Does this WAC impose any restrictions on the work of staffers at your facility who have not had a completed and clean criminal background check received by the employer?"

"They can't work alone," Splenda said, sadly. Lorna started to speak. "Just settle down," Splenda said to Lorna, putting a hand on Lorna's quaking shoulder.

"Did Burris Smalls work alone with Linda Lou at your facility at any time before the date of the, um, alleged rape?"

She nodded. "Yes, he did."

"Looking at the police report, was that one of those dates when he worked alone with Linda Lou?"

She flared. "Yes but that was the day all the kids were going to the zoo, and we were short-staffed, and Linda Lou was sick. You don't think we should let a sick teenager stay in the house alone?"

I kept my voice even. "It would have been better if you did," I said.

Linda Lou nudged my knee under the table. I'd given her a pad to write on. I looked over. She'd just drawn a bunch of daisies, with bumblebees and birds flying over them. I nudged her back.

"I have another objection," Lorna said. "You asked her about a section of the WAC. That calls for a legal conclusion."

I pulled out my copies of Civil Rule 30 and had Fabulous Hal mark one. Then I read it into the record. "Instructions not to answer are improper, except as to the existence and extent of a privilege. Objections shall not be framed so as to coach an answer. Counsel for the parties shall conduct themselves with the same decorum used in the courtroom."

I then said, "Okay Hal, please make Civil Rule 30 part of the record. I may need to request sanctions."

This was what I'd learned. Be courteous. Keep your voice down. Never look at the misbehaving attorney. And patiently drill down until you get to the rotten gummy center of the True Disaster. The more the defense attorney leaps around and yells, the closer you are getting. Just keep drilling, and never raise your voice.

I pulled out another exhibit, but held it up to my face, letting Splenda guess what it was. "Did your agency pursue any alternatives to getting a criminal background check on Burris Smalls?"

"What do you mean? DSHS is supposed to do that."

"True, but we have established they did not. Did you pursue any alternatives?"

"There's no reason we should."

I turned and looked at Linda Lou. "I can think of one reason," I said.

Lorna said, "Objection! Counsel is testifying!"

"Okay," I said again, looking at Splenda. "But just to be clear, ReachKids did not pursue any alternatives for getting a criminal background check on Burris Smalls when DSHS didn't respond on time?" I kept holding the exhibit up to my face. I was holding my hole card. Splenda knew it.

"No we did not," Splenda said, slumping. She knew what was coming. Lorna apparently did not. Hypothesis confirmed. Lorna Weiss hadn't read her own document dump.

I had Hal mark the exhibit I'd been holding up. I handed one to Lorna. Hal handed his to Splenda. I handed an extra to Linda Lou.

Ever since I'd found out how my parents died, I wanted my clients to see what I was doing. Whether I won or not, I wanted them to see somebody fighting back for them. I wanted them to have that feeling because I hadn't had that feeling.

If you're an adequate person you want to leave the world better than you found it.

I needed to be super formal with this one. "Madam, do you recognize this document?"

Splenda said, "Um-hmm."

Hal said, "I'm sorry but I need a yes or no from you." Hal only intervened when the defendant was on the ropes and he could appropriately ask them to use actual words. He'd only done it four times in all the depositions I'd hired him for.

"Yes, I mean yes," Splenda said.

"What is that document?" I asked. I kept staring at her. My eyes were starting to itch, because I wasn't even blinking.

"It's an email I received from SmartEyeFacts.com and my response."

"Can you read it aloud?"

"Objection. The document speaks for itself," Lorna trumpeted.

"Not unless somebody reads it aloud, Counselor," I said evenly.

Splenda cleared her throat and took a big drink of water. Displacement behavior. She was not a very happy camper. "SmartEyeFacts.com emailed me a week after Mr. Smalls was hired and offered to do criminal background checks on employees for twenty-eight dollars apiece, with a two-day turnaround."

"Thank you," I said. "And what was your response?" This I did need her to read verbatim.

"I said given the number of our employees with overdue criminal background checks pending from DSHS, I could not justify the cost to my Board," Splenda said, reading from her email.

"How many employees did you have as of that date awaiting criminal background checks from DSHS?" I took another exhibit from my folder. I was only about a tenth of the way through the pile. I'd brought all my ammo but I wouldn't use it all. I wanted Splenda staring at that big pile of exhibits in my accordion folder, tabbed with color-coded Post-Its. By now she knew I wasn't bluffing

Lorna glanced at my folder with distaste and furiously scratched her elbows. Furious people itch. Ask me how I know.

To her credit, Splenda didn't flinch. She'd figured out that I'd read the whole document dump. "As of the date of this email we had forty-two unscreened employees."

"Thank you," I said. I was on the home stretch. I pulled out yet another exhibit and held it up to my face, so only I could read it.

I was dealing from the bottom of the deck. Totally illegal in poker. Totally legal in depositions. "Madam, how much money do you make per year as president of ReachKids?"

Lorna slapped her palm on the table. "Objection! This witness is not an individual defendant and she has no personal liability! This is absolutely OUTRAGEOUS!"

Goddamn this was going to look good on video.

I kept staring at Splenda. She actually had a sliver of decency left in her, because she saw what I was driving at, and she didn't weasel. She had guessed that I had the ReachKids salary spreadsheet. "I make $220,000 a year," she said demurely. "It's in line with our peer institutions."

"And twenty-eight dollars per background check, for forty-two background checks, totals $1,176," I said. "By my reckoning, you make $4,230 per week. So the cost of these criminal background checks would have been one and a half days of your salary?"

Splenda slumped again. "Yes."

Linda Lou tapped my knee. One of her bumblebees was smiling.

I sighed. "And that was too expensive?"

Splenda sighed, matching me. "Well, I said it was, anyway."

I pulled out another exhibit—the nuclear one. "Did you eventually get a criminal background check for Burris Smalls?"

"Yes," Splenda said.

"What was the result?"

"He had disqualifying criminal convictions."

I had Hal mark the document and hand it to Splenda. "What were the criminal convictions disclosed in the criminal background check?"

Splenda squinted down at it.

Lorna said, "We're going off the record."

"No we are not," I said. "Conferring with a witness when a question is pending is strictly forbidden. Madam, your answer?"

Splenda held it up close. "Assault 2 with Firearm. Residential Burglary. Possession of Narcotics with Intent to Distribute."

"Does the document say which are felonies?"

"They're all felonies."

"Would any of them prohibit Burris Smalls from working for ReachKids?"

"Any one of them would prohibit employment with us."

Lorna just fumed. I expected to see steam boiling out of her ears.

"Nothing further," I said. "I will order the video and the transcript."

Fabulous Hal pointed at Lorna. "Reserve signature, or waive?"

"Reserve," Lorna said.

She wanted to reserve signature so she could "pretty up" Splenda's testimony. Which violated Civil Rule 30 and could be used to impeach Splenda at trial. Another one of my traps. I actually wanted Lorna to change the substance of the testimony, so Splenda could try to weasel out of it on the witness stand in front of a jury.

I worried that Linda Lou, whose deposition was next, would get it in the neck for this. But Lorna intended to torture her anyway, no matter what I did.

There's only one good thing about the worst case scenario. Once the bad guys hit you with the worst case scenario, they haven't got anything left.

When they haven't got anything left, you can do whatever you need to.

We took a break before Linda Lou's deposition. I walked her to the water fountain in the elevator lobby near the fire alarm. They'd really done a nice job remodeling the old building—dove-gray carpets, Muzak, even a sprinkler system.

Linda Lou took a long drink. "Trip to the ladies' room," she murmured. I went to the men's room. Whenever I'm tense I splash cold water on my face. This time I did it twice.

The worst thing in my life is to see somebody I care about getting hurt, and not be able to stop it. That was on tap now.

I prayed I'd prepared Linda Lou enough. I expected life had prepared her better than I could have. Her rotten upbringing was finally going to do her some good.

Because she was used to being treated like a human piece of shit.

***

Romeo Pursuit helped Linda Lou clip the mike onto the collar of her demure tan sweater. Fabulous Hal took out a box of tissues. I couldn't guess who they were for. Maybe they were for everybody.

Lorna had her sworn in and started with a crisp manner. "What is your legal name?"

"Linda Lou Lawson."

"Current age?"

"Fourteen."

"Where do you currently reside?"

"Objection," I said calmly. "This person is currently the subject of a Run Report and I will not allow her to incriminate herself by admitting she is not living in a DSHS-approved facility, so due to the Fifth Amendment to the United States Constitution, I am directing her not to answer. The right against self-incrimination is a privilege that permits me to do this," I said.

Lorna clenched her jaws. I knew she was trying to get Linda Lou to incriminate herself. Her firm did rape defense, among other squalid types of criminal defense. They loved to blame the victim.

Lorna asked, "You were not a virgin when you had sexual relations with Burris Small, were you?"

My jaw dropped. Lorna started needling right where I had.

"That is none of your business, lady," Linda Lou said, putting a frown on a bumblebee on her pad.

"It goes to damages," Lorna said. She told Fabulous Hal "mark that place." This was an archaic phrase. Depositions come out now in searchable PDF files, and nobody marks a place in a deposition anymore. Apparently Lorna had read an old book on depositions. "I may move to dismiss based on her lack of cooperation," she told me.

I gave her a faint smile. "Bring it on."

Lorna flipped to another page of her script. "Describe this alleged incident when Burris Smalls supposedly raped you," she snapped.

Linda Lou looked down at her pad. Now she was obliterating the frowning bumblebee with sharp crosshatching. "The other kids went to the zoo, with all the staff. I was left alone with Burris because I had an upset stomach. I thought maybe my period was starting early. It was my birthday."

Lorna squinted. "I did not ask you about your birthday. Next describe what happened. Just describe the whole whatever in your own words."

Linda Lou stared at her pad. She was focused beyond it now. She was back there, in the room, all right. I knew what it was like to re-visualize a bad moment so clearly it was a film running. "I was in my room. Actually I shared it with three other girls but they weren't there. My mom had brought me a clock radio and I had it tuned to Jack FM. It's my favorite station. They were playing Paula Abdul's song 'Straight Up.' I used to love that song."

Linda Lou took a big drink of water, then returned to staring down at her pad. "I heard the door open. It was Burris. He said it was time for lunch. I stood up. I'd been in bed with the covers over me but I had my sweatpants and my tank top on. The tank top had a Hello Kitty on it." Pause.

I could feel Fabulous Hal getting upset. He didn't flinch, didn't change expression, but I could feel it. Friends are like that.

"So I stood up and I walked to the door. Suddenly Burris was behind me and he had me in a choke hold, around my neck. They told us at Resident Orientation that the staff is definitely allowed to physically restrain you if you are damaging things or hurting people and they can put you in the Time Out Room which is basically a padded cell with a deadbolt on the door but they are in no situation allowed to choke you and he was choking me. He put his mouth to my ear and he said, 'Bitch you know what I want and you gonna give it up to me.' Then he carried me over to the bed."

Her voice had gone monotone. I knew that monotone. I'd spoken in it for years when I was living at the Malletts' Therapeutic Foster Home.

"He shoved me down on my back and he put his hand on the front of my throat and it was so big it reached halfway around my throat and then he squeezed some and the room got kind of gray and he pulled down my sweatpants and my panties and then I heard the clink of his belt buckle coming undone and then he was inside me and it hurt and after some kind of time he nutted in me."

Lorna recoiled. "He what?"

I cleared my throat. "He ejaculated, Counselor. Surely you are familiar with the concept given that you defend rapists."

Lorna glared at me. "He nutted in you?"

"Yes. I felt him nutting in me. It's a splash. A hot splash. Then he took his hand off my throat and said, 'That's my girl, we're gonna keep this on the DL.'"

"What is the DL?"

"The down low. That means I couldn't tell. He made me lunch. It was baloney and cheese sandwiches and tomato soup just like my mom made me once when I got chickenpox. He was nice, after. He called me his Little Sweetheart. I could feel that stuff seeping into my panties. I kept telling myself don't wash up, don't wash up, because the cops will need that stuff. So I didn't wash. The other staff and kids came back from the zoo about two hours later, and I asked for a Phone Privilege because I was on Level Three because I'd been good and did all my chores that week and it was my birthday and then I called 911. The police took me to the hospital and did a rape kit. I heard later that Burris had pled guilty to Rape of a Child in the Second Degree and he went to prison. But by then I had run away."

Lorna frowned down at her script. "So you admit you ran from your authorized DSHS placement?"

"I sure did," Linda Lou declared, her head held high.

Lorna frowned at her and paused. "You don't respect any adult, do you Linda Lou?"

I could have interjected, but I thought Linda Lou was doing fine for herself.

I was wrong. A tear spilled from her eye. Then several more.

"Hal, can I get a tissue?" I asked.

Hal slid the box over.

"Counselor, are you telling the witness not to answer?" Lorna growled.

"I am not," I said. "But she is crying. I think common decency says she gets to dry her eyes when she's crying about her rape before you ask your next question."

Belatedly, Lorna glanced at Romeo's camera. She seemed to have forgotten the camera. Too bad. She waited a moment, and then, because she was stubborn and not very smart, she repeated: "You don't respect any adult, do you, Linda Lou?"

Linda Lou looked sideways at me and smiled through her tears. "I respect my lawyer," she said.

That one hit me in the guts. I teared up too. "Now I need a tissue," I said, and Linda Lou slid the box over to me. I needed four of them. I wasn't ashamed to cry. I'd be ashamed if I didn't.

"Ahem," said Fabulous Hal. It was working on him too. He loved romantic comedy and he had a big heart.

Lorna continued. "So you're hoping that you will get a lot of money from the insurance company for ReachKids, aren't you? That's why you brought this suit?" Lorna was apparently forgetting that the litigation guardian ad litem had actually hired me and authorized me to file suit.

"Yes I am," Linda Lou said. "If somebody pays for this then somebody is going to change what they do. And I would like to start all over in life. If that's even possible."

Lorna flailed a little more but she'd run out of bad ideas. Or so I thought. "Nothing further," Lorna said. "We will order."

"I want a copy of the transcript and the video," I said. "We will reserve signature."

Lorna got a text on her smart phone, and she tapped out a short reply. "Have a nice day," she said to nobody in particular and left.

I asked Linda Lou, "You okay?"

"They can't hurt me," she said, with more conviction than she felt. Remarkable. She was trying to make me feel better even though she was the wounded one in the room.

"You were a champ," I told her.

"True dat," Romeo Pursuit said, abandoning every convention of the professional videographer.

"You were just great, sweetie," Fabulous Hal said, as he was packing up his gear.

"Come on, I'll take you home," I said, even though I had no idea where home actually was. It was probably the storage room at Has Beans where I'd prepped her.

We walked through the conference room door and into the lobby. "And there she is," Lorna said, elbowing a huge Seattle Police officer.

That text. Lorna had set up Linda Lou to be arrested on the Run Report when she left her deposition.

The officer cracked his knuckles, frowned, and started walking across the lobby toward us. Linda Lou gave me a wild look. I glanced around us, checking for anything useful.

Then I lifted up my litigation case and said loudly, "Damn I was sure I remembered that." I opened the litigation case and started rummaging around in it.

Then I stumbled, accidentally-on-purpose, and the corner of the litigation case hit the fire alarm.

I put my mouth on Linda Lou's ear. "Run," I said.

The fire alarm detonated and, white strobes flashed throughout the building, and the sprinklers erupted, drenching us all in a deluge of cold water. and Linda Lou ran off to the left, away from the lobby, where the Exit sign marked the stairwell.

The Seattle Police officer looked up and smiled ironically. "Man, that's a cold shower," he said.

"You did that on purpose!" Lorna yelled at me. "Officer! Arrest that man for tampering with fire control equipment!" Her mascara was beginning to run. We were all drenched. The alarm and the strobes kept right on going.

"Looked like an accident to me, ma'am," the Seattle Police officer said, dropping me a wink where she couldn't see. "Some of you lawyers are plain clumsy."

"I'm sorry," I said, lowering the litigation case. "I must have slipped."

Lorna glared at me. "You son of a BITCH!"

The SPD officer tapped her on the elbow. "Now there, ma'am. Let me call the hose-draggers so they can get all this stuff turned off." He walked a few feet away and started speaking into his shoulder mike. Of course the fire department was already en route. He just wanted an excuse to ignore Lorna.

I could do the math. He'd been dispatched to arrest a juvenile who had a warrant out for her because of a Run Report because she'd fled from her DSHS placement. When he got there, he realized he was being used by defense counsel.

From his manner I knew that he knew Aloysius Miller. He knew that Aloysius defended criminals, and he knew that Lorna defended criminals too. He'd probably been cross-examined by both of them in criminal trials. Because this was Seattle in 2007, and Miller & Associates defended many accused persons of color, they had probably called him a racist too. It was the standard criminal defense move in Seattle.

I wasn't the only person in the world who disliked the Guilty Peoples' Department.

The fire department arrived with their magic keys and turned everything off. I walked out with Romeo Pursuit and Fabulous Hal. Romeo lit up his vape. He was dripping still. Fabulous Hal's tweed suit looked like a burlap sack.

"Gentlemen, your cleaning bills are on me," I said.

Fabulous Hal straightened my lapels. "You devious bastard," he said with charm.

"I'm just clumsy," I said.

Romeo Pursuit snorted. "True dat," he said.

All the way home, as I shivered in my soaked gray suit, I remembered Linda Lou saying, "I respect my lawyer." I felt like crying again. Next week, Lorna and I were going to McNeil Island, the Washington State Penitentiary, to take the deposition of Burris Small.

It was going to be on video again. I wanted Linda Lou to be able to watch it, so I'd make a DVD just for her.

She deserved that much.

Strange. Linda Lou's song was the saddest song I'd ever heard, and she hadn't sung a single word.

CHAPTER TWENTY-SEVEN— FABULOUS HAL IS A TEN-IN-PRISON

Linda Lou didn't get arrested, so she didn't have to spend Christmas at Juvenile Hall. I got coffee from her on Christmas morning at Has Beans, then spent the day obsessing over the video deposition of Burris Smalls. He was imprisoned at McNeil Island Corrections Center—a high-security prison on a small island in the middle of Puget Sound.

Puget Sound's waters are lethally cold year-round. The US government built the prison there because nobody could swim to the mainland and live. Washington State took it over in the 1970s to house sexually-violent predators and other violent felons. It was served by a small ferry filled with the felons' depressed relatives.

The day before the deposition I called Duvonda to get some coaching. She told me to come over. It cost me a mocha with extra whipped cream. When I was prosecuting, I'd never been assigned to the Sexually Violent Predators Team. Duvonda did a year, and then asked for a transfer to Trial Teams, with a focus on robbery and homicide.

As I set down her mochas in front of her, I asked her why.

"Because I hate sexually violent predators," she said, taking a spoonful of whipped cream. "I wanted them all to get the death penalty. I was going through Maalox like a fiend."

I knew she'd also done civil commitment proceedings where the state tried to keep sexually violent predators locked up once their sentences had run, on the theory that they had dangerous mental illnesses and should be held until treatment had resolved their mental illnesses, which caused them to rape people.

I asked her, "I've never done a prison dep before. What should I know?"

Duvonda sat back and smoothed down her zebra print top. Her face went as severe and regal as a queen's. Her prosecution face. "First, you wear a clip-on tie, not a regular tie. Those guys sometimes try to strangle men wearing regular ties."

"Check. I'll have to go to K-Mart and buy one. What else?"

She took a long sip from her mocha. "That's the good stuff, Sam," she said, smiling at me. I knew she wanted a little moment of tasty happiness before the next part. "Next, when you are asking them questions, don't look at them. In prison, eye contact is perceived as a challenge. When you had the Notice of Dep served on the inmate by his counselor, did you learn whether he's in Ad Seg, or Gen Pop?"

"He's in Gen Pop." General population is where most prisoners live. Administrative segregation is reserved for child molesters ("chomos") and informants ("snitches").

"Too bad. You'd be better off if he were in Ad Seg. If he's in Gen Pop, probably none of the other inmates in his housing unit know he pled guilty to raping a child. If they did, he'd probably get a beat-down or get shanked in the shower. Since he's in Gen Pop he'll be trying to project an aura of dominance, of menace. How big did you say this cat is?"

I pulled out the stuff I'd gotten through public disclosure. "Six-two. Two-forty. Age twenty-six. Before he pled out to Rape of a Child he had convictions for Assault 2 with Firearm, Residential Burglary, and Possession of Narcotics with Intent to Distribute."

"That's quite a sheet," Duvonda said. "Is he a soul brother?"

I handed her the booking photo. Burris Smalls was a light-skinned Black man who wore cornrows and held his head high with a cold sneer. He had one gold tooth in front. "Now that's one nasty piece of work," she said, handing the photo back. "Who knows? Maybe people even know he's a tree jumper who likes short eyes. Fella like that could scare a dead kitty cat. Never ever look him in the eyes when you ask him a question. Be small and boring."

"Okay," I said.

"Still, some chomos get murdered in prison. The inmates consider it a badge of honor. Remember that molester priest in Massachusetts, Father Geoghan?"

I remembered. Geoghan had probably a hundred victims—all young Catholic boys. The inmates formed a plan to kill him, and a convicted murderer who'd been molested himself got the honor of the performing the execution while four other convicted murderers distracted the guards and secured the cell door. After the killing, the murderer gained a lot of status in prison.

"I know I'm always telling you this, Sam, but this time it goes double. Auntie Duvonda says watch your ass."

I put my stuff back in my briefcase, then had a closing thought. "Duvonda, if I decide to leave Mammon & Associates, will you give me some pointers on finding office space and running a practice? Like who to use like a bookkeeper, and stuff?"

Duvonda laughed. "Sam, if you do that, I'll throw you a party, and then hook you up with everything you need. When you go out to McNeil Island, remember—those criminals are Rodney Mammon's clients. He advertises for DUI cases. But if the defendant has money, he defends rapists and murderers too. Those who lie down with dogs, get up with fleas."

***

I picked up Hal and Romeo and wedged their stuff into my battered Outback. Fabulous Hal wore a white suit with a pink carnation, off-white shirt, pink bow tie. As we drove down to the ferry Fabulous Hal regaled me with Christmas stories. I was ashamed to admit I'd spent the day obsessing over this deposition. But Romeo was unusually silent. "So what's up, Romeo?" I asked.

Romeo flinched. "My girlfriend wants to open the relationship. She says she's polyamorous now. She says she wants to play with others, both girls and boys, with a bit of S&M flavor."

Fabulous Hal turned around and looked at him, in the back seat. "So what does your heart tell you, sweetie?" he asked.

Romeo hung his head. "My heart tells me no."

Hal smiled at him. "Then you can tell her no. That is your absolute right. If you violate your values, you will hate yourself."

Romeo said, "It's easy for you to say. You're a handsome gay dude who dresses like a Burberry ad and you are never at a loss. Especially since you live on Capitol Hill."

Hall nodded. "All true. But it's better to be alone than be in a bad relationship. Just look at Sam. He's had the worst online dates I've ever even heard of. He won't pair up until it's right."

"That's true," I said. I held up my right hand. "As long as I don't get bursitis, I'll be able to survive without a girlfriend."

We all laughed. All men, gay and straight, know that masturbation can be an excellent placebo.

We rode the ferry out to McNeil Island in silence under the totally cloudy sky, the uniform silver clouds punctuated with drizzle. As we approached the landing a group of sea lions barked. The prison stood at the top of the only hill. Because it was a weekday the small ferry was almost empty.

As we walked up the wide paved path toward the Administration Building, between two eighteen-foot fences topped with concertina wire, it seemed one of the "housing units" was outside for an exercise period. Maybe a third of them were playing basketball, and the others were talking in huddled groups. As we walked, one of them elbowed the others, and they strolled over to the fence. "New fish," called one.

"NEW FISH," they all chanted. More inmates came over. "FRESH FISH," they all chanted.

A huge white guy with a shaved head in the back yelled, "Sweet meat! Sweet meat!"

Romeo and I glanced at each other and sped up. Fabulous Hal gave them all a theatrical wave, his crisp white suit flapping in the breeze.

"Sweet meat!" yelled the huge white guy again.

We waited for Romeo at the door. "You shouldn't taunt them, Hal," I muttered. "Those guys scare the hell out of me."

Hal patted me on the shoulder. "They're behind the fence. Besides, I do have certain resources."

"Even so," I said. I opened the door. I'd been to jail before, but this prison gave me a towering case of the heebie-jeebies.

Jails and prisons have a special smell. I could be reductive and say it's disinfectant and sweat and urine. But the smell is also a rich stew of fear and rage. Like the smell of a dead body decomposing, nobody who smells it can ever forget it. Smell, more than the other senses, can conjure up memories. I remembered once I'd been incarcerated, briefly, at juvie. I was glad I would get to leave here in an hour or two.

We checked our wallets and phones and keys, and the guards carefully inspected Romeo's gear and Hal's machines. The corrections officer lead was a huge white guy with a shaved head who looked just like the inmate outside who'd yelled, "Sweet meat!"

"Keep very careful track of your electrical cords," the lead said. "Inmates have been known to steal them and strangle people. We'll count them all on the way out, of course, before this inmate is escorted back to his housing unit." He flipped the switch on the electric mantrap. "Okay, go ahead."

A mantrap is a medieval doorway and it's very effective. You step inside one door, into a small cubicle as big as about four phone booths. The outer door behind you locks. Then the inner door is unlocked. Only one person at a time goes through. One door is always locked, either behind you or in front of you.

Inside, the smell of sweat and fear and rage and urine filled my nose. The Administration Building wasn't separate from the "housing units"— what ordinary people called cellblocks. They both branched off a main corridor. The guard led us down the main corridor.

In the distance, bouncing off the concrete and steel, I heard a man yelling, "Agnes! GOD DAMN you, Agnes! I'm gonna get out someday, AGNES!" Then distant slapping sounds. I guessed the corrections guards were "establishing control over the inmate."

A guard met us and led us left, through another man trap, down a carpeted hall. He turned left, opened a door, and flicked the lights. It was a small conference room seating six, with a drab Formica table and six all-plastic chairs. "The inmate will be up in about twenty minutes."

Romeo set up at the foot of the table. Burris Smalls would sit at the head, to give a frontal view of his face. I sat immediately to the left of the witness chair, and Hal sat across from me so he could hear well. Romeo put coiled mike cords and lapel mikes in front of us all. I remembered the guard's caution about the cords.

Hal winked at me. "In prison, I'm a ten," he said.

"Aw Hal, you're a ten anywhere," I said. I appreciated him trying to break the tension.

The door opened and Lorna bustled in. She looked nonplussed. She'd been to prison many times before because she did criminal defense. The guards probably even knew her name. We all exchanged muted greetings.

Then the door opened, and two guards led Burris Smalls in. "Here's your inmate," they said. "Just holler if you need anything. Coffee. Cigars." They snickered.

Then they left.

I raised my eyebrow at Lorna. She too thought it was strange that no guard stayed in the room. Duvonda hadn't told me what to do in this situation. But we were in the administration area, not a cellblock, and there weren't any other inmates around. The place had to be swarming with guards.

Burris Smalls looked like a true bodybuilder now, still wearing cornrows. He had on Oakley mirror shades. He held his head high. In his short-sleeved coveralls, his arms showed as cables of muscle. This guy could have forcibly raped two Linda Lous without breaking a sweat.

Romeo did the video read-in, and Hal asked him to raise his right hand to be sworn.

Burris Smalls raised his right hand, but in a fist. He said, "I'll tell the truth." He acted bored.

Lorna said, "Mr. Smalls, I'm your defense counsel. Would you remove your sunglasses?"

He turned to her, and I could see two Lornas reflected convexly. "Lady, I don't think so."

I shrugged. In personal injury, the worse it is, the better it is.

Burris Smalls looked like somebody who should never in a million years get paid to work with teenaged girls. Linda Lou's case was becoming more repulsive—therefore better—every time I turned another corner.

I kicked off: "Sir, can you state your name and spell your last name for the record?"

He made me wait a good ten seconds. "Burris Smalls."

I was using my customary dep intro, and maybe in retrospect, the next question was kind of stupid. "What is your current address?"

He smiled viciously, showing his gold tooth. "I live in a gated community."

Hal chuckled.

"Please play it straight," Lorna said.

Burris turned his head toward her. "Lady, I'se always straight. Even on the inside."

It's a little-known fact that many criminals hate their defense attorneys. Why shouldn't they? It's not like they were going to take the blame themselves for being thrown in prison.

I plowed on. I stared down at my notes, never looking at Burris. I wanted to project submissiveness, so he would feel confident and try to school me. It had worked many times before. "So you currently reside at the McNeil Island Penitentiary in Washington State?"

"Sho. For five more years."

"Are you receiving any counseling while you are incarcerated due to the nature of your conviction?"

"I call bullshit on that. I got to do my months. I don't got to do therapy."

"Understood. Are you currently taking any medication?"

"I call bullshit on that too. No meds. I'se not a patient."

I wrote a few lines of gibberish just to create my own artificial pause. Burris liked to use silence to create tension. Two could play that game. Very often, the mark thinks he is conning the con.

"Can you describe how you came to work with ReachKids at the Wedgewood group home?"

"Saw an ad online. Put in my papers. I'se part of their diversity initiative and that gave me points. Not a bad job, cuz."

"How much did you make?"

He sat back and smiled viciously again. "Not enough, considering I had to clean up puke and tampons sometime. But I done all right."

I had his earnings on the ReachKids salary table, of course. I was just trying to soften him up with softballs. He had loosened up about ten percent. He was a hard case, all right.

"Can you recall the first time you met a resident named Linda Lou Lawson, a fourteen-year-old girl?"

Long silence, this time. I broke my rule and looked at him. He was sitting totally straight and totally still. "Nope," he said.

I reached down into my accordion folder and pulled out Exhibit 1, the Statement of Defendant Upon Plea of Guilty he had signed.

I set it down on the table. I slid a copy over to Lorna Weiss and another to Fabulous Hal to be marked as Exhibit 1. I could feel Burris Smalls reading it upside down.

"Now I'm going to have my first exhibit marked so we can review it together, all right?"

Burris Smalls lunged and grabbed my clip-on tie, which pulled off, and then he twisted my collar in his maniacally strong hands, and the room turned gray, and I was choking, and I saw a white flash, and then the hands at my throat released and then I coughed and coughed, and when the gray vision cleared, I saw Burris Smalls collapsed on the table, unconscious.

Hal was just sitting down. There was a pink flush across the knuckles of his right hand.

"SAVE THAT TAPE," Lorna was yelling. "SAVE THAT TAPE! I need to make my record. Mr. Smalls made a move toward plaintiff's counsel, and then the court reporter violently assaulted him! I need this video so I can seek relief from the court."

I burst out coughing again.

"I didn't see that," Romeo said from the foot of the table.

"Me neither," I said, making sure Hal was taking everything down. We were still on the record in the deposition. "After Mr. Smalls began choking me, I blacked out. Lorna, your client tried to kill me. And you just watched."

Burris Smalls groaned on the table but didn't move. Romeo darted out the door and yelled, "Guards! Quickly!"

A guard came in. Romeo whispered urgently in his ear, and the guard came back with two more—huge guys, all beefy arms and barbed-wire tattoos. The High Power Squad. The guys who could outmuscle the convicts.

The High Power Squad handcuffed and shackled Burris Smalls. They dragged him away like a sack of dirty laundry. He didn't even struggle.

Fabulous Hal had laid some knowledge on Burris Smalls.

I motioned to Hal. "Okay, Mr. Smalls choked me, and after that, he apparently hit his head in some manner in the struggle and lost consciousness. He has been removed by the guards. I am going to recess this deposition, not adjourn it. I reserve the right to return and conduct a further examination of Burris Smalls. He is a defendant, along with ReachKids, and I have a right to perpetuate his testimony for trial." I nodded at Lorna.

"Defense vigorously protests the assertion that this deposition may be taken again and will request a protective order from the court, along with an order prohibiting this court reporter from reporting any further proceedings in this case. Also Defense will be filing a police report against this court reporter."

I made sure she was finished. "I want to order the transcript and the video," I said. "Does Defendant Burris Smalls reserve signature or waive signature?"

"We reserve signature," Lorna said, even though it didn't seem likely that Burris Smalls would correct the transcript in the required thirty days. With the video, it wouldn't make any difference what he did.

That video was gold. I'd gotten choked out. If he'd fractured the hyoid bone in my throat, I'd be dead.

But I'd gotten gold for Linda Lou. I couldn't wait to show her the DVD.

Then, I was walking out with Fabulous Hal and Romeo Pursuit down the long walkway to the ferry dock. Lorna was about a hundred feet ahead of us, marching with staccato precision in her high heels. Even her back looked furious.

The inmates had gone inside. For that, I was grateful.

"Okay, Hal," I said, edging closer. I was still shaking. "How the hell did you do that?"

"Do what," he asked innocently, motioning for Romeo to go ahead. Romeo went. We stopped.

I said, "He was choking me, and I was certain I was a dead man, and everything turned gray. I saw a white flash. The sleeve of your linen suit. How the hell did you do that?"

Hal shrugged. "Taekwondo. I practice three times a week. I'm gay and slender, and I don't intend to ever be a victim. Not again." He winked at me. "You're not the only one with a backstory, Sam."

So we strolled down to the ferry, and Fabulous Hal filled me in. He was from New York City. When he'd come out in the '90s, he'd been gay-bashed and had his jaw broken. It was three Guidos from Jersey. They got caught, and they did time. Hal started learning Taekwondo and moved to Seattle.

There are a lot of things wrong with Seattle, and I think I've covered them. But hate crimes were not common in Seattle.

I asked, "So, what belt do you have now?"

"Black belt, but only first degree. I'm working on the second."

Something else was bugging me. "What did you mean about how I'm not the only one with a backstory? Who told you I have a backstory?"

Fabulous Hal patted me on the shoulder, condescending to me. He'd earned the right. "Sweetie, Duvonda probably knows more about you than you know about you. I do reporting for her, too. Gossip is a regrettable habit of mine. But I keep my friends' secrets."

I hung my head. So, he knew about the Malletts' Therapeutic Foster Home. He knew how my parents had died. He knew I'd been in love only once, and I probably never would be again because of my mission.

But it was all okay. I trusted Fabulous Hal. He'd just saved my life. There was no way in Hell I could have broken Burris Smalls's hold on my neck.

"It's okay that I know," Hal said. "Now you know something about me. Friends protect friends' secrets. You see Romeo down there, using his vape? I'll bet you my next hot date that the video recording cuts off right when my sleeve starts to enter the picture." He lifted my chin with his fingers. "Friends protect each other. You have friends."

I nodded. Duvonda again! She'd been looking out for me in ways I hadn't known ever since I'd met her. Her practice was busier than mine, but she didn't miss a trick. She knew Fabulous Hal. And Don Meissner. I wondered if she knew The Ghost.

Strike that. My distinguished nose told me she knew The Ghost as well. It just had to be that way.

God is a clever novelist.

As the ferry rumbled toward the dock, I said: "Guys, you know what's so special about this job? It's the *people* you meet."

Romeo Pursuit burst out laughing and dropped his vape overboard.

Fabulous Hal winced theatrically. "So you're feeling better, Sam?"

Romeo interjected, "Of course he is. He's back to being a sarcastic bastard."

When I got back to the office, Rodney was in the lobby, joking with the ex-football players and ex-cheerleaders of the Guilty Peoples' Department. "So, how'd you like being in prison?" he asked me as they cackled like crows.

"Remarkable," I said. "You know, Rodney, you're missing out on the best part of this job."

"The money? Au contraire, homeboy, I'm not missing out on the money at all!"

I walked back down the hall to the Innocent Peoples' Department, where Nicky would want to hear how it went. "The clients, you moron," I whispered to myself.

It's a truism among prosecutors and police officers that criminal defense lawyers are more than half criminal themselves.

It's a truism because it is true. He who lies down with dogs gets up with fleas.

When I got the DVD from the deposition a week later, Hal's prediction was correct. The video cut off right as a white flash entered from the left.

I went to Has Beans with the DVD and my laptop and showed it to Linda Lou.

At the end, she touched my throat. The bruises were dull yellow. "So now he's choked you too," she said. "Poor Mr. Uncle."

I anonymously sent Romeo a gross of high-end cherry vape juice and sent Fabulous Hal a gift card for Burberry. After all, he'd risked ruining his suit.

CHAPTER TWENTY-EIGHT— EAVESDROPPING

The Ghost sent me a draft in our Gmail account, and I saw her the next night. She wore a stylish brown corduroy dress and horn-rimmed glasses, and she had a pencil stuck in her flyaway blonde hair, which was up in a bun.

"Ooh, the librarian, look," I said. "Hot date tonight?"

She tossed her head, feigning indifference. "The playmates haven't been playing much lately."

"Sorry to hear that." But I wasn't actually sorry.

Pirate jumped in my lap, and I scratched the back of his neck. He blinked his mint-green eyes at me and purred. The Ghost watched as I stroked Pirate's ears. He closed his eyes, stretched out, and purred louder. "Pirate's a champ," I said. "I've always liked gray mackerel tabby cats."

The Ghost made us gunpowder tea—a Chinese green tea that did smell like gunpowder. I watched the clenched leaves uncurl. The Ghost said, "So I felt like I didn't do a deep enough dive on that guy down in Rockingham County. Ron Porcine, the mayor of Stonington?"

"Okay, so you dug deeper?" After The Ghost produced my parents' medical examiner's report, I suspected she could find unfindable things. And she looked scrumptious.

"Indeed. I used some of my more…occult…resources. Government employees, and hackers who are comfortable on the Dark Web."

I tried my tea. Piquant. "I have a story, too, but you go first."

The Ghost went back to her bedroom. I stroked Pirate. Then she brought out a Redweld—the brown expandable accordion file that lawyers love. I knew she was teasing me.

She took out the first document. "First, Ron Porcine is a member of a family corporation. It's called PorCo."

"Shut up," I said, clapping my hands. "You can't make this stuff up!"

She pushed the document across to me. It was PorCo's federal tax return. Almost impossible for anybody but an IRS employee to get. Very illegal to get. There was a "playmate" behind this.

Then, The Ghost laid out a fan of documents on the table as if she was dealing cards. But they were all aces of spades. She smiled with pride as I read them.

PorCo was quite diversified. They had the contract with Rockingham County for garbage and recycling hauling. They also did it for Stonington. Remember, Ron Porcine was mayor of Stonington. PorCo also owned the landfill the hauling went to and the gravel pit used by the county and the city. And the vehicle maintenance workshop, which was used by the county and the city, was staffed by PorCo employees. And the security guard agency that was used exclusively by all government agencies in the county and city, and which also turned out to be used by most of the big businesses in town. And the bookkeeping agency that helped out the city during tax season. That was the same company which prepared PorCo's own tax returns.

Then she showed me Ron Porcine's personal tax return, and his wife's, and his brother's, and the tax returns for all of these companies. All of the companies were wholly owned by PorCo.

PorCo's shareholders? Take a wild guess. J. Charm was a shareholder. Judge Pluffington was another. Most of the city council had a few shares, too.

This stuff glowed in the dark.

"You know I can't use this stuff," I murmured. "It was all obtained illegally."

The Ghost looked over the rim of her teacup and winked. "I know. But now you know who owns what. So when you get a big judgment against Ron Porcine, you'll look like you're psychic when you can mysteriously locate and seize everything he owns." The Ghost gave a faint smile.

"This stuff makes me so happy I could kiss you," I murmured.

"So kiss me," she murmured.

I set Pirate down and, knelt in front of her and kissed her on the lips.

She tilted her head sideways. Just like before, her tongue darted into my mouth, and her mouth became a happy universe. I felt my blood softening. I put my hand on her cheek. Then I kissed her on the forehead. "I wish I was wired the way you are," I whispered.

"Damn it, why aren't you," she pleaded. Her eyes shone.

"I wish I was. I know what you need. I wish I could give it to you. But I could never call a woman I'm having sex with bad names. I could never hit her. I could never degrade her." I spread my hands, helpless. "For me personally, it would be like taking a shower with my clothes on." I stroked her cheek.

"All right," she said with mock severity, putting a palm on my chest and pushing me away. "But you can't tease me anymore."

"I don't mean to."

"That's why it's effective, Sam. It's sincere. Everything you do is sincere. That's what makes you a weirdo in this town."

"Granted." I sat back down in my chair, and Pirate leaped into my lap and blinked up at me. "No petting from now on. Except for Pirate."

Pirate blinked his mint-green eyes at me. "Meow," he said.

The Ghost finished her tea. "You're my kryptonite."

I said, "you know, I've only had one real girlfriend. The perfect Suzanne, right? My law school girlfriend. She looked like Penelope Cruz. She was wry and witty and very smart. When she said she was moving back to New Jersey, and I should come with her? Did I ever tell you what I said?"

"Nope."

"I said I never wanted to poison a woman with too much of myself."

"Sam Strait! You did not!"

"I did. I used to think I was bad for anybody to get close to. But through my work I'm starting to feel like a halfway decent guy. I guess I'm doing myself as much good as I'm doing for my clients. Strike that. I'm doing myself more good than I'm doing for my clients."

The Ghost took my hand. "That's not the point. Any good interaction between people is good for both of them. That's the only kind of interaction worth having." She stroked my hand. "Its…synergistic."

I nodded. "Synergistic. Once again you've helped me untie a knot in my tortured psyche. And you've helped me open up a defendant like a can of tuna fish. Thank you, friendly Ghost."

"That's pretty vanilla," she said, with gentle mockery.

"My favorite flavor," I said. "My only flavor."

Then I remembered to tell her about my prison deposition. "Okay, so I took the deposition of the rapist in my street kid case," I said. I filled her in on what happened to Linda Lou, and the deposition of the ReachKids president. "I got some good intel before I went to McNeil Island. Child molesters, or chomos as they're called, are hated by the other inmates. They either go into Administrative Segregation—Ad Seg—or they hide out in General Population—Gen Pop. But if they're in Gen Pop, they have to keep it secret that they are chomos. Otherwise they might get a beat-down or get shanked in the shower. Some even get murdered. You see, an inmate who attacks a chomo moves up in the hierarchy. They get status. So this guy was in Gen Pop, but he had pled guilty to raping a fourteen-year-old, so he was a chomo. He's a big guy and super strong. The prison people put us in a conference room with him, and then—get this—they left us alone without a guard."

The Ghost nodded. "I'll bet they hated you for taking his deposition. I bet they thought it would just lead to an escalated inmate that they'd have trouble with afterward."

I nodded. "That's the only thing that makes any sense. So I'm just coming around to the subject of the rape when he leaps across the table and chokes me with both hands, and I start to pass out."

The Ghost covered her mouth with her hand. Her eyes went wide. "What did you do?"

"I tried to break his grip on my throat, but he had me with both hands. He's much stronger than I am. The room was turning gray. I tried to twist my head, but it didn't do any good." I looked down. "Then my court reporter Fabulous Hal gave him a karate punch in the temple and knocked him out."

The Ghost applauded. "Fabulous Hal? I've heard of him. But where did you get so much intel about chomos and prison? I don't remember you being in the Sexually Violent Predators Unit when you were prosecuting for the County."

"I wasn't. But Duvonda Marshall was. I went to her for advice before the dep. She is kind of my mentor."

I watched her. There was just a flicker in her eyes.

Yup. She knew Duvonda. They had talked about me. Suddenly, I was surrounded by a conspiracy of friends. It felt oddly warm and warmly odd.

"Anyway, it's all on video—except for the end where Fabulous Hal knocked out that guy. So, I showed it to my client Linda Lou afterward. She's an incredible kid." I told The Ghost the story of her dep and the dep of the president of ReachKids. "You know what she told me? She said now we've both been choked by Burris Smalls."

The Ghost smiled. It was like the sun coming out. She seldom gave me, or anybody, a broad smile.

"I think I would like to meet this kid."

"I'm sure you will. I told her after the case is over I will file her Petition for Emancipation of Minor, for free, so she won't have to live in a DSHS placement, or with her druggie mother. But after that, I'm going to treat her as my niece. She already calls me Mr. Uncle. I will watch over her as long as I live, if she wants me to."

The Ghost nodded. "That's the best thing about this job," she said. "Some of the people you meet."

I almost burst out laughing, thinking of my snide remark on the ferry. But then something else struck me. "Something Linda Lou said sticks with me. She said now both of us have been choked by Burris Smalls."

"Exactly. Sam, I work for other personal injury attorneys. Most of them have no idea what their clients experience. They don't want to. I had one plaintiffs' lawyer who fell on ice last winter and broke his arm, and he needed an operation with surgical hardware. Know what he told me? You'll never guess."

I shook my head. "I definitely will never guess." I knew she savored her surprises.

"He said, 'You know, orthopedic surgery really hurts!' He was surprised! He'd been doing personal injury at a high level for thirty years, and he was surprised. He also told me that the painkiller medications they gave him caused constipation. He was surprised about that too."

"Hell, even I know that. I learned that my first year doing personal injury."

"But that's the point. You wanted to know what these people were experiencing. He never did. He's made many millions doing the same work as you, but he never put himself in their shoes before. When he gets a new client who's crippled or burned, he says they have a good injury."

I burst out laughing. "Are you fucking kidding me?"

"Nope. It's a good injury, he says. He says for every inch of medical records on a file, he expects to pocket a minimum of twenty grand in fees. He says his last fatal burn case paid for the new wing on his house. I dropped stuff off there recently. I can assure you his French Provincial mansion did not need another wing. So you're not exactly mainstream." She leaned back. "So when are you going to start your own firm, Vanilla Boy? I don't feature you sticking with Rodney Mammon much longer. Surely you've considered that he defends people like Burris Smalls, if they have an awful lot more money than Burris Smalls has."

I shrugged. "I expect it'll be soon."

She patted my forearm. "All right. But if you don't jump ship soon enough, someday you will get pushed."

I shrugged again. "At least Nicky, my paralegal, has agreed to come with me."

She raised her eyebrows. "Aha. Complications ensue. Tell me about this Nicky."

"It's not like that. She's smart, and pretty, she plays piano, and she actually gives a damn about the clients too. But she's got a pretty boyfriend named Fred, and I know she's happy with him, because she blushes whenever I mention him."

"Oh Sam. Haven't you ever considered taking a girl away from a boy?"

"I've considered it. I consider lots of things I wouldn't do. My fertile imagination is constrained by my ethics."

This time, she shrugged. "I once had a playmate who said he never broke up with a woman until he had lined up another woman and had her securely hooked."

"Okay. I think we've established I'm not like your playmates."

"More's the pity."

She walked me to the door and hugged me. Then she turned me around and gave me a playful swat on the butt. "Go get 'em tiger."

"Rowr," I said.

As I drove home, I regretted not asking The Ghost about knowing Duvonda. I would love to be a fly on the wall watching those two talk.

***

A couple of days later, the office was bustling. The Guilty Peoples' Department was going to a weeklong continuing legal education seminar called DUI Dojo. Rodney came into my office and sat on the corner of my desk. His sandalwood cologne made my eyes water. His gel-stiffened porcupine hair quivered. He handed me the brochure. "You should come, bro. Just look at the topics: 'Beating the Breathalyzer.' 'Fifty Ways to Suppress a Blood Draw.' 'Field Sobriety Tests are Junk Science.' It's at an outdoor lodge with private cabins up in the mountains. I'll even pay. It's going to be epic."

I paged through the brochure, feigning interest. "Sorry," I said, waving my hand at my huge pile of documents to read. "I'm kind of slammed."

"Your loss," he said.

DUI Dojo started tomorrow. For a week there would be no accused drunk drivers, domestic violence defendants, and the other marvelous people who sat in the lobby along with my innocent and injured clients.

Such a pity. I was looking forward to not having the unpleasant smell of criminals and their lawyers in my nostrils for a week.

I dove into documents. In the Park case, I got a sweet report from Don Meissner explaining how he'd calculated the truck's speed at the time it walloped Mr. Park in the crosswalk. In the Stone Gamble case, I read Don Meissner's technical journal articles showing how he could prove Ron Porcine's speed based on the compartment intrusion in the Toyota. As always, I gave everything to Nicky to scan into PDF files. Mammon & Associates was mostly paperless. I was grateful, given the huge amount of documentation in my cases. If I had them all in hard copy, in my office, there wouldn't have been room for me. Let alone my desk.

Around noon, Nicky came into my office and shut the door. She reached over and unplugged the phone. We always did this when we had important stuff to discuss. I didn't want any of the criminal defense people picking up anything on the intercom.

"Let's go out to lunch," she said. "I heard something you need to know about," I noted her wide dark eyes and the furrow between her eyebrows. Something major was up. "Let's go out to lunch" for us was code for "let's get away from our sketchy coworkers."

"Okay," I said. I put on my jacket. She plugged the phone back in, and we drove out to my favorite seafood place near the Magnolia Marina. A few months after the placenta soup date, my taste for seafood had finally returned.

I ordered the ginger salmon and she got the Penn Cove mussels. I asked, "Okay, what's up?"

She looked around the room and hunched forward and whispered. This was something hot, all right. "I overheard Rodney talking with Seattle Police about Kandy's death," she murmured.

I swallowed hard and took a long drink of water. "Do tell."

"The SPD detective said, 'Mr. Mammon, I want to tell you our conclusions about the death of your receptionist at your house.'"

"It was at his house? Jesus. I knew they'd been on a few dates. He definitely didn't tell anybody at the firm it happened at his house, right?"

"Nope. Nobody. You know how support staff gossip. It would've been all over. I'd transferred the call, but I didn't hang up, I just put my headset on mute so nobody could tell I was still on the line. I was eavesdropping. The lobby was empty because they're all going to DUI Dojo, so there aren't any new clients coming in. So then Rodney asked what is the manner of death according to the medical examiner? The SPD detective said accident. He said the toxicology report showed she had heroin and Rohypnol in her system, and heroin residue in her sinuses. She had sorted heroin and taken this stuff called Rohypnol too."

Rohypnol. The most common date rape drug. I had prosecuted some rapes before with Rohypnol being slipped to the victim.

My blood was pounding in my ears. "Okay, before you go on, do you know what Rohypnol is?"

"Nope. Not a clue."

I looked around the room and leaned forward and spoke quietly. Now I was more spooked than she was. "Rohypnol is a powerful anxiety drug, related to Valium, but much stronger. It was developed as an anti-anxiety medication long ago and was commonly prescribed for insomnia too. But then the doctors discovered it caused virtual paralysis and temporary amnesia in many patients. It has been outlawed in the US. But it's still legal in Europe. Typically the rapist puts it in the victim's drink, usually crushed into powder, when the victim isn't looking. Then the rapist keeps them drinking, watching them carefully. When the victim starts to get disoriented and clumsy, the Rohypnol is kicking in. They call it 'getting roofied.' Then the rapist rapes the victim. The victim can't resist and often can't even remember it. The newer version of the prescription medication has a dye included, so the drink will turn green. But there's a black market version with no dye. It is sold illegally in the US. It is almost never used as a recreational drug, because paralysis and amnesia aren't considered particularly recreational."

Nicky pulled out her smart phone. "Let me search for the term 'roofies' and 'roofied.' I need to catch up here."

I went to the bathroom and splashed cold water on my face.

I did it again. Because I was enraged.

Rodney had killed Kandy.

After that I stood by the big windows looking west. The gray overcast was ripping open over the Olympic Mountains, and Mount Olympus shone white. The Greeks believed that Mount Olympus was the home of the gods. In the foreground a pod of whales surfaced and blew and dived.

A little girl clutching her mother's hand said, "Look, Mama, it's the whale!"

Mama crouched next to her and stroked her silky hair. "Yes honey it's the whale!"

I seldom believe in omens. But these omens were undeniable.

When I came back Nicky was still reading about Rohypnol. Half her Penn Cove mussels sat neglected. I finished my ginger salmon and let her finish.

Finally, she looked up, her face pale.

"So what else happened in the call, Nicky?" I asked.

"The SPD detective said Kandy had expired due to an OD of snorted heroin and Rohypnol, 'but there was no evidence of your involvement, Mr. Mammon.' He said that carefully: 'No evidence of your involvement.' The evidence does not contradict the presumption that she consumed both drugs voluntarily. The detective said, 'So it looks like you're in the clear, Counselor.' From his tone I could tell he wanted to arrest Rodney, but he didn't have evidence to support a charge. Now that I know about getting roofied, that makes sense. Even Kandy wouldn't take something that would make her unconscious and give her amnesia. She is—was—a stripper and an addict. But she wasn't stupid. I'm guessing that Rodney didn't know she was snorting heroin, so he didn't count on the drugs interacting and Kandy dying. But Sam, when we put all this together, Rodney roofied her. He intended to rape her. The roofies interacted synergistically with the heroin and she died instead. He wasn't trying to kill her. He was trying to drug her and rape her. But Sam. Rodney killed Kandy."

It was airtight. It was exactly the reasoning that had zapped through my head. Rodney had killed Kandy. I couldn't prove it, and SPD couldn't prove it, but it was true.

I remembered the day Rodney took Nicky and me out for jumbo shrimp. I remembered the green pill he had dropped. I remembered I had picked it up and it was still in my home safe, in a sealed envelope, with my signature and the date across the flap. That pill was glowing in my mind. I would bet last week's lunch money it was Rohypnol. I would bet next week's lunch money that it was the kind of Rohypnol pill with no dye.

I could give it to the police and tell them where I got it. There was an outside chance that they would be interested in prosecuting him for possession of an illegal drug, or even manslaughter. But then I considered the chain of custody.

The pill had been in my custody for months. The police couldn't prove with certainty I got it from Rodney. Rodney would get the pill suppressed at trial. He was very good at keeping damning evidence away from juries—that was half his entire job.

Also, SPD had already cleared him, and the medical examiner had ruled the manner of death as "accident."

I would have to get the SPD and the medical examiner to change their minds, then get the King County Prosecutor to file charges, then be a witness in a brutal evidence suppression hearing where my boss would grill me and probably get the evidence suppressed.

It was impossible. Sun Tzu once said, "Never start a battle you can never win."

But this made something hideously clear.

I could not keep working for Rodney Mammon.

I remembered what The Ghost had said the last time I talked to her. "If you don't jump ship, you're going to get pushed."

I'd just gotten pushed. I could not physically tolerate the idea of working for Rodney Mammon anymore.

Sometimes there is only one possible option.

I gave Nicky a faint smile and ordered coffees for both of us. "Honey, I've got a suggestion," I said, taking a purifying scalding swallow of the coffee.

I loved Nicky's intelligence. She'd put the Kandy situation together as quickly as I had. I loved her loyalty. Now I was calling her "honey" and focusing on what I loved about her. I needed to focus on jumping ship, not on Nicky. I'd never taken a woman away from a man, never even tried to. The Ghost loved chiding me for it, but I'd be Vanilla Boy forever, even if I never got to make love to a woman again.

Nicky finished her coffee and tilted her head, quizzical. "So what's the suggestion for us?"

I liked that. Us. "We rent an office, set up an LLC, buy computers and phones, and get all of our clients to sign new contracts. All while Rodney and the Guilty Peoples' Department are out of town." I looked down at my hands. "Are you sure you still want to come with me? If you want to stay at Rodney's I'm sure I'll make it okay."

Nicky shook her head and laughed. "Sam. Sometimes you won't take yes for an answer. I already told you I'll come with you. Now that I know I could have a pill slipped into my morning coffee and wake up after being raped by Rodney? Did you really think that would make me want to STAY?" She raised her voice. "Jesus, Sam. Take the win!"

I burst out laughing, and she laughed too. I paid the check and left a good tip.

Apparently Sam Strait & Associates LLC was going to spring into life in the next couple of days. I would leave a polite letter of resignation on my desk, and take all the files with me on a flash drive, assuming the clients were willing to come.

Rodney had never even met most of them.

I'd met them at their houses, visited their loved ones' graves, looked through their photo albums, and listened. It's astonishing how much good listening does.

I loved my innocent injured people. I was going to gamble my career that they knew that.

CHAPTER TWENTY-NINE— JUMPING SHIP

"So Strait & Associates PLLC is about to become a thing," Nicky mused, as I started the battered Outback.

I was so excited I could barely drive. "Thank God for technology," I said. "First stop? Best Buy."

I bought two HP desktops with maximum storage, two big monitors, two printer/scanners, a one-terabyte portable drive with USB cable, and a bunch of flash drives. (At the Innocent Peoples' Department we usually only had eight or nine active client files at a time, but some of them were massive, because of the photos and video clips and mountains of medical records.) I also got a big package of collapsible bankers boxes and two folding hand trucks.

We'd both been frustrated by Rodney's refusal to buy good computer equipment. He spent like a drunken sailor on advertising, but our tech was just lame.

As we loaded the Outback, I mused, "I want to depend on machines, not people."

"Present company excepted," Nicky teased me.

"True dat," I said, quoting Romeo Pursuit.

Strait & Associates PLLC was fully equipped with tech for under six thousand dollars.

Next we went back to Rodney's office. I plugged in the big portable hard drive and asked it to copy everything from the Civil Litigation folder on the firm server to the drive. Wonder of wonders, it took only twenty minutes. While I was doing this, Nicky put all the clients' Basic Files—the master files with contracts and investigation documents—into bankers boxes on a hand truck.

"We'll use my condo as a base for now," I told her, "but I really need to scare up office space."

I wondered if Duvonda would have good advice on office space. I felt ashamed that I turned to her whenever I was in over my head. But that's what mentors are for.

I called her cell and she was at the downtown courthouse, waiting for a Superior Court verdict. The jury had been out for a day. It was a pretty terrible burn case. I'd seen the photos. Burn cases will ruin your appetite every time. Jurors think so too. This was a scalding injury from an apartment hot water heater that was set about seventy degrees above the mandated safe level. I'd seen the photos when Duvonda did a mock jury and included me in the panel. The plaintiff's forearm was just cooked. It was a miracle he didn't need an amputation. Because the defendant landlord had violated a clear safety rule, and damages were big, we'd both been optimistic about the result.

"So, how's the verdict looking?" I asked her.

"Sam, first rule of personal injury litigation?"

I remembered. "You never know before you know."

"Exactly. The client asked me for my prediction. I said we've done a good job, but I never make predictions. Between you and me, I'm feeling somewhat optimistic. I don't ever get further out over my skis than that. So what's up?"

I sighed. "Remember you told me I need to jump ship from Rodney's firm before I get pushed? Well I just got pushed."

"How so?" Duvonda always found my predicaments amusing. I think I reminded her of herself when she'd jumped ship herself from the King County Prosecutor's Office.

I said, "Long story short, he had our receptionist over to his place. You know, Kandy the stripper. He slipped roofies into her drink while she was in the bathroom. Turned out she was in the bathroom snorting a bump of heroin. The two interacted, and she overdosed, and she died. I just found out."

Duvonda gave a low whistle. "So Rodney's going to get himself incarcerated, then? That's the biter bit."

"No, he won't. Nicky overheard the detective telling Rodney they couldn't prove that Kandy had not ingested the Rohypnol voluntarily, so they were going to chalk it up to an accident. You know, death by misadventure. Cause of death, lethal intoxication. Manner of death, accident. They couldn't prove that Rodney dosed her. But I know. I'll tell you later how I know."

I thought of that little green pill in my safe at home that he'd dropped during the jumbo shrimp lunch. I knew in my guts it was Rohypnol.

In the law sometimes you know things that you cannot prove.

The thought of ever again looking at Rodney's glassy eyes, his studio-tanned face, his gel-stiffened porcupine hair, made me nauseated.

"So I'm looking for office space," I said. "You've told me you have some extra room in your suite since the family law attorney you were subletting to moved to the suburbs last month. Is it still available?"

Duvonda chuckled. "Yes, so far. It's only two rooms—front room for a paralegal and a conference table, back room for the lawyer. Not very big—about six hundred square feet. Because it's in Two Union Square it's not cheap, but I'm not getting anything for it now. The market rate rent isn't too bad, since it's kind of small." She named a figure that was twice the mortgage payment on my condo. I could swing it. Besides, I had True Disasters nearing resolution—if the clients agreed to hire me—and a hunch that Duvonda would throw me some overflow cases.

One True Disaster fee would meet my basic expenses for four years—including my basic salary, Nicky's basic salary, office rent, and a whole bunch of whatnot.

"The price sounds right," I said. "Let me have a look at it. I'll bring Nicky too."

My mind was racing. Rodney's big spending on advertising had brought in a huge flood of DUI and criminal defense, a huge caseload of shrimps and Barking Dogs for the Boiler Room, and a handful of True Disasters.

He'd trusted me with all of the True Disasters because only I could handle them. He'd refused to pay my profit sharing, despite our contract. He'd told me to fire my paralegal. He'd even made a veiled threat to my parrot.

Rodney was about to lose his biggest profit center. Couldn't happen to a nicer guy.

"Okay, how much do you need for a down payment?" I asked. She quoted me a figure. It was about three months' mortgage on my condo. "Done," I said. "If I like the place, can I bring you a check tomorrow?"

"You can bring me a check tomorrow," Duvonda said. "Silent Mike is at his office down the hall from my place right now. He's got a key. He can show you around."

"Is it okay if I move a few things in right after he shows me around? I'd bet my left testicle that I'm going to love it."

Duvonda chuckled again. "You don't have to bet any portion of your junk. And yes you can move some stuff in. But Sam, how the hell are you going to get the files out of Rodney's office with his nifty staff of former football players hanging around waiting for guilty people to represent? Sounds kind of conspicuous. Maybe you should wait until tonight."

"No need," I said airily. "They're all gone to the DUI Dojo. They're learning how to crush the Breathalyzer and stomp blood draws."

There was muffled conversation on the other end. "Judge wants to see me," Duvonda said. She hung up.

I could sublet from Duvonda. I guessed the number of favors I owed her now was above twenty. I definitely needed to pay them off. When you do business with a good lawyer, favors are bankable currency. I would need to start remembering that. Most lawyers were nothing like Rodney. He was an outlier.

Check that. He was a liar.

Nicky and I left our loaded hand trucks in my office, closed the door, and went over to see Duvonda's suite.

Silent Mike met us at Duvonda's reception desk and led us back. It was two rooms, a front windowless room for an assistant, and a smaller back room window for the attorney.

The south-facing window had a view of Mount Rainier. It would get the meager sun that Seattle receives all year long, except between July and September when the overcast finally clears off. The carpet was beige Berber, the walls light cream. It was furnished with Danish modern desks in blonde wood, a blonde wood conference table seating six, and a cream-colored leather couch in the front room, by the front door. The chairs were stark and modern with black leather seats.

I inhaled. It smelled faintly sweet. It was totally quiet.

Unlike Rodney's office, there was no racket from constantly-ringing phone and the Boiler Room or the Guilty Peoples' Department. I'd never realized how much noise there was at Mammon & Associates—so much noise that I'd bought the big Mickey-Mouse style ear protectors that are used for people wielding chainsaws or firing pistols at the gun range.

"What do you think, Nicky?" I asked.

Nicky strolled around the two rooms, musing. She was wearing her blue paisley skirt today, and a black turtleneck. She moved like a ballerina. I caught a faint whiff of her rose perfume. I could tell she was delighted just from her flowing movements. Silent Mike raised an eyebrow at me, and I raised one back.

"I'm really more of a Chippendale girl myself," she said.

Silent Mike said, "The furniture style or the male strippers?"

She winked at him. "Both."

Silent Mike and I high-fived. "Sam, you got a live one here."

Nicky nodded at me.

"We'll take it," I said. "Can I get a key? We're going to be moving in some stuff. Right now."

Silent Mike reached into the chest pocket of his blazer, and pulled out an envelope. "Card keys for the building and the elevator. Card keys for the front door of Duvonda's suite. Your suite doesn't have separate locks. I hope that's okay. If not I can have the super put them in."

I said, "We have no secrets from Duvonda." I took the envelope and put it in the chest pocket of my suit jacket. "I'll bring by the check tomorrow for the first month, and half a month's rent for the damage deposit. One more thing. What about phones and high speed internet?"

"It's all included," Silent Mike said. "Phones are live and the Web connections are too. You get receptionist service and use of the copier included. You also get free coffee from the break room, but it's terrible."

"No thanks. I'll stick with my iced Americanos."

Then Nicky and I unloaded the Outback into the new office, drove back to Mammon & Associates, and loaded up the hand trucks with bankers boxes. While I was doing that Nicky disappeared.

We drove the Outback over to the new office, hauled everything up to the new suite, and presto. I ran around hooking up the computers. Nicky unpacked the boxes and lined the basic files up on the conference room table. Then I connected the terabyte drive to my new HP desktop, and it started backing up. Nicky then backed it up to hers while I downloaded Microsoft Office to both machines.

I asked her to subscribe us both to Carbonite for cloud backup. There are more hip cloud-based backup services, but Carbonite is bulletproof. That was what I needed. Bulletproof.

Nicky sat me down at the conference room table. During the flurry of activity she'd made a list on a legal pad. "Next comes bank accounts, setting up your LLC on LegalZoom, and setting up signing meetings with the clients. I'll take care of the LLC and the bank accounts. You just reach out and get the clients signed."

I stammered: "I wonder who will come with me?"

Nicky cocked her head at me. "Probably most of them, Sam. And we can afford to lose one or two."

"Definitely. Anybody who declines to come with us, I'll return the basic files to Rodney and delete the electronic files. But I had to secure the files so Rodney couldn't phony up new contracts that said they couldn't leave me if I departed from the firm, and put my signatures on them with some artful cutting and pasting. He's fully capable of that."

"I know, Sam. We're about to find out if we have clients or not."

"One last thing. I need to go back to Rodney's to return the key and leave a letter of resignation in his inbox, under everything else. Would you like to come?"

"Of course. I need to return my keys and resign too. I'll try hard to play it straight. You know, not any snarky comments about thanks for not dosing my coffee so he could bang me in the break room while I was unconscious."

"I'm also going to need a logo," I said. "And a basic website. And business cards. And a bookkeeper; probably we'll just use Duvonda's. It's a lot. We'll work hard."

Nicky pointed to her legal pad. "Here's your logo." It was an arrow, pointing up, with *Strait & Associates PLLC* underneath. "It says you're straight, and you're going up. I thought it might work."

I stared at it. Genius. "Might work? It's perfect." I paused. "Nicky, I've thought this over ever since I started playing with the idea of leaving. Attorneys aren't allowed to do formal profit-sharing with non-attorneys. It's against the Rules of Professional Conduct. But every time we recover funds on a case, I'll give you a discretionary bonus for your performance. It just might have a relationship with the amount of fees. I want to cut you in on the revenue, Nicky."

She clapped with glee. "This is perfect. You know why? Rodney alienated you by not paying profit sharing you were entitled to under your contract. You're starting out by paying me profit sharing even though you don't have to." She beamed, with Mount Rainier in the background. "We're going to do everything differently, Sam. You may have gotten pushed out of Rodney's firm. But it's going to turn out to be a huge piece of luck." She shook my hand. "Everything starts here and now."

I held her hand a little longer than I needed to. A piano-playing hand, long slender fingers, warm, magnetic. Everything was starting here and now.

When we finished up at Rodney's and left our keys in our desk drawers, Nicky gave a mock frown as we got on the elevator. "One thing I'd like to bring up with you, boss, even though it's a sensitive subject."

My nerves were so frayed I didn't know if she was teasing me or there was an actual problem. "Okay, shoot."

"I really think the office needs a parrot."

***

I brought Buster into the office the next day, and started calling the clients to set up meetings to sign my contracts with them. All but one said yes. The holdout was an elderly woman whose case wasn't quite a True Disaster. She'd been rear-ended at medium speed and needed a hip replacement, but she'd already had the other hip replaced for non-traumatic reasons.

Nicky put her basic file in a corner of the conference table with a Post-It on it that said, *Hard Pass.*

Stone Gamble's mom sent the new contract back as a scanned PDF with no hesitation. I told her we were closing in on the defendant. I asked her about grief counseling. "I've been spending a lot of time at church," she said. "Will you come with me next Sunday? It's really working."

Of course I would. I'd never been a regular churchgoer. But the past few days I'd prayed a few times, with my neck stuck out a mile like this. It felt good.

Bonus Malone took Nicky and me to lunch and signed the new contract on behalf of Linda Lou. I'd sent over the videos of the depositions. "I watched those things last night, with popcorn," he said, stroking his silver goatee. "When the defendant came across the table at you in the prison dep, I nearly choked. Have those hosers booked a mediation yet?"

"No, those hosers have not," I said.

Bonus had done personal injury in the past, but quit when he started developing an ulcer. "Here's a tip. Send the videos on DVD to the adjuster for ReachKids. The defense attorney probably wants to keep billing the file even though the defendants are basically dead as a doornail. That's what you get with Outhouse Counsel."

I smiled. My snide little phrase was being widely adopted.

Nicky asked, "But isn't that communicating with a represented party? Isn't that a violation of the Rules of Professional Conduct?"

Bonus shook his head. "No. The insurance company isn't a party to the lawsuit. They aren't on the caption. It's fine to communicate over the head of the defense attorney and go straight to the adjuster. The defense attorney won't like it. They could lose the chance to bill lots of yummy hours and make lots of yummy money and delay resolution for years. But it's perfectly legit. Besides, Lorna Weiss will hate it."

I laughed. "Then I'll love it. I'll do that. Maybe the adjuster will want to put an offer out there rather than let Lorna keep milking the thing. Besides, I want to get Linda Lou emancipated."

Bonus ate the last of his veal piccata. "Good news. Linda Lou's mom keeps calling me wanting to know when her check is coming in. The last time, once I was sure Linda Lou wasn't in touch with her, I told her she would need independent counsel for her potential loss of consortium claim due to the damage to the parent-child relationship. Even though, between you and me, Linda Lou's better off without her. She screamed at me and hung up. Apparently she'd wanted to go to the casino and expected I would have her money on tap whenever she demanded it."

"Or else she wanted drugs," I said. "The kids were all removed from her house due to neglect caused by PCP use. For years Linda Lou was the only one cooking and changing the diapers and doing the laundry. This kid deserves to be an emancipated minor."

Bonus signed the contract with a fountain pen and handed it back to me. I folded it and put it in the pocket of my jacket. "So you're still going to file the Petition for Emancipation at no charge?"

"Sure," I said. "Now that I don't work for Rodney anymore, I can give clients some freebies and some discounts without hiding what I'm doing."

Bonus folded his hands and leaned forward. "So that leaves Park. The wife of the deceased called me today and said she wants to meet before Genevieve signs the new contract."

Nicky frowned. "I thought there was a reason why Genevieve hadn't called back. Parental fealty. She wants to be sure her mother is on board, even though she's the personal representative."

"Fair enough," I said. "After lunch we'll call Genevieve and set a meeting. I have no objections to making my pitch. If we get Park, then we got all the cases we wanted out from under Rodney."

Bonus cackled. "Out from under Rodney? Word on the street is, it's tough for a woman to get out from under Rodney."

"You've heard something," I wondered.

"Just that Rodney, the legendary hound dog, has been chasing skirts with more aggression lately. The ladies who do criminal defense in my office suite are telling their friends—never get in an elevator with Rodney alone."

Nicky drank her tea, looking nonchalant. I was grateful I'd gotten her out of that hellhole.

That afternoon I called Genevieve and asked if it was okay with her if I went to see her mother, and she agreed. "She worries about everything," Genevieve said. "Just tell her how you'll handle it. She thinks Rodney must be good because he has TV commercials."

"Okay, I'll tell you how it went," I said. "If it's okay with her, you'll sign?"

"Most definitely, sir. It's my decision, but with all my sisters and my mother wringing their hands, I want to make sure nobody has anything to squawk about afterward. I've gotten the emailed contract, and I'll sign it and return it as soon as my mother is settled down."

So Nicky and I went out to see Mrs. Park. Her English was not good.

"So what money you get?" she asked again.

"It will be a lot," I said. I summarized what I'd gotten from the high-speed Mazda crash down in Kent—the Massive Impact case.

I suspected she'd relied on her husband to make most of the financial decisions, and she didn't want to get tricked. That was fine with me. I didn't know what it was like to lose a spouse, and I didn't want to know. She had one final question. "Can you get me more money than Mr. Mammon?"

"Of course. Rodney's never tried a personal injury case. Not one. I handled all of the personal injury for him. You're better off with me."

Then Mrs. Park called Genevieve and spoke to her in rapid Korean, darting her eyes at me. I gathered Genevieve was being told I was actually acceptable.

When Nicky and I drove back to the office, she said, "We're getting everybody we really wanted. Somehow this feels too easy."

I'd learned to trust her instincts. Rodney and his criminal defense minions were due back from DUI Dojo soon.

He'd probably sue me. Clients had the right to choose me, so it would be a bogus lawsuit—but he'd try to extort something out of me. He'd lose the suit, but he might try it.

He might file a Bar Complaint. Again, clients had the right to come with me. That was a nonstarter.

There was a big chance that he'd call the clients and tell them I was incompetent, or an alcoholic, or whatever. But I'd armored them against that. They were expecting it.

Or he'd try something…furtive.

The smart money was on furtive.

The next morning Nicky and I had just gotten in when the receptionist buzzed us. "There is a Mr. Rodney Mammon here to see you," the receptionist said. "Shall I show him back?"

"Definitely not," I said. "Tell him to wait there. And buzz Silent Mike. I'm going to need a witness when I speak to Mr. Rodney Mammon."

I knew Rodney could hear this on the intercom. Excellent. "Come on, Nicky," I said. "I'd like you to see what happens. But please stand back. This thing could go sideways quickly." She stood and pinned back her hair. I asked her, "Is this okay with you, or would you rather wait here?"

She stood up straight. "I'll come. I want to see it through."

I picked up the hip replacement lady's file, so I'd have something to give him. It was the only thing I was willing to let go of. I'd give him a face-saving victory to perhaps satiate his bloodlust.

Nicky and I walked out to the reception area. Rodney fidgeted at the desk in a loud houndstooth-checked suit with a lavender tie and matching handkerchief in his breast pocket. Behind him were two guys in blue coveralls—their chest patches read, *Major Moving*.

"Hello Rodney," I said. "This is the one client who refused to sign with me." I handed him the binder. "Who are these two strong-looking guys?"

Rodney looked at me, his glazed eyes burning. "They are the movers who will carry the files you stole from me."

He'd hoped to spark an emotional reaction.

From now on I would suppress my emotional reactions to him. Every time. Take no action until my loyal cerebral cortex had a chance to think, rather than letting my impulsive limbic system call the shots. He was trying to escalate the situation. It was the only way he could win.

"The other clients all signed my contracts," I said. "The files are their property under the Rules of Professional Conduct. Therefore I stole nothing. The one file you are entitled to is in your hand." I turned to Nicky. "Nicky, would you go copy the contracts of all the clients who have signed with us?" I wanted to get her out of the blast radius.

Nicky gave me an alarmed look and fled.

The air crackled with potential violence.

For all I knew, the moving guys were thugs that Rodney had gotten acquitted, and who had to "work off" their fees by doing whatever he said. Rodney liked to do that. But they really looked like regular noncriminal mover guys. They were shifting from foot to foot, not pleased to be put in the middle of some dispute.

They weren't backup. They were props.

I stood there and raised my eyebrows at Rodney. I could smell his rage. It smelled like an electrical fire. My loyal cerebral cortex told me not to move or speak. If I could stand still and not speak? Only then would I deserve to have my own firm.

Behind Rodney, the receptionist stared. She'd been with Duvonda for years, but she'd never had a showdown at the OK Corral in her lobby before.

Behind Rodney the front door opened, and Silent Mike walked in. God bless Silent Mike. He slowly walked past Rodney, stood by me, and turned around. He spoke in his customary low growl. "Sir, is there a reason you are in our lobby with a couple of movers? Are you here to repossess our furniture or something?"

Nicky appeared by my side with an accordion with the signed contracts. "Here you go, boss," she told me. "The Rules of Professional Conduct governing client property and choice of counsel are right on top."

I stepped up to Rodney and handed them to him. He reshuffled the binder under his arm, and took the accordion.

His hands were shaking. He was a millimeter from violence. "I'm going to sue you for my fees and for return of my client files," he said in a lazy monotone. He was also ignoring his limbic system and using his cerebral cortex right now. Rodney had made his whole career on brazening it out. He was much better at it than I was.

"Duvonda will represent me," I said, sticking my neck out again. "I've researched the ethical rules and contract law. Until an offer is made on a case, the contingent fee personal injury lawyer has no lien on the file, and no right to recover fees. You are entitled to a refund of the costs you've spent so far. I will send an itemization and payment within seven days. I presume a check will be sufficient. I want a written record of you depositing it. That will be accord and satisfaction. You will not get another dime from me."

I looked him up and down, ignoring my thundering pulse. "I think we understand each other."

Rodney turned red, and dropped the binder and the accordion. His fists were clenched. He was about to lose it.

Silent Mike stepped forward and let his leather blazer fall open. Next to his badge clipped to his belt showing he was a licensed armed private investigator was his holstered Glock 17. "Sir, are we about to have a situation up in here?"

Rodney stared at the gun.

I suddenly realized that there was only one way to stop Rodney from manipulating and exploiting people.

Force.

"Boys," Rodney said, indicating the dropped accordion and binder. The moving guys picked them up. They were just movers. Rodney was going to pay them a couple of hundred bucks to carry two objects he could easily carry himself. Just to avoid the submissive act of picking them up himself.

I understood something else about Rodney, then.

I wasn't conceited. I didn't have a lot of pride. I didn't think I was anybody special. I still don't.

It's a terrible mistake to think you're somebody special.

Rodney thought he was special. His pride was his tragic flaw. His pride would narrow his options. His pride would make him screw up. His pride was terribly dangerous to him.

Silent Mike nodded at Rodney, his jacket still hanging open. "If this concludes our business, then I wish you good day."

Rodney glared at me once more. Once more, I saw him override his overwhelming desire to strangle me.

Then one of the movers opened the lobby door, and said, "After you sir." Rodney stalked out, and the door swung shut behind the movers.

I turned to Silent Mike. "I would like to pay you for an hour of your time, for backing me up," I said in a shaky voice.

"Seemed like five minutes to me."

I looked into his eyes, and saw the hidden glee there. "But it felt like an hour to me. Come on back. You'll get the first of our pretty blue checks."

We walked back to our happy new Innocent Peoples' Department. I took him back to my office and unlocked the drawer where the checkbooks were.

Buster said, "Give 'em the whole nine yards!"

Silent Mike laughed. "Hey, I didn't know you had a parrot!"

I laughed too. "That's Buster. I inherited him from a client in a fatality case. I got my ass kicked, but I got Buster. I've been teaching him some new catchphrases."

I handed Silent Mike the check, and he tucked it away. Then he said, "Hey, do you know where that phrase comes from? The whole nine yards?"

"Nope. I hope there's a story behind that." I wanted to get Silent Mike talking. I felt that after-combat need to chatter.

"Sure is. This one's from my uncle Chester Arthur, who's still got a V-shaped Toyota in his barn if you recall. See, during World War II, American fighter planes with fifty-caliber machine guns had ammo belts that were nine yards long. So when you gave your enemy the whole nine yards? You put every bullet you had into his ass. That's the whole nine yards."

I looked at Buster, who was listening closely, then back to Silent Mike. "Buster's got an eerie way of saying his catchphrases at the right time. He's a very smart parrot. But don't tell Duvonda just yet. I need her to be sure my check cleared before I tell her about Buster."

Silent Mike winked at me. "No worries. I'll just tell her you've got an emotional support parrot. Then under Seattle's disability laws it would be insensitive to make you take him home."

I'd never gotten Silent Mike talking before. This was a rare privilege. "So how'd you wind up as a private investigator?"

He sighed. "Well sir, I was on the Seattle Police SWAT Team for six years. You know how the community and whatnot likes to say all cops are racist and they disproportionately shoot people of color and so on? They picked me for two reasons. One, rumor has it I'm a person of color."

"Okay, what's the other one?"

"I was with Delta Force in the Army."

I gawked. "No shit Sherlock?"

"I assure you, no shit."

"So then, why did you leave SWAT and go private?"

He looked into the distance, with the same expression Bonus Malone had had when he talked about giving up personal injury because he didn't want an ulcer. "I'm proud of what I did. We were resolving about twenty violent standoffs per year. I kept track of the number of hostages I got out unhurt. But Sam," he said, with a trace of sadness, "eventually you realize that the odds are stacking up. Eventually you might decide you want to do something that isn't quite as high stakes. I'm older than you. You'll see."

I nodded. "I'm sure I will. But I've never done anything as dangerous as you. Personal injury isn't dangerous."

He squinted at me. "Physically? No. But you have to deal with snakes like that Rodney Mammon all the time. And under the current state of the law you can't shoot them."

I smiled. "Thanks for your help. Do you have a phrase I can teach Buster?"

He walked over to the cage and bent down. Buster leaned over. Silent Mike said, "Gun control means using both hands."

CHAPTER THIRTY—FRED

So I took Bonus Malone's advice. I sent a DVD of the video depositions in Linda Lou's case to the adjuster for ReachKids with a cover letter requesting an offer. Nicky said, "Let's send it FedEx through their fastest possible delivery option, so it makes a splash." We walked it down to the FedEx office together. It was a beautiful windy day, unusual for January in Seattle. I just wanted to be out of the office with Nicky, making our first big move to settle our first big case.

During the walk I actually saw Nicky. I'd looked at her countless times. But this was the first time I'd really seen her.

The wind whipped her shiny black hair around her face until she put it back in a tortoiseshell barrette. I caught a whiff of her rose perfume. Her warm brown eyes flashed. Her face was alive with wit and perception, and the slight tinge of past bitterness and past sadness from her weird upbringing.

All this was catnip to me. By the time I got back to the office there was a short sentence in my head but I didn't have the guts to say it.

Three days later, Lorna called. "How dare you go over my head, Sam," she demanded.

I took a deep breath, the way Nicky had suggested—breathe in through the nose, out through the mouth, and then pause. That's how she'd soothed herself growing up with her bipolar New Age fruitcake mother.

Then I said, "Hello Lorna, nice to hear from you. What can I do for you?"

"You can stop contacting my adjuster and stop sending my adjuster cherry-picked evidence from the ReachKids case. Your behavior is entirely inappropriate."

Then I said the thing that stops drama queens and drama kings dead in their tracks. "I have done nothing wrong, and I am not going to apologize." I kept my voice low and even.

"I am the contact point for this case. Not the adjuster. The adjuster works through me."

"The insurance company is not a party to the litigation," I said evenly. "I can contact the insurance company directly whenever I want. Perhaps the insurance company needs to know that ReachKids is getting hammered. You're hourly counsel, so you have an incentive to bill hours. I'm sure you're not going to tell them you're losing."

She gasped.

I said, "You have a nice day." Then I hung up on her.

When you calmly tell somebody throwing a tantrum that you've done nothing wrong, and you will not apologize, it drains all the heat from the conversation. They hope to start a wrestling match.

Instead you present them with a steel wall. No emotion. No defensiveness. Just a steel wall. I'd learned this as a prosecutor.

Doing plaintiff's personal injury work is very much like being a prosecutor. You confront people who did bad things and hurt other people. You're pursuing damages rather than prison time. But the defense attorneys are really the same—some of them, like Lorna, actually defend both kinds of cases. They yell and rant and posture to put you on the defensive.

If you give them absolutely no emotion in return, they get deflated.

I wanted them deflated.

I wondered in passing how I'd ever stayed so long working for a tool like Rodney Mammon.

A day later I got a call from the adjuster. "Mr. Strait, I had a chance to review those video depositions," he said. "It seems like there is a colorable claim for negligence on the part of ReachKids. Perhaps we can set up a mediation."

"That would be great," I said. "But I need an opening offer first. If we go to mediation without an offer from the defense? Then the defendant's attorney will tell us our case has absolutely no value. I've seen that movie before, and I'm not going to see it again."

He cleared his throat. "You must understand your demand is totally unreasonable. There's no way a single sexual assault which did not result in pregnancy or sexually transmitted disease is worth two million dollars."

I inhaled through my nose, and out through my mouth. Simple. If you think before you speak, you speak better. "I think a good jury verdict would be that much, and maybe more," I said, keeping my voice level. "A bad jury verdict would be a lot less. What do you think a bad jury verdict would be?"

He snorted. "A bad jury verdict would be a defense verdict. A bad jury verdict would hold that ReachKids could not have known Burris Small was going to rape your client and would award you nothing."

I looked over at Buster. He was staring at me, his head cocked, with a cynical parrot eye. "I don't think that's possible," I said. "Remember the part where the president of ReachKids decided not to spend less than two days' pay to get criminal background checks? When DSHS didn't follow through? Do you remember that part of her deposition?" I let the silence build. "We can set a mediation as soon as you make an offer, of whatever amount, that is payable in actual dollars."

He snorted again. Clearly he'd wanted to go to mediation with the position that we would get nothing. Then he'd try to wear us down without naming a number. He knew and I knew that we could win a Plaintiff's Motion for Summary Judgment of Liability with what I already had. He was testing me to see if I was desperate or stupid.

I had enough money in reserve to run Strait & Associates PLLC for four years without making a dime. I was neither desperate nor stupid.

"Okay, we can put fifty grand on it, purely as nuisance value," he conceded.

We were both anchoring. Anchoring is when you start a negotiation with an extreme figure, knowing that gives you plenty of room to move toward compromise without giving up anything vital. I knew something he didn't know.

I would love to try this case.

Linda Lou was very resilient. The defendants' depositions would probably horrify the judge and the jury. And the video deposition of Burris Smalls? Pure gold. This case was a beauty because something terrible had been done to an innocent kid and the fault was crystal clear. It was a True Disaster.

But there's one more thing you need to win a True Disaster case. A client with the guts to fight back.

I tossed out the names of my three favorite mediators, and he picked one. We hung up, and I realized Nicky had been standing in my doorway, listening.

"So the negotiating has started," she said, tilting her head at me. She did that when she was curious. I liked it.

"Yes, they made an opening offer of fifty thousand," I said.

"Fifty thousand? That's chicken feed!"

I explained to her about anchoring. "It is chicken feed. But they'll come to a reasonable figure, or we'll try the case. Nicky, you and I have the football and we're charging toward the end zone. The only way they can stop us from getting a touchdown is to put a big pile of money in our way."

Nicky tilted her head further. "How much?"

I pulled out a manila folder. I'd gone on a couple of jury verdict websites and found comparable cases. "At the low end, two hundred thousand. At the high end, over two million. That's for a single act, with force, committed against a minor of course. The range is very wide. But I don't think we should accept less than a million. We have a really terrific client. I think the adjuster called me largely because Linda Lou did not back down one inch when Lorna tried to humiliate her in her deposition. Linda Lou is a really great kid. She fights."

Nicky nodded. "I've noticed you've started saying 'we' a lot. We are going to trial. We are setting up a new firm. Can I talk with you about something?"

My heart sank. "Okay," I said, following her out to the front room, where her desk was.

She sat down on the cream-colored leather couch by the front door and patted the cushion next to her. "Sit," she said, arching her eyebrows at me. Then she went over to her desk and took down the picture of Fred that was taped on the wall over the printer.

Fred. Always Fred.

"I've been thinking about we a lot too," she said, blushing, "or us, if that is better grammar. So I need to talk to you about Fred."

"All right," I said. I had truly seen her for the first time on our walk to the FedEx office. She had seen me seeing her. Our grammar was getting tangled up now. We were trying to capture Jell-O concepts with wire words, and it was getting messy.

I admitted that I loved her. I admitted that I had to tell her.

"Here he is," Nicky said, handing me the photo. I hadn't looked closely at it before. I didn't want to consider my rival. Yes, he was my rival. You figured it out long before I did. Nicky did too.

Fred was a preppy-looking guy, tall and lanky, late twenties, with glossy brown curls, merry blue eyes, and a white cable-knit sweater tied by its sleeves around his neck, with a background of maple trees blazing autumn red. Fred looked like prep school and lacrosse and sailboat races and golden retrievers at the family seaside cottage and a frosty shaker of martinis on a wicker side table. Fred looked like everything I could never be. He'd come from a background I could never have. I had no chance against Fred.

"Turn it over," she murmured.

I turned it over. It said *Copyright Marston Inc. Ltd.*

"Great, so he's a model, too," I said. "The guy's a winner. I get it."

Nicky took the photo from me. "Sam, this is a stock photo. There is no Fred."

I looked at her, my jaw dropping.

She laughed and clapped her hands. "If you could see your face now, Sam," she said.

Everything was rearranging itself in my head. I was never so shocked as when something important turned out right. I was on a first-name basis with disaster. Success was harder to get comfortable with.

"I went to the drugstore and bought a picture frame," she said in a rush, "and threw away the frame. Fred was the stock photo in the frame."

"Why?" I asked.

Nicky blushed and looked down at the photo. Now I understood why she blushed when she talked about Fred. Because Fred was a fib.

"When I got hired by Rodney," she said quietly, still looking down, "I worked for the personal injury attorney before you, who was a total wolf. Then there were all the criminal defense football player guys, who get handsy at the best of times. Then there was Rodney. Whenever I look at Rodney, I don't see a man. I see a snake."

"I get it," I murmured.

"But then you showed up," she continued, still looking down, "and I needed Fred for a different reason."

Now, I was starting to understand. "You didn't want to give up the shield of Fred until you got to know me better," I said.

I took a deep breath. I was going to jump off a cliff and I didn't know how deep the water was beneath it. "Nicky, I hope this doesn't mess us up with your work. But I love you."

She looked up, her brown eyes alight. "I didn't want to give up Fred until I knew that you loved me too," she said.

Long silence.

Back in my office, Buster said, "Well, that's a fine howdy-do." He really did seem to understand when to drop the right catchphrase.

I took both of her hands in both of mine. "Seriously?"

She pointed at her blue paisley skirt and my blue paisley tie. "Seriously. Come on, throw a girl a lifeline, won't you?"

I smiled at her. "Nicky, you aren't a woman. You are *the* woman."

The cream-colored leather sofa was an island in the universe, and we were the only two people alive. and every moment there was both very long and very short, and my heart was trying to climb up into my brain and make itself a cozy nest in there.

I kissed her and smelled her hair. It smelled like roses and cardamom and mystery. I was so happy that I had to do everything slowly. I kissed her again.

"I was wondering when you were going to figure it out," she murmured into my shoulder.

"I suspected it out a while ago," I murmured back, "but it seemed too good to be true. I've only had love once, Nicky. Only once. I've been on a lot of bad dates since then."

"Three cheers for TopFliteSingles.com," Nicky said into my shoulder.

The door opened behind me. I turned. Duvonda was standing there looking like she wanted to bounce something off of me.

Duvonda looked at us, and a huge smile spread across her face. "Sam, as your landlord, I approve," she said.

She closed the door quietly. I could hear her laughing to herself as she walked away.

It was starting to look like nothing could go wrong, which is always a dumb thing to believe, given my personal experience.

CHAPTER THIRTY-ONE—LINDA LOU'S SONG PART TWO

After we scheduled mediation in Linda Lou's case, I filed Plaintiff's Motion for Summary Judgment of Liability. I asked the court to hold Burris Small civilly liable for sexual assault and ReachKids liable for negligence—for hiring him, for letting him work alone without a clean criminal background check, and for failing to spend a little money to get a criminal background check from the private vendor.

I included Burris Smalls's Statement of Defendant Upon Plea of Guilty, the relevant parts of Splenda O'Malley's deposition (showing that ReachKids had failed to get a completed criminal background check on him before allowing him to work alone), and Linda Lou's forensic rape exam report from Harborview. They'd found "vaginal tearing." That phrase enraged me.

I also included Burris Smalls's video deposition. I counted on the judge's curiosity.

Lorna filed Defendant's Response, arguing that Burris Smalls's actions were not foreseeable and paraphrasing the Washington Administrative Code while saying that criminal background checks were recommended, not required.

But I had quoted the WAC section verbatim and attached a copy. Judges vary widely. But none of them enjoy being lied to.

Lorna's mediation statement consisted only of a short letter and two sample jury verdicts showing institutions not being held liable for their employees' sexual misconduct—with adults, not kids. Both were decided before *Christiansen v. Royal School District*. That case held that a school or other institution with custodial care of minors is always civilly liable if an employee has sex with a minor in the institution's care. I quoted *Christiansen* verbatim. I also included a copy of the case with my Summary Judgment Motion. I was assuming Lorna would lie about everything. Because she would.

When you pay people to do something—anything—they are more likely to do that thing.

I was going to try to do the nastiest thing I could do to a defense lawyer. I was going to try to cut off her ability to keep billing hours. I was going to try to break her rice bowl.

I planned to take the DVD of all of the depositions to the mediation and show them on my laptop if we made any progress. We agreed on a mediator—Hernando Suarez. I predicted he'd spend most of his time in the defense room, trying to make the adjuster listen to reason. And trying to get Lorna to just shut up.

On the morning of the mediation, I got to work early, but Nicky was already there. We loaded up, and then she asked me to come over to the window behind my desk. I noticed nothing other than uniform slate-gray overcast and scurrying people below.

"Before you came in, I was standing there watching everybody going to work," she said. "I had a beautiful and weird thought."

"Do tell."

"I've told you my sad childhood story. You've told me yours. It occurred to me—we are two of the luckiest people alive right now. We started out with rotten childhoods, and yet now we're here, doing this for these people." She nodded at the scurrying pedestrians. "How many of those people would you guess are delighted to be going to work today?"

I shrugged. "Probably not many. I'll bet most of them aren't as stoked to get started today as we are."

Nicky leaned her head on my shoulder. "It's like that every day for me. We started so low. We have both climbed so high. We can appreciate it because of the huge distance. See what I mean?"

I kissed her forehead. "I see what you mean. Let's go."

As we walked out of the revolving doors, I noticed a couple of paramedics bending over Street Monkey, the homeless junkie in the fleece jumpsuit who habitually begged in the plaza in front of our building. He was a white guy in his twenties with dreadlocks and a sharp wit. We'd trade sarcastic quips, but I never high-fived him because he was, to put it mildly, filthy. I never gave him money—I knew he'd just take it right to his drug dealer—but I sometimes gave him food.

The paramedics' radios crackled. The male paramedic was starting chest compressions on Street Monkey, who was as limp as a rag doll. The female paramedic was readying a syringe of Narcan. I watched—I was a sucker for watching skilled paramedics work.

The female paramedic pushed up Street Monkey's sleeve and showed me the inside of his elbow. It was covered with scabs and abscesses where he had shot up. "I can't find a vein," she said. "Let's try the ankle." His ankle looked just the same—scabs and abscesses and ulcers in the veins. Finally, she punched his calf and managed to raise a vein. She started injecting the Narcan.

"This is the second time this month we've revived Street Monkey," she said. "I'm not optimistic about this time."

Nicky put her hand over her mouth. "Second time this month?"

The female paramedic nodded. She asked the male paramedic, "Are you getting anywhere?"

He shook his head. He said, "That's the thing about IV drug abusers. They keep trying to kill themselves. We keep trying to stop them. The voters want us to keep trying to stop them. But unless the addicts go to jail? They all go to the morgue in the end."

Nicky frowned. "That's because they haven't gotten their neurochemistry straight," she said.

The female paramedic finished the injection. "You got that right, sister. Nobody forces them to start using. Nobody forces them to continue using. People who say they just need more services are nuts. The free stuff just attracts more junkies to Seattle. We have a saying in the Seattle Fire Department—feed the pigeons? Get MORE pigeons! What they need is to get locked up before they kill themselves." She asked the male paramedic, "Any heart response? "

The male paramedic looked down at his portable EKG and shook his head. "Guess we gotta shock him. Give it the old college try, anyway. But I bet he's toast this time." He pulled out the portable defibrillator. "CLEAR!"

The female paramedic raised her hands, and the male paramedic triggered the device. Muffled zap. Street Monkey's body arced about four inches off the concrete. "Nothing," the male paramedic said. "Again. CLEAR." The female paramedic raised her hands again, and the male paramedic shocked him again. "Nothing. I'm calling it. Time of death: 8:22 AM."

We had just watched Street Monkey die. Cause of death? Suicide by addiction.

Nicky nudged me. We started walking down Fifth Avenue toward the mediator's office. "You know something funny? Everybody who gave money to Street Monkey was just subsidizing his drug dealer. He probably didn't hang on to the money for twenty-four hours before he bought his next fix. The so-called compassionate people, with their white progressive guilt? They helped him kill himself." She shivered. "God, I wish people could just understand that."

I hugged her. "Me too. But sometimes people don't learn things because learning might hurt their feelings. You could tell every single client of Priestess Esmerelda that she's a fraud and there's no such thing as soul retrieval. They look at you and pretend to might listen. But then they'd give her another three hundred bucks and another pound of cornmeal. The cornmeal part still stops me in my tracks."

Nicky chided me. "Sam, now it's five hundred. Soul retrieval is a booming industry in this town."

I nodded over my shoulder. "Apparently, so is selling heroin and meth."

Nicky tapped my arm. I knew she was going to quote me back to me. She was wise to me now.

"The truth doesn't care if you believe in it or not," she said.

My favorite saying. I was going to have to be consistent with her.

"So, Sam," she said with feigned casualness as we walked, "what would you say to a little coed slumber party this weekend?"

We'd made out but hadn't taken it any further. "I would say hell yes," I said, smiling down at my feet.

"Splendid. I'll wear my best long flannel nightgown."

"And I'll wear my long johns with the flap in the seat of the pants."

"It's a date, then."

By the time we got to the mediator's office I was pretty charged up.

***

Hernando Suarez, the mediator, was a veteran insurance defense lawyer at a firm I'd come to respect. Recently, he'd retired to live on his sailboat and do mediations. I liked him. He'd never tried to give me a snow job, and he could talk turkey with the insurance adjuster because he'd done it for thirty years.

I needed to keep going over the head of Lorna Weiss, so maybe we could get a decent settlement without her billing lots of hours and wasting lots of time. I needed to do the one thing that Outhouse Counsel hated the most. I needed to break her rice bowl.

Hernando was looking tan and fit in his cream-colored suit. His silver crew cut shining. Retirement was agreeing with him. I introduced him to Linda Lou and, Bonus Malone, and Nicky. To my delight, Hernando had already gone to the other room where Lorna Weiss and the adjuster, Ricky Tartan, were set up.

When Hernando sat us down, I first went over to the phone and unplugged it. "Okay, Sam, what's that about?" he asked.

I said, "I have a friend who found out after mediation that the defense lawyer had turned on the intercom in the plaintiffs' room so he could hear everything the other side was saying. I'm not letting that happen to us." I didn't tell him that the plaintiffs' lawyer who'd been tricked was Duvonda.

"Interesting," Hernando said, as Bonus winced. "So their opening position is that fifty grand is nuisance money and the costs of expert witnesses. They say you're not going to do any better."

I pulled out my mediation statement. "There can be a big swing in cases involving sexual assault of a minor," I admitted. "But there's only one issue in evaluating defendants' offers. Can we do better at trial? I'm confident we can do better than fifty grand at trial."

Hernando nodded. "It's an opening offer. So is yours."

I decided to pull the best move I had with good mediators. "So what do you suggest to get their best offer? Then we know if we're going to trial or not. I'd like to send out a sonar ping and see what comes back."

Hernando rubbed his hands together. He liked it when attorneys asked for his expertise. "Well, I recommend you drop one hundred K and see how they react. That's a sonar ping that is a big enough drop to get their attention, but you're not giving away the store." He wrote on the notepad in his leather portfolio. "Let's say you drop one hundred grand, but that offer expires at the end of the mediation. With a big insurer like these guys, you never want to leave an offer on the table very long."

"Brilliant," Bonus said. I agreed.

"Let me see what I can do," he said, leaving.

Bonus looked at all of us and squinted at me. "I'd never heard about the intercom thing before."

I shrugged. "It happened to a good friend of mine. I won't say who. But now, I always do that at the start of mediation. We need to make sure our discussions are private. Also, this time, the defense room is all the way at the end of the hall. Please, nobody say anything important outside of this room. We're sending signals right now, and we need to be cautious. Me more than any of you."

Linda Lou was drinking orange spice tea. She pulled off her hoodie. "Could you go to the front desk and tell them not to let any police officers back here?"

"Sure," I said. "I wouldn't put it past Lorna to try that trick again."

Nicky started telling Bonus what happened at Linda Lou's deposition.

I went to the front desk. The receptionist looked at me quizzically, but she agreed. Mediators and their staff see all kinds of weird behavior. Especially in big cases.

When I came back, Hernando was back too. Another thing I liked about him? Unlike some mediators, he didn't waste time until the mediation was almost over in an attempt to create false urgency. He liked movement. "They went up to a hundred," he said. "They're also suggesting they won't go to three hundred."

Nicky and Bonus threw up their hands. Linda Lou looked at me with alarm.

"Don't worry, guys," I said. "If they top out below three hundred, we'll just leave. They control their offers. But we decide what is enough. Last night, I added up the four most similar jury verdicts, the verdicts I included in the mediation statement, and divided by four. If we can't get close to that number? We won't settle."

"What's your counter?" Hernando asked.

"I'd like the adjuster to do a meet and greet with Lorna," I said. "No discussion, just look her in the eye and shake her hand. Sometimes, it helps thaw them out."

"I concur," Hernando said, and he left.

I smiled at Linda Lou. "Just say pleased to meet you and shake hands. Don't respond to anything Lorna says. Lorna wants to escalate conflict to increase revenue. Just ignore her."

Nicky added, "Give her the steel wall. Polite expression. No talking. It's all you can do with a toxic person." She'd learned that one the hard way.

The door opened and Hernando came in, followed by Lorna Weiss and Kyle Tartan, the adjuster. Mr. Tartan wore a khaki cardigan; he was cadaverous and about fifty. Like most big-time adjusters, he looked chronically depressed. If I got a decent settlement, my fee would be more than he earned in two years. He knew it.

"Mr. Tartan, I'm Sam Strait," I said, shaking his hand. His hand was cold and thin, but his grip was good. "May I present my client, Miss Linda Lou Lawson."

He shook hands with Linda Lou. "My pleasure, young lady," he said with a deadpan expression.

"Pleased to meet you," Linda Lou said. She was a foot shorter than him. Even though she was a minor rape victim with an arrest warrant out due to her Run Report, she looked happier than he did.

Lorna held out her hand to Linda Lou. Linda Lou squinted at it. "We've met," Linda Lou said, refusing to shake her hand.

Hernando ushered out the defense team, and returned. "Okay, so where do we go from here?"

Bonus said, "Maybe you should remind them that any settlement has to be approved by a minor settlement guardian ad litem and a commissioner at King County Superior Court. If the court doesn't approve it, then nothing happens."

Hernando scribbled a note. "Good point. Okay, here's one thing they say that is actually pretty solid. They say that the harm was much less bad than it could have been." He motioned to Linda Lou. "May I speak plainly?"

"Yes sir," she said, pulling her hood over her head again. It was her signature move of withdrawal.

"Okay. The harm would have been greater if you had become pregnant or if you had contracted a sexually transmitted disease. You didn't, did you?"

Linda Lou retreated into herself. "I didn't get pregnant. I got clean STD tests, except one hasn't been done. The HIV test. I have to wait another two months for that. You have to wait six months until the date of exposure."

My blood ran cold. I'd forgotten her HIV test hadn't been done yet. It was even in the forensic rape report from Harborview. I'd even included it in the mediation statement.

I felt like an utter moron.

Hernando nodded. "That is an excellent point," he said, scribbling. "How long did the pregnancy and STD tests take to come back? Other than HIV, I mean?"

"I got my period two weeks later, so the pregnancy part cleared up fast. The STD tests took several weeks. Except for the HIV test. It's still not done. I might be HIV positive."

Hernando scribbled again. He murmured, "Six months of waiting. No negative HIV test yet."

Bonus said, "I recently had a colonoscopy, and it took a week to find out if my polyps were benign. It's hard to imagine waiting six months for an HIV test. You've had a long road, kiddo. I'm sure glad Sam insisted you be here."

I was too. Since I'd made a boneheaded mistake by not focusing on the pending HIV test.

Linda Lou looked up at Bonus. "Sam says only you can sign a settlement agreement, and then the court approves it or denies it, but it's my life. Sam says he won't accept anything unless I agree."

Bonus replied, "It's not just that, kiddo. You just gave us a gold-plated argument that none of us had thought of. Am I right?"

I sighed. "True. The waiting period for the HIV test still hasn't expired." I swallowed hard.

What would I do if Burris Smalls had given Linda Lou HIV? I couldn't do…anything.

But I'd sure like to kill him.

Linda Lou drank the rest of her tea. "That's okay, Mr. Uncle. You haven't been in my shoes."

Actually I had kind of been in her shoes, but I wasn't going to say that. I didn't just want to get Linda Lou her settlement; I wanted her to get some of her autonomy back. A parentified child learns to be independent very early. Since she was eight she'd been mostly in charge of a herd of younger brothers and sisters.

Hernando finished writing. "I'm going to use that HIV test waiting period argument in every sexual assault case I mediate from now on," he said. "Young lady, you aren't just doing this for yourself. You're doing this for everybody who's in the same shoes, as you put it."

Linda Lou looked at her feet and blushed. "I see."

I said, "I recommend we reduce by fifty K, and again make the expiration set for the end of mediation. Bring up the HIV issue. It's time for them to get serious. That's why I booked a half day mediation. In full-day mediations, the plaintiffs often get worn down, while the defendants' room gets paid and answers emails and talks about other cases. Also, please remind them that the Plaintiff's Motion for Summary Judgment is up for argument in nine days."

Hernando snapped his portfolio shut. "I agree. This is a louder sonar ping. It's time to see what they are actually going to do." He left.

Bonus asked me, "So what do you think they're gonna do?"

I said, "You never know until you know. I bet they don't go to three hundred. That wouldn't be anywhere near enough anyhow. I doubt this mediation will succeed. But we'll give it another round of offers, maybe two, and then walk if they didn't get to my figure."

"What is your figure?" Nicky asked.

I pulled out my sheet with the four comparable jury verdicts added up and averaged. "It's just a shade over $801,000," I said. "But given the HIV issue, maybe I should bump it up higher. We'll certainly bring that up if there's a trial."

Bonus whistled. "I know the court would approve the eight hundred," he said.

"But I personally will soften up if Linda Lou doesn't want to go to trial," I said. "However…big however. I checked out the Order Setting Civil Case Schedule last week. Now in a case like this, the defendants virtually always pay the fee and file a Jury Demand. They want to tell the jury that the plaintiffs are greedy and prevent the jury from learning that defendants have insurance. It works very well in Seattle. But—it turns out that Lorna Weiss missed the deadline for filing a Jury Demand. In rare cases I file one, if the defendants haven't done that. But I didn't do it this time. So this case will be tried by a judge." I looked at Linda Lou.

"Kiddo, it's much less humiliating to testify in front of a judge, rather than a jury. Judges have seen some awful stuff. They are usually very considerate to plaintiffs under eighteen. So if we go to trial, I will be with you every step, and the judge will make sure Lorna doesn't misbehave."

Bonus said, "I'll be there too. Whenever you are on the stand, I will be there. As your litigation guardian, I can get pretty obnoxious if I need to."

Linda Lou smiled shyly at him. "I'd like to see that, Bonus. You being obnoxious. You seem like a teddy bear."

"Remember, I used to do personal injury, too," he said. "I can go from teddy bear to grizzly bear when I have to."

Hernando returned. "Okay, they went up fifty more. They're at one fifty. They again say they won't get to three hundred." He looked around the table. "I'll let you confer," he said, leaving.

"Okay, gut check," I said. "Linda Lou, do you feel comfortable going to trial with the judge, but no jury? Bonus and me will be right there with you."

Linda Lou looked sadly into the distance. Then she looked at me, and Bonus, with a fierce expression. "Yes, let's do it," she said.

I said, "Bonus? Do you think it's in her best interest to keep litigating?"

Bonus stroked his gray goatee. "I do."

Nicky said, "How about you, Sam? I know it's the client's decision, and Bonus is the legal client, but what do you say?"

I slid my accordion file back into my briefcase. "Yes, I think we should go to trial. When I have a big decision to make? I put myself six months in the future, and then ask myself: Which choice will I be proud of? I couldn't be proud of taking their chicken feed. I say we go."

We all got up. I plugged in the phone. Hernando came back. "So what does the plaintiff say?" he asked me.

I shook his hand. "Plaintiff says we refuse. No counter offer. They're smoking crack. We're leaving. Is there a chance you'll circle back with them after our summary judgment hearing?"

Hernando smiled. "I can do that." He shook hands with Linda Lou. "It's been a pleasure, miss," he said.

I reached into my accordion file. I had made copies of the Order Setting Civil Case Schedule, and highlighted the Jury Demand deadline. I made sure we were all ready to leave and then handed two copies to him. "Hernando, when we're safely out the door, would you give this to Kyle and Lorna? This is going to be a bench trial. Lorna missed the deadline to demand a jury. I thought Kyle Tartan should know that the defense won't get to try any hocus pocus with jurors on this one."

Hernando's eyes went wide. "Jesus, Sam, that's a Sunday punch. Sure, I can do it. Why didn't you raise this before?"

I said, "I just knew in my bones that they wouldn't offer anything serious. So I wanted to start a vigorous discussion between the adjuster and Lorna after we left," I said, casually.

Hernando slapped me on the back. "You are a wicked, wicked man." He laughed, a short crack.

When we got to the elevators, Linda Lou said, "I like that about the judge. I had to testify a couple of times when DSHS was taking us kids away from my mom. I think I can hack it, talking to a judge." She made sure her hoodie covered all of her hair. She was still living underground. I could have kicked myself for not remembering to give her a ride to mediation. She was sure getting a ride home. Complete with ice cream.

"One more thing," I told her. "I'm going to file the Petition for Emancipation of Minor today. I want to get you out from under DSHS. I don't want you to be scared of being arrested again. Email me your last paycheck stub, okay? You've got months of earnings history now, and it's clear you should never be in a DSHS placement again. So let's clear that up before anything else happens, all right?"

I drove Linda Lou and Nicky back to the University District, where we stopped by a Baskin Robbins. Linda Lou liked Cookies and Cream. Nicky got Mocha Fudge. I just got black coffee, to get me jazzed up for writing the emancipation pleadings.

That afternoon, as I was writing the emancipation pleadings, I kicked myself repeatedly for not bringing up the HIV waiting period in the mediation statement.

But would it have done any good? No. I would use it as another Sunday punch when the time was right.

When I electronically filed the Petition for Emancipation of Minor, I noted it in Juvenile Court. Just an hour later I got a kickback message setting it before Judge Gloria Palacpac, the assigned judge for our civil case, including the Summary Judgment Motion.

The Petition for Emancipation of Minor was re-set for the same date and time as the Summary Judgment Motion. The next day, Lorna filed a Motion to Extend Deadline for Jury Demand, also setting it before Judge Palacpac at the same date and time.

This hearing was for all the marbles.

***

On the day of the triple hearing, Nicky and I picked up Linda Lou, then we met up with Bonus Malone in Judge Palacpac's courtroom. Bonus didn't have to be there, but he decided to tag along "out of a morbid sense of curiosity." He was keeping track of billable hours, but saving the bills for the Minor Settlement Hearing, if there ever was one. He'd gotten hooked on Linda Lou's case, just like me.

Lorna Weiss had brought the adjuster, Kyle Tartan. This is very unusual. Nowadays adjusters attend depositions or motion hearings only when the stakes are very high and they think the case is going off the rails. We all nodded to each other but said nothing.

I should explain about Judge Gloria Palacpac. She was appointed to an unexpired term of a department at King County Superior Court about four years ago. I was at the prosecutor's office. My two office mates made snide remarks about how she must be a "quota queen" because she was a Filipina lesbian in a wheelchair. But she'd come straight from running the Felony Trial Team at the Whatcom County Prosecutor's Office, up north near the Canadian border.

I like it when prosecutors take the bench. Prosecutors hear so much nonsense from criminal defense lawyers that they usually know how to cut through the emoting and get down to facts and logic and law. I was optimistic.

Since then I'd tried two criminal cases before her, and one civil case. She was my favorite judge out of all sixty-five on the King County bench. Every judge says, "I've read the materials" at the start of a hearing. But not all of them do. Judge Palacpac always did.

But—isn't there always a but? Duvonda had warned me that Judge Palacpac had her heart set on sitting on the Washington Supreme Court. "She won't risk getting reversed by the Court of Appeals," Duvonda had said. "She might be turning into a political animal. You need to give her ample cover to rule in your favor. If it's risky she'll probably punt the football."

Judge Palacpac liked to run a "hot bench," where she peppered both sides with tough questions. There was none of that "Seattle nice" sympathizing with bad guys.

The bailiff stood. "All rise. King County Superior Court is now in session, the Honorable Gloria Palacpac presiding."

Judge Palacpac wheeled in, threw her shoulders back, and smiled. Her bronze face shone in the lights, accented by her silver crew cut. She had laugh lines. "Be seated. We're here on three motions in the case of Bonus Malone as litigation guardian ad litem for LLL, a minor, versus ReachKids et al. Parties and counsel, please identify yourselves."

I stood. "Sam Strait for the plaintiff."

Bonus stood. "Bonus Malone, Litigation Guardian ad litem for the plaintiff."

Linda Lou stood. "Um, I'm LLL, Your Honor."

Nicky stood. "Nicky Schwartz, paralegal for Mr. Strait."

Lorna stood. "Lorna Weiss for the defendants."

Kyle Tartan stood. "Kyle Tartan, claims adjuster for the defendants' insurer."

Judge Palacpac nodded at him. "Not often we see a claims adjuster at a motion hearing. Welcome. First, let's take up Defendants' Motion to Extend Deadline for Jury Demand. Ms. Weiss, can you explain more fully why defendants did not file a Jury Demand before the deadline in the Order Setting Civil Case Schedule?"

A little inside baseball knowledge here. Each county Superior Court adopts and publishes its own Local Rules. It's a very, very, very bad idea to violate them. The judges love their Local Rules, because the rules let them manage a flood of complicated cases. Without the Local Rules, cases get tangled up, and judges get overwhelmed.

In the law, it's more important to be organized than to be smart. We all resent it when others try to derail a case. Judges more than anybody.

Lorna stood. "Your Honor, I didn't file the Jury Demand because I had not received permission from the insurer to pay the fee. I needed the sign-off to spend that kind of money."

Judge Palacpac frowned. "It's only $240. You work for Aloysius Miller, correct? Why couldn't Aloysius Miller see it clear to spend the $240 and request reimbursement from Mr. Tartan here?"

Lorna looked down. "Your Honor, I'm just an associate. Mr. Miller made that decision."

Judge Palacpac drilled in. "Is Mr. Tartan here to testify that he was ready to pay the fee, and he simply wasn't asked?"

Lorna bit her lower lip. "Your Honor, we weren't anticipating testimony from him today."

Judge Palacpac sighed and looked at me. "Counselor?"

I jumped to my feet. "I have nothing to add to my briefing on the jury demand deadline, Your Honor."

Napoleon once said you should never interrupt your adversary when they are making a mistake. Lawyers love quoting that one.

"I'm going to deny the Motion to Extend Jury Demand Deadline," Judge Palacpac said. "No good cause was shown for missing the deadline set forth in the Local Rules. Furthermore I am retaining jurisdiction. This will be a bench trial before me. If my schedule requires limited adjustment of the trial date, my bailiff will inform you."

Judges only retain jurisdiction when they've decided a case is their baby. It's rare in King County. Judge Palacpac wanted to make all the pretrial rulings and preside over the trial.

We'd whetted her appetite.

"Next, let's turn to the Plaintiff's Motion for Summary Judgment," she said. "Mr. Strait, my first question is how is this case different from *Christiansen v. Royal School District*, where a school district was liable for the sexual abuse of a minor committed by an employee against a minor?"

I stood. "*Christiansen* establishes that an institution with custodial control over a minor is automatically civilly liable for the sexual abuse of a minor in its custody. But this case is even worse than *Christiansen*. LL was ordered to live in the ReachKids group home nonstop, around the clock, 365 days a year. If she ran away, she could be arrested. She had nobody else in a parental role she could turn to. The abuser, Burris Small, has pled guilty and his Statement of Defendant Upon Plea of Guilty is before the court, as is his video deposition."

I'd stuck my neck out submitting that. It wasn't necessary, but it was short and very lurid. Most of us can't resist a short video showing terrible behavior. Trying to strangle me on camera certainly qualified.

Judge Palacpac smiled at me. "How is your neck, Mr. Strait?" She'd watched the Burris Smalls deposition, all right.

I smiled with relief. "It's fine now. Fortunately, my friend Duvonda Marshall advised me to wear a clip-on tie whenever I go to prison, so it turned out okay."

Lorna spoke up. "Mr. Strait should be disqualified as counsel, Your Honor. He was allegedly assaulted by the defendant and therefore he is a witness and cannot serve as plaintiff's attorney."

I watched Lorna clacking her puppet mouth.

Judge Palacpac squinted at her. "Allegedly? For real? I watched the video deposition and you were right there, Ms. Weiss." She turned to me. "Mr. Strait, have you filed any sort of personal injury claim against Burris Small?"

"No, Your Honor. And I won't. I formally waive any such claim."

Judge Palacpac turned back to Lorna. "There, you see? Motion to disqualify is denied. Bailiff, put that on the docket." The bailiff typed busily. Lorna had goofed. She was trying to be too clever. I used to make the same mistake.

Judge Palacpac said, "I'm inclined to grant Plaintiff's Motion for Summary Judgment. Ms. Weiss, can you tell me why the motion should not be granted?"

Lorna stood. "Yes, Your Honor." I had to hand it to her, she could take a punch. "As the court pointed out, the Christiansen case is a school case. The public schools are a unique statutory scheme for education of all children of the general public, and they are governed by unique truancy laws. Group care is a whole different animal, governed by different statutes and different sections of the Washington Administrative Code."

Judge Palacpac tilted her head. "I read in the briefing that one WAC requires group home employees to receive a clean criminal background check before they work alone with kids. The president of ReachKids's deposition showed that this WAC was not complied with by the date of the sexual assault."

Lorna nodded. "True. DSHS was backlogged."

Judge Palacpac drilled in. This was what I loved about her. "But the president could have gotten the background checks from a private vendor, for all forty-some employees whose checks were overdue, by spending less than two days of her pay. Yet she did not. Then ReachKids allowed the abuser to work alone with LL. There was nobody else in the house when the abuse occurred. I note in passing that LL was raped on her birthday. So how are the facts in this case less egregious than they are in *Christiansen*?" Judge Palacpac pinned Lorna with her eyes.

"The staffing situation was an unfortunate emergency, and we will show at trial that it was an unavoidable circumstance that prevents liability," Lorna said, soldiering on.

Judge Palacpac looked down at a document. "I'm reminded of the case Plaintiff's counsel cited about custodial care called *Niece v. Elmview Group Home*. The organization providing custodial care is responsible for a universe of potential harms, limited only by foreseeability. That's pretty strong language from the Washington Supreme Court."

She paused, to let us all take a breath. "Plaintiff's Motion for Summary Judgment is granted. Madame bailiff, please hand up the Order."

Lorna was rocked back on her heels. Her clacking puppet mouth was shut. I would have felt sorry for her, if she hadn't been a first-class shit to Linda Lou in her deposition. Which was part of the record in this motion.

Judge Palacpac signed my Order. "Now we turn to the Petition for Emancipation of Minor. Ms. Weiss, you and your adjuster are excused. These particular hearings are closed to anyone but the participants."

Lorna gathered up her things, and she and Kyle Tartan trudged to the door. The door swung shut with a loud click. The courtroom was suddenly very small and very big, very hot and very cold.

Judge Palacpac motioned to Linda Lou. "Please remove your hoodie, dear," she said.

Linda Lou pulled down her hood and took the witness stand and was sworn.

"Young lady, I have read your Declaration in support of your Petition for Emancipation that Mr. Strait filed. Are all statements in the Declaration true, under penalty of perjury?"

Linda Lou lifted her jaw. "Yes, Your Honor."

I'd used overkill in Linda Lou's Declaration.

She signed it, but I wrote it while meeting with her. It described how Linda Lou's mother had been a drug addict since before she was born. How Linda Lou took care of the younger kids since she was eight. How Linda Lou had been removed from her mother's home by DSHS due to neglect caused by her mother's PCP use. How she'd been forcibly raped in DSHS-paid group care, resulting in "vaginal tearing" according to the rape forensics report. I described how she had a job now, and a place to live. She was still frightened she would be arrested due to the Run Report and sent to juvie, prior to being placed in another "group care facility." I'd spent two hours with Linda Lou writing it. Even though it was only three pages. This thing had to be ultra-tight. We wouldn't get another chance for a year, maybe more.

No matter what happened with her civil case, I couldn't let Linda Lou be arrested and put back in one of those DSHS hellholes.

Judge Palacpac re-read the Declaration. She shook her head twice. Every prosecutor or ex-prosecutor remembers the child victims. Don't let anybody kid you about that.

She raised her head, and gave Linda Lou a motherly smile. "It is my pleasure to announce that the petition is granted. Young lady, you are now a legal adult. You don't have to live anywhere you don't want to. You can decide to retain Mr. Strait as your attorney, or to get another one. I will look forward to receiving an Amended Complaint. I wish you the best of luck."

Linda Lou stood up, and tears flooded her eyes. "I'm definitely keeping Sam Strait," she said.

Judge Palacpac said, "Madame bailiff, please give this party one copy of the other orders, and two copies of the Order Emancipating Minor. I want Ms. Lawson to have something to show the police if they contact her. We will stand adjourned."

"All rise," the bailiff called, and we leapt to our feet.

Linda Lou hugged Nicky. She hugged Bonus. She hugged me.

I told her, "I'll find out how to quash the arrest warrant from the Run Report."

Bonus chided me. "Already covered, Counselor. One of my office mates does criminal defense. He had it all teed up if we could get the Order of Emancipation. By the end of the day, Linda Lou, you'll no longer be a wanted criminal for running away. You can even stop wearing your hoodie. Unless it's a fashion statement."

Linda Lou pulled her hood over her head. "You know, I've kind of gotten to like it. But let me know when all that stuff comes through."

As we walked through the homeless people thronging the sidewalk in front of the courthouse, I thought about what Nicky had said about her and me.

We really were the luckiest of people.

Nicky and I drove Linda Lou back to Has Beans. "Since you're emancipated, and you can't be arrested," I asked her, "could you at last tell me where you're living?"

"Sure," Linda Lou said. "I'm living with Amanda Febrile, the owner. She has a three-bedroom house nearby. She lets me crash on the fold-out sofa in exchange for a small rent. We call her Demanda because she's kind of bossy. But that's only because the shop is for sale and nobody's making offers. She wants to go to New Mexico and become a chiropractor."

Linda Lou jumped out. "Sam, thanks. You're The Shit."

I laughed. "I assure you, kiddo, I am not The Shit."

"Nope. You are The Shit." She slammed the door and walked into Has Beans, looking six inches taller than when she was in court.

I looked at Nicky. "I'm formulating a devious plan," I said.

"Does it involve a coed slumber party? Flannel nightie and long johns?"

"I stand corrected. I'm formulating another devious plan, besides that one."

"Sam Strait!" Nicky grabbed my hand. "Tell me everything."

I took her hand in both of mine. "When I finally get Linda Lou's case resolved, I would love to see if she wants to buy Has Beans. I'm guessing she'll have more than enough. She would be one hell of a business owner."

Nicky kissed me. "That is a wonderful and devious plan."

That night we had our first coed slumber party. I won't tell you anything except her lips tasted like morning in Heaven.

CHAPTER THIRTY-TWO—LINDA LOU'S SONG, PART THREE

A couple of days later Bonus called. "My colleague got Linda Lou's warrant quashed. She's in the clear."

I stood at my window, watching a rainstorm blow in from the south. "Can you email the document?"

"Already did. By the way, I called that lady you told me about and found out about the price of entry. It's thirty. But she owes twelve to her bank on top of that. So once you get Linda Lou's money we've got an opportunity here."

"I'll probably have to go to trial—but once I get her money, we have a good option for her. Bonus, you'll be getting all my guardianship and probate work. You up for that?"

"Does a bear go Number Two in the woods? Hell yes. I'm just glad you're doing the personal injury and risking the ulcers instead of me."

I opened my email and printed the document showing the warrant had been quashed, then saved it in Linda Lou's file folder named Emancipation. I tapped the edges together and stapled it. I'd been looking for an excuse to go see her. Nowadays when she called me Mr. Uncle, I only heard the uncle part.

Outside in the front room, Nicky was huddled with our new bookkeeper Cassandra. Cassandra was Duvonda's hourly bookkeeper. She had a string of about thirty small law firms. Cassandra was fiftyish, brunette, funny and sarcastic, and always cheerful. She'd told me my handwriting was "regrettable" and liked to explain what she was doing: "You take your happy check register, and your happy bank statements, and give them to me as scanned PDFs. Then I make sure everything matches in your happy trust account and make sure you're paying enough in federal and state taxes so the happy government stays happy." Nicky thought Cassandra would have been a better mother than Priestess Esmerelda.

I'd noticed this since I lost my parents. You can create a healthy family from the right friends. I liked to tell Nicky: "My family is anybody who likes me."

I went out and interrupted them. "Nicky, could you print the Excel spreadsheet for Linda Lou's costs? I need to know how deep we are into this case."

Nicky printed it and handed it over. "So far we're under ten thousand. But it's going to get expensive from here."

"You bet. We'll have to hire two expert witnesses—a gynecologist to talk about the rape injuries, and a psychiatric social worker to talk about the long-term consequences of forcible rape of a minor in state care. If she turns out to be HIV positive then I'll need another expert for that."

Cassandra's eyes widened.

I plunged ahead: "The defense will hire the same types of experts. Then everybody gets deposed on video and we have to pay them to read records, prepare, and testify. I think we're going to burn fifty or sixty grand in the next two months. I can hack it, but I want to know what we're spending so my poor old savings account doesn't give out. Outhouse Counsel loves to fight a war of attrition."

Cassandra asked, "You haven't gotten any revenue in the door yet, have you?"

I shrugged. "Not yet. But I have enough money saved to run the firm without revenue for around four years. The only thing that can put us in trouble is spending too much on client costs. So while you're here, Cassandra, can I go downstairs and get you a mocha? Nicky, can I get you anything? It's not Has Beans, but the espresso stand downstairs is pretty good."

Nicky said, "I wouldn't say no to an almond latte."

Cassandra said, "I could go for a triple mocha with extra whipped cream."

I wrote it down on a Post-It. "That's exactly what Duvonda likes."

Cassandra winked at me. "She got me hooked. She's a bad influence."

I went downstairs and got the drinks, along with a giant iced Americano for myself. I had to read a couple hundred pages of medical records this afternoon. It was the only part of the job that bored me, but there's no substitute for it. Some lawyers don't read all the evidence. It shows.

When I came back, Nicky and Cassandra fell silent as I opened the door. They'd been talking about me, I suspected. I set down their drinks. They both looked at me with curious expressions.

"What," I asked.

Nicky said, "You just got a call from Hernando Suarez."

Holy smoke. Linda Lou's mediator. He'd said he would follow up with the insurance company. It couldn't be bad news. Either they were willing to increase their offer, or we'd keep grinding toward the bench trial with Judge Palacpac.

"This could be big," I murmured.

"No lie," Nicky said.

I went back into my office with the iced Americano. I took a long pull. Rain started spattering the window. I looked at the costs spreadsheet, then called Hernando.

"Sam, we've got some movement on the other side," he said. "I just spoke with Kyle Tartan, the adjuster. Before I let him get a word in edgewise, I told him Linda Lou has two months to go before she finds out her HIV status. If she's HIV positive, then ReachKids is looking at a multimillion-dollar judgment. I told him to take a step back from the brink."

"Holy smoke. Thanks Hernando. What did he say?"

"Well he told me how they lost Summary Judgment and the Jury Demand extension issue. He's doing the big adjuster fan dance now. He said if he can get you seven hundred ten, would the court approve it?"

Seven hundred ten. We were going to spend a fortune on expert witnesses in the new few weeks. I let the silence build.

Hernando chuckled. "He said to remind you that their insurance policy is a wasting policy. Their limit of a million is being depleted by the defense attorney's billings, and the litigation costs. He said it he can get this for your client, they won't pay anything more. Not the cost of mediation, nothing. This is the highest offer they will make before trial. A lot of the policy limit will get used up from now on."

I took another pull on my iced Americano. I decided to do a little mild bluffing. "ReachKids does own some valuable real estate. The Ravenna group home alone has to be worth a million plus. But I don't know how big the mortgage is on it, and we'd have to get a bond and execute on it by selling it. I hear what you're saying about the wasting policy; I was thinking of that too. Did he say anything about a confidentiality provision or a non-disparagement clause?"

"He did. He said those were the usual terms. I told him I didn't have permission to speak for you or Linda Lou, but I bet you would not agree to keep the settlement secret or promise not to say anything negative about ReachKids."

I took another pull on my iced Americano. My pulse was speeding up. "That's probably true. But the insurance company won't get hurt by any disparagement—only their crappy insured ReachKids will. So I bet the insurance company doesn't really care about that. And they're writing the checks, so Lorna Weiss probably won't care about that either. I should tell you—Judge Palacpac emancipated Linda Lou. She gets the final say on settlement. No court approval is needed now. So I will lay out the numbers in front of her and take her temperature."

Hernando chuckled. "Okay, that streamlines things. When I told Kyle he probably couldn't get confidentiality and non-disparagement, he didn't protest. They try for it, in cases like this, but the real settlement term for both of you is the number. That stuff about seeing if he can get that for you? He round-tabled it with the other senior adjusters. I've been to those things. He can get it for you. If Linda Lou wants it, it's there."

The rain was splattering the window now. "Thank you, Hernando. Most mediators don't circle back like this. I'll let you know."

Hernando concluded "Would you send me a copy of your Motion for Summary Judgment? Just for my own amusement? It sounds like you made quite the impression."

"Will do." I hung up.

The case wasn't settled yet. But I'd bet it was going to.

So I stood in my window and did The Crane.

This was a really good deal. I'd leave the choice up to Linda Lou, but it was a really good deal.

I looked over at Buster. "Holy frigging smoke," he said.

"You can say that again."

"Holy frigging smoke," he said again.

Controlling myself, I wrote up the Settlement Memo. I was going to give her some discounts. I would write off my litigation costs. I'd trim my one-third attorney fee to get the "price of entry" Bonus and I had talked about.

Linda Lou would net $496,000.

I double-checked the figures, printed it, and slipped it into my briefcase along with the costs spreadsheet. I could feel eyes on me. I looked up.

Nicky and Cassandra were in the doorway, looking nonchalant.

Nicky asked, "Got some news?"

I got up, ran to her, and threw my arms around her. I whirled her around twice, set her down, and gave her a big kiss.

"The defense in Linda Lou's case just offered $710,000," I said.

Nicky went pale. "Jesus. That's almost as much as a good verdict. And we wouldn't have to hire the expert witnesses either."

Cassandra said, "Forgive me for interrupting, but what would be your happy fee from this?"

I said, "I'll give her a discount of thirty thousand for a certain project I have in mind, so we'll net $206,000."

Cassandra smiled. "That is a happy fee."

I said, "I would have had to work for Rodney Mammon for over two years to make that much. But I have to put this in front of Linda Lou. She's a legal adult now, so it's her decision."

Nicky looked around at our office, so new we hadn't put anything on the walls yet. "Our practice is going to make it, isn't it?"

I kissed her on the forehead. "Sure looks like it."

Cassandra said, "As your bookkeeper, I approve." It wasn't clear whether she was talking about me kissing Nicky, or our practice turning a profit. Maybe both.

I drove the battered Outback out to the University District. The rain was sweeping across the pavement in white waves now. I grabbed the umbrella and sprinted into Has Beans. Linda Lou was running bar.

"Can I see you for a second?" I asked her.

"Course."

We went into the storage room and sat down on adjoining sacks of coffee beans.

"What's up, Mr. Uncle? You seem kind of keyed up."

I took a deep breath. I didn't want to push her.

"The defendants just offered $710,000 in your case," I said.

She put her hand over her mouth. "Jesus Christ on a cracker," she said. Then she sat up straight and looked straight at me. "That's close to what we would have taken at mediation. Is this a good deal?"

I opened my briefcase. "I think so. I'm estimating we will spend at least fifty thousand on expert witnesses and video depositions of the other side's expert witnesses between now and trial. All that comes out of your share. There is a possibility that Judge Palacpac will award more than the $810,000 we demanded as our bottom line at mediation. But defendants' insurance policy is a wasting policy."

Linda Lou looked at the floor. "What is a wasting policy?" She was looking for the bad news. She was a hypervigilant kid. She'd always had to look for bad news.

I looked down at the floor too. Sometimes during a serious conversation, eye contact overwhelms people. "The policy limits are one million. Because it's a wasting policy, the costs of Lorna's billable hours and the defendants' expert witnesses come out of the policy limits. So the available policy limits by now have been reduced to nine hundred thousand, or even eight hundred thousand. I don't get to see Lorna's billings, of course. But she's been billing up a storm. If we go to trial she's certain to spend fifty on costs, just like us, and she's certain to bill another hundred in attorneys' fees. So the limits will be severely depleted by the end of trial. However. We could go to trial, go for a maximum verdict, and then slap judgment liens on ReachKids's group homes like the Ravenna house. If they aren't mortgaged too badly, we could sell them to satisfy our 'excess judgment,' meaning the judgment in excess of the available insurance policy." I looked up at her. "I can show you the figures for what you get if you settle."

"Okay, Mr. Uncle," Linda Lou said in a choked voice.

I knew what was happening with her. She was basically an orphan too. With orphans, good news is very confusing. It's disorienting. We orphans don't know what the hell to do with good news.

I handed her the settlement memo. She took out her phone and checked the numbers. I respected her for that. She didn't need a court order to make her an adult, she just needed a court order to keep her from getting arrested, and to open a bank account, and to settle her case.

She pointed at the line below my fee that said, *$30,000 courtesy discount to favored client for possible project.*

"Okay, so you're giving me thirty thousand extra of your own money," she asked. "And what is the possible project?"

I looked down at the floor again. I did not want her to thing there were any strings attached to this. We orphans see strings attached to everything—including things without strings. "Bonus called Amanda and asked what she would take to sell Has Beans. It's thirty thousand, plus twelve thousand to pay off the banker."

I risked a glance at her. Her brow was furrowed. "Wait, are you buying Has Beans? Is Bonus buying Has Beans?"

"Oh no. If you want to…you are."

Linda Lou's eyes went wide. "Jesus Christ on a cracker," she said, leaping to her feet. "Of course I want to buy it! Be my own boss? Run the show? Mr. Uncle, I've been running the show all my life, in my mom's house, but I never got paid for it before!" She clenched her fists, closed her eyes, and jumped up and down a couple of times.

I smiled down at the floor. "Okay, so if you want to settle, I can get the money in about two weeks. The fee discount to buy Has Beans is my gift to you, whether we go to trial or not. You can spend it on Has Beans or anything else. It's just a discount to a favorite client."

Her eyes went wide.

I looked down at my hands. "I was a kid in state care too. I was sexually abused too, not as badly as you. I'm guessing you have a bright future. I'd sure like to help get it started."

Linda Lou sat down again. Then she scooted away from me. I could read the signals.

"One last thing," I said. "You remember Nicky?"

"Uh huh."

"Nicky and I have gotten together. So I finally found a good girlfriend. It's probably TMI to you, but I thought you should know."

"That's great, Mr. Uncle," she said. Her whole posture changed. "Now all I have to do is take care of my arrest warrant."

I reached into the briefcase and handed her the document quashing the arrest warrant. "Bonus already did. His office mate got it done. He'll send me a bill, and I'll pay it from my fees. It can't be more than a thousand dollars. You're helping Nicky and me get our practice started, Linda Lou. I'd still go to trial if you want me to. But if you want to settle, I'll have forms to sign in a week or so, and the money in a week after that."

Linda Lou shook her head. "This is a lot of good news to take in. I feel pretty dizzy."

I held up my hand, and she high-fived me. "You and me both, kiddo. Now that you aren't a dangerous wanted fugitive anymore, I'd like to take Nicky and you out for some good food to celebrate. Which do you like better? Indian or Thai?"

Linda Lou pondered. "I think Indian would be more special."

"Me too."

We went for Indian food the day Linda Lou signed the Release and Hold Harmless. I got four-star Vindaloo and it made my eyes water.

At least, that's what I told Nicky and Linda Lou.

I was probably lying.

CHAPTER THIRTY-THREE— PARAMEDICS AND DETECTIVES

About two weeks later I was asleep with Nicky at my condo. I woke up as suddenly as if somebody had fired a gunshot outside. But everything was quiet. I checked my clock radio. It was 5:32 AM.

Just then my cell phone started ringing, and I went out to the kitchen to get it. I looked at the Caller ID.

THE GHOST.

The Ghost had my number. But she had never called me before.

"Hey," I said, alarmed.

"Hello, um, Sam, I'm feeling all sick and because somebody gave me a drug," she mumbled. "And for some reason, it seems I am bleeding."

"Are you at home?"

"Yes I mean affirmative I am at home."

"Do you need an ambulance? Should I call 911?" The Ghost valued her privacy so highly she would never call 911 herself.

"No but if you please would come over," she mumbled.

"I'll be right there," I said.

I pulled on jeans and a T-shirt. Nicky sat up rubbing her eyes. "Sam?"

"I need to go out for a bit," I said. "Go back to sleep."

I broke the speed limit and violated a few other traffic rules in my battered Outback on my way to The Ghost's condo in Magnolia.

I ran up to her door and tried it. Unlocked. Strange.

I opened the door. Her pink lamp was on, which made the scene even more unreal. I smelled sandalwood. Muted Sinatra came from the Bose Wave.

The Ghost was lying by the coffee table in front of her couch wearing nothing except a black garter belt and fishnet stockings. There was a pool of vomit next to her. She had a long slash down her right cheek from beside her eye down to under her chin and onto her throat. A sheen of blood flowed down her face, dripping onto the carpet next to the vomit.

Her cat Pirate sat on the kitchen table looking at me, his luminous green cat eyes saying: *Do something.*

I knelt by The Ghost. "Honey, can you talk?" I asked her.

She opened her eyes but she couldn't focus. "Why are you… Sam?"

I ran to the bathroom and got a hand towel, then pressed it on the slash on her face. "You're bleeding. I'm pressing on the wound."

The Ghost tried her sentence again. "Why are you…here, Sam?"

I pressed harder on the wound. "You called me. Remember? You asked me to come over. You said somebody had drugged you. What drug is it?"

She blinked at me. Her short-term memory didn't seem to be working. I noticed there were two martini glasses on the coffee table, both mostly empty. "I'm not sure why you are here, Sam," she said, trying to sit up.

I kept pressing her wound. "Honey, you're bleeding. You've been drugged. You need more help than I can give you."

Then I risked our entire friendship. I picked up The Ghost's landline and called 911.

"911, what's your emergency?"

"I'm at my friend's house. She's been drugged and assaulted. Somebody cut her with a knife down the side of her face and it's bleeding pretty badly. She's probably been sexually assaulted too. I need the fire department and police. Do you have the address on your screen?"

"Yes sir, I have the address on your screen. Is there an apparent offender at the scene?"

"No I just got here and she's all alone except for me. She's in and out of consciousness. Please get the fire department here because I don't know if she's had a lethal overdose and I'm afraid she is going to die."

I was reciting the magic words to get a quick response. But she could actually die.

"Sir, fire department is coming, about two minutes out, and Seattle Police are close behind. I show your location is a three-story condominium building so you will need to watch and bring the EMTs to the unit."

"I will do that." I hung up. I went back to The Ghost.

"I'm right here," I said, pressing down on the hand towel again. It was soaked through. She must have lost two pints of blood by now.

She looked at me again, quizzically. "And why are you here, Sam?"

"You called me," I said. I had a bad suspicion growing. But there was no point sharing it with The Ghost. She couldn't focus on my face, let alone my words.

Red and white strobe lights flashed through the living room window. I ran outside onto the concrete walkway and down the stairs. Two EMTs were getting out of the fire engine with their plastic tackle boxes. (Seattle Fire always sends a fire engine with EMTs first, to evaluate and see if Medic One is required. They dispatch Medic One unit if more intensive first aid or transport are needed).

"Up here," I called, waving to them. I ran back up the stairs and they followed. I knelt down by The Ghost and applied pressure to the hand towel again.

"I'm Sam Strait, and this is my friend," I said, using The Ghost's real name. "About half an hour ago she called me at home. She said she had been drugged and she was bleeding. I got here as fast as I could and found her like this. She's incoherent. I think she was sexually assaulted too."

The EMTs jumped right in. One took out a handful of gauze pads and pressed them to the slash on The Ghost's cheek, then taped them down tightly to apply pressure. The other took her blood pressure and listened to her heart with a stethoscope, then shined a penlight into her eyes. "Sluggish pupil reaction," he said. "I'll call it in."

He muttered into his shoulder mike. He told me, "Medic One is two minutes out. We're lucky they just had a cancellation in West Queen Anne just a few miles away." Then he took out his penlight again and examined The Ghost's crotch.

She was shaved. There was glistening semen there.

"Yup, positive for sexual contact, possibly sexual assault. We'll tell the paramedics to ask for a rape workup at Harborview."

Another set of red and white strobes flashed through the window. I ran outside and motioned to the paramedics just climbing down from their Medic One rig.

King County Medic One was the first paramedic program in the nation. The trauma doctors at Harborview Medical Center train the paramedics in Advanced Trauma Life Support, pronounced "Atlas." The idea is to make the best use possible of the Golden Hour. Trauma surgeons say the first hour after injury is the Golden Hour, when people either get lifesaving treatment or they are much more likely to die. In most of my biggest cases, treatment started with King County Medic One. Each time I started reading one of their reports I got a jolt of adrenaline.

The EMTs repeated my history to the paramedics. One of the paramedics replaced the gauze on The Ghost's face with a thicker bundle and taped it down tighter. Then they took her blood pressure and pulse and checked her pupil reaction again. Still sluggish.

I cleared my throat. "You should know she has multiple sclerosis, and she's on immunosuppressive medication for it. So, I guess there's a heightened risk of infection. Will you tell the ER people about that?"

"Sure thing," one paramedic said, giving me a reassuring smile.

The EMTs left and returned with the stretcher from the Medic One rig and folded down the wheels. They flipped the restraining straps aside, gently lifted The Ghost onto it, and covered her with a warming blanket. Then they strapped her down and took her out.

I wished I hadn't seen her slashed face, her pale body in nothing but a garter belt and fishnet stockings, the splatter of semen on her labia.

You can't unsee some things.

I went outside because I realized that The Ghost's condo was a crime scene, and I had to avoid contaminating it. I sat down on the concrete walkway.

A Seattle Police patrol car pulled in. I went down and told the officer my story. She said, "Okay, we will roll Sexual Assault Unit detectives on this one. I will come with you and secure the scene until they arrive."

She took a yellow roll of Crime Scene tape and put it across the door. "I did have to go in to help stop her bleeding and let in Seattle Fire," I said.

"That's all right, sir. Just sit tight outside here until SAU arrives."

SAU. Sexual Assault Unit. Those initials were used by the Seattle Police and, the King County Prosecutors, and Harborview Medical Center. The three agencies meshed well together. I'd only prosecuted a couple of lesser SAU cases. But Duvonda had done SAU trials for two years. She'd told me a bunch of war stories.

The SAU detectives arrived in a black Crown Victoria. The uniformed officer went to their car and talked for a few seconds, then left. The detectives got out.

The driver was a man in his fifties, with a gray crew cut, gray fleece pullover, and gray chinos, whose face was stamped in a permanent expression of wry wit and sorrow.

The passenger was a muscular lesbian woman with a strong jawline and a black crew cut in her late thirties, wearing a beautifully tailored suit, with a toothpick in the corner of her mouth.

"Al Broccoli," said the fifty-ish man, shaking my hand with a warm grip.

"Cam Cookie," said the lesbian, shaking my hand with a strong grip.

We went up to The Ghost's unit. Detective Cookie read me my Miranda rights, and I waived them. I signed the waiver agreed to make a statement.

Then, I narrated everything into her digital audio recorder before we went in.

I was glad to. I naively thought if I told it, that story wouldn't be inside me anymore.

Dawn was approaching—a stripe of weak orange under a sad January overcast. The story I'd given the detectives reminded me of something. But what?

It reminded me of being picked up from summer camp when I was seven years old by a state trooper. It reminded me of the medical examiner technicians on the front lawn of my family's house, wheeling out two bulging body bags on wheeled stretchers just like the wheeled stretcher they'd taken The Ghost on.

It reminded me of that smell—rotten eggs and roadkill. That smell gushing from the windows propelled by the fire department's fans.

Detective Broccoli cut the crime scene tape with his penknife, and we went in. Detective Cookie opened her shoulder bag, produced a box of latex gloves, and held it out. We all put them on. Then she said, "Stand here," and walked through the condo, taking flash photos with her digital 35mm SLR. She took more photos of the couch and coffee table than anywhere else, particularly of the pools of blood and vomit. Then she circled back and nodded to Detective Broccoli. "At first blush, looks like everything happened here in the living room. But there's one odd note—a Scrabble game in the kitchen. It's in the box, not set up."

I shivered. "She and I play Scrabble a lot. We're just friends. But she's into polyamory and BDSM. She likes three ways, golden showers, humiliation, some light bondage and sadism. I'm a personal injury lawyer. I hire her sometimes because she's a very good private investigator. But her sexual preferences are abhorrent to me."

They were watching me with neutral expressions.

I got it. Very often the person who reports a rape or murder is the attacker. I'd been with Nicky at the time. The Ghost would of course clear me if her memory came back. But I needed to get them started on finding the real attacker.

Detective Cookie took the lead in questioning. She turned on her recorder again. "So Mr. Strait, you did not in any way physically harm the victim tonight?"

"No ma'am. She called me. I came over. She was already naked and bleeding and incoherent. She had already vomited. I tried to stop the bleeding. I called 911 and asked for fire aid and police. When she was attacked I was in bed at home with my girlfriend Nicky Schwartz. So I did not harm her or drug her or rape her."

Detective Cookie kept looking at me, her gaze carefully neutral. Police investigation has a Golden Hour, too. "Have you ever had sexual relations with the victim?"

I shook my head. "No. We kissed a couple of times. Both times she told me I had to call her a filthy whore or she wouldn't go to bed with me. I'm just not like that. So we flirted and remained friends. We never had sex. She took me to the swingers' club she likes called The Switching Yard once, and it wasn't my scene. When we got home it turned out her cat had died. That was a bad night for her."

Detective Cookie glanced over at Pirate, still sitting on the kitchen table, staring at us. "Not that cat?"

"No, that's Pirate, her new cat. He must have seen everything tonight. I sure wish we had a human witness. Besides the victim."

I thought of The Ghost at Harborview. I imagined her getting sutures in her face, getting blood and saline, going through the humiliating process of the rape exam and vaginal swabs and blood draws for every sexually transmitted disease. I knew her MS made her more vulnerable to infection.

Like Linda Lou, she would have to wait six months until she could even get an HIV test. The Ghost had a long wait ahead of her, too.

I thought back to the night Guinevere, her previous cat, died. The night we went to The Switching Yard. If only we had a human witness.

"God, I'm so stupid," I said to Detective Cookie. "I almost forgot. The night her previous cat Guinevere died, she showed me her hidden video camera. It's a motion-activated digital pinhole camera that covers the couch and coffee table, really the whole living room. It has a wide-angle lens. She ran back the video for me so we could see what happened to Guinevere. Can I show you?"

"Sure," Detective Cookie said, with a gleam in her eye, "but don't touch anything."

I turned to the entertainment center opposite the couch. "The camera is inside a little hole right at the top of the entertainment center, in the middle. The camera is connected by a wire to the hard drive that stores the video. That's down at the bottom of the entertainment center. You swivel forward that little panel at the base, and there it is."

Detective Cookie and Detective Broccoli shared a look. I knew what they were thinking—this could be the real thing, or it could be a clever rapist—me—trying to alibi myself with video from some other date, when The Ghost was with some other playmate. I would just give them everything I knew and let the chips fall where they may. I had the best ally in the world—a clear conscience.

Then I realized I had to give them cover against a claim of unlawful search and seizure. "I used to be a prosecutor with King County," I told them. "I'm a personal injury lawyer now. The condo owner invited me in voluntarily before the medics took her. I invited you in as her guest. I have apparent authority to give you consent to search the premises and gather evidence. So I think you're clear to look into this without having to get a warrant." I made sure I was speaking into the audio recorder when I said that.

Detective Cookie said, "Fair enough."

Detective Broccoli took out a Leatherman tool and opened the panel at the base. He found the ten-terabyte drive. It was only the size of a pack of cigarettes. The Ghost had always used the best tech. It was her secret sauce.

We all sat down on the floor. Detective Cookie took a small laptop from her bag and connected a mini-USB cord to the hard drive. She skewered me with her eyes. "I would like you to narrate into my audio recorder what you see while I play back the video. Maybe we can identify the offender. It's possible you met the guy at The Switching Yard or someplace else. We'd like an ID to jump start this case if you can help us out."

"Anything I can do," I said.

I did not want to watch this video. But The Ghost needed me to. She once told me: "if you want a friend, be a friend."

I was going to watch her worst playdate.

A video file popped up on the laptop, and Detective Cookie clicked on the Play icon. Then she scrolled back several hours. I saw a male figure in a suit and The Ghost's figure, in the little box above the scroll bar, jumping around.

Finally Detective Cookie stopped at the right place. She clicked Play. For the first time, I realized this was all going to be soundless, and that was part of why they needed my narration.

The Ghost was sitting on the couch wearing her red satin dressing gown, the one with the golden dragon embroidered down the right side. The video had exceptional detail.

The Ghost was smoking a cigarette, and her legs were crossed, and she was bouncing one foot up and down, a clear sign of anticipation.

She lifted her head and walked to the door, slowly, the red satin shimmering over her curves. She opened it. A blond man stepped in wearing a houndstooth checked suit, his back to the camera. He was about as tall as her.

She held out her hands, and he took them and kissed her cheek. She twirled on her heel and went to the kitchen. She brought back two full martini glasses, and motioned for him to sit. He sat on the edge of the couch, his face still turned away from the camera.

"Just sing out if you recognize him," Detective Cookie said. I nodded. A horrible thought was forming in my head.

He bent in to kiss her again, on the lips.

She playfully pushed him away. She motioned with her open hand: *Say it.* I could read her lips. I knew what she was saying. It was her warm-up line.

"She's telling him to call her a filthy whore," I said, my heart sinking. The way she motioned to him, it was clear this wasn't their first play date. She was feeding him his line.

His head moved a little, and she clapped her hands and smiled. Apparently he'd said it, so it was all systems go. She motioned—wait here—and disappeared back toward the bedroom.

He turned to the camera and grinned wolfishly.

It was Rodney Mammon.

"Jesus Christ," I said, "That's Rodney Mammon, the criminal defense attorney."

Detective Cookie pressed Pause. "Are you absolutely certain? Take a careful look at his face."

"God, yes I'm certain. I ran his personal injury department until a few weeks ago. Do you two know him?"

Stupid question. They looked at each other and smiled. They knew him. He defended rapists, after all.

I kept talking, trying to bleed off some of my swelling outrage. "When I worked for him, my paralegal Nicky and I—she's my girlfriend—we used to say we work in the Innocent Peoples' Department, and Rodney and all his well-dressed goons work in the Guilty Peoples' Department."

Detective Broccoli and Detective Cookie gave each other a fist-bump.

"Okay, let's continue," Detective Cookie said, starting the video again.

I was suddenly filled with a ball of rage as tall as a skyscraper, again. It inflated as quickly as an airbag after a crash.

I would need to be very careful now. Until I could start crushing it down into a glowing golf ball of nuclear fuel. I would need that glowing golf ball to do what was needed.

Most of us orphans learn how to control our emotions until we can channel them, to do what is needed.

In the video The Ghost was still gone when Rodney reached into his pocket and took out a small box, about the side of a matchbox. He took out two tiny objects, smaller than Tic Tacs. Then he took out a small plastic device. I recognized it as a pill crusher, an item that powdered pills so they could be snorted by addicts. He crushed the pills and dropped the dust into The Ghost's martini glass.

I kept narrating, keeping my voice level. "It appears to me that Mr. Mammon has just powdered two pills and put them in her drink," I said.

Rodney sat back, his hands behind his head. The Ghost came back, and as she came into focus, she was wearing nothing but a black garter belt and fishnet stockings, her delicious body shining like living marble. She paused behind the couch and lifted her hands like a referee signaling a touchdown. Ta-da!

Rodney applauded.

The Ghost sat down on the couch and kissed him. He raised his martini glass—a toast! She toasted him and drank deeply.

He watched her to make sure she emptied the glass. Pirate the cat sat on the kitchen table beside the Scrabble box, watching all of this.

Rodney sat back down and toasted her again. They started kissing. He ran his hands up behind her neck, and cupped her breasts, and playfully pinched her nipples. She took off his tie, unbuttoned his shirt, and threw them over the couch. Then she took off his pants and shoes and socks, kneeling before him.

Then she took off his briefs and began performing fellatio on him.

I felt like I was covered in poison ivy. My skin itched with fury.

Nobody needed any narration for this.

She leaned left, and almost fell. Rodney took her hand and helped her climb onto the couch. *Now it begins*, I thought.

The Ghost put out her hand to steady herself, and shook her head. Rodney sat back and watched. She shook her head again, confused.

Then she slumped back on the couch, fell over, and her eyes rolled back in her head.

Rodney took a fold of her forearm and pinched it. Hard. She didn't stir. He did it on the other forearm. Again she didn't stir.

Rodney turned away from her and grinned wolfishly again, not knowing he was looking at the camera. He did not put on a condom.

Then he sat her up straight, lifted her ankles to his shoulders, and forcibly thrust himself into her.

He only lasted about thirty seconds.

Then he stood, his relaxing penis still nodding. He dressed quickly and patted his pockets. He hit his forehead. He'd forgotten something. He grinned wolfishly again. His pupils seemed big.

He went into the kitchen and came back with a ten-inch chef knife. He tested the blade against his thumb, and drew a thin line of blood. He wiped it on the back of the couch beside The Ghost's head.

He cupped her head firmly under the chin and held the chef knife firmly in his other hand. Then he stabbed her by the corner of her eye and drew it down, slowly, a rich stream of blood in its wake. He licked the edge of the knife, smiled, and put it in his pants pocket. Then he left. The video didn't stop because it was motion-activated—the stream of blood running down The Ghost's face turned into a river, flowing down her face, across her right breast, and onto the couch beside her.

After a very long time she stirred, and tried to rise, and fell off the couch. She crawled across the floor and got her phone. She crawled back to the coffee table and leaned on it with one arm.

She bent over away from the coffee table and vomited copiously. Then she squinted at the phone, trying to make out the numbers.

She fumbled three times trying to dial. Then she raised the phone to her ear.

I hadn't known The Ghost had my phone number memorized. She'd never called me before. But I guess she was always ready to.

After she talked for a few sentences, she dropped the phone and slumped over again. After a long time I came in the door.

Everything from that point on was just what I'd told the detectives. They looked at each other and nodded again. They were agreeing that I was innocent. And Rodney was…not.

"I thought of something else, if that's okay," I stammered.

"It's okay," Detective Broccoli said.

"When Nicky and I were out to lunch with Rodney months ago, he dropped a pill and I picked it up and took it home to my safe. It's a small green pill. Then after that, our receptionist Kandy died of an overdose at his house. Nicky overheard the detectives talking with Rodney at the office. They said she'd died of a mixture of Rohypnol and snorting heroin. They couldn't prove that anybody had given her either drug, so they couldn't pursue charges against Rodney. But I still have that pill. I think that Rodney used Rohypnol again last night. Would you like me to go get the pill?"

Detective Cookie smiled at me for the first time. "Sure thing. I'm not sure if we can get it into evidence due to chain of custody issues. But it's worth a try." She looked at Detective Broccoli. "I've been doing SAU for three years, but this is the first rape I've gotten on video. So we have Rape 1, Assault 3, Unlawful Administration of Controlled Substance, and Burglary."

"Burglary," I murmured. I saw where she was going. I'd prosecuted burglaries.

"Sure," Detective Broccoli said. "Entering a residence with intent to commit a felony. That one's kind of a reach. But the rape, assault, and controlled substance charges are pretty solid. We'll need to get Crime Scene in here to get the martini glasses and run a tox screen on them, and also sample the blood and vomit. Including the little blood smear on the couch from the attacker's finger when he tested the sharpness of the knife. If we get Mr. Mammon's blood from that sample, that will be pretty good."

I shook myself all over like a wet dog. This night would stay with me for a long time. "I'll definitely testify. Is it okay if I go home to get the pill in my safe?"

"Sure thing," Detective Cookie said, giving me her business card. "Give me a call when you have it." She put the small hard drive in an evidence bag, sealed it, and marked it. "Given the nature of the defendant, I'll bet my boots this one's going to trial."

I had a sickening thought. Would Rodney defend himself?

Of course, he would defend himself. Rodney was a magician in criminal trials. So, The Ghost was going to be cross-examined by Rodney Mammon.

So was I.

CHAPTER THIRTY-FOUR—GOING UNDERGROUND

Two weeks later, on a Saturday night, Nicky slept at home to do laundry and give us breathing space.

The next morning, I walked down to my condo lobby to get mail and pick up the Sunday paper. I heard sirens in the distance. I was glad that, for once, they had nothing to do with me.

Then I stepped outside, looked to the right, and saw my battered Subaru Outback was engulfed in flames.

I called Detective Broccoli and he picked right up. "Detective, this is Sam Strait. My car is on fire. Have charges been filed against Rodney Mammon?"

"Yes, they filed on him Friday. We took him into custody at his office and served a search warrant on his house and his office. I'm not allowed to tell you anything else."

The sirens came closer. "Does he have representation? Has he gotten the Affidavit of Probable Cause? Because that's the only explanation I can think of for what I'm looking at."

The fire truck pulled up in front of my Subaru. Four firefighters jumped down. Two started in with fire extinguishers and the other two ran hose to the hydrant.

Detective Broccoli said, "I think we'll send our arson investigator out. In the meantime, Mr. Strait, I'd like to share an old police saying with you."

"Shoot."

"Every place is safe until it's dangerous. You and your girlfriend had better hole up in a motel somewhere under fake names for a week or two." He paused, but I couldn't speak. "Sorry we can't offer you witness protection, Mr. Strait, but we're not the Feds."

I'd been silent only because I was planning quickly. "I understand. I'll vacate my office and my condo and get Nicky safely underground, too. This isn't your problem. You can still reach me at this cell or through email."

"Keep your head down, Mr. Strait. Maybe we can get Rodney Mammon in witness intimidation."

I said goodbye. I knew they would never get Rodney on witness intimidation. He'd been in jail whenever this had been set up. All jail phone calls are recorded.

I called Nicky next and filled her in. "Will you hole up with me until this blows over? I couldn't stand it if Rodney got to you."

Nicky's voice was shaky. "Yes, okay. I'll pack two weeks of stuff and bring my shock wands—you know, handheld tasers. I have two of them."

"Two?"

"I got them when Rodney and the other wolfish guys started circling, right about the time I invented Fred. Since then I always have one in my pocket and one on the charger."

I told her I'd pick her up within an hour. "Until then, please draw the shades, lock the door, and don't open it for anybody."

"What's our code? I need a code to know it's you at the door and you don't have a gun in your back."

She'd gotten there before I did. "How about, well, dog, my cats."

"Okay," she said. I could tell she was still scared because she didn't laugh at Buster's catchphrase. "Remember, we'll need the computers and files from the office. Don't forget Buster. I love you."

She hung up.

Next, I called Duvonda. I had her cell number, but I'd never used it before. Silent Mike answered, and he sounded like he was in bed. I told him everything. I heard muffled voices, and he handed the phone over to Duvonda.

"Okay," Duvonda said. "I worked narcotics for a while, so I can rough out a plan with you. We need to get you and Nicky to an extended-stay hotel under a fake name. You'll need your stuff from the office. I'll put an ad in *King County Bar Bulletin* and online saying your office is for sublet again, but tell anybody who calls that it's already been taken."

"Al Broccoli said basically the same thing."

"He would. He's the one who taught me this stuff. We worked narcotics together."

It was turning out that everybody I liked was acquainted with everybody else I liked. I decided on a ploy to verify if she really knew The Ghost. "How's The Ghost holding up?" I'd only talked with her twice by phone since she was released from Harborview.

"She's doing okay, and I set her up with a rape survivors confidential support group," Duvonda said. Then she gasped. "You caught me, Sam. That doesn't happen often."

"Only when it's early Sunday morning, and you're in bed with that total stud Silent Mike."

She chuckled. "Okay, we'll get a hotel reservation. Silent Mike will round up a couple of his crew to load up your office computers and files into his van and bring it out to the hotel."

"Don't forget, Buster," I said.

The firefighters had broken the Subaru windows and drenched the inside with water. It was a charred wreck, but the fire was out. The street reeked of burning oil and plastic. Eventually, I'd be in the market for a new Outback.

"We couldn't forget Buster. Mike likes to go back to your office and teach him new catchphrases when you're not there. And Sam? Keep your pretty head down, okay? Don't leave the hotel for any reason. Do you have a gun?"

"No. I didn't think I needed one until today."

"Well, if you don't have a license, don't get one. But when you can resurface, both you and Nicky should get concealed pistol licenses and start carrying. Silent Mike can teach you to shoot. He's the one who taught me."

The surprises were piling up. "You carry a gun?"

"Always, unless I'm going into the courthouse or getting on a plane. What we do is a contact sport, Sam. Welcome to the NFL. I'm sorry you had to learn like this."

I told her everything Al Broccoli had told me about the arrest and the search warrant.

"Okay, so Rodney's on custodial hold, but it's only a forty-eight-hour deal. Then he'll try to bail out. Almost everybody gets bail unless they're charged with murder. So you can expect more unpleasant surprises unless you stay hidden. Got any relatives in town?"

I swallowed hard. "My sister Catherine. But I never mentioned her to Rodney, and he certainly never met her. She's on the eastside, not far away."

"You at least need to give her a heads up. But now Mike and I will get the van and the hotel in motion. Don't go anywhere alone, Sam, until this is over. In fact, don't go anywhere if you can help it. If you have any court hearings I'll cover for you. You got that?"

"Copy that."

I went over to a firefighter, trying not to breathe the reek of my burned Outback. "That's my car. I'm a witness working with Seattle Police. They're sending an arson investigator, and I'm guessing it'll be towed away. Is it okay to leave it here until then?"

"Well, sir, the fire's out, and it's not blocking traffic, so I don't see a problem. Too bad. I have an Outback myself. They'll go anywhere."

I ran upstairs and, threw two weeks' worth of clothes into a duffel bag and then ran back down. About half an hour later, Silent Mike pulled up in a black Yukon Denali. I tossed my stuff in the back. He asked, "What's Nicky's address?"

I told him, and he roared onto Northgate Way. He drove confidently. "Did I ever tell you the real reason I quit SWAT?" he offered.

"Nope."

"After my last breach of a structure with a hostage taker inside, I overheard my team commander talking to my best friend on the force. He said I ought to be called Violent Mike because of how I shot the hostage taker in the forehead as he held a carving knife to the throat of a four-year-old girl. Just like that? I knew I was done. Not scared or regretful, but just done. It was time for a new chapter." He squinted at me. "You thinking it's time for a new chapter, Sam?"

"No way. I'm not done with my mission. I just need Rodney incarcerated so I can start up again."

"That's my boy."

We got Nicky and drove to an Extended Stay America up north over the Snohomish County line near the freeway. "I thought a little distance would be beneficial," Silent Mike said, pulling up. He went in with us to register. We spent a little cash to be listed under fake names. After we finished, a white van pulled up. "Okay, Cyrus and Reckless," he said.

Cyrus and Reckless turned out to be two young Black men with major muscles. They took out a hand truck and carted our file binders and computers up to the suite. Nicky took Buster's cage. In the elevator, Buster said, "That's OG!"

I looked at Silent Mike, and he winked at me. New catchphrases, indeed.

Within an hour, we had the office set up in the small dining area of the suite. Nicky looked at the melon-orange carpet, the orange bedspreads with concentric circles like bullseyes, and the cliche painting of a clipper ship in a storm. "It could do with some plants," she said, her hands on her hips.

I embraced her and swung her around in a circle, her feet in the air, as she squealed with delight. "Thank God you're safe," I said.

She looked at me and became serious. "Do you believe in God?"

I nodded. "I do now."

CHAPTER THIRTY-FIVE— WILL IT GO?

Oe morning when we'd been in hiding a few days, I was answering emails when Nicky got a text. "That's funny," she said. Her tone meant it wasn't humorous funny; it was weird funny. "Sam, what do you think of this?"

It was from Priestess Esmerelda. *HONEY NEED TO SEE YOU URGENTLY THE ENERGIES ARE DISTURBED.* It ended with a bunch of emojis, as was to be expected.

"What's funny about it?"

Nicky frowned down at the text. "This is the first time in years she's contacted me when she wasn't asking for money."

I remembered the day Priestess Esmerelda had been bugging Nicky at work. "Well, the one time I met her, that's what was up."

Nicky kept frowning down at the text. "After you escorted her out of the office, she told me later that she'd run into Rodney, and they had a nice chat. So she's had some kind of contact with Rodney. Maybe he's given her money."

"Nicky, if he ever gave her money, he'd get more than his money's worth out of it."

"But what could Rodney want from Priestess Esmerelda?" Nicky clapped her hand over her mouth. "Oh Jesus. He's using Priestess Esmerelda to draw us out into the open. It's a setup." Tears came to her eyes.

That had to be it. Rodney knew peoples' bait so he could maneuver them. Priestess Esmerelda's bait was money. Nicky's bait was guilt over not being a good daughter to her totally vile mother.

My bait? My bait was Nicky.

"I've got a plan," I said. I laid it out for her. She laughed and clapped her hands, then she added a couple of beautiful touches.

Nicky sent the following text: *Mama honey I'm so depressed because Sam and I broke up and his new firm failed. He can't pay me or anybody. I'm trying for unemployment. Could you maybe spare about two thousand dollars?* Then she added a bunch of emojis, because Priestess Esmerelda, like many morons, communicated mostly in emojis. She hit send.

So now Priestess Esmerelda and Rodney would hopefully think Nicky and I were no longer lovers, and my firm had failed. If it worked, Nicky and Duvonda were safe. I was the only one Rodney had to intimidate (besides The Ghost).

And he had to intimidate me. I was the one who authenticated the video from The Ghost's condo. I was the one who picked up on him having Rohypnol long before he drugged and raped and slashed The Ghost. The prosecution could make a case without me, but it would be much harder.

Anybody I cared about could be in danger. I was radioactive.

Two days later Catherine called me up. "Sam, while Jerry and I were on a cruise, somebody broke into our house. It's weird, Sam. They didn't take anything. They just took a big dump on the oriental rug in the living room. What does that mean?"

I told her everything about Rodney's attack on The Ghost and his upcoming trial. "I didn't think he even knew you existed," I stammered.

"Maybe you and Jerry should hide out, the way I'm hiding out with Nicky."

Catherine snorted. "Fat chance. Jerry's sitting on the couch cleaning his Mossberg 12-gauge shotgun. But there's one thing we can do. The neighbors breed Dobermans, and they're lending us a pair to roam around outside the house. Also we've put up a driveway alert sensor and some motion detectors. Jerry's actually kind of hoping they try it again. He's pretty ballsy for a bald psychiatrist."

"He sure is. The dogs are a great touch. I didn't even know he had a gun."

"He has four. So there. What about you, Sam? Do you have a gun?"

"No. I should have gotten a concealed pistol license when I was prosecuting, but I just didn't think I needed it."

"Jerry says it's better to have a gun and not need it, than to need it and not have it."

"Copy that. It'll all be over soon, Catherine. But at least consider going into hiding like me. You're one of the few people I care about, and apparently he knows it."

"No sale. Jerry won't do it. But I'm guessing the Dobermans will do the job."

A couple of days after that, Silent Mike called. He was with Duvonda in her office late, with the lights out in the reception area.

Somebody put a crowbar into the suite's front door and started prying it open.

Silent Mike turned out the lights in Duvonda's office and crept down the hallway as the burglar was prying the door open, splintering it. Silent Mike reached into his pocket. As a head with a ski mask on it came through the door, Silent Mike drew his handheld Taser and zapped him. Then he climbed on top of him, zapped him again, and cuffed him.

"So I turned him over to the Seattle Police. The responding officers were old buddies. The burglar gave them a fake name, and he had no ID, but turns out his name is Bran Wheatley."

"You must be joking. Bran Wheatley?"

"Yup, and he's got a couple of prior felony busts. You get three guesses who his defense counsel was in the prior busts. The second two don't count."

My heart sank. "Shit."

"Guess Rodney wanted to see if you had really moved out or not. So that motherfucker is still trying to play angles."

"The only way that motherfucker will stop is when he's in prison."

After we hung up, Nicky pulled out a portable hard drive from her purse. It was the good kind that held ten terabytes and was the size of a pack of cigarettes. The same kind The Ghost had stored her video on.

"Sam, now it's time for my secret stash," she said.

"What is that?"

"Well, before we jumped ship, I went into the server and downloaded Rodney's criminal defense files, including the unpaid bills ledgers. So now we'll know who we're looking at. Bran Wheatley, huh?" She ran a USB cable into her laptop.

"Nicky, this is serious," I said. "We had the right to copy the personal injury files, because we worked on them. But we never did any criminal defense. This is computer trespass."

Nicky winked at me. "Not if nobody finds out." She double clicked on some boxes, and some more boxes. "Bran Wheatley. Age twenty-two. Residence is Darrington Washington, way up in the mountains. Hillbilly country. Priors—two residential burglaries, one count possession of methamphetamine with intent to distribute. Whaddya know? He owes Rodney seven thousand dollars. You told me Rodney liked having clients in debt to him, so he could make them do stuff."

It all fit. And I was impressed with Nicky's boldness. "But we can't go after Rodney for witness intimidation because of how we learned about Bran Wheatley's connection with Rodney."

Nicky mused. "Maybe the Seattle Police will pressure Bran to find out if somebody put him up to it. Maybe he'll flip on Rodney to save his skin."

Nicky had learned the finer points of law quickly. "Oh honey," I said, "you would make one fine lawyer."

She tucked her hair behind her ears and looked at me. "Do you think so?"

"I know so. You could do this."

She looked down. "Then I have another legal issue for you. Rodney's trial. Will it go?"

When lawyers ask, "will it go," they mean will it go to trial and verdict? When a lawyer answers, "yes, it will go," that lawyer gets a jolt of adrenaline.

"Yes," I said. "It will go. The prosecutors have him on video. They don't have to offer any deal. Rodney is a psychopath. So he can't admit fault for anything. It's the irresistible force versus the immovable object."

We both sat, quiet, in a pool of fear.

Nicky gave me a lush kiss. "Good. Then we can get out of this dump. Not that I have any major prejudice against orange carpet and concentric circles on the polyester bedspread."

Buster said, "That's OG." We looked at him. His vocabulary was improving.

***

A couple of nights later I got a call from The Ghost. It was delightful but still weird that she was calling me. But her privacy had been blown to shreds by the charges against Rodney. She sounded unnaturally calm—which meant in Ghost-speak that she was very upset.

"I've had a disturbance at my place," she said.

My heart sank. The last disturbance at her place had turned everything upside down. "Since I'm hiding out with Nicky," I said, "could I put you on speaker? It would save time because I tell her everything anyway."

"All right. Duvonda likes her, so go ahead."

I hit speaker. "Okay. The disturbance at your place."

The Ghost said, "Since your car got burned, and Duvonda's office got burglarized, I've been really on edge. I suspected there might be blowback from Rodney's indictment. So I installed another motion-activated pinhole camera outside my door, overhead, and I've been geared up ever since. I don't leave the condo. After all, no victim, no crime."

I swallowed hard. "So, what was the disturbance?"

"Last night I was playing Words With Friends on my phone after midnight. It's a poor substitute for Scrabble with you. Pirate was pacing around mewing. I swear that cat is clairvoyant. Anyway, the laptop screen turned on showing this moose of a guy outside my door. I turned off the lights and made sure I had my gear on. The guy bent down to the lock; I guess he tried to pick it, but it didn't work. Then he tried a plastic shim but couldn't slip the deadbolt. So he took a crowbar out from under his trench coat. Brute force approach, just like at Duvonda's office. He put the straight end into the doorjamb above the lock and leaned on it. There was splintering. I went over to the entertainment center beside the door because it's darker there. More splintering. The crowbar came in, and then he must have leaned hard because the door splintered more and opened. I could smell him. He must smoke four packs a day. This guy was huge—maybe six-five and three hundred pounds. Big white guy with scraggly hair and a bushy mountain man beard. He took two steps in the door, and I took my bear mace out from the pocket of my fleece jacket and I emptied it into his face. He yelled but he didn't stop. He swung a wild punch and hit me on the right cheek, right where my scar is. Man, that hurt. I saw stars. Then I drew my Glock 17 and pistol-whipped him across the face four times until he went down. I jumped on his back and cuffed his hands and feet with the zip ties in my other pocket. I called it in. Not more than twenty minutes later, Detective Broccoli and Detective Cookie showed up. They're handling my burglary and Duvonda's burglary and your Subaru arson too. The Seattle Police know they're all connected. They're building a case for witness intimidation."

"Jesus," Nicky blurted out. "You GHOSTED him."

The Ghost burst out laughing. I had only heard her laugh a few times. It was like the sun came out. "Okay Nicky, that is solid. Now I see why Vanilla Boy likes you."

"But how did you know how to do all that?" Nicky said.

It was time for The Ghost's backstory. I'd heard it all, but Nicky needed to know. "I was with the Tacoma Police on patrol for six years," The Ghost said. "I really liked it. But I liked the investigation part better than the muscling people around part. One day when I was off-duty I went to the bank to deposit a check. Two robbers came in with revolvers out and masks on—Bugs Bunny and Porky Pig. Bugs Bunny said, 'It's a holdup, everybody down on the floor.' He jumped the counter, pointed the revolver at the tellers and told them to back away, so they couldn't push their panic buttons. Porky Pig slowly turned in a circle as we all got down. I was next to an elderly woman who had a hard time getting down to the floor; she was stiff. She had to be eighty or more. Porky Pig came over and kicked her in her hip, and she fell on her side. Bugs Bunny was stuffing cash in a pillowcase. 'Wassup pig,' he yelled. 'Oink oink,' Porky yelled back. Then the old lady moaned and turned onto her stomach; it turned out he'd broken her hip when he kicked her. So Porky Pig sees her roll over. He must have been hopped up. He said, 'I said don't move bitch,' and he shot her in her low back. Then Bugs jumped up on the counter because I guess he thought one of the customers fired the shot, and he fired a shot into the ceiling. Then Porky shot the old woman again, I guess thinking somebody shot at him. I had my holdout weapon, a small Glock nine millimeter, in my ankle holster. I curled up as if I was wincing from the gunfire and got it. I aimed for Porky's belly, but I was high and hit him in the chest twice. Bugs turned toward me and I aimed for his belly too, but I missed him once and hit him the second time in the left eye. They both died at the scene. Well, that tore it. I was put on paid administrative leave. Eventually I was cleared, but it took forever. They called it a good shoot. It's the only time I ever shot anybody in the line of duty, but I killed them both. While I was on leave, I was very stressed. It was weird. I knew I did the right thing but I still felt just awful. Anyway, I started getting blurry vision in my left eye, and my right foot started going numb sometimes. Then my right leg got weak, and I was put through some fitness for duty medical examinations. After a bunch of doctors hemmed and hawed, they sent me to a good neurologist. Turned out I was developing multiple sclerosis. So I took a medical retirement and got my private investigator license. Maybe that's a good thing. Turns out I'm more equipped to be a snooper than a shooter."

Nicky was weeping. I'd heard this story in pieces but she'd gotten it in one dose. She'd never even met The Ghost, but she'd heard many of our tales we called Ghost Stories, about The Ghost finding unfindable people and unfindable evidence.

I hugged Nicky and stroked her hair.

The Ghost sighed. "I guess you're off the market now, Vanilla Boy," she said wistfully.

"I guess I am," I said. "So what do you hear from the detectives? How's the case against Rodney developing?"

Nicky sniffed and pushed me away and gave me a brave smile.

"Well not to shock you, but it's turning out weird. Rodney was denied bail. In a case that doesn't involve murder, that's unusual."

I did a quick search on my laptop. Aha. Criminal Rule (CrR) 3.2, Release of the Accused. "Okay. Bail can be denied for several reasons. First, there's a risk that the accused will not appear for trial. In other words, he's a flight risk. Second, there's a risk he'll commit a violent crime. Third, there's a risk of witness intimidation."

The Ghost said, "Detective Cookie seems to think Rodney intentionally got denied bail, by implying that one or more of those risks was present. He took a dive. Why would he do that, Sam?"

There was a sickening jolt in my stomach. "Because being incarcerated is a perfect alibi. Since he was in custody he couldn't be blamed for the attack on you, burning my car, or any of the other stuff. He must be using some kind of code word to control his goons. Also I'll bet my lunch money he won't waive his right to speedy trial. He wants to rush to trial hoping the prosecutors won't be ready."

"That fits. What could he possibly have, Sam? Let's game this out."

Nicky said, "Game this out?"

The Ghost said, "When Sam brings me a case that is totally twisted, we game it out. It means we speculate about what the enemy is doing and why they are doing it. It's a kind of brainstorming. We list every single idea we can think of, no matter how bizarre. Then we weigh them and eliminate the dumb ones. But before we go further, Nicky, I need you to agree with me about something. This conversation never happened. We never spoke about any of this. With Sam, it's understood. But I need a promise from you."

Nicky's eyes went wide. "I promise. I won't refer to this nonexistent conversation."

"Okay," The Ghost said. "So let's start with some basic premises. Rodney is a psychopath. He won't accept responsibility and he won't plead out. He won't hire a lawyer either, because he's the Ultimate Super Criminal Defense Lawyer. So he'll represent himself. If Rodney were in fact innocent, what the hell could be going on here? That's the situation he will try to fabricate. I'll bet he's not going for a hung jury. He's going for an acquittal."

I took out a legal pad and a pen. "Okay, so he tries to show he's been framed. Either you framed him, or I did, or both of us. What's our motivation? Why did we frame him?" I made a heading—*Motivation*—and got ready to intuit twisted motivations from the twisted mind of Rodney.

The Ghost said, "Maybe I framed him because I'm hopelessly in love with him, and he won't commit to me, so I want to wreck his life so nobody else can have him."

Nicky burst out laughing.

"Seriously, that's how he thinks," The Ghost said.

"I know," Nicky said. "I worked for him for two years, remember? I'm laughing because that's just how he sees the world."

I said, "Maybe I framed him because I envy his professional success and wanted to ruin him so I could have you all to myself."

The Ghost said, "Good one. Of course Nicky is an inconvenient truth, but he could always allege you're a two-timer and Nicky doesn't know that I am your One True Love."

Nicky snapped her fingers. "Maybe both of you framed him. You're secret lovers and you both wanted to frame him. So you could sue him for the rape and take his precious money. You're setting him up so we can rip him off after he gets convicted."

I winced. I wrote it down.

The Ghost said, "That smells so bad it's probably true; given that we're working in Rodney World, he'll probably go with that one— both of us are conspiring against him to get him convicted and rip him off. That way if either of us looks bad on the stand, his theory still has some plausibility."

I said, "Now for the hard part. HOW did we frame him?"

The Ghost said, "The case has four pillars: the semen, the video, your testimony, and my testimony. He has to knock down pillars—all four if he can do it."

"Okay, the semen. He can allege he had consensual sex with you. Or he can challenge the DNA findings."

"I don't see him challenging the DNA findings. Detective Cookie told me they forced Rodney to get swabbed, and they got a rush job at the State Crime Lab. The DNA matches."

"Okay, then he alleges consensual sex."

"Exactly. I am ashamed to admit I played with him a couple of times before. So he can allege consensual sex. Or better yet, he accuses me of keeping a used condom and planting the semen. Since that's wicked? That's what he'll allege. This is how a psychopath works. Everything that he is doing, he accuses other people of doing. Classic reversification— accuse the opponent of what you are doing."

"Okay, so that covers the semen. How does he take you and me out of the equation?"

The Ghost said, "I should tell you, the burglar who broke into my place had four commando knives on him—two in belt holsters and two in tactical holsters strapped to his thighs. It's a solid bet that Mr. Burglar was going to kill me."

Nicky gasped. "Why knives?"

The Ghost said, "You can't do ballistics on knives. They're silent and they never need reloading. If the murderer is much stronger and catches the victim by surprise, knives are better weapons than guns. By the way, these knives had woven cloth hilts so fingerprints can't be lifted from them."

Nicky said, "Excuse me," in a small voice. She fled into the bathroom. I could hear her vomiting. Poor Nicky. I'd sure dragged her into my accidental shit show.

The Ghost continued: "So, his plan is to have us killed. Has he made an attempt on you besides the Subaru fire? That had to be a warning, unless the pyrotechnic device malfunctioned."

"I'm guessing the Subaru was a warning. But recently Nicky's mother was in touch with her, wanting to meet up with her for no apparent reason. I think Rodney was trying to draw Nicky into the open and either kidnap her or me."

"Or both. Either of you would do. Both would be better. You would not survive. Nicky is your bait, Sam. When you love someone, you give the psychopath a lever."

"I know," I said fervently. "But it's worth it."

Nicky returned with a glass of water. She was pale white. I kissed her on her forehead and promised myself that Rodney would never get a crack at her. The thought of her being kidnapped made me want to vomit too.

The Ghost said, "Sam, we need to agree on something. This thing has escalated all the way. Either we destroy Rodney or he destroys us."

Nicky took a sip of her water and asked, "How about if we game that out? What happens if Rodney gets convicted and imprisoned? What happens if he gets acquitted?"

The Ghost said, "Yes, I've thought that through. If Rodney gets convicted and imprisoned, we win. He'll be locked up for years. He'll be automatically disbarred. I will sue him for every goddamned penny he has—assuming I can find his pennies. Once he gets disbarred his goons won't do errands for him because he'll be of no use to them anymore. So that's the best-case scenario."

Nicky said, "But what if he beats the charges?"

I said, "Then we all leave the state and change our names, or we eventually get murdered."

The Ghost said, "Correct. It's him or us. So now we need to understand how he can explain away the video. The video is really lethal to him unless he can get it excluded from evidence or he can attack it at trial. I don't see it getting excluded because it's soundless, so it doesn't violate the wiretap statute."

I said, "He'll probably allege the chain of custody is broken because I was alone in the condo with the hard drive before the medics and police showed up. He'll allege it could have been planted. I'll bet he's already filed his Motion to Suppress. But I'll bet my boots he'll lose."

The Ghost said, "Okay, so if it's not excluded, he'll have to allege it's a fake. How can he show reasonable doubt about the authenticity of the video?"

I shut up. I was too deep in Rodney World and couldn't find my way.

The Ghost drummed her fingers. She only did that when she was very agitated. Finally she said, "I've got it. He'll use an expert witness to attack the video. He'll claim the video is a clever fake. He'll bring in somebody who knows a lot about digital video production to say look at this, look at that, it's a fake and Sam planted it when he was at the condo before the medics and police came. He'll show it over and over to desensitize the jury, then give them a bunch of technical BS."

I swallowed hard again. It was brazen distilled bullshit. Therefore it was true. Rodney never got embarrassed about lying. He had the conscience of a snake.

"God damn it," I said. "That has to be it. Maybe he'll bring in the company that produces his cheesy TV commercials."

The Ghost shot that down. "No, it'll be a video forensics witness who does criminal defense trials all the time. It'll be a professional witness—like the kind who says surgeons commonly leave instruments inside patients, or that false positive alcohol tests on the Breathalyzer are a usual finding. It'll be the most-skilled and highest-priced whore on the market."

I scribbled everything down. "I'll bet that's it. The County almost never pays for expert witnesses, so Rodney's expert will be unopposed. He or she will be super friendly and have great credentials. Probably will have worked on a TV show for a season or two. Somebody that will dazzle the jury. We can't be certain. But it smells right."

The Ghost said, "Yes, it smells right. It smells like an outhouse in August with a dead skunk inside. This is the only good thing the three of us ever got from knowing Rodney Mammon. We have a firm sense of what kind of a waste of oxygen he is."

I was so relieved she used our old phrase, waste of oxygen.

Now The Ghost saw him as a defendant. Not an enemy, just a defendant. When she called somebody a waste of oxygen? She had the detachment to study him like a chessboard.

"So, has the prosecutor prepped you yet?" I asked.

"Not yet. We're meeting tomorrow. She's Harriet Hatchet. She's run the Sexual Assault Unit for ten years. She's an original member of the Bitch Squad."

"What's the Bitch Squad?" Nicky asked.

"It's the original Sexual Assault Unit crew of reformers," I said. "They helped push through the rape shield law that prevents pre-rape sexual history from being admitted into evidence. They're all women, about half of them gay. Truly committed. Duvonda was on the Bitch Squad for about two years, but she left because she wanted to branch out."

Nicky said, "Wait, I just figured something out. Every last one of you is ex-law enforcement of some kind. Cops or prosecutors."

The Ghost laughed. "Don't you forget it, Nicky. But what did we agree about this conversation again?"

Nicky recited dutifully: "This conversation never occurred and the words used never happened."

This time I laughed.

"Close enough," The Ghost said.

"So, did they ID the guy who broke in?" I asked.

"Sure. Gran Cornwall of Darrington. Convicted meth cook and burglar. I'll bet my boots he's had Rodney as his defense attorney."

Nicky typed quickly on her laptop, searched Rodney's deadbeat clients list, and gave me a thumbs up.

I said, "You get to keep your boots. Besides, I don't wear women's shoes anyway."

"See what I said, Nicky? Vanilla Boy. I hope you don't have any unusual carnal tastes."

I took that one. "Her lips taste like morning in Heaven," I said.

"Oh brother," The Ghost said. I knew she was rolling her eyes.

Nicky kissed me and proved me right.

CHAPTER THIRTY-SIX—THE GOON SQUAD

Silent Mike called me the next evening and I put him on speaker so Nicky could hear. "We need to get out in front of the opposing team," Mike said. I liked that he had become more talkative.

"I'm doing witness prep with the prosecutor later this week," I said.

Silent Mike laughed mirthlessly. "I mean these hillbilly motherfuckers that broke into Duvonda's office and The Ghost's condo. Rodney's goon squad. I heard it through the grapevine that Nicky has some intel on these crackers. But before we go further, can you two agree that this conversation never happened?" Hypothesis confirmed—he was in touch with The Ghost—and was using the same phrases.

Nicky said, "I'm not sure to what nonexistent conversation you are referring."

Silent Mike laughed. "I did not have a nonexistent conversation with either of you at any time. So, what do you know about them?"

"Okay, we have two names," I said. "This is thanks to Nicky being a bit of a data kleptomaniac." Nicky elbowed me. "Ow," I said. "Bran Wheatley is the guy you tasered breaking into Duvonda's office. Two prior felony arrests—meth possession and burglary. Last known address is a PO box in Darrington." I read off the PO box number.

Silent Mike paused. "Darrington. The logging town way up in the Cascades, otherwise known as the Appalachia of Washington. And the other one?"

"Gran Cornwell, the guy who broke into The Ghost's condo. Six-five, three hundred pounds, prior busts for—you guessed it—meth cooking and burglary. Meth cooking times five, burglary times three. Heavy smoker; reeks of tobacco. Last known address?"

Nicky said, "The same PO box in Darrington."

Silent Mike said, "Correct me if I'm wrong. Both were represented by Rodney before?"

Nicky said, "Yup. Both former clients of his. Both owe him money. Both currently on probation."

I said, "For the time being. These new arrests will eventually void their probation and get them pulled into custody again. The same address means they're part of the same crew."

"Rodney's goon squad," Silent Mike said. "I'll bet there's more of them. Any way to find out if there's anybody else on that PO box?"

Nicky said, "I can't find out, but I'll bet The Ghost can. Are they still in jail?"

Silent Mike said, "A little bird told me Gran Cornwell is about to bail out. I'm heading down to the jail in my grubby clothes and a hoodie to loiter around the exit port and tail him. I've got his mug shot. I've looked up some stuff you aren't privy to that shows this clown is Not A Very Nice Person. I'll let you know what I find out."

Silent Mike called back five hours later. It was late and Nicky was pulling back the ugly bedspread with the concentric circles while I fed Buster. "Okay, I followed him back to his truck. It's a fifteen-year-old diesel crew cab pickup with a gun rack, spray painted olive drab. Just what a hillbilly meth cook would drive. I put a GPS tracker inside the rear bumper and fired it up. Get this. It went up to Darrington, then out a Forest Service road, turned onto another Forest Service road, and stopped about a hundred feet off that road. So I'm going up there tomorrow to send up my drone and see if I can get some video of where he's holing up."

I said, "No kidding? You have a drone?"

"Quadcopter with digital video camera, digital still camera, and infrared video. Perfectly legal. Sometimes a private investigator needs the tools, you feel me?"

"I feel you. That's sweet tech. What's the range?"

"I can make it go out ten miles and return without sweating it. I'll let you know what I find out."

"Okay Mike, but the pit of my stomach says there's a whole nest of them. Don't get close, okay?"

"Okay. I'm engaged now, so I won't get close."

Nicky and I exchanged delighted glances. He'd popped the question to Duvonda.

Silent Mike called back the next evening. He sounded somber. "I didn't get too close. But that's the only good news."

"Okay, what's the other news?"

"Drone worked perfectly. I pulled way off the road to launch it and flew it out of a clear-cut. Gran's truck hadn't moved since he bailed out of jail and drove there. You were right, Sam. There's a whole nest of them."

Nicky said, "Enough suspense."

"Well the drone comes over a low ridge, and there's a little valley with a creek running through it. There's a sort of homemade road coming off the Forest Service road, only a hundred feet or so long. At the end of it? Twenty-one RVs. Some of them so ratty they have tarps over them to keep the rain out. There's a portable garden shed well away from the RVs, with drums and whatnot around it. And there's a flatbed with a camouflage tarp over it. There were ten of these guys with long mountain man beards standing around a firepit, smoking and drinking beers. I also saw a very fat woman with tattoo sleeves and a toddler. I'm sure there's more people, but that's who was outside."

"Did you get in closer?"

"Yeah, first I came over their RVs at one hundred feet and went right over, recording, but then I circled back at fifty feet because I wanted the infrared camera to get real close. There's a nice thermal bloom on the gardening shed and there were fifty-five-gallon drums next to it. Any ideas what was in the drums?"

I shrugged. "Probably acetone. And the thermal bloom? They are cooking meth."

"What's acetone?" Nicky wondered.

I said, "It's an industrial-strength solvent. Used to make meth. Carcinogenic as hell. It's also very explosive. Acetone is what makes meth labs blow up, which they often do."

Mike said, "But that's not the headline news, Sam. As the drone came in toward them the second time at fifty feet, two of the guys pointed and ran toward the flatbed with the camo tarp. They pulled off the tarp. Any guesses what was under that?"

"At this point, I don't even want to guess."

"It was a tripod-mounted fifty-caliber machine gun."

Long silence. I looked at Buster and he looked at me. I looked at Nicky and she looked at me. The situation had…escalated.

Silent Mike said, "They whipped off the tarp, then the biggest dude pulled the charging handle—all quick, well practiced. Then shot at my drone. I dodged it all over, managed to get it down low, and then told it to return to base. One shot grazed it. If they'd gotten a solid hit they'd have blown the drone to pieces. But holy fuck. A fifty-cal?"

"What's a fifty-cal?" Nicky asked me.

I felt sick inside. "A fifty-caliber machine gun—a heavy military machine gun. I qualified on the fifty-cal when I was in the Coast Guard. A fifty-cal can send a torrent of bullets as big as my thumb at a target up to two thousand yards away. That's over a mile. Minimum rate of fire is 450 rounds a minute, which is seven and a half rounds per second."

"Damn straight. Sam, this goon squad is a little army. We've got major trouble up in here."

"So, how about if you call the Forest Service? They're squatting on federal land."

"Right government, Sam, but wrong agency. The Forest Service ain't equipped for that. I gave everything to the Bureau of Alcohol Tobacco and Firearms, and the Drug Enforcement Agency. Meth cooking plus a heavy machine gun equals lots of puckered assholes down at the federal building. I have contacts at both places from when I used to do SWAT. Both agencies said they are looking it over."

"Any timeline on when they might go in there?"

"Sam, you know—this is the federal government. They might be up there right now—or they might get around to moseying up to Darrington in about six months. This would be a good score for them, but it's a little dangerous. Feds are like pretty ladies—you can't rush them."

I was thinking about how quickly a fifty-cal could shred this whole Extended Stay America.

If they pulled up in the parking lot outside with that flatbed and knew which room was ours, everything in the room including us would be mincemeat in five seconds. Tops.

"So what's the next move, Mike? I think Nicky and I are hid out all right. But how about you and Duvonda and The Ghost?"

"Sam, I am not chickenshit. But I'm taking Duvonda and The Ghost down to my uncle Chester Arthur's place until this stuff is settled.

I'm pretty sure Rodney doesn't know about Chester's place or he would have made a move to steal the Toyota wreck from your Rockingham County case for leverage. Besides, Uncle Chester has five Presa Canario attack dogs at over a hundred pounds each. And more guns than a shark has teeth."

I sighed. "That's a good plan. Should we go with you? Should all of us hole up together?"

"Sam, I think not. There are two witnesses who can get Rodney convicted. The Ghost, and you. We can't put both of you in the same place. That way if one of you gets killed? The other gets to testify. But there is one—just one—bright spot in the picture."

"Oh yeah, what's that?" I asked, stroking Nicky's hair. She was staring into space. She'd had lots of trouble as a kid. But she was a stranger to violence.

Silent Mike said, "Why are all these lethal crackers willing to help Rodney anyway?"

"Because they owe him money?"

"Use your head, fool. It's because Rodney is a criminal defense attorney, and they are criminals. If Rodney gets convicted, he'll get disbarred. If he loses his license to practice, the goon squad won't even answer his phone calls anymore."

I shivered. "So it's him or us," I said. The Ghost had convinced me.

"Him or us baby. This is a dirty war. We damn well better win."

We hung up. I hugged Nicky and stroked her hair. I was probably more scared than she was.

I'd trained on the fifty-caliber machine gun with the Coast Guard. Once at a firing range I got to use it on a standard Ford van. After twenty seconds there was nothing left but a gnawed-on chassis, a lump of broken engine block, and a bunch of shredded steel. The range? A quarter mile away. I was competent with it—but I wasn't an expert. Stinky Bill was the expert in my crew.

My story had started with a massive impact. But I didn't want it to end with a bunch of them.

Nicky murmured something into my chest. "How's that, honey?" I asked, stroking her hair.

She lifted her harrowed face to me and said, "They really are the Guilty Peoples' Department."

I looked at Buster again. He didn't say anything. He could smell the vibe.

After I held her for a long while, she said, "What if Rodney gets acquitted? What will we do then?"

"I'm thinking we could move very far away and change our names. I've got enough seniority and a good track record, so I can get admitted to the Bar just about any place. If that can't be done with the name change, I could swallow my pride and get hired as an insurance adjuster. That's if you would come with me."

"I'd come with you." She said it without hesitation.

There was only one good thing about my desperate position. I had the best people right in the morass with me.

I asked Nicky, "Are you sure you could stand me as an insurance adjuster?"

"Maybe I'd become one too, and we could get adjoining cubicles. There's just one problem."

"What's that?"

"I'd miss the unwavering support of my nurturing mother."

We both smiled at that. Buster said, "Word up."

CHAPTER THIRTY-SEVEN— HATCHET JOB

The morning I was scheduled for trial prep at the prosecutor's, Nicky wore an impish smile.

"So you said you were going to get me a disguise," I said skeptically. "What did you come up with to get me in and out of the courthouse without being recognized by Rodney's goons?"

"Close your eyes."

I heard crinkling. Nicky put something on my head, leaning close enough that I smelled her rose perfume. I tried to kiss her.

"Tut tut, Sam. You're in wardrobe and makeup. Don't harass your stylist."

Then she put glasses on my face. "Now I'll give you the hand mirror, but don't open your eyes until I tell you," she said.

I did not expect a very flattering disguise.

She folded my fingers around the handle of the mirror. "Okay, open."

I was wearing a red trucker's cap with fake black hair sewn into it—a mullet. The "business in front, party in the back" haircut. And mirror shades tinted dark pink.

"You look so distinguished," she said, straightening the fake black curls on the back of my neck.

"Nobody will recognize me," I said. "But I look like a fucking idiot."

"That's why nobody will recognize you." She sent me off with a kiss.

Silent Mike had a friend named Fritos—yes, Fritos—who owned a used car lot. Fritos had rented me a banged-up white Geo Metro with only one hubcap. I liked it—nobody could take the driver seriously. It was damn near invisible. It ran, but the engine grumbled in Armenian under its breath.

Because there was a pileup on Interstate 5, I drove the Geo Metro south toward Seattle on Highway 99, the old pre-interstate Pacific coast highway. Back when I was a prosecutor, we used to call it the Heroin Highway.

The Heroin Highway had not improved one bit.

Once I reached the Seattle city limits, the picture darkened immediately.

At every bus stop, a bedraggled crew of addicts slouched under cover, squinting at the rain and smoking hungrily. Teen hookers in miniskirts and plastic platform sandals walked with their faces toward traffic, their gaunt faces painted up like clowns. One held up a fist and made an "O" of her lips, pumping her fist. Mimicking fellatio. Marketing.

Every three or four blocks on a vacant lot or in a parking lot festered a homeless encampment of dome tents surrounded with tents and shopping carts and fields of trash and junk carpeting the environs. All had one or more cars which had been stolen and stripped for parts.

Scraggly men and vacant-eyed women meandered through the carpets of wreckage they had created. Some rearranged junk. Some tried to remember what or who they were.

Seattle had cancer. The homeless encampments were the tumors. They were growing and spreading.

Anybody who mentioned societal chemotherapy was labeled "insensitive"—the worst epithet that Seattle progressives could devise.

How did Seattle get this cancer? Lax law enforcement and tons of free stuff for "our most vulnerable neighbors"—who were addicted criminals.

They weren't vulnerable. Everybody else was vulnerable. The addicts stole stuff, attacked people, broke into cars and houses. Seattle's government kept saying, "our homelessness programs are underfunded."

The programs were overfunded. They attracted addicts from all over the US.

Silent Mike once explained why the city government was doing this. "They're afraid that high-paid tech people might just vote the wrong way. So they're counterbalancing them with addicts who will vote more free stuff for themselves. Then, they demand more funding for the programs—to attract more addicts. The city bureaucracy expands and takes a lavish cut of the homeless services budget for yet more staff. The city knows what it's doing, all right. They just won't admit it. As the firefighters say, "Feed the pigeons? Get MORE pigeons.""

For the first time, I decided I would leave Seattle even if Rodney got convicted. I would buy a house in the suburbs for Nicky and me.

The balance had tipped. Seattle had gone too far into decadence to recover. The city spent almost a billion dollars a year on "homeless services." They kept saying their programs were "underfunded." More homeless people kept flooding in from across the country. I remembered Street Monkey, dead in the plaza in front of my new office building.

I remembered the EMT working on Street Monkey telling me: "Most addicts are going to jail or to the morgue." I thought it was better to send them to jail than to the morgue. This marked me as "insensitive."

I parked the Geo Metro near Pioneer Square. I doubted anybody would steal Fritos's car—nobody would be that desperate. I checked my stylish mullet hat and pink mirror shades, and walked to the courthouse.

For the first time as I threaded through the crowd of addicts in front of the Fourth Avenue entrance nobody asked me for money. Wardrobe and makeup indeed.

I rode the elevator up to the prosecutor's office. People looked at me out of the corners of their eyes. I knew why. I looked like a defendant.

I checked in with the receptionist and sat down in a hard plastic chair to wait. I mused about Rodney, and about psychopaths generally. I'd learned quite a lot about them when I was prosecuting.

Bear with me here. This next part is important.

The amygdala is the brain structure that governs the fight or flight response. Psychopaths have abnormally low amygdala response. In the extreme cases, they are basically fearless. It takes extreme stimuli to make them feel anything at all. So they tend toward extreme and impulsive behavior. The worst of them become sadistic, enjoying inflicting pain on others to spark a pleasurable emotional response in their brains.

Rodney was one of the worst. He was a high-functioning psychopath with the drive to inflict pain, and the intellect to conceal his abnormality.

To be blunt, he delighted in being evil.

Psychopaths were rare. High-functioning psychopaths were even more rare. Thank God.

This explained Rodney's curious emotional blankness and flatness. This explained why he was laughably implausible when he attempted to convey sympathy. He couldn't feel sympathy. It was all clearly fake.

As very advanced primates, humans are generally good at detecting insincerity. A high-functioning psychopath has to learn to mimic normal emotions. Rodney was a snake posing as a man.

Psychopaths see other people as…objects. Other people aren't people to them. They are talking puppets available for the psychopath's sick pleasure.

Because of all this, Rodney would look for any opportunity in trial to horrify me, and the other witnesses, to throw us off our game. To Rodney, trial was a game. His brazen quality made him good at reading and humiliating people. He had an excellent trial record.

I thought I'd gamed out the worst things he could say to me, and about me, to show that the charges against him were false. The video was solid proof of what he had done. He would have to prove the video was fake, with an expensive digital video production expert.

 But I was tangled in the chain of custody of the video. He would have to prove I was using a faked video to frame him, for disgusting motives of my own.

I would have to present the Steel Wall to him. I would have to calmly resist his attempts to smear me. A truly innocent person often gets angry when falsely accused. But he would twist my anger to show the jury I hated him and had framed him.

Rodney World was an inside-out and upside-down place. I would need to be completely unflappable even though his attack on The Ghost enraged me.

Finally Harriet Hatchet came out and led me back to the small conference room by her office in the Bitch Squad suite. Only then did I take off the mullet hat and the pink mirror-shades.

Harriet Hatchet was a fiftyish woman, slim and spare, with a severe librarian vibe. Her long gray hair was back in a bun, and she wore a blue skirted suit with a severe cut. I'd heard the intel on her and her husband, a guy on Felony Trial Teams who I'd known during my rotation there. They were prosecutors-for-life. I'd once wanted to be one myself.

"I see you're being careful," Harriet said, as I placed my mullet hat and pink mirror shades on the table. "I approve. Did you know I have the burglary cases on The Ghost's condo and Duvonda's office? And the arson on your Subaru? I'm handling all of these cases as a bundle because it all counts as witness intimidation. If Rodney's minions will roll over on him I can add charges. In the meantime the jail guards have stockpiled audio of his in-custody phone calls. Detective Broccoli and Detective Cookie will review them looking for coded messages if I lose the upcoming trial. We'll get two bites at the apple if we're desperate. But this is the bite that counts."

"I know you can't tell me much about the case against him," I said, "but can you list out the charges in his trial?"

"Sure, that's public information," she said, putting on her reading glasses. "I'll give you the shorthand because you once worked here, so you'll get the gist. Count One—Rape in the First Degree. Count Two—Assault in the First Degree. Count Three—Burglary in the First Degree. Count Four—Delivery of a Controlled Substance."

I nodded. Quite a lineup. Also they hadn't added any "chippy charges" that might trivialize the trial. "I've never been on the witness stand," I said. "So give me the ground rules."

She said, "First off, never lie or exaggerate. Every single thing you say must be totally true. If you don't know, say so. If you don't remember, say so. I've got a transcript of your recorded statement from the detectives. The night before you testify, absorb that statement completely. The statement is the Bible."

I nodded.

"Second, do not show any emotion whatsoever. Don't laugh. Don't raise your voice. Don't swear or argue. You must play this totally straight. You are the authenticator of the video. If your words are true? Then the video is true. Their razzle-dazzle attack on the video only works if you seem like somebody who would fabricate the video."

"So my guess is correct? Rodney hired somebody from Hollywood to testify about how the video could have been faked?"

"I'm sorry, I can't say," Harriet said, but she winked. I approved. Smart prosecutors always held their cards close to the vest.

It's a dirty secret of the law—both civil litigation and criminal litigation—that if you hire an expert witness with splendid credentials and pay them a boatload of money, then usually they will testify however you want them to. If they won't, you hire another one. If you don't like what they say in their report before any testimony is given, you designate them as "consulting experts" and trash the report. They never testify and the opposing party can't hire them for the case either. If you do like the report, you designate them as "testifying experts" and pay them three times as much per hour after they take the stand.

Lawyers gossip a lot. Experts who don't play ball don't get hired again. Between ourselves, many lawyers think of many experts as prostitutes. That's why one good lawyer I know once anonymously sent a notoriously flexible testifying medical expert a Victoria's Secret gift card so he—yes he—could be properly dressed when he testified. I steadfastly deny it was me. (It was Duvonda.) But I sure wish I had thought of it first because I still smile when I think of that.

Harriet brought me out of my reverie. "So here's an overview of my direct examination."

She deftly led me through an abbreviated biography, the basics about my work at the prosecutor's office and in civil work, and the short version of why and how I'd left Rodney's firm. She questioned me closely about my relationship with The Ghost. She confirmed that I was not particularly tech savvy and knew jack shit about how to counterfeit a digital video.

"Now, on to the cross," she said. "I've tried four cases against Rodney. All rape cases. I won three and lost one. That one was in a video courtroom, so I pulled the video and looked it over to get a sense of his style."

I said, "I hope you took a long shower afterward."

She nodded indulgently. "All right, but don't make any smart remarks like that on the stand."

"Copy that."

Then she put me through a witness prep that made my prep of Linda Lou look like a Sunday school picnic. In a flat and authoritative voice she accused me of every vile motivation and act she could fabricate. "I need to get you desensitized, Sam," she said.

Several times, even though I knew she was just prepping me, I turned red and started to interrupt. Each time she calmly redirected me and restarted the entire line of questioning.

She'd prosecuted a lot of rapists and prepped a lot of victims. I was in the hands of a maestro.

By the end of it, I was breathing hard. I was sweating. My blood pressure was so high I expected to squirt blood out of my ears and eyeballs.

But I could respond to anything with an even tone. If she had accused me of having sex with corpses I could have said without batting an eyelash, "I have never had sex with a corpse, Counselor." Because I was an idealist, it took her a long time.

She gave me the details about when I would testify, and I confirmed my cell number with her. She had her paralegal come in and formally serve my Subpoena for Trial. I signed the Acceptance of Service and waited until the paralegal left.

"One final thing," I asked. "Why didn't the prosecutor's office want to keep me? I did pretty well on Felony Trial Teams. Nine convictions and one hung jury. After that I had to rotate to the Filing Unit, fair enough. You guys always do that after a trial teams rotation to prevent burnout. But why was I sent to juvie after that? Why didn't I get another rotation on Felony Trial Teams?"

Harriet looked at me with compassion. I guessed it was rare to have a former prosecutor as a complaining witness in a significant criminal trial. "I wasn't on the Management Committee then," she said, "but my husband was. He was in your corner, Sam. But a couple of the members thought you were so idealistic that you might morph into an overzealous prosecutor."

I nodded. I was a zealous prosecutor. I read everything, did thorough witness prep, and worked my ass off. But an overzealous prosecutor was one who might cut corners, hide discovery from defense counsel, even encourage perjury among witnesses. I wasn't one. But they'd thought I might become one.

For the first time ever, I was relieved I'd been sent to juvie—Siberia—by the prosecutor's office. I liked personal injury a lot better. They hadn't meant to do me a favor, but they had done me a favor.

"Fair enough," I said. "They were wrong. But I like my present job better anyhow."

"Get a good night's sleep before you testify," she said. "Eat a large breakfast before you come in. People who are being tormented burn a lot of calories."

As I put on my mullet hat and pink mirror shades, I realized that was why I'd been skinny all the time I was living at the Malletts' Therapeutic Foster Home.

CHAPTER THIRTY-EIGHT— STATE V. MAMMON

On the day of my testimony at Rodney's trial, Silent Mike insisted on driving me to and from court. I wore my best charcoal gray suit with my trademark blue paisley tie. Nicky kissed me goodbye as Silent Mike pulled up to the Extended Stay America in his rented black SUV. That reminded me that he and Duvonda and The Ghost were still in hiding too—down at his uncle Chester Arthur's place.

As I got in, I noticed Silent Mike wore a Glock in a shoulder holster and another in an ankle holster. He smiled at me. "It's better to have a gun and not need it, than to need a gun and not have it," he said.

"True dat," I said, unconsciously echoing Romeo Pursuit.

"Now here's how this will work," he said, accelerating rapidly. "I drop you on the far side of the King County Administration Building from the courthouse. You take the elevator to the bottom floor. Go into the courthouse through the tunnel, and go straight to the courtroom. That way you avoid the big crowd of homeless addicts at the street-level entrances. Rodney could have hidden a couple of his goons in the crowd. They could take you out easy as gutting a fish."

"Okay, copy that. What's the procedure when I'm done?"

"You call me on your cell before you even leave the floor where the trial is. I'll be waiting on the far side of the King County Administration Building, motor running. But the big danger is going in. Our mutual friend would really like to prevent you from testifying."

"Is that what you're doing for The Ghost?"

"She's done. She was on the stand the past two court days. It was rough, but she held up. Let's not get into any of that until after the verdict, okay? You need your head in the game."

I nodded, turning off my cell phone so it wouldn't ring in court. I remembered that Silent Mike had done lots of "hostile structure breaches" when he was on SWAT. I was in capable hands.

I took the tunnel into the courthouse and went up to the fifth floor and found the courtroom. I looked at the name plate next to the door.

Judge Palacpac.

Holy shit—Judge Palacpac was the trial judge. This trial was the vortex of everybody I respected and loved, and the one person on earth I feared. All the players were here.

Harriet Hatchet's paralegal came out and fetched me after about ten minutes. "You're up," she said, opening the door.

When I stepped in, I felt my body temperature go up ten degrees in an instant. The jurors and Harriet and Judge Palacpac looked up and noticed me. Then Rodney's head swung around. I met flat and glazed eyes. Rodney wore a Savile Row chalk stripe gray suit, and a lavender tie and matching handkerchief. He'd always had better taste in clothes than I had.

"State calls Samuel Strait," Harriet Hatchet said.

"Please step forward to be sworn," Judge Palacpac said.

I walked slowly up to the witness stand and, stood in front of the chair, and raised my right hand, and I was sworn in.

"Be seated, Mr. Strait," Judge Palacpac said, not unkindly. "Ms. Hatchet? Your witness."

Harriet Hatchet came up to the podium. Judge Palacpac liked to have attorneys question witnesses from the podium, and not to roam the courtroom except during argument. She made attorneys get permission to approach witnesses to hand them exhibits. She was running a tight ship. I belatedly realized that if Rodney was convicted—of anything—he would automatically appeal.

Judge Palacpac was trying the case with one eye toward the jury and one eye toward the Court of Appeals.

Harriet asked my name and address. I gave her my name and the address of the condo. By now it had probably been ransacked, so there was no reason to be coy. Harriet and Judge Palacpac exchanged a significant look. I belatedly realized something else.

Judge Palacpac had somehow learned from Harriet, or somebody, that Rodney had attempted to intimidate the witnesses. Probably that came up accidentally-on-purpose when The Ghost testified. Only the jury didn't realize the subtext here. Rodney squinted at me, then began writing busily. Behind him was a public defender, a guy I'd known when I was a prosecutor.

Sometimes, when non-attorneys represent themselves in trial, the court appoints a public defender as "standby counsel." I'd never heard of this being done when an attorney defended himself.

Come to think of it, I'd never heard of an attorney defending himself in a serious criminal charge. There were levels of complexity going on here that I couldn't suss out. Judge Palacpac was carefully defending herself from whatever bizarre appeal theory Rodney would advance.

Harriet started off examining me about how my parents died when I was seven, and how I was raised in foster care. I was surprised that I was able to be calm. A courtroom looks entirely different from the witness stand than from counsel table. It's like when you're a kid, and you visit the family across the street? Your house from that perspective for the first time.

Then Harriet deftly moved me through my Coast Guard service, my time at the prosecutor's office, and my switch to personal injury.

"So you are an attorney, Mr. Strait?"

"Yes, I am," I said. But I wasn't that day. I was a pawn in a game of chess. I had to cooperate while I was being moved.

Harriet got permission to approach, then handed me the transcript of my recorded statement which I'd given to Detective Broccoli and Detective Cookie the morning after The Ghost was attacked. "Is everything in this statement true, Mr. Strait?" she asked.

I adjusted the mike. "Yes it is," I said.

"Is there anything in this statement that you wish to amend or correct?"

"No I do not."

"Move to admit state's Exhibit 47," she said.

"Objection," Rodney said, standing. "Evidence is cumulative and prejudicial and therefore is barred by Evidence Rule 403."

Judge Palacpac said, "If the jury will excuse us, we will need to discuss this a bit." The bailiff led the jury back to the jury room.

"You may approach, Counsel," she said to Rodney. I got it. She was calling Rodney Counsel and calling the prosecutor Ms. Hatchet. She was playing to the Court of Appeals, all right.

Rodney came forward to the bench in front of the clerk's desk. He was only eight feet away. He wore sandalwood cologne. He was impeccably dressed and groomed. His gel-stiffened porcupine hair gleamed. "Your Honor, this witness can testify about what he said to the detectives," he said, spreading his hands…the soul of reason.

Harriet said, "Your Honor, the statement has already been admitted through the detectives, in explaining why they arrested Mr. Mammon. The audio has been played too, at Counsel's request, to show Mr. Strait's tone and demeanor when he made the statement. I think this is locking the barn door after the horse has gone."

I liked that. An earthy cliche to bring us back to earth.

"I agree," Judge Palacpac said. "Counsel," she said, turning to Rodney, "your objection was previously noted. I also ruled that it is an ongoing objection for purposes of appeal. The statement is in. Your objection is noted but it is overruled. However you are going to get significant latitude on cross examination, which I presume you will use wisely."

Rodney darted a glance at me, and licked his lips. He was going to use it wisely, all right. We were going on a trip to Rodney World together, starting soon.

The jury came back.

After that, Harriet led me carefully through The Ghost's bleary phone call to me, how I found her drugged and raped and slashed, how I called 911 for paramedics and detectives, and how I showed Detective Broccoli and Detective Cookie where The Ghost's video camera and hard drive were. She pinned down that I did not touch any of the equipment, I just showed the detectives where it was, to seal up the chain of custody argument.

Next Harriet did something that all wise trial lawyers do. When there's a fact that can hurt your case, make sure you are the first one to bring it up. If the opposition brings it up, it looks like you've been hiding something. Juries do not like people who've been hiding something.

"Mr. Strait, is it true that you were employed by Mr. Mammon's law firm until recently?"

"Yes, that is true."

"Why did you leave?"

"I wanted to start my own practice, focusing solely on personal injury law. Mr. Mammon only practices criminal defense law."

"Was your parting friendly?"

"Well not very friendly, because he didn't want me to leave," I said timidly. A single juror stifled a laugh.

"Did any of the personal injury clients from Mr. Mammon's firm accompany you to your new firm?"

"Yes, they did. I gave them a choice of counsel, as I am required to do. All but one of them decided to come with me. I was moved by their support."

Harriet looked at me, and gave a subtle nod. Now she had to throw me to the enemy. "Nothing further, Your Honor," she said.

Rodney stood and went to the podium. He had a big binder, just like Harriet. He opened it and flipped it to a new tab. I had a feeling the tab in the binder read *Rotten Little Worm*.

So here's what I'd figured out so far, on the witness stand. Harriet knew about Rodney's witness intimidation. Judge Palacpac knew about Rodney's witness intimidation. Detectives Cookie and Broccoli had shown the video, and my witness statement had been admitted into evidence through them.

Therefore? I was the last witness for the state.

This was Rodney's final chance to derail the state's case. After that, what would he have? Probably just a video expert to say the video was a fake. And his own testimony, if he chose to testify. How would that even work? Would Rodney get on the witness stand and ask himself questions?

Then I realized Rodney probably would not testify. He always advised his clients not to testify, and argued, "The state has not met its burden." He would probably do that here too.

Rodney looked up from his binder, and locked eyes with me. I'd looked into his eyes many times before, and just saw a kind of blankness.

He blinked. For an instant, I glimpsed the viper inside.

"Mr. Strait," he said mildly. "Why are you jealous of my success as an attorney?"

"I'm not, Mr. Mammon," I said.

He paused, and wrote officiously. He was portraying somebody catching a liar in a lie. It was an Oscar-worthy performance.

He looked up again. "Why did you steal my clients when you left my firm?"

I adjusted the microphone and said evenly, "I gave them the choice of which attorney they wanted. I practice exclusively personal injury. You practice exclusively criminal defense. All but one chose me. As I said before, I am honored and humbled to have been chosen. For the one client who chose you, I personally handed you her file when you came to my new office."

I was two people. Underneath I wanted to leap on him and strangle him. On the surface, I was correct and polite. I didn't like being two people.

I realized that Rodney was two people all the time.

Rodney finished writing, and smiled to himself. He was portraying the truth seeker cornering the liar.

He looked up again. "How long before this alleged attack had you been having sexual relations with The Ghost?" he asked, staring at me to see if I would flinch.

"I've never had sexual relations with The Ghost," I said. "We kissed once, the night her cat died, and that was it. We would not work as a couple." I looked over at the jury. They were engrossed. I had no idea how I was doing.

I did what Harriet Hatchet specifically ordered me not to do. I added more. "She's an excellent private investigator," I said, "and she is my friend."

Rodney pounced. "So you have never performed oral sex on her?"

"Never."

"She has never performed oral sex on you?"

"Never."

"You have never had vaginal or anal intercourse with her?"

"Never."

"You have never touched each other's genitals with hands or objects?"

"Never."

Rodney wrote, and smiled to himself again. He had nothing. But he was trying to make the jury believe he had something. Then he glared at me. "So what do you and The Ghost do in your time together during this, uh…friendship?"

"We talk. Often we play Scrabble. She's pretty good," I said, lamely. I blushed. I could feel the jury staring at me. I hoped to hell I wasn't letting The Ghost down.

Rodney said with a flat tone, writing, "She is pretty good at Scrabble," as if this was the dumbest thing anybody had ever said.

"Oh yes," I said, like the naive bozo I was. "She hits triple word score lots more often than I do."

Rodney kept writing, ignoring this. I blushed darker.

Then he looked up again. "Why did you plant that fake video in The Ghost's condo," he asked in a level tone.

I sat up straight and took a deep breath. "I didn't plant a fake video." Again I violated Harriet's instructions by adding more. "The night of the attack, she called me for help, and I went over. I found her drugged and slashed and raped. I called 911 and the paramedics and police came. After the paramedics took her to the hospital, I waited outside for the police, because her condo was a crime scene. Then Detective Broccoli and Detective Cookie came, and I gave them a statement which they recorded on audio. Then I showed them where the video camera and hard drive were. They showed me the video. I identified you on the video as the attacker. I never touched the video equipment. I did not plant a fake video." I stopped. I was breathing hard. "It's real, all right," I said. I was tearing up now. "There's no way I can ever unsee that."

Rodney smiled indulgently and kept writing. I was completely screwing up. Harriet had told me not to narrate. Just answer the question asked as narrowly as possible. I was doing what I'd told every witness in every one of my cases not to do.

Rodney finished writing and looked up again. His next question was really out of left field. "Isn't it true that The Ghost has retained you to sue me for personal injuries if I am convicted of these false charges?"

My jaw dropped. "What? No, certainly not."

He looked down and leafed through his notes theatrically. "You are a personal injury attorney, correct?"

"Definitely."

"In fact, you are currently working on a personal injury case involving the rape of a minor in a group home, a case you stole from me. Isn't that true?"

"I recently finished up that case. I certainly didn't steal it from you. The litigation guardian ad litem chose me."

"And you do have this, this friendship with The Ghost, where all you do is innocently play Scrabble, isn't that right?"

"Yes. Oh, and sometimes we go for walks. I also get to play with her cat. Her cat's named Pirate. Pirate is really cute."

"I thought her cat died, Mr. Strait."

"That was Guinevere. This is her new cat."

Rodney said, "Her…new…cat." He wrote this stuff down as if he'd discovered the law of gravity.

He looked up again. "And so you state now, under penalty of perjury, that you have no intention of representing The Ghost in a personal injury case against me if you get the conviction that you so fervently desire."

I adjusted the microphone again. "Correct. I have no such intention. In fact, I hereby waive on the record the right to represent The Ghost in any civil case against you. The video is real. I am not testifying falsely to create a phony civil case against you, Mr. Mammon."

He looked up at me again and blinked. Again, he let me see the viper behind his eyes. "And you stand by your statement that you have not had sexual relations of any kind with The Ghost? Not even one time? She is a most attractive woman."

"Yes, Mr. Mammon, I stand by my statement." I looked over at the jury. "We are good friends. I'm proud to call myself her friend."

He murmured "Friends" while writing, as if that was a ridiculous thing to say.

Then he looked up. "Nothing further on cross, Your Honor," he said.

I felt like he'd cut me to ribbons. I waited for Harriet to do redirect and rehabilitate me.

Harried stood. "No redirect, Your Honor."

My jaw dropped. Was I so terrible that she couldn't even patch me back together? But I couldn't exactly volunteer to say anything I hadn't been asked.

My testimony was done.

I had an instant of flashback, seeing my parents' bodies being carted out of my childhood home the day they died. Now, I'd lost somebody else I really cared about.

Judge Palacpac cleared her throat. "Mr. Strait," she reminded me gently, "you may step down."

I stood. My knees were weak. I almost stumbled as I stepped off the stand and walked down the aisle. I felt like I was on fire. I felt like the jury was watching my back, thinking What An Obvious Loser.

Kurt Vonnegut once wrote: *If we got rid of all our weapons, we could still embarrass each other to death.*

After I got through the courtroom door and heard it click behind me, I realized somebody was waiting for me. Silent Mike.

"I saw the whole thing, Sam," he said. He handed me an iced Americano. "I've come to take you home."

We went down the elevators, through the tunnel to the King County Administration Building, and then to a parking lot on the other side. Silent Mike opened the rear hatch of his SUV, opened his gun safe, and put his big Glock in his shoulder holster and his small Glock in his ankle holster.

I was grateful for his silence. I was also grateful that I didn't own a gun myself. When Rodney was acquitted? It would be my fault.

If he walked, there was a danger I would shoot myself.

If he walked, there was a danger that I would shoot him.

As we drove north out of downtown, Silent Mike said, "I watched the whole thing. I was in the back, but I didn't want you to feel self-conscious, so I didn't tell you I would be there. Duvonda wanted me to see your entire testimony."

I put my head in my hands. "I think I crashed and burned," I said. "I have a giant headache."

When I looked up, Silent Mike was smiling. "When I did SWAT, after a takedown, we used to get headaches. We said we were suffering from ARPS."

"What's that?"

"Asshole-Related Psychology Syndrome."

That got a weak smile from me.

Silent Mike socked me on the shoulder, a welcome gesture. The gesture a brother would make if I'd ever had a brother. "Sam, you don't hate the rattlesnake. You just avoid the rattlesnake. Rattlesnakes bite. It's just their nature."

I drank my Americano. This small gesture meant a lot to me. "What if you can't avoid the rattlesnake?"

Silent Mike nodded, watching the road. "Then you kill the rattlesnake."

Rodney was going to walk. Nicky and I would have to leave Washington.

I could refer all my clients to Duvonda. She would take good care of them. She'd tried to make something of me. She had failed, but I appreciated her.

Maybe being an insurance adjuster wouldn't be so bad.

CHAPTER THIRTY-NINE— SECONDARY EXPLOSIONS

In the days after I testified, Nicky and I developed a bad habit of watching local TV news for word on Rodney's verdict. After we wrapped up work for the day, we watched it while eating TV dinners that I bought in bulk from Costco. Fortunately, we were at Extended Stay America, so we had a kitchenette.

After the third night of watching TV news, Buster started saying, "Ask your doctor about erectile dysfunction."

I kissed the back of Nicky's neck. "That's the only problem I don't have," I told her. "Luckily, I'm hiding out with a total fox." I hugged her and smelled her hair. "So honey," I murmured, "after we get out of here, I want to buy a house in the suburbs. Would you like to live with me?"

Nicky held me at arm's length, astonished. "Sam Strait, are you asking me to shack up?"

"Damn right I am," I said.

Her eyes teared up. "That's the only good thing that's happened lately," she said helplessly. "Now I know we really belong together."

I kissed her. Call me yucky, but I still thought her lips tasted like morning in Heaven.

"The answer is yes," she said. "When it's safe to come out, I'll start packing. Assuming there's anything left to pack. It's a fair bet that both our places have been ransacked."

"Yup," I said. "I haven't heard from the condo Homeowners' Association, and you haven't heard from your landlord. But if they got in using lockpicks, we wouldn't. So whatever's left, we'll pack it up and move it. I'm thinking about Edmonds. It's just north of the King County line but close enough to the city. And there are no homeless addicts living in tents there. I've gotten the heebie-jeebies about those people."

"I've always had them," Nicky said. "I just don't want to live near homeless people."

Buster said, "Well, dog my cats."

Then the news came on. "Our top story tonight! In a daring raid at dawn, agents of the Drug Enforcement Agency and the Federal Bureau of Alcohol, Tobacco, and Firearms raided an illegal RV encampment with a methamphetamine lab in the national forest just outside of Darrington."

The temperature in the room seemed to drop twenty degrees. Nicky grabbed my arm so hard it hurt.

The newscaster furrowed his brow. "Our chopper picked up radio traffic and was nearby when the raid went down. We got video of the raid."

He rolled the video. It showed a clearing with a circle of RVs, some with blue tops over the tops of the RVs. A flatbed truck with a tarp over the back stood just outside. Beyond it was the metal garden shed Silent Mike had described, with a row of fifty-five-gallon drums next to it.

The video camera zoomed in as agents with DEA raid jackets approached the clearing. The video was silent because the news chopper's noise would drown out any sound from the ground. Four pit bulls ran toward the agents, and they were all shot. The guns made little white sparks. Then, four men ran out of the RVs. They all had bushy mountain man beards.

One bearded man ran to the flatbed and whipped off the tarp, revealing the fifty-caliber machine gun. He jumped up on the flatbed, got behind the fifty-cal, and pulled the charging handle.

More little white sparks from the DEA agents. Three red dots appeared on the chest of the man behind the fifty-cal. He fell. It was Bran Wheatley.

Another bearded man ran toward the garden shed, then turned and fired a pistol at the agents, with the garden shed and drums just behind him. His pistol made little white sparks.

The DEA agents fired more little white sparks. A red dot appeared on the bearded man's forehead. It spurted red. Two more red dots appeared on his belly. He fell. That was Gran Cornwell.

Behind him, dark dots appeared on the side of the garden shed, and several more appeared on the sides of the fifty-five-gallon drums beside it.

"Oh hell, those drums are acetone," I said. Nicky just gripped my arm harder.

Then the barrels and the garden shed exploded in a giant marigold of flame a hundred feet high that nearly reached the RVs. The marigold was fully fifty feet in diameter.

The DEA agents threw themselves flat. Then, the steel framework of the garden shed started folding up as the fire melted the steel.

The announcer said, "Seventeen adults and two minors were taken into custody. Two adult males died in the confrontation. Two DEA agents were wounded by gunfire, and one was bitten by a pit bull, which did not survive the encounter."

The newscaster rolled video showing three passenger vans pulling up to a federal jail and handcuffed suspects being led out. I didn't recognize any of them. All were white males with bushy mountain man bears, except for two obese women wearing tank tops with tattoo sleeves.

The newscaster said, "All of the adults are being held in federal custody on charges ranging from manufacturing methamphetamine, possession of four illegal machine guns, possession of other illegal firearms, felony drug possession charges, and attempted murder. Arraignment is scheduled for next week."

I kissed the top of Nicky's head. "So Bran and Gran are dead," I said. "Looks like Rodney's goon squad is out of business."

"Those two," Nicky said, "but there are lots more criminal defense clients who owe him money. I counted while you were testifying. There are over two hundred. We won't really be safe, Sam, until he's been convicted and disbarred."

My phone rang. Silent Mike. He asked, "Are you seeing this?"

I said, "Yup. Whoever your friend with the Feds is, he or she really got rolling."

Silent Mike said, "It's a true pleasure to see a good takedown by law enforcement. And given my advanced state of burnout, it's a true pleasure not to be in on it."

I said, "So how's The Ghost? I didn't want to huddle with her until I had testified. Is she doing all right?"

Mike said, "She's right here."

"Hey Vanilla Boy," The Ghost said. She sounded weary and sardonic and delightfully normal.

"Hey," I said. "I hope I did okay as a witness. I told the jury that you and I weren't having sex. We just played Scrabble. Rodney treated me like I was an idiot. I'm hoping I didn't let you down."

The Ghost said, with a smile in her voice, "I hope you told them I usually won."

I laughed. "I did. I said you kept hitting the triple word score."

She said, "So what is your backup plan if Rodney is acquitted?"

I looked at Nicky. "Nicky and I were thinking we move to a new state far away, legally change our names, and get hired as insurance adjusters. How about you?"

"I'll do the same. But I can keep my current profession. I can work as a private investigator doing computer searches for the local attorneys whether I'm in Seattle or Houston or Kuala Lumpur."

I relaxed. "I just hope I didn't blow it. I won't really draw a deep breath until we have a verdict."

We exchanged a few more polite nothings and hung up. Nicky straightened my collar. "I think you would make a very handsome insurance adjuster," she said.

Buster said, "Ask your doctor about erectile dysfunction."

CHAPTER FORTY—THE VERDICT

We kept watching the TV news after wrapping up our workday. The Park case was really firming up. Don Meissner had gotten the black box data from the airbag control module and had finished up his collision reconstruction. The delivery van driver who had hit Mr. Park was almost nailed on fault. Now we'd just do the elaborate and cynical dance with the insurance company about what Mr. Park's life had really been worth.

The Stone Gamble case against Ron Porcine down in Rockingham County was firming up too, but the defendant didn't know it yet. Don Meissner had finished his collision reconstruction on that case too. The Ghost had found more properties and corporations tied to Ron Porcine and his family and the merry band of insider crooks down in Rockingham County. But she thought there was more to sniff out. I wouldn't file suit until I knew everything they had, so I could at least try to seize it all with a Prejudgment Writ of Attachment.

While we watched the evening TV news, Buster broadened his repertoire of commercial taglines. "Where winners play," he would yelp. "Some lucky dog's gonna win it!"

As we watched a few days after the goon squad raid, my phone rang. It was Harriet Hatchet. I muted the TV. I felt faint. Nicky could tell who was on the line just from my expression.

Harriet spoke for about ten seconds. Then I dropped the phone.

"Sorry," I told her. "Can you tell me more?"

She talked for another couple of minutes, then hung up.

I went over to the window. I drew the drapes—the first time they'd been open since we holed up there.

Then I did The Crane.

Nicky came over and did The Crane beside me. I'd never had a partner in doing The Crane before. "So is that what I think it is?" she asked.

"Yup," I said, still balancing on my left foot. "Rodney was found guilty of Rape 1, Assault 1, and Delivery of a Controlled Substance. They had a hung jury on the burglary charge because they couldn't unanimously agree he intended to commit felonies when he entered The Ghost's condo."

I sat down on the couch, and Nicky sat beside me. She put her head on my shoulder. "So they believed you after all," she said.

"Yes. But Harriet said she was worried because the County didn't authorize her to hire a digital video expert witness. They didn't want to spend the money. So Rodney brought in a hired gun from Hollywood, who must have cost an arm and a leg. He charmed the jury. He went minute by minute through the video, pointing out irrelevant little things, talking about pixels and resolution and whatnot. The real reason he did that, playing the video slowly, and repeatedly, was to systematically desensitize the jury."

"What is systematic desensitization?"

"If you see a disturbing video repeatedly, at different speeds, and you have somebody explaining What It Really Means, it leaches out the emotional impact of the video. There have been studies done on it. Harriet tried to rein it in, but Judge Palacpac wanted to let Rodney put on his complete defense in hopes of appeal-proofing the case."

"Yet somehow the jury didn't buy it?"

"Nope. They were only out for three hours. That's a pretty fast verdict." I put my head in my hands. "I thought I was totally blowing it. Talking about how The Ghost and I didn't have sex, we only played Scrabble. I said she was my friend. Rodney kept looking at me like I was a square egg. I felt like the dumbest man alive when I got down from the stand." I shuddered. "It worked. The system actually worked."

Nicky ran her hand through my hair. "So can we come out from hiding now?"

I looked at her. My eyes were wet. "Yes. Rodney will get disbarred, so he can't represent any more criminals who might do ugly favors for him. We can go home."

Nicky wiped my tears away. "And then we can go looking for our new home. And we won't have to change our names and move to Tennessee or Arkansas and work as insurance adjusters."

All this was still sinking in. "I can't believe it," I said.

Nicky messed up my hair. "I know how you feel. Those of us who had a rotten upbringing are always shocked by good news."

That reminded me of something. I went to my laptop, took out a new flash drive, and started copying forms onto it. Then I called Duvonda. "Did you hear?" I asked.

"Yes," she said. "This development calls for a nice dinner out, for all of us."

I pulled the flash drive out of my laptop. "So Duvonda, I've got an idea for you, and a present for you," I said.

"Do tell."

"I can't sue Rodney for personal injuries because I'm a witness. But you can. Will you do it? I'll help out any way I can."

"Way ahead of you, Sam. I signed her three days ago. We'll sue him, all right. The Ghost went online and turned him inside out. She knows where his accounts and properties and stuff are. He's got four rental houses, about three million in stocks in his Schwab account, and a nice tidy million stashed away in a bank in the Cayman Islands. We know where his stuff is."

I burst out laughing. "That is a bucket of awesome, with some awesome running down the sides," I said.

"So, what's my present?"

I put the flash drive in my pocket. "You can definitely do a better job on her case than I could. But I just copied all my forms and briefing onto a flash drive for getting a Prejudgment Writ of Attachment. I want to help you two open him up like a can of tuna fish."

Duvonda said, "That is very thoughtful, Sam. She wants to see you. I want to see you. I have a message for you from Silent Mike," she concluded. "Even if you think you've avoided the rattlesnake, keep watching the rattlesnake."

I sighed. "Copy that," I said.

We set a dinner. Nicky and I made passionate love that night, our last night at Extended Stay America, at one point throwing off the ugly bedspread with the concentric circles on it.

As we drifted off to sleep, Buster said quietly, "Some lucky dog's gonna win it."

CHAPTER FORTY-ONE—A MEDICAL DILEMMA

So Nicky and I went home.

My condo had been broken into. The lock had been picked, badly. My computer was stolen; I'd had nothing on it but personal stuff. I made sure my Norton LifeLock identity theft protection was still working, and forgot about it. They hadn't stolen anything else and showed exceptional restraint by not taking a dump on my rug.

Also they had spray-painted *FUCKER* on the wall over my computer. I got a roller and paint, and painted it sky blue. Big improvement actually. A locksmith replaced the lock in twenty minutes.

Nicky's apartment had been burglarized too but they hadn't stolen anything—just left a little plastic coffin on her kitchen counter. Classy.

A week after the verdict came in, Duvonda set up a big celebration dinner at my favorite seafood place in Magnolia, overlooking Puget Sound, not far from The Ghost's condo. Rodney had gotten an early sentencing.

Judge Palacpac gave him eighteen years—at the top of the standard range. He was remanded into custody.

Rodney got hammered.

I hadn't seen The Ghost since the night she called me for help—and I found her slashed and incoherent and raped. I took a deep breath when Nicky and I got out of my rental car. (I was in the market for another battered Subaru Outback. The insurance covered it. But I hadn't found the right one yet.)

The Ghost stood in front of the restaurant, dressed in a long black velvet dress, her flyaway blonde hair whipped by the wind. When she turned toward me, I felt a strong pang.

It was the first time I'd seen the long pink scar down the right side of her face.

I was glad I'd brought the contact info for a plastic surgeon I'd used before, for clients who needed scar revision surgery.

The Ghost ran up to me, her face alight, and hugged me. I kissed her on the cheek. "This is Nicky," I said, introducing them.

"Pleased to meet you," Nicky said, a little wary.

The Ghost gave her a two-handed handshake. "So you're the little vixen who took Sam Strait off the market," she said, puckishly.

"Guilty," Nicky said. They both laughed.

I gave The Ghost the note with the info for the plastic surgeon. She tucked it into her cleavage. We went inside.

Duvonda had told us all to dress "to the nines." Silent Mike wore a black Pierre Cardin suit with a black collarless shirt with pearl buttons. Duvonda wore an evening gown of lime green. I wore an ordinary gray suit, because as we have seen, I have no fashion sense. Nicky looked smashing in a low-cut blue paisley sun dress.

I don't think I've ever had a better time with any group of people.

As we were filing out, Duvonda took me aside, and we hung back in the lobby while everybody else streamed across the windy parking lot. I handed her my flash drive with my Prejudgment Writ of Attachment forms on it. "We'll be back in the office next Monday," I said, "but I wanted you to have this now."

"Thanks Sam," Duvonda said, putting it in her clutch purse. "But there's something I want to make you aware of without everybody else hearing this. Especially without The Ghost hearing this."

"What's up?"

"Right after Rodney got sentenced, Harriet Hatchet got a Notice of Appeal."

I sighed. "Oh boy. We knew this was coming. Is he representing himself?"

"Nope. He brought in Chucky Scalpthorne."

"Crap. He got the best."

"Yes. Chucky is arguing two things—first, Rodney has diminished capacity due to mental disease or defect. Second, because of his mental disease or defect, he provided ineffective counsel…to himself."

I was stunned. Rodney could do that. "But he was his own lawyer! There was a public defender right there on standby, but Rodney insisted on defending himself. Everybody has the Constitutional right to defend themselves. What a load of industrial-grade bullshit!"

Duvonda said, "I know, Sam. I really doubt the appeal will be granted. I don't think that's what he's angling for."

"So what could he possibly be angling for?" I mused.

Duvonda waited, while the February wind whipped around her. She waited to see if I could do the math.

I snapped my fingers. "He wants a transfer to a psych hospital," I said, "while the appeal is pending. That way he can escape from custody."

Duvonda pursed her lips. She was quietly livid with rage. "That's the way I figure it too. He's requested emergency relief transferring him to Western State Hospital for so-called necessary psychiatric treatment. You remember the audit they did of Western State Hospital a couple of years ago? They found that six thousand—repeat *thousand*—master keys were missing. They refused to re-key the place due to what they say is inadequate funding." She pursed her lips again. "Sam, a mentally retarded water buffalo could escape from Western State. That's the play. He's planning to make a run for it."

I was so pissed my whole body was trembling. "So do you think he'll make a run for the border? Do you think he wants to leave the US and hide out somewhere with no extradition treaty, like Brazil?"

Duvonda snapped her clutch purse shut. I remembered again that she carried a gun there. "I'm not willing to gamble my safety on that. Are you?"

I looked at Nicky, leaning against my rental car in her blue paisley sundress, the wind molding it to her splendid body. She made a sassy remark to Silent Mike and The Ghost. They all exchanged high fives. "No, I'm not," I said. "Any chance that Silent Mike would give me some firearms training? I need my concealed pistol license. It's time I got a gun."

Duvonda tapped me on the shoulder. "You do that," she said. "I spoke with Harriet about all this, just as former colleagues. Of course they'll fight any transfer to Western State. They're countering by filing a motion to have him remanded to McNeil Island as a sexually violent predator. They offer treatment there. But McNeil Island is pretty much escape-proof."

I nodded. "I'd forgotten for a second that you worked with Harriet back in the day. I'm very impressed with her. Does she think they'll win? Can they stash him on McNeil Island?"

Duvonda tapped me on the shoulder again. "Remember what you always tell clients when you're waiting for a verdict?"

I looked down, reproved. "You never know until you know."

"Exactly. Oh, and Silent Mike knows about this. I haven't told The Ghost yet. Poor dear. We offered her to stay with us at the house in Bellevue, but she wants to go back to her condo and live with her cat Pirate. At least she's well-armed. But I'll have to tell her tonight. I want you to be there for her, Sam. You're in love with Nicky, and you two will start house hunting, all well and good. But stand by her. That poor lady is going to need you more than ever after she hears this."

"It goes without saying," I said. "I gave her the name of my favorite plastic surgeon for a scar revision surgery. She doesn't look bad, really, but I bet she'll want to get it worked on. Poor thing. Every time she looks in the mirror, she's got Rodney's handiwork looking right back at her."

"That's not all, Sam. Her STD testing from her rape kit came back. I'm not authorized to know the result, but Harriet gave me the heads up. It's possible Mr. Mammon left her with an STD to remember him by."

I shook my head, helplessly. Would this whole thing ever truly be done? Would Rodney ever be securely incarcerated? Would The Ghost ever be truly healed?

"I'll stand by her," I said.

Duvonda said, "Harriet debriefed me on how you handled yourself on the witness stand."

I blurted out, "I felt like the biggest moron on Earth. I told the jury that The Ghost and I never had sex; we were friends and we played Scrabble. The way Rodney handled me on cross, I came out of there convinced I had blown it."

Duvonda hushed me. "You didn't blow it. You were an idealistic and likeable guy. Rodney was shown up by the contrast. But The Ghost still needs you, Sam. Now go drive your lovely girlfriend home."

***

Three days later The Ghost called me at the office and asked if I could come to a doctor's appointment with her at the end of the week. "I'm going to see my neurologist, Sam, and it might get somewhat heavy," she said, in a forlorn tone. "I'd sure like you beside me if there's bad news to be had."

"Sure," I said.

The Ghost was having more trouble walking and driving because her right leg was going numb due to her multiple sclerosis. She used her cane all the time now.

So I picked her up and drove her to her neurologist at Swedish Hospital up on First Hill. Her neurologist turned out to be a very short Hispanic woman named Dr. Rivas who'd been treating The Ghost for her MS since the beginning. "And who's this?" Dr. Rivas said, turning to me.

The Ghost said, "This is Sam Strait, my dear friend."

Dr. Rivas shook my hand and turned to The Ghost. "He's not your spouse, right?"

"Oh no," I said. Somehow it seemed strange to think of The Ghost as a wife.

The Ghost looked at me with a touch of her old sass. "Sam is my emotional support animal," she said.

I picked up on it. "I identify as a Labradoodle," I said.

Dr. Rivas winked at me. "Very well," she said, leading us to an exam room.

Dr. Rivas sat us down on those funny rolling stools they have. "Okay, so we got your STD testing back from the rape kit," she said, pulling up The Ghost's chart on her iPad. "It's too early for HIV testing, but everything else was negative. Except one. The assailant infected you with Human Papillomavirus. HPV."

The Ghost brushed her flyaway blonde hair out of her eyes. "What's the harm in HPV?" she asked.

"Ordinarily, not much. Most people clear the virus. It can cause genital warts, and warts of the vulva, vagina, penis, and throat. In bad cases it can cause cancer of the throat, cervix, or other areas."

The Ghost said, "I know your signals, Doc. There's a reason my MS doctor is talking to me about HPV."

"True. Here's the dilemma. Most people clear HPV without major illness. That's for people who have a normal immune system."

The Ghost picked it right up. "But I don't have a normal immune system. My MS is caused by my immune system attacking my nerves. My MS medication suppresses my immune system."

"Right, so here is the dilemma. We can reduce your MS medication to give your immune system more power to fight the HPV. But your MS will progress. Once you've lost nerve function with MS, it never comes back."

I hunched forward, hanging on.

"But if you don't reduce my MS medication…" The Ghost said.

Dr. Rivas sought refuge in her iPad. "Then the HPV will probably get a real foothold in your body. Then you are at heightened risk for cancer. And the immune system roots out early-stage cancer. So if you get cancer it'll really get rolling."

The Ghost drilled in on that. "How much increased risk is there, Doc? Of cancer?"

Dr. Rivas looked her straight in the eye. "We don't have firm numbers, my dear," she said. "We know there is a significant increase in the risk of cancer if you continue your current dosage of MS meds. But we don't have firm numbers."

The Ghost nodded. I realized—that, like me and Nicky—bad news didn't surprise her. It confirmed to her that life was sometimes really rotten.

She nodded again, deciding. "I'm already using my cane every day. I'm not going to cut my MS meds. If I get cancer, I'll just have to fight it like hell. Does that sound like a smart decision to you?"

Dr. Rivas punted. "I respect any decision you make, my dear. We've been together quite a while now."

The Ghost asked, "But if I was your sister? Would you approve of my decision?"

Dr. Rivas patted her hand. "I see you more often than I see my own sister," she said. "Yes I approve of your decision. But if you want to change your mind, I'll cut the dosage of the MS meds. You're in the driver's seat."

The Ghost stood and took my hand. She thanked Dr. Rivas. As we walked back to my car, with her leaning on her cane, she murmured, "I'm in the driver's seat? I'm afraid it doesn't feel that way, Sam." She smiled sadly at me. "Thanks for being my emotional support animal today."

I gave her a long hug.

When we got back to the car, she put her hand on my hand as I put the key in. "Can I explain something, Sam, before you start the car?"

"Sure."

"I wasn't into kink before I got MS. But my nerves are dying. Each time I take a step down with MS? I will never come back up. I can't feel anything, sexually, without kink being involved. I didn't want to become this way. I just turned out this way."

"You're great just the way you are. Other than my sister Catherine, you're the closest woman friend I have ever had."

The Ghost looked down. "I just wanted to explain to you why I can't be a one-man woman. Why I can't get turned on without some extreme stimulation. I'm not physically capable of it, because of my dying nerves. I think I've been calling you Vanilla Boy because I wish I could be with you. Or somebody like you."

Well that shut me up. As I drove her home in silence, I remembered what Silent Mike had said—about what to do if you couldn't avoid a rattlesnake.

CHAPTER FORTY-TWO— WHEN YOU CAN'T AVOID THE RATTLESNAKE

After Nicky and I returned from hiding out, she said we should take a break to make sure we were ready to live together.

I felt crushed, but only for a few minutes. Then I realized something.

Pilots talk about "the point of no return"—the point in a journey where they've come too far to turn around and go back. I was at that point with Nicky. If I moved in with her, I would ask her to marry me. If she said yes, I could never leave her, no matter how things turned out. Because of my weird childhood, I could never approach the subject of marriage lightly.

I was Vanilla Boy for real now. I wouldn't ante up on this relationship unless I put all my chips on the table.

After I sat brooding for a few minutes, with her pushing back her cuticles and fidgeting, I said, "All right. If we go further into this relationship, I will never be able to let go."

Nicky looked down and nodded. Her hair formed a curtain around her face. This reminded me of my sister Catherine. That's why Nicky was irreplaceable—I trusted her as much as I trusted Catherine.

That night at my anonymous condo, it was just me and Buster. I fed him some treats and taught him a new saying: "rip off the Band-Aid." He mastered it pretty quickly.

That night I obsessed about Rodney and The Ghost. I had severe insomnia. I took a Benadryl, then another one. No dice. Every time I started to fall asleep, I had a flash of The Ghost's drugged, raped, bleeding body on the floor.

Finally I went out in the living room. Although the cover was on Buster's cage, he heard me. "If you have to rip off the Band-Aid, do it fast," he said.

I'd reached the point of no return with Rodney.

The Ghost and I had talked several times about Rodney's appeal and his motion to get transferred to Western State Hospital. The Ghost was quiet and formal whenever she discussed it, the way she always was when she was afraid. I didn't tell her I was terrified.

Rodney's appeal had the stench of effrontery that marked his worst impulses. I knew in my bones he'd get transferred to Western State. I knew in my bones he'd escape. I knew in my bones he wouldn't leave the country with his unfindable stash of cash until he'd made a final move against The Ghost and me.

At this one moment in my life, I had everything to gain…right when I had everything to lose.

I curled up in the fetal position on my green leather couch and let my mind stir all the options, like that paint-mixer machine you've seen in the hardware store.

Option One—I somehow get at him and kill him. Maybe when he went to the Court of Appeals? He'd no longer be a threat to The Ghost, or Nicky, or everybody I loved.

But I'd get caught, and I'd go to prison. Ever since the Malletts' Therapeutic Foster Home? I'd rather die than go to prison.

I would breathe free air until I died. Any risk to my freedom was not an option.

Option Two—I could kill Rodney and then kill myself. Also no good. If you put Rodney aside, my life had never been so good. I loved Nicky. My work was the mission I'd been born for. I'd never had such good friends as The Ghost and Duvonda and Silent Mike and Fabulous Hal and Don Meissner and Romeo Pursuit. I couldn't do that to them.

I was going to stay alive. I was not going to prison. But I was going to stop Rodney—for keeps.

Then, my brain just kept churning like the paint mixer for three hours.

Then I got a fantastic and weird idea: a chess move that would make all the chess commentators say, "how bold and outrageous." It was a permanent solution. It was even probably legal. It wasn't a sure thing, but it had a good chance of success. But if I did this, nobody could ever know. Nobody but The Ghost. Not even Nicky.

I got up and stretched, then took a long, hot shower. I sang "Straight to Hell" by The Clash. I slept like a rock after that.

The next morning, I called The Ghost and drove my replacement Outback over to her condo. On the way, I stopped at a drugstore and bought a box of disposable surgical gloves, two books of forever stamps, and a large packet of postcards showing women in bikinis.

The Ghost met me at the door. She was using her cane. She always used her cane now. She was still wearing her Glock on her hip. She wore jeans and a fleece pullover.

Her scar was red, not pink. It turned red whenever she was upset. When she was calm? It was pale and less noticeable.

"I called your plastic surgeon, Sam," she said, leading me over to the kitchen table. I sat down, and Pirate jumped into my lap and looked up at me. The Scrabble set was still there. "He says he can revise the scar so it's less noticeable," The Ghost said, bringing me a cup of orange spice tea. "But he can never make it completely go away."

I knew the scar was a metaphor—for how Rodney had given her the medical dilemma between fighting MS and fighting HPV. And for Rodney, destroying her dignity and her privacy.

I took a deep drink. "I once had a case where a nice young woman had her nose bitten off by a pit bull," I said. "The surgeon said the same thing. Doctors are taught by their malpractice insurers to never give false hope, because disappointed patients sue doctors."

I let her ruminate. "So, how did her nose turn out?" The Ghost asked.

I met her eyes. "I was astonished at how good it was. After three procedures, you couldn't tell anything had happened unless you looked at her nose from six inches away in bright light. Rodney was disappointed because we got less money for it. I was delighted because this pretty woman got a splendid nose."

The Ghost took Pirate from me and stroked her. "And there's the real issue," she said, her voice forlorn.

I got out the Scrabble board and the bag of tiles. "Precisely. But I have an idea. Can you turn off your video camera? Can you turn off your cell phone?" I took out my smartphone. "I'll do the same. What I'm going to say is so private that we can't whisper it down a well at midnight, as they say in Arab culture."

The Ghost turned off her video camera (even though it didn't record audio) and her cell phone. I needed to give her some buildup so she wouldn't laugh in my face and throw me out of her condo.

"Enough mystery, Mr. Strait," she chided me. "What's the plan?"

I held up a finger. "Next, I need you to promise you will never tell anybody about this. Not for the rest of your life. Some secrets we must take to the grave."

The Ghost said, "Okay, I promise. But what about you? What about Nicky?"

I drank my tea. "Not even Nicky. I also promise I won't tell anybody about this until I die."

Pirate jumped down from The Ghost's lap and jumped up onto my lap. She blinked at me with her mint-green eyes.

"Okay," The Ghost said, chiding me again. "Now you're just teasing. What's the plan?"

I fished through the Scrabble tiles and spelled out the word POSTCARDS. I put it on the triple-word score.

"I'm going to need a little more detail, Sam," The Ghost said. But her voice was brightening. "Don't tease me."

"Okay," I said, warming to my subject. "Rodney's currently in prison. I have a sick feeling he's going to succeed in faking a psychiatric illness and getting transferred to Western State. I have a sick feeling he's going to escape. With me so far?"

"Totally," she said.

"But for now, he's in the new prisoner intake facility at Sheldon. They send all the new prisoners there for a few months to figure out which ones are security risks, which ones need medical care, and which ones need Ad Seg."

"Okay, what is Ad Seg?"

"In prison, there are two basic classifications of housing—General Population, or Gen Pop, is for most prisoners. Ad Seg, or Administrative Segregation, is for prisoners who are in danger from the other prisoners. Prisoners in Ad Seg get single cells and very little yard time. But they're protected from the prisoners in Gen Pop."

I drank more tea. Pirate began purring. "So the really violent prisoners like multiple murderers and gang trigger-men know they're going to be there a long time. If you're incarcerated for decades? You need to build up status. The best way to build status is to kill a rapist or a child molester."

"Very well. Now postcards."

I put my little bag on the table. "In prison, the mail is not sorted by guards. It's sorted by trustees—the inmates who've earned the privilege of an easy job. Inmates gossip incessantly. It's one of their few forms of entertainment. So here's the plan. You put on the surgical gloves. You write a postcard to Rodney, starting with his Department of Corrections number. Then you write something like, 'Hey Rodney—I'll bet you're glad none of the convicts on your cellblock know you're a child molester! It'd be a damn shame if that got into general circulation, wouldn't it?' Then you mail it off. Always use gloves. Never say anything that links the postcard to you or me. Eventually, the trustees will gossip. The word will go out that Rodney is a child molester."

The Ghost put her hand on my hand. "And then somebody will eventually kill him to gain status." She thought it over. "And the postcards will get read immediately by the trustees because prisoners aren't allowed to receive pornography. But bikini postcards are the closest thing to pornography allowed."

She sat back and nodded. She smiled. Her scar went pale. "Jesus. That's a devious plan, Sam."

I smiled, too. "I know. But here's the thing. It's totally anonymous if done correctly. It's probably even legal. But if anybody found out we were involved in this? I bet you would lose your Private Investigator license, and I would be disbarred."

The Ghost zeroed in on the flaw, of course. "Sam, there's no guarantee this will work."

I finished my tea. "I know. We're taking a long shot. It's the only option I could dream up that didn't involve me killing him and going to prison or me killing him and then killing myself. I had visions of myself waiting at the Court of Appeals with a gun when he came in for his appellate argument."

The Ghost said, "Not even in jest, Sam, do I want you to talk about going to prison or killing yourself."

I ran my hands through my hair. "I had bad insomnia when I came up with this. This is the best shot I can take at Rodney without destroying or ending my life."

The Ghost took my mug. She gave me more hot water to freshen up my tea. "I notice something curious about your options, Sam," she said. "You didn't even consider doing nothing."

The guilt hit me again.

This next sentence would determine whether The Ghost and I continued being friends. Or if it ended right here. "I didn't consider that because I think Rodney came after you to get even for me leaving his firm," I confessed.

The Ghost took my hand. "Look at me, Sam." I did. "I've been playing a dangerous game for a long time with my playmates. I took my own risks."

I started to feel better. Right then. That's what a good friend can do. "But still," I said.

"No 'but still,' Mr. Sam Strait said. I made my own decisions. I took my own risks. I had played with Rodney before. I knew you were leaving his firm and taking clients with you. I am a free woman who charts her own course. You cannot take my autonomy away from me."

Damn, she was good. She outsmarted me into almost feeling innocent. This was why I hadn't considered doing nothing. Some wise man once said, "In order for evil to triumph, it's only necessary that good men do nothing."

She cleared her throat. "Okay, I have two conditions."

I sighed. Here goes. The Ghost was smart and stubborn. She never adopted a plan of mine without changing it.

"First off, you don't touch the postcards. I do everything. I don't want your fingerprints on this, literally or metaphorically."

"Agreed."

"Second, I'm having a hard time driving with my right leg acting up. The postcards have to be mailed from someplace far away, so the postmark is nowhere near where we live. Doesn't that make sense?"

"Definitely," I said. "I agree to both."

The Ghost took the bag. It crinkled in her hand. "So you got your new car? It's all good?"

"Yes. I got another aged Subaru Outback. Because I'm a man of superior taste."

She rolled her eyes. I noticed something else about her two changes to the plan. They gave her total control over the execution. But she would get my company for reassurance.

I couldn't fault her for wanting to take back her power. I'd wanted to do the same thing when Benny tried to molest me at the Malletts' Therapeutic Foster Home. That's why I kept daring Benny to do stuff that eventually got him killed.

So that's what we did.

Each Friday around two, I would leave the office early, telling Nicky I needed to drop in on The Ghost. Then, The Ghost and I would drive to Mount Vernon, a county seat about an hour north of Seattle. The Ghost would be wearing surgical gloves from start to finish.

We'd pull up to a drive-up mailbox. She would drop in the postcard. She would say, "That's that." Then we'd drive back.

Meanwhile, I pieced my life back together. Linda Lou called and said her HIV test was negative, and I took her and Nicky for Indian food. She was set to close on buying Has Beans later that month. I went to see my sister Catherine, and we sat on hay bales beside her paddock. Her shy racehorse Jenny grew to like me. I sent a big stack of financial documents to a mortgage broker to prequalify myself. I started to favor mid-century modern houses with four bedrooms in Edmond, north of Seattle on Puget Sound, but Nicky was reluctant to talk about them.

In the Park case, Don Meissner outdid himself with his accident reconstruction report, getting the calculations from the black box in the delivery van matched up with the calculations showing why Mr. Park's shoe flew such a long way from the impact point. I went over it with Genevieve Park, and it went to the defendant's insurer with a thorough demand package. Genevieve told me I needed to start running after I told her a little about the Rodney situation, so we started doing a three-mile loop around the Lynwood Golf Course every night before dinner with Nicky.

Also, Stone Gamble's mother got pastoral counseling and made a fairly nice recovery from her grief. The Ghost at last finished chasing down all the assets of Ron Porcine, Judge Pluffington, and the rest of the crooked cabal in Rockingham County. It turned out every major player in the corruption ring was doing business with every other player in the corruption ring. Judge Pluffington invested in Ron Porcine's businesses, which did business with the County, and J. Charm incorporated everything, served as the registered agents for all the companies, and invested in them, too.

The Ghost said, "It looks like a bucket of incestuous octopi down there."

I said, "That accounts for the unique smell." I started preparing a Motion for Prejudgment Writ of Attachment.

Six weeks after we started driving to Mount Vernon, I drove to The Ghost's condo one fine spring afternoon. Robins sang from blooming cherry and redbud trees. Yellow forsythia blazed under a mild blue sky.

The Ghost invited me in for tea. "It looks like we won't have to go for a drive today, Vanilla Boy," she said. She wore a gray velvet smoking jacket and black velvet lounging pajamas. She'd put on a touch of Chanel No. 5. She looked like the pretty cat that ate the annoying canary.

She said, "I have good news and better news."

I gulped. "Give me the good news first. The better news might not be better."

She handed me a mug of orange spice tea. "Spoken like an orphan," she said with faint amusement. "Very well. The good news? Rodney's emergency motion to be transferred to Western State Hospital for treatment was denied by Judge Palacpac. Instead, she transferred him to McNeil Island Penitentiary—because that's where the Sexually Violent Predator Center is. She didn't put him in the SVP Center, but she said in her Order that McNeil Island was best suited to meet his unique treatment needs while preserving public safety."

I was flooded with delight. "That's awesome news! That means we're all safe! When did this happen?"

The Ghost said, "Four weeks ago."

I stammered, "But we didn't stop driving to Mount Vernon. Don't you see? This means our problem is solved."

The Ghost's face went solemn. "This wasn't a solution, Sam. It was only a reprieve."

"Why didn't I find out about this?"

"Harriet Hatchet told me because I'm the victim. She didn't tell witnesses, only me."

I sighed. "Okay, but why didn't you tell me?"

The Ghost sighed, too. "This news wasn't a solution, Sam. You know how devious Rodney is. He could try again in conjunction with his appeal. The Court of Appeals might even buy it." She paused. "Rodney Mammon is a waste of oxygen."

Pirate began purring and circled The Ghost's ankles.

"So what's the better news?" I asked. I had a hunch.

The Ghost said, "You never looked at the postcards. You kept driving me up to Mount Vernon, and I kept mailing them. So, after he was transferred to McNeil Island? I sent them there."

"All right. Again, what is the better news?" Pirate jumped onto my lap. I looked at The Ghost. Just then, a sun break appeared. Her flyaway blonde hair blazed. "What could be better news than Rodney getting transferred to McNeil Island?"

She turned her laptop around and hit the space bar to light up the screen. There was a story from the *Seattle Times* on it. Here's what it said:

MCNEAL ISLAND PENITENTIARY—Prison officials announced today that two inmates have been murdered in apparently linked attacks. Rodney Mammon, a convicted rapist and suspended attorney, was stabbed 57 times in a community shower room by another inmate and succumbed to his wounds.

One prison guard, speaking not for attribution, said, "Mr. Mammon got hooked up with a prison gang and was giving them free legal advice because he was an experienced criminal defense attorney. Another opposing gang heard a persistent rumor that he was a convicted child molester. The rival gang's hitman stabbed him to death to increase the rival gang's status in the prison. Then, the hitman was stabbed to death just moments later as he returned to his cell. The hit man's name was Burris Smalls, a convicted child rapist serving a sentence for sexually assaulting an underaged female in a group home in Seattle."

The murderer of Burris Smalls has not been identified but is thought to be the hitman for the gang that Mr. Mammon had become associated with. The warden said, "Here at McNeil Island, we take intra-inmate violence very seriously. The murderer of Mr. Smalls will be located, and he will be brought to justice." Remembrances for Mr. Mammon or Mr. Smalls may be made by contributing to the Indigent Prison Canteen Fund for inmates who do not have funds to purchase items needed at the prison.

I looked at The Ghost. She was trying unsuccessfully not to smile. "Well, dog, my cats," I said, unconsciously quoting Buster.

She couldn't help herself. She smiled now.

"What," I asked.

"Wordplay is our thing, Sam," she said, shaking her head. "There's a phrase that captures this situation."

"Do tell."

"Looks like we killed two rapists with one stone."

ABOUT THE AUTHOR

Sam Strait is the pen name of a personal injury attorney in the Seattle area with over twenty years litigating wrongful death, sex abuse, and medical malpractice cases. In his free time he enjoys running and chess.

www.ingramcontent.com/pod-product-compliance
Lightning Source LLC
Chambersburg PA
CBHW060600300726
48975CB00005B/1394